Still Life

ALSO BY SARAH WINMAN

When God Was a Rabbit

A Year of Marvellous Ways

Tin Man

Still Life

SARAH
WINMAN

VIKING

VIKING

an imprint of Penguin Canada,
a division of Penguin Random House Canada Limited

Canada • USA • UK • Ireland • Australia •
New Zealand • India • South Africa • China

First published in the United Kingdom by Fourth Estate,
an imprint of HarperCollins Publishers, 2021.
Published in Viking paperback by Penguin Canada, 2021.
Simultaneously published in the United States by Putnam,
an imprint of Penguin Random House LLC.

Grateful acknowledgment is made to reprint from *A Room with a View*
by E. M. Forster and *Selected Letters of E. M. Forster, Volume One,
1879–1920*, courtesy of the Provost and Scholars of King's College,
Cambridge, and the Society of Authors.

www.penguinrandomhouse.ca

*Publisher's note: This book is a work of fiction. Names, characters,
places and incidents either are the product of the author's imagination or
are used fictitiously, and any resemblance to actual persons living or dead,
events, or locales is entirely coincidental.*

LIBRARY AND ARCHIVES CANADA CATALOGUING IN PUBLICATION
Title: Still life / Sarah Winman.
Names: Winman, Sarah, 1964- author.
Identifiers: Canadiana (print) 20210092564 | Canadiana (ebook) 20210092599 |
ISBN 9780735241411 (softcover) | ISBN 9780735241428 (EPUB)
Classification: LCC PR6123.I62 S75 2021 | DDC 823/.92—dc23

Book design by Katy Riegel
Cover design and illustration: Ellie Game © 2021 HarperCollins*Publishers*
Cover image: (parrot) Passakorn Umpornmaha / Shutterstock

Printed in the United States of America

10 9 8 7 6 5 4 3 2 1

Penguin
Random House
VIKING CANADA

For Mum

For Patsy

For Stella Rudolph (1942–2020)

Two people pulling each other into Salvation is the only theme I find worthwhile.

—E. M. Forster, *Commonplace Book*

One of the primary objects of the enlightened traveler in Italy is usually to form some acquaintance with its treasures of art. Even those whose usual avocations are of the most prosaic nature unconsciously become admirers of poetry and art in Italy. The traveler here finds them so interwoven with scenes of everyday life, that he encounters their influence at every step, and involuntarily becomes susceptible to their power.

—Karl Baedeker, *Italy: Handbook for Travelers*, 1899

Still Life

Man as
the Measure of
All Things

1944

Somewhere in the Tuscan hills, two English spinsters, Evelyn Skinner and a Margaret someone, were eating a late lunch on the terrace of a modest *albergo*. It was the second of August. A beautiful summer's day, if only you could forget there was a war on. One sat in shade, the other in light, due to the angle of the sun and the vine-strewn trellis overhead. They were served a reduced menu but celebrated the Allied advance with large glasses of Chianti. Overhead, a low-flying bomber cast them momentarily in shadow. They picked up their binoculars and studied the markings. Ours, they said, and waved.

This rabbit's delicious, said Evelyn, and she caught the eye of the proprietor, who was smoking by the doorway. She said, *Coniglio buonissimo, signore!*

The *signore* put his cigarette in his mouth and raised his arm—part salute, part wave, one couldn't be sure.

Do you think he's a Fascist? said Margaret quietly.

No, I don't think so, said Evelyn. Although Italians are quite indecisive politically. Always have been.

I heard they're shooting them now, the Fascists.

Everyone's shooting everyone, said Evelyn.

A shell screamed to their right and exploded on a distant hill, up-rooting a cluster of small cypress trees.

One of theirs, said Margaret, and she held on to the table to protect her camera and wineglass from the shock waves.

I heard they found the Botticelli, said Evelyn.

Which one? said Margaret.

Primavera.

Oh, thank God, said Margaret.

And Giotto's *Madonna* from the Uffizi. Rubens's *Nymphs and Satyrs* and one more—Evelyn thought hard—ah, yes, she said. *Supper at Emmaus.*

The Pontormo! Any news about his *Deposition*?

No, not yet, said Evelyn, pulling a small bone from her mouth.

In the distance, the sky suddenly flared with artillery fire. Evelyn looked up and said, I never thought I'd see this again at my age.

Aren't we the same age?

No. Older.

You are?

Yes. Eight years. Approaching sixty-four.

Are you *really*?

Yes, she said, and poured out more wine. I pity the swallows, though, she added.

They're swifts, said Margaret.

Are you sure?

Yes, said Margaret. The squealers are swifts, and she sat back and made an awful sound that was nothing like a swift.

Swift, said Margaret, emphasizing her point. The swallow is, of course, the Florentine bird, she said. It's a Passeriform, a perching bird, but the swift is not. Because of its legs. Weak feet, long wingspan. It belongs to the order of Apodiformes. Apodiformes meaning "footless" in Greek. The house martin, however, *is* a Passeriform.

Dear God, thought Evelyn. Will this not end?

Swallows, continued Margaret, have a forked tail and a red head. And about an eight-year life expectancy.

That's depressing. Not even double digits. Do you think swallow years are like dog years? said Evelyn.

No, I don't think so. Never heard as much. Swifts are dark brown but appear blackish in flight. There they are again! screamed Margaret. Over there!

Where?

There! You have to keep up, they're very nippy. They do everything on the wing!

Suddenly, out from the clouds, two falcons swooped in and ripped a swift violently in half.

Margaret gasped.

Did everything on the wing, said Evelyn as she watched the falcons disappear behind the trees. This is a lovely drop of Classico, she said. Have I said that already?

You have actually, said Margaret tersely.

Oh. Well, I'm saying it again. A year of occupation has *not* diminished the quality. And she caught the proprietor's eye and pointed to her glass. *Buonissimo, signore!*

The *signore* took the cigarette out of his mouth, smiled and again raised his arm.

Evelyn sat back and placed her napkin on the table. The two women had known one another for seven years. They'd been lovers briefly in the beginning, after which desire had given way to a shared interest in the Tuscan proto-Renaissance—a satisfactory turn of events for Evelyn, less so for Margaret someone. She'd thrown herself into ornithology. Luckily, for Evelyn, the advent of war prevented further pursuit, until Rome that is. Two weeks after the Allies had entered the city, she'd opened the front door of her aunt's villa on Via Magento only to be confronted by the unexpected. Surprise! said Margaret. You can't get away from me that easily!

Surprise wasn't the word that had come to Evelyn's mind.

Evelyn stood up and stretched her legs. Been sitting too long, she said, brushing crumbs off her linen slacks. She was a striking presence at full height, with intelligent eyes, as quick to the conundrum as they were to the joke. Ten years before, she had committed her graying thatch to blond and had never looked back. She walked over to the *signore* and in perfect Italian asked for a cigarette. She placed it between her lips and steadied his hand as she leaned toward the flame. *Grazie*, she whispered, and he pressed the packet firmly into her palm and motioned for her to take it. She thanked him again and moved back to the table.

Stop, said Margaret.

What?

The light on your face. How green your eyes are! Turn a little to me. Stay like that.

Margaret, for God's sake.

Do it. Don't move. And Margaret picked up her camera and fiddled with the aperture setting.

Evelyn drew on the cigarette theatrically (click) and blew smoke into the late-afternoon sky (click), noticing the shift of color, the lowering of the sun, a lone swift nervously circling. She moved a curl of hair away from her frown (click).

What's eating you, dear chum?

Mosquitoes, probably.

I hear a touch of Maud Lin, said Margaret. Thoughts?

What is old, d'you think?

Cabin fever talking, said Margaret. We can't advance, we can only retreat.

That's old, said Evelyn.

And German mines, silly!

I just want to get into Florence. *Do* something. Be useful.

The proprietor came over and cleared their plates from the table. He asked them in Italian if they would like a coffee and grappa and they said, How lovely, and he told them not to go wandering again, and he told them his wife would go up to their room later and close the shutters. Oh, and would they like some figs?

Oh *sì, sì. Grazie.*

Evelyn watched him depart.

Margaret said, I've been meaning to ask you. Robin Metcalfe told me you met Forster.

Who?

Him with a View.

Evelyn smiled. Oh, very good.

The way Robin Metcalfe tells it, you and Forster were best friends.

How ridiculous! I met him across a dining table, if you must know, over dinners of boiled beef, at the ghastly Pensione Simi. We were an impoverished little ship on the banks of the Arno, desperately seeking the real Italy. And yet at the helm was a cockney landlady, bless her soul.

Cockney?

Yes.

Why a cockney?

I don't know.

I mean, why in Florence?

I never asked.

Now you would, said Margaret.

Now I certainly would, said Evelyn, and she took a cigarette and placed it between her lips.

Probably came over as a nanny, said Margaret.

Yes. Probably, said Evelyn, opening the matchbox.

Or a governess. That'll be it, said Margaret.

Evelyn struck a match and inhaled.

Did you know he was writing a book? asked Margaret.

Good Lord no. He was a recent scholar, if I remember rightly. Covered in the afterbirth of graduation—shy, awkward, you know the type. Entering the world with no experience at all.

Weren't we all like that?

Yes, I suppose we were, said Evelyn, and she picked up a fig and pressed her thumbs against the soft, yielding skin. I suppose we were, she repeated quietly.

She tore the fruit in half and glanced down at the erotic sight of its vivid flesh. She blushed and would blame it on the shift to evening light, on the effect of the wine and the grappa and the cigarettes, but in her heart, in the unseen, most guarded part of her, a memory undid her, slowly—very slowly—like a zip.

Strangely charismatic, though, she said, surfacing into the present.

Forster was? said Margaret.

When he was alone, yes. But his mother's presence suffocated him. Every reprimand was pressure applied to the pillow. Odd relationship. That's what I remember most. Her with a parasol and smelling salts, and him with a well-thumbed Baedeker and an ill-fitting suit.

Margaret reached for Evelyn's cigarette.

I remember he'd appear in quiet moments. You wouldn't hear him, just see him. Tall and lanky in the corner. Or in the drawing room with a notebook. Scribbling away. Simply observing.

Isn't that how it starts? said Margaret, handing back the cigarette.

What?

A book.

Yes. I suppose so.

Those little moments that nobody else notices. Little sacred moments of the everyday. She picked up her camera (click). Like that moment (click). Or that.

Good God, will you stop now, Margaret? What's got into you?

Margaret lowered the camera. You don't see what I see, she said seductively.

You have something in your teeth.

Why didn't you say?

I did. Just now.

Margaret turned away and hid her mouth behind her hand. She ran her tongue back and forth across her incisors.

Better? she said, baring them.

Yes, said Evelyn.

Margaret suddenly swapped the positions of the ashtray and figs and wineglass. She altered the aperture (click). She moved a wineglass, the packet of cigarettes (click) (click) (click) (click).

I was twenty-one when I first came to Florence, said Evelyn. Did I say?

Yes, I think we all knew that, said Margaret.

Oh.

Evelyn continued: The landlady at the Simi had a maid who did a little of everything. She could always be found in the dining room, in the corner as we ate. Always watching. Waiting to serve, waiting to clear. Working us out.

(Click.)

She was eye-catching, said Evelyn. Astute. Pretty.

(Click.)

Margaret sat back down. How pretty? she asked.

She was a Leonardo, said Evelyn.

Which one?

Lady with an Ermine.

Oh, said Margaret, raising an eyebrow.

Not in attire, of course—mostly black and white in the evenings, white during breakfast service. Very buttoned up, but those were the times, of course. We all were, I suppose—but her skin and eyes. The drape of hair across her forehead. The blush on her cheeks.

It seems you were quite taken with her?

Everyone was taken with her, said Evelyn.

Even Forster?

No, dear. He's a queer.

Evelyn paused the story. She flicked ash off her cigarette and Margaret watched her intently.

He wasn't there the night I'm thinking of, continued Evelyn. The night of my birthday. He hadn't arrived yet.

What was her name? interrupted Margaret.

I don't rem—

Oh, let's give her a name—

—let's not—

Something like Beatrice!

For God's sake, Margaret! It's not about a name. It's about a *moment*. That's all. It's not about her name.

Apologées, said Margaret, leaning back theatrically and retreating with the remains of her grappa. *Continuez*, she said.

Evelyn continued: She knew my birthday was approaching because it had been the talk of our group for days, and although she spoke little English, she understood what we said. A curious worldliness. Saying nothing but understanding everything. And she asked the cockney *signora* if she could take over the cooking that particular night, to give us all—*me,* really—a feast like no other. The cockney *signora* was thrilled, of course, and retired early.

Which was no great loss, said Margaret.

None at all, qualified Evelyn. I remember my feelings of excitement as I came down the stairs and—

Weren't you traveling with anyone? interrupted Margaret.

No. Unchaperoned until Rome.

Unchaperoned? How on earth—?

Margaret. Please. We were an unconventional family. Scandal was a rite of passage. May I continue?

Margaret gestured that she might.

Evelyn said, I should have realized that something special was brewing. I walked into the drawing room and there was a hush. Constance Everly was smiling at me and she took my hand and—

Constance Everly?

Yes.

The poet?

Yes. Constance Everly the poet, Margaret.

Evelyn sat back, exhausted. She could never get through a story without interruptions.

And? said Margaret.

And what?

Constance Everly took your hand . . . ?

And. Squeezed. It, said Evelyn.

Why are you talking oddly?

In case you want to interrupt again. I'm leaving gaps. Between. Words. So you can slip in, and not disrupt the—

Oh, just tell the bloody story, Evelyn.

Evelyn laughed. She said, Constance led me into the dining room.

Candles were on every surface, and running down the center of the tables were small tubs of Parma violets—so rare, that early in the season—and sprigs of rosemary and the smell was intoxicating. This was a room that had been thought about; the effect it would have on those who entered. And there was wine in large earthenware flagons, and *fiaschi* on the table—bottles wrapped in straw—and the young woman poured out the wine for me and bade me sit. And the other guests followed and gasped at our moment of beauty, of *bellezza*. Our night, finally, of Italian authenticity and grace. She fed us a simple *pappardelle* with a *ragù*—

She probably used the boiled beef, said Margaret.

—and rabbit with white beans, and bitter greens that she would have collected from the roadside in Fiesole or Settignano, which she cooked *ripassati* style with garlic and oil. And when we were all served, out she came from the kitchen and stood in the corner, in the shadows, and watched us eat. Our enjoyment being her enjoyment. I couldn't take my eyes off her. I was twenty-one when this moment was presented to me. The gift was beyond my comprehension. Only later did I come to understand what she was offering.

Oh? And what was she offering?

A door into her world. Priceless.

Margaret poured out another glass of grappa and sipped it. Her mouth was tight. She said, You've never told me this story before.

Have I not?

I think I'd remember. Why now?

Yes, why now? thought Evelyn, and she said, The rabbit.

The rabbit?

Yes.

Have you not had rabbit since?

And the music.

What music?

The overture to Spontini's *La Vestale*. The *signore* played it this morning. A simple memory of the Teatro Verdi.

And that's how it ends, is it?

Almost, said Evelyn. After dinner, guests retired as they always did. There was a faint sound of a piano in the background. I told Constance I wanted to stay and give my thanks to the young woman and she went on ahead to the smoking room. And there I stood, between the grave-yard of glasses and the wilting nubs of candles. The maid came out shortly after. I don't think she noticed me at first. She looked hot and rather distracted. But then she saw me. She picked a violet and handed it to me. *Per voi*, she said. For me. The evening was *for me*. I knew that. I thanked her. I took the violet from her hand and left the room. Later, I pressed it in my Baedeker.

Do you still have it?

The Baed—

The violet.

I doubt it. All those years, Margaret. Why would I? Evelyn lit a ciga-rette and they sat in silence. She could feel Margaret's gaze haunting her. The blunt edge of her jealousy.

What adventures you've had, said Margaret coolly.

The sun was lowering. The shadows lengthened. The temperature surrendered shallowly to the breeze. The sound of a sewing machine coming from indoors: the *signora* mending sheets. A radio played qui-etly. A clandestine channel keeping contact between the Allies and the Resistance.

Margaret said, I think I may go in and read. You?

I'll be here a while longer. Finish the ciggie. Touch more grappa.

Don't wander off.

I shan't. I'll just go to the edge of the road over there. Where I shall stand. Obediently. Hoping for a horse and cart to trample me.

She watched Margaret depart through the doorway. She could feel the tension ease from her shoulders. She got up and downed the grappa and went over to the side of the road. The sudden drone of Allied traffic in the distance made her look toward the edge of land. She raised her binoculars. Cypress hills were already in shadow. It wasn't cold but the tilt of light, the mauve tinge to the landscape, made her shiver. Almost forty-five years ago, she'd fallen in love with a young maid called Livia.

The distant rumble of guns sounded like thunder. Brief flashes of artillery split the sky. Of course she'd kept the bloody violet.

In a wood, somewhere between Staggia Senese and Poggibonsi, Allied troops were waiting to enter Florence. Dusk was looming, and through the trees came the sound of an accordion stolen from a factory near Trieste.

Standing by his jeep, peering into a broken mirror with the lower half of his face covered in soap, was a young man. He was running the blade carefully across his upper lip, avoiding the scar that had risen two years before.

He had blond hair that revealed a hint of red under the early-evening sun. No one in the family knew where the red had come from, both sides being dark, and his father often joked that the winter his son was conceived, he'd eaten his fill of beetroot. You were stained, his father liked to tell him.

His features were his mother's: Straight, slender nose, slightly longer than the required ratio of hairline to bridge, or chin to tip, that would have signified a face in perfect symmetry. Eyebrows at an upward angle conveyed a good listener, and his ears, though not wildly protruding, were definitely alert. When he smiled, which he did often, a dimple appeared in either cheek, which was immediately disarming.

His wife, Peg, said he should've been better looking seeing as he'd inherited all his mum's best bits. She'd meant it as a compliment, but her words danced both ways, hot and cold, kind and cruel, but that was Peg. Unknown to everyone, his apotheosis would come in later years. He would be a fairly handsome middle-aged man. An eye-catching elderly man.

The squeal of birds overhead delighted him. He and they had traveled hundreds of miles north against all odds to arrive at that place in time—swifts at the end of March and him in June—and the catalog of near misses and lucky escapes that had accompanied his journey across Africa, Sicily and up the Adriatic would have astonished priests and astrologers alike. Something had been watching over him. Why not a swift?

He looked at his watch and rinsed his face. He threw his pack and rifle into the jeep just as Sergeant Lidlow was coming out of the mess tent.

Where you off to, Temps?

Picking up the captain, Sarge.

Bring us back a bottle or two, will you?

Ulysses turned the ignition and the old jeep caught the first time. He drove into the hills, leaving behind the silhouettes of tanks and men. He passed different Allied divisions, young men like him worn old. The soft light moved with him across the groves and meadows, until the sky held only ripples of pink and the night chasing in from the west. He'd tried to practice ambivalence toward this land, but it was futile. Italy astonished him. Captain Darnley had seen to that. They'd traveled up the country together, mostly reconnaissance, but sometimes mere wandering. Through remote villages, seeking out frescoes and hilltop chapels.

A little over a month before, they'd driven up to Orvieto, a city built on a huge rock overlooking the Paglia valley. They'd sat on the bonnet of the jeep and drunk red wine out of their canteens as bombers roared overhead toward Mount Cetona, the boundary of Tuscany. They'd stumbled into the cathedral, into the San Brizio Chapel, where Luca Signorelli's masterpiece, the *Last Judgment*, could be found. Though neither of them was a believer, the images had still held them to account.

Darnley said that Sigmund Freud had visited in 1899 and had somehow forgotten Signorelli's name. This he'd called the mechanism of repression and it became fundamental in Freud's *The Interpretation of Dreams*. God—but you probably know this already, don't you, Temps? And not waiting for an answer, Darnley marched out into the crisp June sun, leaving Ulysses giddy in the whirl of information, and in Darnley's unwavering belief in him.

The road straightened out and from the trees in the distance, a glint of light flickered across his face. He slowed and came to a stop with the engine running. He reached down for his binoculars and saw it was a woman standing by the roadside watching him through hers.

She waved him down with an unlit cigarette, and when the jeep came to a halt, she cried, Oh thank God! Eighth Army?

Just a tiny fraction of it, I'm afraid, said Ulysses, and she held out her hand.

I'm Evelyn Skinner.

Private Temper, said Ulysses. Where've you come from, Miss Skinner, if you don't mind me asking?

Rome, she said.

What? Now?

Good Lord, no! From that *albergo* behind the trees. Came up a week ago with a friend and stopped off in Cortona to assess the damage to the Francesco di Giorgio. Miraculously untouched. We've been waiting ever since.

Waiting for what?

I'm trying to contact the Allied Military Government.

For what purpose, Miss Skinner?

To liaise with the Monuments, Fine Arts and Archives officers. They know I'm here, but they seem to have abandoned me. I'm an art historian. I thought I could be of use once they've located all the works from the museums and churches. They've been sequestered around these hills, you know. All the masterpieces. The whole gang—even dear old Cimabue. But I suppose you know that, don't you?

Ulysses smiled. I did hear a rumor, Miss Skinner.

Do you have a light? she asked.

I wouldn't recommend it. Look what happened to me. And he pointed to the scar at the corner of his lip. Sniper, he said. A near miss.

Evelyn stared at him.

But it *hit* you, she said.

But not the important bit, he said, tapping his head. Nearly took my lips off, though. Then where would you be?

Struggling with my plosives, Private Temper. Now, light me up. Please.

Ulysses leaned across and struck a match.

Thank you, she said, blowing out smoke in a perfect circle. She raised her arm and looked about. See? No snipers. So, do you think you can help me? I'll be no trouble at all. And my lips, still perfectly intact, will be forever sealed. What do you say?

You're putting me in a bit of a bind, miss.

Oh, I'm sure you're no stranger to that.

Do you believe in fate, Miss Skinner?

Fate? It is a *gift*. According to Dante, anyhow.

A gift? I like that. Come on then, miss, hop in.

Oh, drop the "miss," for God's sake, said Evelyn, sitting down next to him. My name's Evelyn. And yours?

Ulysses.

Ulysses! How wonderful! And is there a Penelope waiting for your return?

Nah. Just a Peggy. And I doubt she's waiting. And he turned the ignition and the jeep pulled away.

The rogue shelling that had accompanied the afternoon had ceased and a soft, almost believable, peace lay across the wooded hills and hill-top refuges, across the dark symmetry of vines that terraced the slopes.

Ulysses lit a cigarette.

So, said Evelyn, tell me a little—

London. Twenty-four. Married. No kids.

Evelyn laughed. You've done this before.

You gotta be quick, right? Could be dead tomorrow. You?

Kent. Sixty-four. Unmarried. Childless. And what of life before all this?

Globes, he said. Dad made 'em and I sold 'em. Then he died and I just made 'em.

You made the world turn!

Find a Temper & Son globe and you'll find my mum's name hidden somewhere on the surface.

A town called . . . ? she asked.

Nora.

How romantic.

Nice, right?

You and Peggy like that?

Nah, me and Peg are the opposite. Left to me, I'd name stars after her. We got married on a bender, only way we could do it. When she woke up and saw the ring, she punched me in the face. Happiest day of my life, though. Then I joined the army and we're strangers again.

Don't you write to one another?

He shook his head. We know what we're both up to, he said. Thing is, it's always been us when the others have left. Always that spark when the lights have gone out. Is that love?

Oh, don't look at me. I've not stayed long on that particular horse.

Never?

Once or twice, maybe.

Once is enough. We just need to know what the heart's capable of, Evelyn.

And do you know what it's capable of?

I do. Grace and fury.

Evelyn smiled, and drew heavily on her cigarette.

So *that*—and she pointed to his lip—was Peg and not a sniper.

No, that was definitely a sniper. Look, he said, and he raised his right arm and showed the scar along his wrist. Shrapnel, he said.

He leaned toward her and parted his hair. Sniper, he said. He pulled up his trouser leg. Evelyn winced. Artillery fire. That one got infected. And then this. And he unbuttoned his shirt.

Good Lord, said Evelyn. Another near miss?

A lucky escape, he said. There's a difference.

How so?

It's all mental. How I see life at that time. This last one was in Trieste, and there's been nothing since. And now I know I'm not going to die. And I'm a lot happier.

Excuse me? said Evelyn.

Not die here, I mean.

Italy here?

War here, he said. It's like having a debt hanging over you. You know it'll be called in, but it's how it's gonna get called in that's the question. What I mean is, all those opportunities to kill me off. I'm still here. There's a reason for that.

Poor aim might be one, said Evelyn.

You're funny, Evelyn.

And you're a very optimistic young man.

I am, he said, I'm glad you noticed that. And he went on to explain that his optimism came from his father, Wilbur, whose wise counsel of "Life's what you make it, son," had been firmly entrenched in him from a young age. The man was a dreamer, he said. Had a loser's luck and a winning smile and was never happy unless he had a churn in his guts that denoted money riding on an outcome. A feeling he often equated with love.

But then one day it happened for real. He walked into the pub, stood on a table and declared he'd fallen head over heels and everyone thought she'd be some tidy young thing, but she wasn't. She was almost as old as him, slipping down the other side of fifty. Tired, kind face with the keenest blue eyes that looked at him as if he was a meadow of wildflowers. And two months later—against all odds—she told him they were having a child, a first for both.

The most beautiful words in the world, said Ulysses.

Having a child? said Evelyn.

Against. All. Odds.

This recognition of double luck—wife, and kid incubating—brought back a familiar taste to Wilbur Temper, like sucking on a coin.

And his palms are tingling, said Ulysses, the soles of his feet too, and he knows this feeling because it's a winning feeling and you can never let a winning feeling pass because that would go against nature. So, he goes to my mum and explains what he needs to do. Last time, she says. Last time, he promises.

Now, his mate Cressy has told him about this illegal greyhound meeting out in Essex, all hush-hush and big money, and they go out there together and study form and he scribbles in his notebook a beautiful constellation of numbers, subtractions, additions, an algebraic formula of luck. Last race. Everything on the black. That's what he used to say. All or nothing. And he places life and savings on a tan and white dog called Ulysses's Boy at a hundred to one.

The rest is folklore. Dog came in first, thus ensuring two things: enough money to set up a modest business in handmade globes, and a memorable name for his sole son and heir.

You were named after *a greyhound*? said Evelyn.

A *winning* greyhound, Evelyn. Winning.

The heavy presence of artillery guns and infantry came into sight long before the villa. At the checkpoint, they were waved on through. Along the driveway they could see military guards and Italian civilians placing *Off Limits* signs at every entrance to the ornate building. Captain Darnley was waiting for them outside. He was wiping his glasses on the tail of his shirt. He looked up, squinting at the sound of the jeep. His dark hair had a premature dusting of gray at the sides that made him appear older than his thirty years, and his dark eyes peered out from dark sockets and gave him a perpetual look of sorrow. Rather like the last panda facing extinction. He put his glasses back on and approached the jeep.

Temps! he called. Temps!

Ulysses parked the jeep and got out.

What's up, sir? he said.

We found a cellar. Jerry must have missed it. We've been drinking all bloody day. I think I've drunk myself sober.

Not yet you haven't, sir. Sir, this is Miss Evelyn Skinner. Miss Skinner, Captain Darnley.

They shook hands. A pleasure, Miss Skinner, said Darnley.

Likewise, Captain, said Evelyn.

Miss Skinner's an art historian, said Ulysses. She's been trying to contact the Monuments officers through the AMG. I thought there was a good chance they'd be here, sir.

Not yet they're not, Temps, said Darnley. But fear not, Miss Skinner, we shall get you your contact. But first, follow me. Come on, Temps, you too.

He led them toward the villa and said, It's quite a haul. Only uncovered twenty-four hours ago.

And as they crossed the courtyard and passed the guards, Evelyn said, Are you saying what I think you're saying, Captain Darnley?

In here, said Darnley, and he pushed open the large wooden Baroque doors into the *salone*. The stink assaulted them.

Oh my word! said Evelyn, covering her nose.

Sorry, Miss Skinner, said Darnley, I should've warned you. The Germans like to shit everywhere before they retreat. Watch your step. It's quite a sewer in here.

It was hard to see anything except for the dark shapes of furniture. The shutters were drawn, and the air was lifeless, and the flies were giddy. Underfoot the sound of broken glass and broken tiles, and brick dust swirled. Wait here, said Darnley as he went across the room to a lamp. He bent down, struck a match, and raised the lamp with a theatrical flourish. The room flared with light, and in the middle, rising out of the stink and gloom, was a large undamaged altar panel.

Oh my, whispered Evelyn.

Ulysses Temper, Miss Evelyn Skinner, I'd like you to meet Pontormo's *Deposition from the Cross*.

Do you think they'd let us take it now, Captain Darnley, and save them the trouble? asked Evelyn.

Darnley laughed and said, Shall we ask?

What is it exactly, sir?

One of the great altarpieces portraying the life of Christ, Temps. Isn't that right, Miss Skinner?

You are correct, Captain. Painted to hang above the altar in the Capponi Chapel in the church of Santa Felicità. Completed in 1528. Give or take. The style is what we would call early Mannerist, Ulysses—a break in tradition, that's all—away from High Renaissance classicism and everything associated with it. You can see it's a deliberate denial of realistic style, calculated, and artificial. The light—you see—theatrical.

And she went on to explain the difference between a deposition and an entombment. The dreamlike use of color, the sparseness of the image, the dance.

She said, It's about feeling, Ulysses, that's all. People trying to make sense of something they can't make sense of.

(The faint sound of laughter trespassed on the room.)

It's simply the dead body of a young man being presented to his mother, said Darnley.

Oldest story in the world, said Evelyn.

Which is?

Grief, Temps. Just a lot of fucking grief.

They ventured into the further reaches of the villa. Military guards and Italian custodians marched past, carrying religious relics and statuary. They stood back as Filippo Lippi's *Annunciation* was maneuvered through as if it was a deck chair.

Darnley stopped outside a small wooden door. Here we are, he said. Worst-kept secret in Tuscany. Shall we?

Candles threw scant light onto the edges of the stairwell. There was a strong smell of damp stone and tallow, and the level of oxygen thinned as they made their descent. The staircase eventually leveled out into a vast cellar lit by oil lamps. The floor appeared bloodied where dozens of oak casks had met their fate. Documents and books lay scattered and the ceiling was propped up by timber. A pathway had been cleared through the rubble toward a wall of shelving, which was, in fact, a magnificent trompe l'oeil. As they got closer, Ulysses could see the incongruous seam of a door.

Abracadabra, said Darnley.

How many more white rabbits can we expect, Captain?

Hat's empty now, Miss Skinner. After you. Please.

Darnley opened the door and conversation and music spilled out. The room was a long narrow corridor, Caravaggesque shadows in the corners where the throw of candlelight was simply too weak to penetrate. Broken glass littered the floor and two plundered walls of wine disappeared into the furthest reaches. Smoke hovered above tables occupied by Allied officers and Italian superintendents and the only air came from a grille in the ceiling, where the fug was sucked out in sporadic gasps.

What'll it be, Miss Skinner? Something red?

Surprise me, said Evelyn.

Darnley went to the rack, flexed his fingers and reached for a bottle. He looked down at the label and gave a thumbs-up.

A 1902 Carruades de Lafite. Pauillac! he shouted. Heavenly! (A word he used a lot, which was odd for a man whose idea of the afterlife was oblivion.)

They sat down at an empty table and a private emerged out of the shadows carrying three crystal goblets, a corkscrew and a small plate of thinly cut pecorino cheese.

You see, Miss Skinner. It's really not much different from the Garrick.

Evelyn laughed.

Darnley did the honors. A neat little pop, the smell of the cork and the comforting glug of the pour.

To what shall we toast? said Darnley. What do you think, Temps?

To this moment, sir.

Oh, very good, said Evelyn.

To this moment.

The conversation went straight to Evelyn and Darnley's love of Florence. Darnley explained that his father had been—for a short while, at least—vicar at St. Mark's English Church. Halcyon days, he said. Summers in the Uffizi were my education. By the time I left school, he said, I had little interest in anything other than art. Brief stint at Chelsea. Brief stint at the Royal Academy. And here we are. I am a privileged cliché, Miss Skinner—

Oh, I think we've all been one of those, Captain—

—unqualified for anything except oenology or the occasional attribution.

And Darnley reached into his jacket pocket and pulled out a mottled notebook and a nub of pencil. He said, Do you mind? It's just notes about wine—memory, you know. Thoughts. Just things.

No, no, indeed, said Evelyn. Go ahead.

Long slim fingers. Hair falling across his brow. Quite childlike. He reminded her of Forster and she leaned across to Ulysses and told him so.

Who's Forster, Evelyn?

What's what? said Darnley, looking up.

I told Ulysses you reminded me of E. M. Forster.

D'you know him, Miss Skinner?

I bought him his first *bombolone* and lent him my Baedeker.

Good God! People get engaged for less! And Darnley tapped out a cigarette and offered it over. What was he like? he asked.

Rather sweet, said Evelyn. He didn't like Rubens and was quite devoted to his mother.

Could've been my twin, said Darnley, lighting up and downing the contents of his glass.

You got time for another drink, Miss Skinner?

All the time in the world, said Evelyn.

And Temps, the music? Something softer to match the wine, please.

Righto, sir. And Ulysses went toward the gramophone. He also commandeered another plate of cheese.

The second bottle was a 1900 Château Margaux accompanied by Joan Merrill singing "There Will Never Be Another You." A singular pairing, all three agreed. Darnley poured out the wine. On the nose was smelled tobacco, truffles, cedar, strawberry. Glasses were raised. *To this moment!*

I was twenty-one, said Evelyn. Not that much younger than you, Ulysses. That was my first experience of Florence. Traveling unchaperoned and ready to fall in love.

And did you, Evelyn?

Evelyn paused as she tasted the wine. I did, as it happens, she said. Once with a person and once with the city itself. You have all that to come, Ulysses. Open your heart. Things happen there, if you let them. Wonderful things.

Suddenly, the cellar lurched to the right as the earth above was blasted by artillery fire. Evelyn gasped. Chunks of ceiling fell and extinguished candles, and men reached across to steady their tables, some diving underneath instead. Glasses and bottles were thrown to the floor.

This is bloody tedious! shouted Darnley, cradling his bottle of Margaux.

Ulysses reached across the table for Evelyn's hands. He began to talk to her, even sing to her. Still singing as the barrage ended. The faint click of a turntable slowing to its inevitable end. The soft fall of white dust in the intervening silence. Darnley laughing.

Out into the night, they breathed air that was fresh and welcome. Darnley settled down in the back, Evelyn in the front, and they pulled away amidst salutes, and drunken soldiers running at their side shouting they'd see them in Florence!

The roads were tree lined, and glimpses of the bright gibbous moon lit their way in the absence of headlights. The dark swallowed them. The overhang of thick trees, and the sloping curve of the road, made them feel they were no longer on the surface of the earth but heading slowly into its muddy, bosky depths. The smell of the air was heavy and verdant. Soon Darnley was in a boozy sleep and the air was perforated by his juddering snores. Ulysses took his foot off the accelerator and they coasted slowly along the shoulder of night.

Evelyn leaned back and looked at Darnley's face. Full of bluster, isn't he? she said. Look at him. Just a boy really. You're all just boys. You care for him, don't you? she said.

I do, Evelyn. I really do, he said, and he pulled over to let an Allied convoy pass. The noise was an assault and they sat back and watched the trucks pass, the pale stony faces of soldiers looking back at them. The sense was one of doom.

They'll be in the city soon, won't they? she asked.

Couple of days, tops. Kiwis first. South Africans. Then us.

Will it be bad? she asked.

I 'spect so, he said. It's always bad.

The last of the dust from the last of the trucks settled. Ulysses lit two cigarettes.

He said, That painting? The Pont—

—ormo, she said. Pontormo's *Deposition*?

Yeah. And he handed her a cigarette. Darnley said he studied it before all this and I said what's to study? It's just a picture, right?

It *is* just a picture. And you *are* right, said Evelyn. Art historians have made gods of men.

So?

So, said Evelyn.

All this fuss?

Evelyn laughed. The fuss, as you say, can certainly be exaggerated. But what it's always about, for me, is response. It's a painting that demands of us a response. All the best ones do.

What response?

You tell me.

I don't know what that means.

You were taken with the cloud back there. It drew you in. It interested you.

It looked separate from the picture, said Ulysses.

Noting the drama that's unfolding below, perhaps. A symbol of heaven? The Holy Spirit? Or a simple reminder that the action is taking place outside. All this is a response, Ulysses. It's not more complicated than that. Of course, we can then throw in execution of the craft—how *well* one paints—and the history of the piece, its provenance, and we can come up with value. But always the value for me will be response. How it moves one.

And that makes it worth saving?

I think so. I really do. To make sure it's around for another generation. Because it is important, Ulysses.

More important than people?

Evelyn let out a long stream of smoke. She said, They go together. It's what we've always done. Left a mark on a cave, or on a page. Showing who we are, sharing our view of the world, the life we're made to bear. Our turmoil is revealed in those painted faces—sometimes tenderly, sometimes grotesquely, but art becomes a mirror. All the symbolism and the paradox, ours to interpret. That's how it becomes part of us. And as counterpoint to our suffering, we have beauty. We like beauty, don't we? Something good on the eye cheers us. Does something to us on a cellular level, makes us feel alive and enriched. Beautiful art opens our eyes to the beauty of the world, Ulysses. It repositions our sight and judgment. Captures forever that which is fleeting. A meager stain in the corridors of history, that's all we are. A little mark of scuff. One hundred and fifty years ago Napoleon breathed the same air as we do now. The battalion of time marches on. Art versus humanity is not the question, Ulysses. One doesn't exist without the other. Art is the antidote. Is that enough to make it important? Well yes, I think it is.

Through the olive trees, the *albergo* came into sight. Here we are, said Evelyn quietly, and the jeep slowed down and stopped. The ticking sound of a cooling engine. The distant call of an owl. Darnley's heavy breath.

Look, said Ulysses as a faint light came on in an upper room. Welcome party? he said.

Oh, I doubt that, said Evelyn as she climbed from the jeep. She bent close to Darnley's ear, and placed her hand on his shoulder. Captain Darnley, she whispered.

He woke, dazed.

It's time to say good night, she said.

Miss Skinner.

No, no. Stay where you are, she said, and she offered her hand. Thank you, she said. For tonight. Keep your head down and stay in the world, if you please.

Darnley smiled. Take care, Miss Skinner. It's been a pleasure.

Likewise.

And I'll give the AMG a nudge, I promise.

Thank you. And Evelyn turned to Ulysses. I'm not sure I can say good-bye to you, young man.

Then let's not, Evelyn.

Ulysses got out of the jeep and offered his hand. She took it in hers.

A gift, right? he said.

A gift, indeed, she said. Dante Alighieri. You'll meet him in Florence, outside Santa Croce. He looks rather grumpy. Give him my best, though.

Will do.

And stay invincible, she said.

He saluted her. Watched her stomp across the parched grass toward the terrace.

It was too dark for him to see her turn back and look at him, but she did. She watched him get into the jeep, watched him disappear around the curve of the bend. She said something quietly, not a prayer exactly, just a little nod to keep him safe.

In East London, Peggy Temper woke with a thumping head on her. She was an hour late for setup, had spent most of it over the sink looking for a memory of the night before. The chatter of draymen outside the window, and she pulled back the curtain and was dazzled by sunlight. She watched Col offload barrels of ale and he glanced up at her window and she darted back but he saw her, she knew he did.

She went to the mirror and groaned. She wet her fingers and tried to encourage a curl here, a curl there before setting it in a haze of lacquer. A quick flannel wash and a spritz of perfume got her back into clothes and she smoked half a fag to clear her head.

She staggered down the stairs and put the place on edge. In the bar, she said, Don't say a fucking word, Col, and he didn't and pushed a neat gin her way. Ta, she said, and downed it in one. Oh Christ, she said, and Col kicked the mop bucket her way.

She was a liability, but a good-looking one at least. Her face and gob brought the soldiers in, and even puking her guts up, she did it with

style. Her arse bucked at each spasm and offered a sweet glimpse of
stocking. Col felt the nudge of an erection push against his Y-fronts. He
went down to the cellar to get a bottle of rum. When he came up, she
was glass in hand at the optics.

Hair of the dog?

Hair of the dog, she thought; she'd need the whole bleedin' pelt to
get moving this morning. What the fuck was she thinking?

Take it out of me tips, she said, and she sat down and lit a cigarette.

He came over and joined her. Good night? he said.

She looked at him and laughed.

No one like you, Peggy, he said, and she smiled that smile and the
bluebirds sang.

Col? (Oh Christ, what now? That face of hers . . .)

What, Peg?

This Saturday.

No way, Peg.

I know, I know, but this one's important.

They're all important. And Col downed his drink and got up. He
said, You've got resilience, I'll say that for you.

That's a good thing, right?

And Peggy stood up and started to dance in front of him. That's a
good thing, right, Col?

Come on, Peg, we're open. And mind you don't step on that bloody
mess you're dragging around you.

Peggy stopped and looked behind her. What mess? she said.

Your liver. Now, open the bleedin' door.

The warm morning air sauntered in, bringing with it the stink of brick
dust and tarmacadam. Ginny Formiloe, Col's kid, was coming back
from the baker's holding a loaf of bread tight against her chest like a
baby. Ginny waved at her. Peg waved back. Ginny loved Peg, told her
that every morning with her funny nasal voice. Ginny was a woman in
body and a child in mind. She collected glasses in the pub and some-

times poured a pint, but mostly it was the glasses and the counting out of coins at the end of the night. Sweet, sweet kid, with her strange brain and her mother's legs and her pretty floral dress. She looked a lot like Col's wife, and that used to break Col's heart in the early days. Ginny wasn't born with the clocks turned back, but something happened, probably that fever when she nearly died. Col's wife left because of his drinking but really it was because of something else and she got out long before the war started. Went up to Scotland to the Outer Hebrides to her sister who farmed. No one said what they really thought, because how bad could it have been to have ended up on a granite rock in the North Atlantic?

Col never did stop drinking when his wife left, but he cut back. Besides, around his daughter his anger turned to mush. He became a soppy drunk, all patriotic songs and teary eyes, because it was just his way.

Ginny stopped at the curb. She looked left looked right looked left looked right before she crossed. Peggy! she screamed. Peggy opened her arms, and Ginny ran into them. Love you, Peggy, she said. Ginny had a strong whiff of the monthlies about her and Peg said, Come on, Ginny, let's go get you changed.

By the end of the afternoon, Peg was dead on her feet. The pub had turned into a morgue and she took her break outside. She looked up and down the street with its bleached front steps and enough gossip to fill a sewer. She plonked herself down on a chair and faced the sun. Kids as young as eight cycling by and whistling, All right, Peg! She raised her arm. Yeah, all right, kid, she mimicked. She'd not long closed her eyes when Old Cress came by. She knew it was him blocking the sun, trying to get her attention. Cress was Peg's rock. Always had been, always would be. He thought her the most beautiful woman alive and he'd have done anything for her. Even given her the moon, if he could. (And what would I do with the moon, Cress? Exchange it for the sun. Think big, girl.)

You get home all right? he said.

You brought me home, you silly sod. I might not remember much but I do remember that.

Cress said, You comin' inside to pull me a pint?

I'm done. And she pointed to the *Closed* sign. Col's on the taps and I'm sunning, she said.

When he'd gone, Peg pulled her dress above her knees. The sun felt warm on her crotch, made her feel wet and easy, same feeling as when she'd set eyes on American Boy.

He was a good dancer. She'd noticed that first. Better than his mate, though to look at them they could've been brothers. Mate peeled away to the bar and Eddie's eyes latched on to hers. Like stars colliding, he told her. And then they danced celestially till their clothes were wet and their appetites raw and afterward, in a café on Old Compton Street, they ate a sorry dish of unidentifiable meat and spuds.

Eddie had lovely hair (thick, shiny, dark) and Peg ran her hand through it and said it felt like silk and Eddie blushed because he was still a boy despite his age. Eddie told her he was going to college after the war to take over his father's business and Peg asked, What business? and he said, Oranges. Peg said she hadn't tasted an orange in two years and Eddie said he'd have to see about that. Eddie asked if he could see her on Saturday and Peg said, Just try and stop me, and Eddie laughed. Eddie had good teeth too. American white. Slight overbite when he kissed her, but nothing that couldn't be sorted out with practice. Eddie paid the bill and asked if he could come home with her and she said, Not tonight, sunshine, and he said, I love your accent, and she said, Still not tonight. That was when Eddie mentioned a hotel room on Saturday night and Peg's knees could've given way there and then. I'm gonna treat you like a princess, he said.

Music from the turntable inside. "Someday My Prince Will Come."

Bloody comedian, Col! she shouted, and she stood up and went back into the bar with a black mood descending.

All week, she was up early wiping down tables and checking the optics. She was sober and charming and still put everyone on edge. What's up with Peg? Fuck knows, said Col, skirting about her as if she was a volcano ready to blow. And yet she didn't. She just smoked. She did the accounts, placed the orders, took Ginny down to the canal to find the kittens Cress said had been born that week. On Thursday night Peg polished the countertop with another coating of Brasso and Col said it shone like a crystal ball. Col said, I see Saturday night. I see you and wonder boy out on the town.

Peg did a double take at first. What's that? she said.

You heard, said Col, and Peg jumped into his arms and straddled his waist with her good strong legs and he felt that nudge again real hard. All right all right, he said, needing to go down to the cellar to finish himself off.

When Saturday night rolled round, it rolled warm and yellow, and the canal shimmered with a million crazy stars and set the dogs barking.

Clack clack clack Peg's heels down the stairs. Col smelled her before he saw her, and she smelled French and flowery, all allure. She entered the bar with blue eyes and red lips and blond hair and skirt tight.

Col said, I hope he's worth it. And Peg said, He's an American, Col. He's worth it.

Col handed Peg a gin and tonic.

You be careful, Peg. Don't you go falling.

Here's to falling and being caught, said Peg, and she raised her glass.

Here, said Col. Kathleen dropped it in for you.

He pushed an envelope across the bar. Peg opened it and pocketed the money.

He say anything? said Col.

We don't do letters, Col, you know we don't. The money says he's alive and that's all I want to know. We'll sort everything else out when he's back.

He's a good boy.

I know he is.

Don't wait up, sunshine, she added.

Peg?

She turned. What? she said.

You're better than the lot of them.

It was a classy restaurant. Violins played and a waiter flapped out her napkin and laid it in her lap. Even called her madam, which was a bloody cut above. Eddie beamed at her, teeth polished and breath like mint. His handsomeness shot straight to her knickers.

He pushed two boxes across the table.

Open them, he said. So you know I'm serious about you.

Peg felt other tables looking at her. She opened the larger box and lifted out an orange. It was the most perfect orange. She closed her eyes and smelled it. Could've bitten into it there and then and when she heard someone laugh it almost ruined the moment.

Next, he said, and she was prepared to feign delight at the little box, but when she opened the lid the brooch was beautiful, so she didn't have to. Eddie took it from her hand and held it up to the light.

Cameo is shell. Did you know that?

Course I did, said Peg (even though she didn't).

I didn't, he said, and he held the brooch to his ear.

Can you hear the sea? she said.

He shook his head. Nope. Just a little voice, he said, screwing up his face.

What's it say?

Let's go back to your place. And Eddie laughed.

Peg didn't laugh.

We can't, though, Eddie. I told you that. I thought we were going to a hotel.

It was the brooch or a room, he said. And I thought you'd like the brooch.

Peg drank past the borders of romantic and ended up against a wall under a railway arch. It was a monochrome night and shards of moonlight scattered across black cobbles and highlighted glimpses of Peg's white flesh. Her American soldier was kissing her hard and he'd promised her a room but got her a brooch instead and there they were, up against a wall with a cheap bunch of flowers at her feet.

He was fumbling around, looking for the Western Front, and she said he'd have to go further south to find it.

There we go, she said, and he groaned.

She liked the way he said baby. Liked the way he said, I've never met a girl like you, Peg. Liked the way he fucked her. But all she could think of was that he'd promised her a room, and she tried to push the thought aside but the more he kept pounding her into the wall, the more that room came back to taunt her.

You promised me a room, she said.

I know, I know, he said, all busy like. Next time, he said.

I don't do next time, she suddenly said, and dropped her leg.

Stop, she said. I'm done, and she tugged on his rich-boy hair.

Jeez, Peg! What ya doing?

I said, stop!

A train passed overhead, and the stones shook. Peg pulled down her skirt and took off across the road.

Peggy! Her name echoed across the bricks. The sound of his foot-steps after her.

Why can't we go to your place? he said. You married or some-thing?

No. I'm not "married or something." I live above a pub. Where I work. I've told you that a hundred times before. You promised me a room and you've suddenly gone cheap.

That brooch wasn't—

Call me when you've booked the sheets, Eddie. But none of this one step away from whore. It's too close.

She walked down to the canal with a hard-as-nails look across her face and even the rats steered clear. The bench was empty, and she sat down and lit a cigarette. A drunk stumbled along the towpath and was about to speak to her, but she said, Don't you fucking dare, and her voice was like a blade, so he didn't. She could handle herself, al-ways had, and the city never frightened her, especially at night. The canal drew the lonely and the dreamers, and in that moment she was both.

She wanted out of here and American Boy was her out of here. California. New World. New Life. She was cupping that dream in both hands, careful not to spill even a drop.

She rubbed her foot. She had the start of a bunion like her mum. The woman'd had big bloody chestnuts on the sides of her feet; God help her if the similarity was working its way up. She lit a match and looked at her watch. Ten minutes past one. Out of the darkness that familiar face.

Come here often? said Cress.

We're making a habit of this, she said.

Wanna go home? Come on then. And he pulled her up and she towered over him. Cressy had once told her that he'd dreamed of being a jockey, on account of his size, but had ended up at the docks. And just once, he'd said, just once he'd've liked to 'ave gone on one of them boats.

You don't have to travel the world to be worldly, she'd said.

You think I'm worldly?

No one worldlier. It's what's in here that counts. And she'd pointed to his stomach. Guts is where we love from, she'd said.

They climbed the steps back up to the street.

You love this Yankee fella? he asked, but Peg didn't answer.

Come on, girl, you ain't a kid no more.

Peg stopped and slipped on her shoes. Yeah, I love him. Like I'd die without him.

Blimey, you got it bad.

So don't ask.

You tell him stuff? said Cress.

I tell him nothing.

Tell him something. Words, Peg. He might not be here forever.

You get told stuff?

Not so much. But words are gold dust to a decrepit old git like me.

You're not decrepit, she said, and opened her handbag. Here, have an orange.

Well, look at that, he said, and held it up against the black sky. You know how this came into the world, Peg?

A couple of navels on a dirty weekend?

He laughed.

This here is the love child of a mandarin and a pomelo.

What in fuck's name's a pomelo?

Citrus maxima.

You seen one?

Nah. Just read about it. It's like a large grapefruit with thick skin and a lot of pith.

Bit like Col then, she said as the dark outline of the pub came into sight.

When you seeing him again?

Day after tomorrow.

Well, you tell him stuff, Peg. You give him hope.

A week after the Oltrarno district of Florence had been liberated, Ulysses and Darnley were in the Boboli Gardens behind the Pitti Palace, where they'd been managing a supply convoy all morning. Darnley was standing on a wall overlooking the city. The sound of gunfire ricocheted across the Arno and smoke rose from the streets below. Ulysses was hidden in a bush, gun sight trained on the Belvedere Fort, where a Fascist sniper had caused havoc all morning.

You still OK with this, sir?

Yes, yes, said Darnley. I die here, I die happy. OK if I smoke?

Whatever you like. You're a mere lure.

I am a lure, said Darnley. I'm a lure unto myself. And he laughed and struck a match. This view, he said. Miracle of right time right place. *"Luce intellettual, piena d'amore."*

What's that mean, sir?

Light of the mind, full of love.

Nice.

Isn't it?

One of yours, sir?

No! Dante. The belief that a combination of intellect and beauty can make the world a better place. You see our sniper yet?

Not yet, sir, said Ulysses, wiping sweat out of his eye. Probably having lunch.

Probably, said Darnley, blowing out a long stream of smoke. He said, And there in the center representing the glory of the city itself—

What are you pointing at, sir?

The cathedral. Brunelleschi's dome. Ushering in the great period of Renaissance humanism. Built in majesty so those seated below it could receive God. And yet, first and foremost it's a testament to the order and beauty of the universe. A universe that is responsive and nonjudgmental, Temps, and in which mankind has a place: man as the measure of all things. And the poets and artists ran with that conviction. Perspective composition arranged around the human figure. The square and the circle became the bedrock of fifteenth-century architecture and in Vitruvian spirit Leonardo placed man inside both. Science and theology living side by side, Temps. The gift of intellect and artistic achievement as God-given as faith. What a moment for these maverick minds to have come together. Yes, it was short-lived, but so what? The explosion of energy from that time destroyed myths and superstitions and revealed the heavens just as they were. Subject to decay and mutability. Just like us.

Darnley flicked away the cigarette. He said, I was thinking. After the war, we could—

We don't do after, do we, sir?

Oh fuck, God no, of course we don't. Sorry. It's this view. It makes me dream.

More rage, sir, please.

More rage?

Yes please, said Ulysses. And a lot more volume. Wave your arms around.

Like this?

That's perfect, said Ulysses. Ah, here we go, I see him—

My life in your hands, Temps—

Always, sir. And he held his breath. He lined the man up in his sight and the trigger moved easily. The jarring crack of a gunshot rang out, and in the distance, a body fell from the tower, then a *panino* a moment later. Darnley cheered and jumped down from the wall. Ulysses crawled out from the bush and brushed himself down.

Darnley said, D'you notice a smell, Temps?

I do, sir. Death and unwashed bodies, I'd say.

That's precise, said Darnley as they headed up toward Neptune's Fountain.

And a touch of the usual, said Ulysses.

When they got to the fountain, a group of women were scrubbing their children and clothes in the same fetid water.

Darnley shook his head. Jesus Christ! he said. Niccolò di Raffaello di Niccolò dei Pericoli would turn in his grave.

Oh, I doubt he'd be able to move, sir, once they'd got his name in.

It *physically* pains me, Ulysses, he said. To see these gardens like this.

I know it does, sir.

You can see that?

I can.

Don't they care?

It's hard to care if you don't have bread, sir. Or water.

Darnley sighed.

Come on, Alexander St. John Darnley. Let's find you a jeep and get you back.

The stench of squalor hit them as they stepped down into the courtyard. The place was crawling like a Naples slum. Thousands of traumatized people with only one source of water as if emerging from a siege. Ulysses and Darnley struggled through the murk toward the supply convoy. To their left an argument erupted over the allocation of flour. Sheets and clothing hung down from the upper balconies of the palace, and under the portico, away from the sun, people sprawled across mattresses holding tight to meager belongings. Makeshift charcoal stoves were firing up, and the air was acrid and fumy. These were the people who'd once lived in the vicinity of the river Arno. Forced to evacuate their homes before the retreating German army blew up the bridges. All except the one, that is.

The Ponte Vecchio was saved by a sentimental Führer, who'd visited the city in '38 and formed an attachment to the famous landmark. Darnley said it proved the man had fucking awful taste. So had invading Poland, added Ulysses.

Let's go, sir! shouted Ulysses. Darnley got in the jeep and they drove into the heat, leaving behind the grand façade of the former ducal seat. At the bottom of the slope, along the Via de' Guicciardini, rubble thirty feet high blocked access to the Ponte Vecchio. Ulysses turned the jeep around and headed west. The stink of broken sewers and seeping gas pipes broiled under an August sun. The air shimmered like liquid.

They'd only gotten as far as Piazza del Carmine when Darnley suddenly shouted, Stop the car!

Sir?

Stop the car, repeated Darnley.

Crowds of returning Florentines passed by, dragging handcarts.

What is it, sir?

You need to spend time in this city, Temps. I promised Miss Skinner, didn't I? Go on, out you get. But back before nightfall.

There was no negotiation. Ulysses grabbed his rifle and got out the jeep and Darnley shifted behind the wheel.

Ulysses watched him drive away, unsure what had just taken place. He unscrewed his canteen and drank. The sun was fierce overhead. The wide expanse of the piazza offered no shade and the stones were baked white. Ulysses backed away from the church and followed a cyclist making slow progress toward a street entirely in shadow.

He felt invigorated by the cool and by the hours of freedom ahead. Men continued to shake his hand as if he were the sole liberator of their city, and women kissed him, left marks of bright lips across his cheeks but he didn't mind. No one back home could understand what occupation did to a people. The deprivation of body and soul. The daily choice to survive, but at what cost and sometimes at what cost to others. He stood back and saluted as Allied tanks passed. A soldier gestured that he was a wanker. He laughed. That was the least of his problems.

The street brought him to the corner of a tree-lined square dominated at the far end by a church. He moved through a crowd that had gathered outside a café and the bells rang out. He settled on a bench in the shade near a fountain, half expecting to hear a familiar gurgle, but the city's water supply had long been cut. He lit a cigarette and watched the path of swifts through the *campanile*, across the terra-cotta dome, that perfect complement to the azure sky. A dog howled. A cyclist passed by. An overwhelming feeling that something bad had happened there, and it was that something other that ratcheted up the tension.

He noticed a group of people gesturing wildly. He stood up and joined them, followed the path of their gaze to a shutter swaying above. Beyond the shutter, a lone dark figure. It could have been a statue except for the slight swing of the man's arm to steady his balance. He was inching himself down the roof until the drop came into sight, at which point he froze. The man's hat took off on the breeze and made a spiraling descent. It took no effort at all for Ulysses to stretch out his hand and catch the dark gray Borsalino pinch-front fedora.

He rushed forward, surprised to find the door to the building locked. He tried each of the neighboring buildings in turn, until a door gave way and led him into an ancient stone vestibule. He ran up the stairs two at a time and set in motion a sequence of events that the locals would gladly recapitulate in the coming days.

There would be many versions of the stairwell dash that would be told later in the café, but it was Signor and Signora Mimmi, an amorous couple in their early sixties, only recently returned to their top-floor apartment, who actually opened the door to the *soldato* and were thus granted special dispensation to tell the story as it was, without interruption or embellishment by the many unreliable narrators who frequented the square.

He was banging on our door, they said in unison. But not like when the Germans arrived, added the *signora*. Could you demonstrate?

suggested the priest, and she made a fist and began banging on the counter. Everybody agreed that the tone was not angry but had a certain consideration to it. Oh yes, said Signora Mimmi, he was very polite. He wiped his boots on our mat. He said *Buongiorno*, but that was the extent of his Italian. He was a kind-looking soldier with lovely eyebrows, and dimples. He kept pointing his finger upward, trying to get us to understand. He was sweating. We had no water, so we offered him a large glass of wine, which he drank straight down. We led him into the kitchen and when he saw the ladder he began to climb up to the terrace, where my husband grows two fig trees and collects rainwater. But there has been no rain for weeks and the fig trees are dead.

Mine too, said the butcher.

It was at this point, both Signor and Signora Mimmi confessed to the gathering, that they lost sight of the soldier when he moved from the ladder to the roof. Weren't you interested? the greengrocer asked. No, they said. We wanted to make love.

So, there was Ulysses. On the roof with a nice little wine buzz, one hundred feet up with a man he didn't know precariously close to the edge and an easy target for the most incompetent sniper.

Signore? said Ulysses. I seem to have your hat. And Ulysses held out the fedora in a casual and unthreatening manner. As an opening gambit, he thought it would establish whether the man could (a) speak and (b) understand English. The resultant silence proved he could do neither. Ulysses left the hat by the terrace and inched his way down the shallow slope. The gasps from below were audible. As Ulysses drew near, he could see that the man was in his fifties, wearing a suit and tie of all things, dressed for his funeral. I wonder what's brought you up here? he thought, and he smiled because everyone told him he had the most disarming smile.

Down below, Michele the café owner had miraculously acquired a pair of binoculars and was reporting the situation to the eager crowd that was growing by the minute.

He's smiling, he said.

Arturo?

No, the soldier. Now he's lighting a cigarette.

Arturo?

Madonna mia, the soldier! And Michele gesticulated wildly and lowered the binoculars.

On the roof, Ulysses brought the cigarette to his mouth and assessed the situation. It was a beautiful summer's afternoon.

The sun was at his back, casting a web of brilliance across the rooftops, and the light fell pink across the Bellosguardo Tower and the Duomo, and the hills shimmered in haze. He was flooded with gratitude. If life was to end there, then so be it. He felt his father by his side. And his father's father. He was grounded by a long line of Tempers, all mild-mannered, decent men, who'd never asked for much except good odds once in a while. He wondered if the name had actually derived from Templar, the warrior priests. Fighting in the name of faith and love, however misguided. There were consequences to actions, of course—

These were his thoughts before he dislodged a tile that sent him hurtling into space.

The crowd below gasped. *O mio Dio!* shouted Michele's wife, Giulia. *O mio Dio!* The priest crossed himself multiple times, and a stranger to the area, who had Fascist tendencies, crossed his fingers and hoped for the worst.

The predicament, as far as Ulysses could see, wasn't that he was half on and half off the roof, but that his gun barrel was caught in the guttering. He was wedged in a rather uncomfortable position, testicles not known for their weight-bearing capacity. Ulysses turned toward the man and, still optimistic that a conversation without commonality of language was possible, said, Now, listen to me, *signore* . . . , and went on to explain that he'd been in a similar situation once before, and apart from the physical discomfort, which was severe, he was still hopeful for a positive outcome, if only—his voice, at this point, was calm and measured with not an ounce of pleading—if only you could bend down and release the barrel of the gun.

The *signore* frowned.

The gun. Ulysses's eyes motioned to the gun. Bang, bang. All that was necessary, he said, was a small movement. A lean forward, a slight crouch and an outstretched hand. An action that demanded nothing more than a bodily counterbalance. No more than you would do, say, to pull a child out of a pond. Nothing more.

Down below, Michele explained to the crowd, The soldier's gun barrel's caught in the guttering.

A murmur of disbelief rose.

They seem to be talking, said Michele.

How can they be talking? said the elderly contessa. Arturo doesn't speak English; the soldier doesn't speak Italian. This is a disaster. Do something, idiot man.

Michele stepped forward and in his strong accent shouted, Oi, Arturo! The gun barrel's stuck! You have to release the gun from the guttering!

The crowd below started to shout, Release the gun! Release the gun! Release the gun!

Arturo bent down.

No, don't close your eyes, said Ulysses.

Arturo looked at him.

That's it. *Sì, sì*. That's it. Almost there. Almost—

He's released the gun! shouted Michele from below. The crowd cheered and clapped. Well done, Arturo! they shouted, and started to chant his name. Arturo looked down at them, confused. It was death he'd been seeking, not acclaim.

Ulysses gave him a thumbs-up before he made a quick assessment of his next move. He found that his body weight favored the roof considerably more than the drop and he began to listen to the building. To its hardened solidity. To the centuries-old terra-cotta tiles. To the guttering. To the lives once lived within. And in this act of listening was a simple question: Can I trust you? It was a question he asked silently of everyone within minutes of an encounter. Peggy: cruel but trustworthy. Evelyn Skinner: trustworthy. Captain Darnley: I'd follow him to hell.

He watched an insect crawl across his arm and thought that was as good an answer as he was likely to get, and he began to swing his leg and the guttering shook. Backward and forward until the impetus of motion had generated enough energy for him to push off—suspended momentarily between roof and sky—and when he landed, there was just a slight wobble backward that evoked a scream from the priest below. But it was mainly traction that he felt beneath his boot: beautiful resistance. He brushed himself down, readjusted his balls, and a crescendo of applause rose from below.

At this point, three buildings along, the Mimmis looked out of the window, completely unaware of the drama that had played out above them, as they'd gone at it on the sofa like teenagers.

Come on, Arturo, said Ulysses. It's over, and he offered his arm, and Arturo took it, and they walked back up the roof together, to the hat, to the small terrace, to the quiet home below.

The euphoria of cheating death gave way to a weary calm and Ulysses left Arturo at the kitchen table and went to find a bathroom. The toilet gave off a strong smell of ammonia, which he regretted adding to.

Out in the hallway, the first room on the left was a bedroom. Ulysses lay down on the bed, and the heavily embroidered eiderdown was cool and enticing. Above him was a fresco. Something classical, not religious, and he recognized the acanthus leaves that Darnley had pointed out to him over the months. The trompe l'oeil effect of cornices, an open sky and birds in flight. A breeze blew and the shutters creaked. He heard the man in the kitchen, and it was a sad, lonely sound.

Three more bedrooms led off from the hallway, two overlooking the church and square, the other a *cortile* in the back. They shared the same simplicity of décor, a luxurious ease of taste and style, frescoes on the ceilings, but only curved lines and clusters of leaves, blue and white, or white and pink, washed out by age or a skillful brush.

In the living room, two walls of books insulated the room and rugs were cast across the terra-cotta floor. An air of conviviality was enhanced by a couple of large sofas, orange in the fading light; no antimacassars, no heavy wooden chairs that were all too familiar in Florentine homes. Paintings cluttered the walls, images of fruit and working kitchen tables, scattered ingredients in various states of decomposition, ordinary domestic scenes he could have placed his mother in.

He sat at the desk behind a typewriter and typed his name over and over and the keys made a heavy percussive sound in the quiet. He picked up the book next to the typewriter, looked at the dense text and old photographs of paintings. *Il Restauro dei Dipinti* large on the cover. He flicked through the pages and stopped at one of the images.

In the doorway to the kitchen, he held the pages of the book open and said, I saw it.

Arturo turned. *La Deposizione del Pontormo?*

Yep, said Ulysses. Saw it—and his finger moving from eye to picture to window.

Dove l'ha visto? said Arturo.

South of here, said Ulysses, and he pulled up a chair and dropped his pack on the floor. He placed the book between them and said, It's about grief. Oldest story in the world. And he placed his hand on Arturo's arm.

He said, They're trying to make sense of something they can't make sense of. People captured in the exact moment Jesus comes off the cross. And in that moment is energy and emotion. It's a bit like stopping a dance. And all you're left with is the silence. And the sorrow. And your pulse races.

Arturo stared at him. Eventually, he stood up, pushed aside his chair and crouched under the table. He removed a couple of floor tiles to reveal the dark maw of a cubbyhole, a hidden pantry that, for a year, had sustained life. He pulled out a bottle of wine, a candle and a nub of cheese.

What a feast, said Ulysses, and he reached around and retrieved a tin of ham from his pack and placed it on the table.

That's when Arturo began to cry.

It's only ham, said Ulysses.

And for two hours the wine was poured, the cheese cut, and the two men talked. Of what? Who knows? Of love, of war, of the past. And they listened with hearts instead of ears, and in the candlelit kitchen three floors up in an old palazzo, death was put on hold. For another night or day or week or year.

Ulysses left as dusk was beginning to settle across the square. The heavy thump of the door behind him set a dog howling. The striking façade of the church glowed and the last of the swifts made a desperate lunge at play. There were a few stragglers aimlessly wandering, but mostly the square was emptying before dark. He'd need to be sharpish to get back to camp before curfew and he ran across the square instead of turning left and found himself down by the river. The water was low, and a squadron of mosquitoes hovered above it, cruising for blood. The old buildings that had once overhung the river had all gone. The balconies, arches, towers were now a giant pile of shattered masonry that littered the embankment or had found settlement on the riverbed. A Bailey bridge, under construction, crossed the stricken stumps of the Ponte Santa Trìnita and the occasional pop of sniper fire north of the city kept him close to the wall in the darkest shadows. On the opposite shore, German tanks drove down onto the *lungarno*. Their bulk, in the twilight, like elephants at a water hole. And the flare of German cigarettes in German mouths; it shouldn't have been beautiful, but it was, daringly so. He stepped back into the dark streets and headed west until he came to the vast space of Piazza del Carmine again, then continued west until the Boboli Gardens were back on his left. If they stayed on his left, he knew he would eventually arrive at the Porta Romana and an Allied unit, and the slow road home.

He heard the sound of English vowels up ahead and quickened his pace. They were battalion stragglers coming from a brothel, and, safety in numbers, they traversed the checkpoint and the threat of court-martial and staggered up toward the villa where they were billeted. The night became fragrant and flowers from lime trees spilled over the wall. The scent draped across them and filled the space between them, dizzied them like bees.

Darnley was waiting in the orchard by Ulysses's tent. The familiar stooped outline, the furtive rise of cigarette to mouth, the furrowed brow lit by the cold blue light of the moon. Darnley turned at the sound of his footsteps. Nice hat, Temps, he said.

Thanks, sir. And Ulysses took it off and showed him. Darnley motioned for him to follow and they walked to the edge of the trees and the remotest part of the garden, away from ears.

Darnley said, We're leaving.

What?

Tomorrow. Back over to the Adriatic. Fifth Army stays put.

Fuck.

Indeed.

All a bit sudden. You all right, sir?

No. Not really. And Darnley ran his hand around the hat band. I don't know, he said. Something's not right. Is it cooler tonight, or is it me?

Bit cooler, sir, said Ulysses, lying.

Thought so, said Darnley, and he placed the Borsalino back on Ulysses's head.

I saved a man's life this afternoon, sir.

You save mine every single day, Temps. You heading in?

In a bit, sir.

Night then, Temps. And Darnley—without thinking—took his leave Italian style. There was a pause, however, before the second kiss, and in that intimate space was a 1937 Brunello di Montalcino. Decanted. And in that intimate space was something unvoiced. No more, sir. And war is over.

You look very handsome, said Darnley before disappearing through the trees back up to the villa.

The following day, on August 11, La Campana del Popolo in the Palazzo Vecchio chimed continuously, encouraging every other bell in Florence to do the same. The sound chased the Germans up into Fiesole and into the surrounding hills.

At the modest *albergo*, Evelyn Skinner, Margaret someone and the *signore* stood on the terrace, listening.

Gloria. Gloriosus. Glorious, pronounced Evelyn.

Margaret said nothing because she was still smarting over Pontormo's *Deposition*, and had moved into the annex the night before, into a somewhat smaller and cooler room.

Liberazione! said the proprietor.

In more ways than one, thought Evelyn.

She went with him to search for bottles of *frizzantino* and the proprietor, overcome by the emotion of the morning, attempted to kiss Evelyn in the old cowshed (not a euphemism, she would one day say). Oh, what the hell, she thought, and offered her mouth. He was surprisingly tender, but the kiss asserted her view that men were still not for her, and after she thanked him in perfect Italian, confirming that the kiss would be their first and last, she turned around, only to see Margaret someone standing in the light-dappled doorway, mouth pinched as if a wasp had unwittingly found entry.

How could you? whispered Margaret.

Get a grip, said Evelyn, passing her swiftly and striding toward the terrace.

The proprietor popped the cork and narrowly missed an unsuspecting swallow.

Evelyn toasted loudly, To freedom and all who sail in her!

The bells guided Darnley and Ulysses out of the city as if they were kings.

Darnley asked Ulysses to pull over to a stretch of road that offered the most spectacular views, and he stood up and named every church and monument he could see.

Ulysses watched him salute the city: his longest, most committed relationship to anything.

Darnley said, Come on, Temps, let's go! and the jeep pulled away and rejoined the convoy heading east. The sun was high and the shad-ows spare. The smell was of dust and lime flowers, and men. Darnley gibbering on about an obscure sculptor whose work had been attributed to someone else.

Ulysses said, I think you're one of the best men I know, sir. The best man ever, sir.

Darnley turned to him and smiled. (Click.) Caught forever.

Captain Darnley was killed in action on September 9, 1944, at Cori-ano Ridge. Three days short of his thirty-first birthday.

Ulysses became quiet that day. He wouldn't talk about him for years.

Somewhere
Between an Atom
and a Star

1946–53

The start of November had Old Cressy staring at a small ornamental tree. A *Prunus serrulata*, a Japanese cherry. No one knew who had planted it, because the area was dominated by plane trees, but some bright spark had once had a bright idea and had given it a home there, as an act of joyous rebellion. Or maybe a bird had long ago shat out the seed that had grown into such startling wonderment. But whoever—whatever—was the cause, the tree had become, for Cressy, a symbol of everything good.

What amazed him most about the tree was that it had survived the Blitz, and also a V-2 bomb blast that had taken out the Imperial Gasworks, which had taken out the windows of the streets around, scattering coal for the taking. Amidst the wail of sirens, and great wall of flames, Cressy had placed his hand on the trunk, reassuring it that the worst was over. For there was little else of interest to bomb in the area. Even the church had gone.

It was after this last act of destruction that Cressy took it upon himself to nurture the tree. Its origins, he'd read, had been the forests of central Asia, and Cress thought that a mighty journey to have undertaken. Cress was deep like that. So he watered it, and talked to it whenever he passed. It didn't matter that the fruit it bore was unpalatable, because cherries upset his stomach, always had; something to do with a mild irritation in his lower bowel. He was on firmer ground with apples.

Every April, as thick clusters of white and pink blossom hung heavy and low and became the talk of the street, Cressy walked methodically, Zen-like, with a glass of stout from Col's and sat under the blossoming tree, knowingly enacting the Japanese ritual of *hanami*—something he'd read about in the library. People passed by and laughed, but Cress closed his eyes and listened to the song of the breeze through the flower heads. He was oblivious to everything except that moment. Cherry blossom and a glass of stout. Hard to beat.

Old Cress had never been Young Cress. He'd been born Alfred Cresswell and soon became Egg on account of his prematurely balding pate. Egg 'n' Cress came next after that culinary marriage, but it was the Cress that stuck. He could fix anything, find anything, and was everyone's go-to man in need. Cress couldn't read till he was thirty. Lot of shame in that empty space.

Peg hated winter.

She hated the smells of damp wool and coal smoke. She hated nights that began at three and days that barely raised their heads from the pillow. She hated the same old same old that winter brought. She hated the bomb sites and the lack and the mirrors that never lied. She hated magazines that showed American life with wide plains and fancy cars and a Hollywood sign that made you dream of something more. She hated the sun-bronzed women in big sunglasses outside big houses with white fences, and advertisements for cigarettes with scowling cowboys and red-mouthed beauties. She hated that Eddie Clayton had disappeared two years before. She hated the wind that whistled through her teeth, and she hated that summer was too far away and that Christmas stood between her and another year.

Coming down the stairs she snagged her stocking and sat down on the last step. Peggy never cried, because she was dry, but it didn't mean she didn't feel. Sometimes she felt like dying but who wants to hear that?

Clack clack clack along the street. Peggy's tune.

All right, Peg? said Old Cress, standing beneath his tree.

Peg nodded and walked on.

It's never as bad—

It's bloody bad today, Cress, so keep it to yourself.

Col stood in the doorway of the pub and smoked. God, the loneliness in his soul. It manifested as acid reflux and it was the winter that brought the long burn to his esophagus, along with the dark misty days and a misty yearning for the woman who used to be his wife. Agnes Agnew, a step up for Col with her Huguenot genes and name. Who was he then and who was he now? That was as far as he got along the byways and stiles of his existential musing. He knew something had gone wrong, but for the life of him he didn't know how to put it right.

Agnes was still out there, somewhere. On a rock, farming sheep or maybe goats. People would have felt more sorry for him had she died, and he would have liked to have had that—a bit more sorry. Thank God he had Ginny to keep him on the straight. Ah, Ginny. She had the look of Agnes about her these days. Cressy called her engrossing and she was engrossing, till she opened her mouth and a kid tumbled out. Ginny was always racing from his sight (the acid begins to roil as he thinks about her absences). There'd been some shenanigans during the Blitz, when he'd caught her snogging a sailor. Sailor didn't understand when Col kept hitting him and saying, She's only ten, you fuck. Sailor spent his shore leave in the hospital.

Col unwrapped a peppermint. A sharp slug of wind rumbled through his small intestine like an underground train.

―――――

This was the London Ulysses walked back into. Winter 1946, two months before the big snows came. A city gray and struggling, like an old fella outside the Mission, all grace and has-been.

Ulysses rode the bus east and jumped off at Kingsland Road, walked behind the flurry of traffic to the bomb site where his dad's workshop had once been. Cressy had warned him of the blast, got a letter to him in North Africa and had written it like a telegram:

ULYSSES. STOP. YOUR DAD'S WORKSHOP HIT. STOP. SAVED A GLOBE AND THE COPPERPLATES. STOP. NO ONE KILLED. STOP. HOPE AFRICA'S INTERESTING. STOP. CRESS.

It was true his old man hadn't died in the bombings; he'd died a couple of years before, diagnosed with a rare blood cancer.

At least it's not my lungs, he'd said as they'd walked out of the London Hospital together.

Two weeks later he was called back in.

It's your lungs, they'd said.

His dad, Wilbur, believed he was going to beat "the cancer," as he called it, with the same misguided surety that had lost him thousands of pounds, and a few trusted friends, over a lifetime. I feel lucky, son, was what he said. A precursor to disaster if ever there was one.

It was September, and they walked over to Tubby Folgate's together to make a final bet, one that said his dad would be alive till the new year. Tubby laughed and said he'd have given him better odds on a white Christmas.

That night, they sat out in the small bricked yard. Neither knew what to say to the other. Mrs. Ashley's soprano voice rose from the neighboring lav and she played her part and added an exquisite sweetness to this scene of father and son on the precipice of farewell. So tender.

Wilbur got out his notebook and quietly said, I've done my calculations, son, and the numbers add up, and his frail finger moved across the page tracing the illegible mystery of chance. See? he said. And then his arm shot up to a midnight sky, revealing the shocking translucency of his skin.

Look, he said.

And there, a sudden clearing in the fog, as if heaven's chenille had been pulled back just for him. Same frail finger moving across the celestial architecture. Across the constellations, and the containment and hopes of all they were. And from gambler to philosopher, he said, I've lived under the fickle movement of planetary adventure. I've encountered long dark nights when the sirens sound. But the moment stars align, and the shift of sweet wind greets you of a morning, this is when mystery becomes knowing and fortune becomes love—

Nora popped her head out the front door.

What's he going on about, love?

Don't know, Mum. I think it's the morphine.

—and the arc of flight settles a small bird a thousand miles from home with heat on its wings and a calm delight at the mastery of navigation.

Wilbur withered within the month; his lungs rattled like an overworked boiler, and he became teeth and bone and essence. Everything on the black, was the last thing he said. He died in the middle of the night on the downstairs sofa.

Ulysses kept vigil in the armchair next to him and when he looked over, his dad was glowing on top of the bed. Glare from a streetlamp had snuck in through the curtain and lit up the old boy like some medieval saint.

The wake was at Col's. Stout and whiskey and tea. Peg buttered the sandwiches and forgot to put the filling in, and Ginny cried because she was always a kid and always would be. It was a good send-off. Tubby Folgate sent a wreath, paid for by his dad's last bet, and a card that said, You were one in a million to one.

End of an era, said Cressy to Ulysses. Up to you now, boy.

Ulysses was seventeen. Big words for slight shoulders.

Ulysses turned the corner and Col's pub came into sight. The Stoat and Parot was a tatty Georgian tavern that had never seen better days. Ragged bunting left over from VE Day hung down from the guttering and there was enough pigeon shit on the bricks to give Nelson's Column a run for its money. For years it had been known as the Stoat, till the eponymous bird flew down the chimney and refused to leave, thus instigating a hasty and careless addition to the pub's name.

The sign swung to and fro in the breeze, a weary creak of indolence. Come in or fuck off, come in or fuck off.

Ulysses pushed open the door, and the fire to his right gave off a ripe old smell, all sour and smarting bodies. The old ones were huddled around the hearth exactly as he'd left them: same faces less teeth. And above the fire on a narrow shelf, the stuffed stoat, looking exactly as it had the day it died: angry and incredulous.

Over by the bar, the large blue-fronted Amazonian parrot guarded the till with a glum weariness. Ulysses dropped his kit bag by the footrest and rubbed the parrot's chest. Hello, Claudie, he said, Remember me, fella? But Claude stared at him mute, eyes glazed by post-traumatic stress. Suddenly Claude ducked low and hit his head repeatedly against a bell. Col came through from the snug.

Well, look who's here! Good to see you, Tempy. We thought you'd forgotten us.

They shook hands.

Peg here? asked Ulysses as he took off his hat and smoothed his hair in the mirror behind the bar.

Nah. She don't work here anymore, son.

Peg don't?

Nah. Not for a while. She's gone up in the world. Typist. Sixty words a minute and that's just her gob. You been to Kathleen's?

Why should I go to Kathleen's?

No reason.

(People were looking at him now.)

Col pulled him a pint. There you go, mate, he said.

Cheers, Col, and Ulysses drank. He looked at the parrot and said, I'm surprised he's still alive, Col.

So am I, boy, so am I. Larger the bird, longer the life—that's what they say. And that parrot's a fat fuck. I reckon he's sixty to the day. He'll bury me.

Don't he talk no more?

Not after the gasworks went up. Lost his feathers and his voice, just like that. Stress from the explosion. Ugly thing he was. Like a pheasant ready for the oven. Ginny pulled him back from the brink. Healing hands, that girl. I wanted him dead, of course. I've always felt he had something to do with Agnes leaving.

Really?

He took sides, Temps. And I can't forget something like that.

Col released a shot of whiskey from the optics and raised his glass. To you, mate, he said. Glad to have you back.

Thanks, Col.

You know what's strange?

Go on.

Last thing that bird said before the great molt: the quality of mercy is not strained. *Strained*. Strange word for a parrot to use, don't you think? Where d'you think he got that from?

Shakespeare.

You reckon?

I know.

Huh.

They drank in silence, staring at the bird.

Ulysses looked about. You got rid of the sawdust then?

Yeah, it was time. Brought in the wrong crowd.

Wallpaper the same.

Yep. But you know what they say. If it ain't broke . . .

But it was all broke, thought Ulysses. The whole fucking place was broke. The wallpaper curled at the seams and the lights flickered as if a storm was approaching. An effect enhanced by the leaded green windows in the upper bays, bringing a watery glow to the afternoon radiance. And, of course, a parrot that didn't speak.

Actually, said Col. One change. I've diversified. I sell aspirin and stamps now. One-stop shop.

Masterful, Col.

That's what I thought. You got plans?

Another pint after this, please.

Comin' up, lad, said Col, over his specs. You look in one piece. You intact?

Ulysses nodded.

There's always a job here for you, you know that. And he pushed the pint toward him. On the house, he said.

Ulysses lifted the glass.

Oh Jesus, said Col. This is doin' me head in. You need to go to Kathleen's. I'm sorry, boy, but—

Ulysses put down the pint and wiped his mouth. Nobody touches that, he said.

Nobody will, mate, said Col, and Ulysses turned and thumped through the door.

He walked down the road. Turned left into the square of gothic villas, then a right. Stood in front of a proud house in a row of struggle.

Kathleen! he shouted, and knocked.

Kathleen!

A sturdy redhead of middle years opened the door and said, Well, look who's here.

Col said I have to see you.

She laughed. Course he did!

Where's Peg?

Not here.

What does that mean?

You wanna come in, sunshine?

I wanna know what's what.

Six years is what's what. She weren't waiting, Tempy.

I never expected her to. We still got the place on the crescent?

Have you hell. The Masons needed that after they were bombed out. Everyone's on a list.

Jesus, he said quietly.

A small child emerged from Kath's side. You a granny now?

Not yet, smart-arse.

What's her name? he said.

Don't you know?

Yeah, I'm a mind reader too. Tell Peg I'm back, and he began to walk away. Tell her—

The kid's Peg's, Temps.

He stopped.

Kath nodded to the kid.

The kid. She's Peg's.

I heard.

Can't you see the likeness? Yankee dad.

Peg all right?

Kathleen shrugged. The kid's called Alys, she said.

Right.

Five minutes later, the doors of the pub opened and Ulysses reappeared.

Been to Kathleen's?

I've been.

Good lad. So you'll need a job and somewhere to live, then?

Col pushed his beer across the bar.

No one touched this, right?

No one at all, said Col.

Ulysses drank. He wiped his mouth and adjusted his hat in the mirror.

Nice hat, said Col.

Ulysses took it off and showed him. It's Italian. See? Anyone round here wears this hat, you know they've nicked it. Simple as. This is my hat. No one touches it.

Like no one touches your drink? said Col.

That's right.

You should put your name in it, he said.

I might.

Any time you wanna talk, son, said Col, and he threw him the keys and disappeared into the snug.

Ulysses walked down to the canal. The immediate familiar whiff of the place, the icy smoggy chug to the air, the gasometers proud and monumental. He sat on a bench. The slow drift of a barge and then silence. He watched the world hardly move at all. So there's a kid, he thought, and before he could think further, he looked up to see Old Cressy rushing down the stairs, calling out his name. Ulysses stood up. Cressy's head smelled of coal dust and cough syrup. You all here, boy? said Cress, holding his face. Mostly, said Ulysses. Thank God, said Cress, punching him lightly on both arms, a playful one-two one-two because the old fella was choked.

They sat down and Cressy raised a bag in his hand and said, Here it is, the only one to survive, and he carefully lifted out a globe the size of a football. He said, It was quite a night, Temps. I heard that all the globes shot into the air when the bomb landed. Hovered in the warm updraft and spun. A mini universe lit by flames. Now, wouldn't that have been something to see? She's in Nicaragua, by the way.

Who is?

Your mum. I looked for her. Took me over a month. But I found her. In Nicaragua. Next to Managua.

Peg's got a kid, Cress.

None of it was mine to tell, boy.

I know, Cress, I know.

Ulysses took out his cigarettes.

You know the bloke?

An American fella. One minute here. Then gone.

You see him? said Ulysses, lighting up.

No one did. Kept him away from here, she did. That was decent.

Cressy took a cigarette.

There were feelings, son. He was no fly-by-night.

Ulysses nodded. Peg in a bad way?

She'd bite her own tongue off before saying so. And Cress blew out a stream of smoke and picked a strand of tobacco off his lip.

Should I go and find her?

You leave her be. She's got a crap hand of cards and has been bluffing all this time. You turning up means she's being forced to show. But it'll be done on her terms. Always is. You forgotten how she works?

They watched a lone swan swim by till it disappeared under the bridge.

Here, said Cress, and he nudged Ulysses. Something for you to think about. Something I read.

Go on.

The scale of man—*spatially*—is about midway between the *atom* and the *star.*

Ulysses looked at him and frowned. Atom and a star? he said.

Cress nodded. Spatially, he said.

That's a lot to take in.

Isn't it? I haven't had a good night's sleep since.

Well, you wouldn't, would you?

Although a stronger candidate for the midway position would probably be a hippopotamus.

What d'you think it means?

Cress thought for a moment.

Interconnectedness, I think.

And they both nodded that time.

They turned their attention to the canal just as the swan reappeared.

Cress said, You're back. I reckon I'll sleep tonight.

You seen who's back? they said to Peg when she returned from the typing pool. Mrs. Lundy the baker had told the butcher, who had told the Cranes, who owned the café. Gloria Gosford who sold haberdashery was having tea in the café and overheard the butcher tell the Cranes. She went straight to Mr. Bellingham who sold furniture. And of course, Mr. Bellingham told me, said Linda, who was having a very public affair with the man.

They walked with Peg along the street yacking. Yeah yeah, it's getting boring now, said Peg to each and every one of them. She was glad to put her key in the lock and close the door.

Later, over gin, Kath said Ulysses had looked reasonable. He's always been fucking reasonable, said Peg, and Kath said he looked a bit more handsome and she said that wouldn't be hard and Kath said, Naughty, and she hated she was such a bitch because what had he ever done to her? Only married her in case he died. You'd get money, Peg—that's what he said. Always looking out for her.

She went upstairs to her room and kicked off her heels. Twenty minutes at the typewriter board flexing her fingers. She was getting good, good at shorthand too. She'd earn her own money in America when Eddie came to get her. He ain't coming now, Kath had said. What the fuck did she know? He'd bought her the Pitman's course; said she could have anything she wanted, and he thought she was going to say a fur coat or something shiny, but she said a typing course, and she noticed he looked at her differently that day, like she had dreams too. Like she was worth something. He'll come because he loves me, she said, and Kath said, I never said he didn't love you.

You saw it, right? said Peg.

I saw it, said Kath.

The kid stirred next to her. The kid who looked like him. Same shiny thick dark hair and bright eyes. Some nights the similarity could have ripped her guts out. She'd never wanted a kid and her mum had never wanted her. Bloody careless, stupid cows. And now Tempy's back.

Over at the mirror, she looked a mess. Her mother would have loved to have seen her like that. Now you know how I feel, she would've said. Thought you had it all worked out, didn't you? Think you're better than me, don't you?

This is what you men do to us women, thought Peg. You make us hate us. For your absence. For your lies. For your violence.

She got up and went to the window. I'm still here, Eddie. And I know you're out there.

For a whole week, the pub was on tenterhooks, waiting for Peggy the gunslinger to enter town and shoot up the peace. Ulysses opened up and the regulars barreled in with coats smelling of mothballs and complaining about the wait. Then they'd stop and look about. She been in yet?

Nah, not yet, said Col.

What she up to, that girl?

What she ever bin up to? said Col.

The tension simmered. The pub had never been so quiet. Mr. Mason had a heart attack in the wait and he was in death's grip before he hit the floor, but at least *something* had happened.

They all knew Peg'd turn up sooner or later, but it was *how* she was going to do it, that was the question. Four evenings later, she didn't disappoint. With an hour and ten minutes of drinking left and Piano Pete warmed up, she pushed open the doors and stood backlit by a particularly bright streetlight. It was all MGM and the lion roared. She dropped her cigarette and stubbed it out under her shoe.

Eh up, said Col.

And Ulysses raised his head from the bar.

Easy, lad, whispered Col. Easy there.

The swing of her hips, the sound of her heels across the floor. Droll Pete tapping B-flat in time with her stride until she headed his way, and the B-flat fell flat. She glanced through the sheet music, but she knew what she was going to sing. This one, she said quietly, and handed Pete his instruction. Slow, she whispered. Real slow. And Pete obliged, fingers dexterous along the keys, ash falling from his moist lips, smoke irritating his bloodshot eyes.

Ulysses watched her every move. He'd had women in Italy, but none like her. Had even loved some of them, but not like her. In Naples, he used to watch the women head over to the American camp. The Yanks had lots of money, lots of charm, the women were sad and beautiful. What a combination, he thought. He never stood a chance.

He felt Col's hand on his back. Col knew he didn't stand a chance.

Peg—you only had to look at her to know she was born to better things. She knew it and he saw it. She was an upriver swimmer, struggling against a contemptible tide, but by God she tried. She sang to no one. Locked eyes with no one. Focused on an empty corner of the room that held a ghost that'd haunt her till the end of her days. Drinks were left untouched and cheeks were glazed by tears. She mesmerized because that was the Peggy spell. She had class. She may have stolen it, but she had it. And she told you so when she sang, because she sang for her life, and for yours too, because the world never turned out the way you wanted it to. It simply turned. And you hung on.

The last notes rang out. Her voice cracked. Piano Pete wept. A standing ovation and whistling and cheering, and boy did she look modest, a look she'd practiced well. Old Cressy sent over a gin and she raised the glass to him, and he raised his to hers, and she downed it in one. Then she turned toward the bar. The sound of thirty heads following. Crack crack crack went the necks. Hips swaying, arms swinging, and by God those cards were on the table now. Cressy said she'd got a crap hand, but everyone could see she was the one holding the aces.

Keep that horse steady, said Col before he disappeared into the snug.

Ulysses and Peg locked eyes, and it was familiar and there was history and also truce.

She walked up to the counter. You could have heard a pin drop.

Hey, soldier, she said, and touched his cheek.

Hey, you, he said, and touched her hand.

I—they said in unison.

You first, she said.

No, you, he said.

OK, she said.

I want a divorce, Tempy.

Blimey, he said.

The sound of thirty mouths exhaling. The sound of Claude manically pecking his bell.

The next morning, Peg woke in his bed because that's what they did. She groaned loudly and gripped him tight with her thighs before he got soft. She rolled off and said, I'm glad you're not dead.

(It was as romantic as she ever got.)

She climbed out from the sheets and he sat up and watched her. Her arse in the early-morning light, moon and sun as one. Her arm across her stomach, hiding the marks that had appeared since he left.

Tell me something no one's ever told me before, she said.

You're perfect, he said.

She laughed and got back into her clothes and he watched.

He said, I could help with the kid—

Not your responsibility, Temps. (Her in front of the mirror now tidying her hair.)

But we can still look after one another. Look out for one an—

You're too good. (Her putting on her lipstick.)

He smiled.

No, Temps. You're *too good*. It's not a compliment. And with one hand on the doorknob and ready to go, she turned and said, I'll see you around.

Same time tomorrow?

We won't be doing that again.

We'll see, he said, and he blew her a kiss.

He listened to her stomp down the stairs. The sound of the front door opening and shutting. Ginny calling after her. He got up and turned the electric heater on. He wrapped a sheet around himself and stood at the window and watched her cross the road. He wondered what he'd come back for if it wasn't her.

Ginny running out now without her coat and Peg rubbing Ginny's arms, her sweet concern. Cressy coming around the corner dragging a large pine tree behind him. A rusty pub sign swinging in December's throaty wheeze, and a traumatized parrot too far from home. This was his world now. Somewhere between an atom and a star was this.

Come February 1947, the snow fell.

Great drifts of the stuff clogged up the city and the canal froze over. Ulysses spent his days clearing paths and keeping the fires going as best he could. Coal was hard to come by and windows grew ice. The streets were silent, and the nights banked by white.

The Eskimos have fifty words for snow, said Cressy, looking out the kitchen window.

And I've got one for idiot, said Col. And I'm looking at it. I thought you were making stew. I've got nine rabbits in the cold box hopping about waiting for a pot for tomorrow's lunch.

Ulysses smelled the milk and poured it into his cup of tea.

And what are you laughing about? said Col.

Nothing, said Ulysses.

You're like one of them monkeys.

A macaque, said Cressy.

A what?

A macaque. He's like a macaque.

Stop saying the fucking word macaque. Jesus. Thousands need a job and I end up with you two.

Get out the wrong side of the bed, didya, Col?

No, actually, Temper. Au contraire.

New lady friend, whispered Cress.

Ulysses grimaced.

This is the first day of the rest of my life, said Col.

And what will tomorrow be, Col? Will it be the first day again, or the second day? said Ulysses.

Col thought. Burped. Fair point, he said.

Jesus, Col. You stink.

Liver sausage, he said, holding up his sandwich. Got it cheap.

Drive the dogs wild, do you?

You seen Ginny? asked Col.

Not upstairs? said Ulysses.

Wouldn't've asked, would I? said Col, and his hand gripped his stomach as a surge of acid banked.

Ulysses said, I'll go, and he downed his tea, grabbed his coat and boots and headed out.

He went to Mrs. Lundy's first, and she said Ginny had been in and bought a loaf of bread as she always did. He detoured to Cressy's tree, but she wasn't there either. He headed on down to the canal even though she wasn't supposed to go there by herself.

It was quiet down there. A couple of barges puffing out smoke, and ducks resting on the ice. He blew on his hands and stuffed them in his pockets.

Ginny! he called out.

He walked the towpath. Followed fresh footprints in a recent dump of snow. The slow movement of a barge carrying coal passed by and broke the ice. Pound for pound it was now more expensive than gold. According to Col, anyhow.

Ginny!

There she was up ahead, on a bench.

Ginny, said Ulysses. He sat down next to her and put his arm around her. Cold, ain't it? he said. You warm enough?

Bread's warm, Uly, she said in her funny nasal voice, hugging the loaf to her chest.

What you doing down here?

Feeding ducks.

The end of the loaf had been torn away.

You're kind, he said, and kissed her head. You talk to anyone down here?

I'm not allowed to talk to strangers.

Good girl, he said, and lit a cigarette. He blew out smoke and realized she was copying him.

I like it down here, she said.

Me too.

She pressed her finger against the scar on his lip.

Hurt?

Not much.

Lying.

He held her finger and grinned. You know everything, don't you?

Peg teached me.

Worse teachers, he thought, and flicked his cigarette away.

Ginny said, You love Peg?

Course I do.

You her boyfriend?

It's complicated, Ginny.

Because you went away?

Not just that.

You look sad, she said.

Yeah.

Feet cold, Uly—

I bet they are. Come on, up we go, Gin Gin. Let's go get you warm.

Carry my bread.

Course, he said. Hey?

Ginny turned.

Thanks for the chat.

Anytime, Uly. I'm always ears.

He laughed and pulled her close.

It was a week before the big melt. A regulars' night, with the same old faces shuffling in for prime position around the fire. They were getting bold and brought sandwiches with them, and Mrs. Lovell snuck in a roast dinner under foil. They absorbed the heat like lizards and left everyone else shivering under coats. Col couldn't wait for them to die.

In the snug, a couple of coppers were lording it, keeping the language clean. Col was on the long pull, generous measures to encourage a lock-in, a ploy to shift the stack of liver sausage sandwiches stinking up the counter.

Piano Pete was warming up with a bit of Beethoven. He'd spent all afternoon playing for a beginners' tap class full of two left feet. Those classes were the septic boil of his wasted life. Pete could've gone to the Royal Academy, everyone knew that. He moved seamlessly on to Wagner, a sure sign that his evening was turning bitter.

Jig it up, Pete, said Col, recognizing the shift in mood. And Pete swung into swing and the pub went from dry to thirst.

The upbeat shift in musical choice affected everyone but most notably Claude. He launched himself into an aeronautical display of rare aptitude and his final demonstration of complex asymmetric hovering brought raucous applause from the usually less than impressed drinking clientele.

That bird's showing off, said Old Cress. That bird's in love.

Talking out of your arse, said Col.

But Cressy knew his birds. And Claude ended up in front of the mirror, rubbing himself vigorously against a bottle of rum.

Disgustin', said Col.

What's he doing? said Ginny.

Bringing relief to his swollen cloaca, said Cress.

That's a word you don't hear often, said Ulysses.

Do you have to? said Col.

By eleven, the lock-in had become official and the coppers had buggered off with a couple of quid in their pockets. It was a man-against-the-elements kind of night, and Ulysses went down to the cellar to fetch a box of candles.

Piano Pete was sitting in the corner making a considerable dent in a bottle of whiskey.

All right, Pete?

Not bad, Temps. You?

Not bad. You want me to say I don't know where you are?

If you don't mind, Temps. Suddenly lost me confidence.

Ulysses smiled. He liked Pete. Always had. Pete was as elusive as they came. Might've been rich or might've been poor. Might've been brought up in a castle or under a bridge. Pete had been a conscientious objector and had done a bit of time. Pete was bruised but Pete was kind.

Here you go, Pete, said Ulysses, and he covered him with a regulation army blanket. He placed a lit candle next to him.

I'll be up in a minute, said Pete.

Stay where you are, said Ulysses.

Bless you, said Pete.

Upstairs, Ulysses set candles on saucers, one on each table. He turned off the lights, and the old ones complained about the power cut, but Ulysses ignored them. He placed a record that Cress had given him on the turntable. Cress had said, I reckon this might be a bit of all right. You know—something special, and he was right. The woman sang in Italian and her voice took him back to a painting and another country and another version of himself. Col came out of the snug into the bar ridiculing the woman's voice. He was full of impersonations that evening, and he pitched his voice high and tremulous. It's what Col did when he didn't understand something—he made it ridiculous and brought it down to an acceptable level; crotch height, usually, so he could piss on it. Peg was a bit like that, and he should have seen it coming, but he'd become daft and a bit moony on account of the music and the candlelight and the soft fall of snow against the windows.

Peg had been drinking up a storm, and there was an edge to her, something cruel in her eyes. On nights like these, beauty made her uncomfortable, as if there was only room for hers. She waved him over and when he sat down, she immediately started talking about Eddie. Told him what she planned to do when Eddie came to get her. I was everything to that man, and he was everything to me. She was in full-on goad mode. Ulysses drank his beer and ignored her. And then she nudged him and said, You ever meet anyone? He thought about the question, the two roads that led away from it, the yes or no that would attract pity or scorn. He said he did actually. And he talked easily about

Evelyn. And there's Peggy laughing at him now, nudging him, all older woman this and that, and he said it's not like that, it was about who she was and what she said and what she knew. And Ulysses knew he shouldn't have done it, but he did it anyway because the music offered a skylight to another dawn. He said stuff about art and paintings and Italy, things that Evelyn had told him, things he'd often thought about in the conflicting sounds of night.

That's when Peg struck.

She said, Tommy Bruskin didn't come back. Mick Dodds didn't come back. John Baines lost a leg. Gary Castle's gone fucking doolally. And you talk about art? What kind of war did you have? You have a nice one, did ya, Tempy? Fucking nice one?

Everyone looking at them now. Everyone thinking: This is more like it, fireworks instead of sonatas.

Ulysses put down his glass slowly. He looked up, said, I dodged bullets for six years, Peg. Yours are a piece of piss.

Stomp stomp stomp. She broke the glass in the door.

You'll have to pay for that, mate, said Col, laughing.

I'll pay, said Ulysses, and the music played on.

The next morning, Ulysses was shoveling snow whilst Col and Cress surveyed the repair he'd made on the door. Suddenly, from inside, a tall shadow approached through the stained glass.

What the fuck! said Col, and he grabbed the hammer and raised it.

It was Pete coming through the door, doing his best impression of Lazarus. I feel like I've lost everything, Temps. Days, weeks—

You're frightening me, Pete, said Col. Look at me.

Pete looked at him, eyes and mouth crusted with drool.

You'll be all right after a good night's sleep, said Ulysses.

And remember, said Col, today is the first day of the rest of your life.

Pete couldn't quite get his head around that and began to cry.

That's just the whiskey working its way out, said Col. You'll feel better in an hour. Keep it flowing, mate.

Come on, Pete, said Cress, I'll help you back home. Lean on me, son.

Col watched them depart. Blind leading the blind, he said. Aye aye, he said as he blew out a thick plume of smoke. Here she comes.

Fuck off, Col, said Peg, approaching.

Fucking off now, said Col, heading back in the warmth.

Peg was sheepish and shivering, a bit cold and a lot hungover. She said to Ulysses, You all right?

He knew that was her apology. He said, Not bad. You?

Oh, you know. (Hunched shoulders, hands in pockets, big furrow between her eyebrows.)

He carried on shoveling and she surprised him by mouthing the S-word.

What's that? he said.

You heard, she said.

No I didn't. Go on. Again.

Sorry, she whispered.

And again?

Sorry.

She laughed and punched him, and he ditched the spade and grabbed hold of her. Peg, he said, I bloody missed you, and you start giving me grief—I know, I know, she said—I got back when loads didn't—I know, I know, she said—and stuff helped me, he said. And I learned things and I met people and I'm proud of what I got to know—I know, I know, she said—and he started to dance with her, and she laughed more, and he'd forgotten that it was the best thing in the world to make her laugh. They stopped their dance and caught their breath. Peg looked warmer; she had color in her cheeks.

You still want a divorce? he said.

D'you mind?

Nah.

So, they did it. They got divorced and got more friendly. Even shared the kid called Alys. Peg kept the name Temper 'cause there was no way she'd go back to Potts. And the weeks and months rolled out ahead of them and ordinary returned. The snow disappeared and the sun shone again, and everyone complained how hot it was, how winter was really better. The kid called Alys grew and Col's new lady friend was called Denise. Peg got a job in a typing pool for an insurance firm off Tottenham Court Road and Ulysses settled into civvy life.

By the summer of 1948, London was ready for the Olympics. Col was happy that neither Japan nor Germany had been invited to take part and Denise agreed, saying that England would probably have a better chance in the shooting now.

Col wanted to increase custom during the fortnight, and it was Cressy who suggested the television. He said he knew someone who knew someone who had access to the back of a lorry, and before long, a small set was moved into the snug, covered to look like a birdcage. Inside was the sweet sound of a nine-inch Pye. Wembley Stadium had never looked so small.

A week before the opening ceremony, Cress walked into the pub all woozy and vacant-eyed, and Col said, You look a bit touched, mate.

I am touched, said Cress.

Here, sit down, said Ulysses, and he pulled out a chair and handed him a small glass of beer.

So what's what? said Col.

I had a vision.

Jesus, said Col.

Not him. Fanny Blankers-Koen.

Who?

Dutch athlete, said Ulysses, feeding Claude a Brazil nut.

She was doing the housework, said Cress.

And she appeared to you? Alfred Cresswell? Out of all the people in the world?

She looked at me and said, Four.

Four?

Actually, she said *vier*. That's Dutch for "four." *Vier* or four. And then she showed me a wedding ring. So I went down to Tubby's and put a bet on.

For her to be married four times? said Col, laughing.

For her to win four gold medals.

What d'you put on her? said Ulysses.

Everything.

Jeez, Cress.

Not much then, said Col, disappearing into the snug.

It's a sure one, Tempy. Your dad was all around me. I could feel him. I could smell him—

Pocketful of loose change?

That's the stuff. You put on what you can afford, son. This one's set to go. Trust me. It's everything on the black all over again.

So Ulysses did. Went on his break down to Tubby's and put on what he had in his wallet and all he'd saved in his tin.

And in the days that followed, the crowds in the snug increased as word got around about Cressy's bet. People stopped him in the street and wished him luck. None of it was about luck, though, he knew that. This was destiny.

On August 2 at four forty-five p.m. and twelve seconds, Fanny crossed the line to win the one-hundred-meter gold medal. Ginny and the kid jumped up and down and Pete screamed and thought he'd coughed up a tonsil. Is that possible, Temps?

I don't think so, Pete.

On the blackboard Ulysses wrote: *One down, three to go.*

Col said, You're dreaming, mate. Never gonna happen. Over my dead body.

Don't tempt me, said Peg.

On August 4 at four p.m. and 11.2 seconds Fanny crossed the line in first place to win the eighty-meter hurdles. The crowds were smaller than in the previous race due to the earlier start, and Col said, Yeah, but who's really interested in women's hurdles? I am, said Denise, hoisting up her skirt and coming a cropper over a bar stool. Ulysses picked up the chalk.

Two down, two to go, appeared on the blackboard.

You've gone a bit quiet, Col, said Ulysses.

Fuck off, birdbrain.

On Friday, August 6, at four thirty p.m. and 24.4 seconds, Fanny won the two-hundred-meter and Cress quietened the snug and urged everyone to raise their glasses to Fanny. To her effortless stride and determination. To her thirty years. To her unassuming beauty. To her singlemindedness. To her—

What is it with him and this woman? said Col.

Search me, said Ulysses.

—bravery, said Cress.

The glasses were raised.

To Fanny, they all said.

Three down, one to go, appeared on the blackboard.

That evening, people passed by and shook Cressy's hand. Wished him luck for the big race tomorrow as if he was running a leg of the relay himself. A reporter from the *Hackney Gazette* came down to do a piece on him, which started well. Ulysses delivered a couple of pints to their table and heard Cressy say, She'd already missed two Olympics because of the war. And most people told her to stay at home and look after the kids. You tell me what's right about that kind of thinking.

Ulysses stood out on the street. The evening was dreary, the promise of summer had deflated. If he won money, he thought he might be able to get away, or help Peg out, more like. Do something for the kid, buy a week of sunshine. Cress and the reporter came out onto the street fighting.

Course there's nothing unpatriotic in my support of Mrs. Blankers-Koen! shouted Cressy. Talent's talent. And you're a pillock!

The story would never run. Ulysses went back inside to change a barrel.

The following day was a Saturday. The clouds had pissed off to Hammersmith, and they were left with blue skies and a sharp sun, all show and no heat. People gathered around the pub as if a wedding was about to take place. The TV was warmed up and Col thought he was masterful charging entry. No one complained, though, and when Old Cressy appeared, everyone in the snug cheered and led him to a chair at the front.

Ulysses looked about for Peg. He asked Col if he'd seen her and Col shook his head and called him a big old muggins and hadn't he got the message by now? The front door clattered open and Peg and Ginny and the kid rushed in, all flustered and sorrys, just as the relay teams took their marks. The pub hushed. And at four forty p.m. all that could be heard was the sound of history in the making.

Bang!

By the time Fanny Blankers-Koen took the baton, she was four meters behind the Australian. Col kept saying she ain't gonna do it, ain't gonna do it, and Ulysses could barely watch. Peg and Pete screamed and the kid was up and down, and Claude had a run on droppings. But Cressy, well, Cressy stayed composed, with not a hint of sweat across his face. Fanny Blankers-Koen crossed the finishing line first—47.5 seconds after the starter gun had fired. It was Fanny's fourth gold. Cressy was lifted into the air like a king and five streets away Tubby cursed and punched his oldest son in the face for having taken the bet in the first place.

Col sidled up to Ulysses and whispered, How much d'you think he won, then?

A bloody fortune, said Ulysses, just to piss him off.

How much Old Cress had won became the stuff of legend and would be talked about long after the pub had gone. No one knew, not really, though speculators were many. Cress bought himself a pair of desert shorts off a veteran in the market, big baggy sandy things that he wore with a jacket and tie and sometimes a sleeveless sweater, and as far as anyone could tell, they were his sole purchase after the Big Win. Everyone wondered what had happened to the rest. Those who'd cheered him on months before soon succumbed to derision. Human nature, right?

Of course, Tubby knew the amount. Tubby felt the pain of that loss every waking hour and one day someone would have to pay. Tubs sent a man out with a magic key to snoop about Cressy's gaff, but Cress always knew because he could see air that had been disturbed by a stranger.

Cress didn't know why he'd got all that money at his time of life. In truth, he thought it was too late for him to make the changes a younger man might have made. But he sat under his tree and listened. He admired his legs sticking out of his shorts and he knew they were his best feature because they were his mother's legs. Thoughts of his mother made him cry.

Nineteen fifty and the turn of the decade was welcomed. Fuck off, the forties, what have you ever done for us? Col lit the last of the fireworks that were to usher in a decade of hope. I mean, how bad can it be? he said, imploring the exploding heavens. Yeah. Just you wait.

British national service conscripts were soon sent off to Korea, and absence and heartbreak were back on the menu. Ulysses joined Piano Pete to march against the war and got drunk in a Soho pub afterward in a wordless show of grief. Kid'd turned into a chatty little thing, with a mouth full of American teeth, and she called Ulysses Ulysses, and he called her kid. Peg got promoted from the typing pool and she played it cool, but Ulysses could see that she was jazzed. Even one rung up the ladder, the air smelled fresher, the view wider. Cressy helped Ginny grow carrots and potatoes in the yard at the back of the pub and she gave the first crop to Mrs. Kaur who had the convenience shop simply because she liked her and the color of her skin. Piano Pete cut a lucky break in a West End show. A small but noticeable part; he played a frontier pianist with a drink problem. Only appearing in the first act meant he could still honor his obligations to the pub. The beginners' tap class, though, could go fuck itself. Col swapped Denise for Elaine, but in the end, she didn't last long. Set his sights instead on a 1930s ambulance because he'd always wanted one. Ever since the day he'd watched his mother driven away in one. Jeez, said Peg. I only asked.

———

Heat grew that first summer of the decade. Made the oldies wobbly and the dogs mad. Queues for the swimming pool extended along Whiston Road, but down by the canal kids were bombing in as kids do, getting a gutful of rat piss, but it was worth it, if only to feel a slight breeze on wet skin.

Peg called out to Ulysses. He looked up and waved. She clacked down the steps and joined him on the bench. They watched the kids in their undies, skinny arms and legs flailing in the air, squealing and daring one another, and cascades of water splashed across the towpath onto their legs and shoes, but they didn't flinch or care.

We did that, he said, adjusting his hat.

Not that long ago, he said.

Peg sighed.

Another world, he said.

As teenagers, they'd made out in the bushes to their left, oblivious to the stink of dog shit and the discarded French letters. She was his first, he wasn't hers, but all of them had borrowed one another to get good at it and to feel good. Pale skin in the moonlight. Peg was the keeper of their history. She knew the names of those long dead and who had done what and who had loved whom.

Not a care in the world, said Ulysses.

What a strange thing to say, thought Peg. She'd never been without a care in the world. Not at that age, not at this age. A whirling dynamo of tension she was, and always had been, propelling bloods and lipids along a never-ending godforsaken circuit. She remembered him as a boy. Stocky and small with the brightest eyes, constantly polishing a silver lining. She used to give him blow jobs just to see his gratitude. Over time, he filled out. Got forearms all the girls went wild over. And his eyes got more blue, and his parents died, and he made globes and spun them on his middle finger. And he said, I want to be somebody someday, Peg. What d'ya say?

But what could she say? Someday was too far away.

She bent down and adjusted her shoe. She said, I've met someone.

Ulysses turned to her. Said, Oh yeah? Turned back to watch the kids.

I think it's serious.

He nodded.

I'm taking it slow. Just wanted you to hear it from me.

Thanks, Peg.

She stood up. She studied him. Always him. They needed to stop having sex. She told him so. Not fair on Ted. Ted's your bloke, is he? And she nodded. OK, he said, but he knew they wouldn't.

Can I take Alys to the gallery tomorrow? he said.

Course you can.

Morning all right?

All day if you want.

He laughed but he knew she was serious.

You're a good mum, Peg.

No I'm not but it's good of you to say. Your mum was a good mum, Temps. That's what a good mum is. Mine was competition.

The next day, the Whitechapel Gallery felt cool out of the sun. Alys ran on ahead and scanned the paintings because she knew what she was looking for. She settled, eventually, on an area of floor where she'd be left undisturbed. She opened her sketchbook and took the pencil sharpener out of her sock. Ulysses knelt down. He collected the shavings in his hand and put them in his pocket because that was his job. And for an hour and a half, out of the corner of his eye, he watched the kid produce her own version of a painting by Joan Eardley: children sitting on a pavement reading a comic. A world she understood.

She was five. Would she remember that moment as completely as he saw it?

Probably not. But she would remember the day because years later, she would tell people about it. The cool of the floor on her bare legs, the lines she'd made on the page. She would remember how a morning became an afternoon, how people stared at the paintings on the wall and talked about them in serious tones. How the gentle murmur became white noise and calmed her. How Ulysses's gaze made her think she was something, or something enough. How she was glad to be away from her mother. How she saw a woman dressed as a man and thought how interesting life could be, might be. The type of day that showed her where she ended and the world began.

Ulysses left the kid drawing. He wandered through the hall of paintings. Sheila Fell, Eva Frankfurter. Dorothy Cunningham.

Since his conversation with Evelyn during that long dark drive back to the *albergo*, he'd thought about the gallery a lot. How Evelyn had laughed at the snobbery of art, said that the responsibility of privilege must always be to raise others up. Standing there now, he equated that conversation with the space around him. Paintings by local schoolchildren were exhibited on the wall opposite, and he thought maybe this was what she'd been talking about. Nearby, an artist began to introduce her work.

From the back the woman could have been a man with her short hair, rolled-up shirtsleeves and high-waisted slacks, but her voice was unmistakably feminine. She was referred to as Miss Cunningham—Dorothy Cunningham, he presumed. He was drawn to the rounded explanation of her craft, her brow intelligent and open to the questions fired at her from the front. From considered to acute spontaneity was how she described her new work. He let those words roll about his tongue.

Ulysses looked over to the kid. Still in her quiet world, sucking a pencil.

The catch of conversation from a passing couple and a brief reference to Spain propelled him back to 1938—a year after his parents had died, and the year Picasso's *Guernica* came to the gallery. It had traveled the world by then, raising funds for the rebels fighting Franco. That's why Ulysses had gone to see it—his first ever exhibition—lured by a romantic and fallacious idea of war. The gallery had been a campaign head-quarters of sorts and the price of admission, for those who couldn't afford the entrance fee, had been set at a pair of boots. He'd gone back the next day and left a pair of his father's just inside the doorway. On the leather tongue he'd written, Good luck.

The voice of Dorothy Cunningham drew him toward the conflu-ence of same thought same time. Yes, she said, I did see the *Guernica*.

A surge of electricity spluttered up his spine.

I agree, she said. We learned the hard way. That there must always be a moral argument against the march of Fascism.

Ulysses wondered what his response to the painting might be if he were to see it now.

Not at all, said Dorothy Cunningham. There was no heroism in Picasso's depiction of war. No victory, only horror.

The deliberate bombing of civilians on market day, said Ulysses.

Dorothy Cunningham turned toward him.

We weren't immune, he said. It wasn't just them who did stuff. We did whatever it took, too.

Everyone looking at him. The kid looking at him.

And it was this she would remember: his voice resonant in the still-ness. People listening to him, not laughing. She stood up, marched over to him and held his hand. Her exquisite moment of ownership. The day when he became hers.

They left the peace of the exhibition and were immediately con-sumed by the noise of the high street. Ulysses bought her a lemonade before they got on the bus. This is my best day ever, she said.

There'll be more, he said.

I know. I'm only five.

That night, Peg watched the kid sleep. Her face still flushed after a day out with Temps. Temps had a knack with her, but Peg couldn't come close. She sat on the bed and flicked through the kid's drawing book. She felt bad, like it was a diary, but not bad enough to put it down. A picture of Temps, the scar on his lip like a digit. The kid had talent, and she didn't get it from Peg. Eddie, of course. All the things she didn't know. Like if he was dead or alive or if he ever thought about her and their nights together. Cress had once told her she needed to tell Eddie things. Words are gold dust, that's what he'd said. So she'd told Eddie stuff, stuff that would make her toes curl now. Laid out her heart on the bed and had cut it open, a full autopsy of love. That's what being in a hotel room could make a girl do. Sex in soft sheets and room service. Making plans. And all the time war was eavesdropping . . .

Peg got up. She spilled gin on the bedclothes. Sometimes it was unbearable looking at the kid. The always reminder of the life she'd lost.

April 1952 had Old Cressy under his *Prunus serrulata*, his Japanese cherry. It was evening, and thick clusters of white and pink blossom hung heavy and low and reflected the flaming gold of a lowering East End sun. Cressy sat with a glass of stout from Col's and listened to the secrets of Mother Gaia.

The voice of Ginny brought a smile to him.

What you doing, Cressy?

I'm enacting the Japanese ritual of *hanami*, my love.

Is that when you fold paper?

Not quite, sweetheart. Come sit with me. And he got up and gave her his chair.

Rain, she said.

Just starting, said Cressy, looking out. Won't last too long. Let's just sit it out, shall we?

Ginny nodded. The smell, she said.

Petrichor.

Ginny repeated the word over and over.

Scent of rain on dry earth, said Cress, and he sipped his stout.

It won't go away, she said.

Soon it will, my love, he said.

This.

What? And Cress turned to her. She had tugged the top of her blouse away to reveal a small love bite, like a thumbprint, floating between her collarbone and breast.

Won't go away, Cressy.

Cressy smiled. It'll go away, my love, if you cover it up and don't show anyone. You shown your dad yet?

Ginny shook her head.

Then don't. Best not to. It'll go away quicker if he don't see.

Thank you, Cressy, she said. Not scared anymore.

He bent down and held her cheek. Good, he said. No need to be.

But Cress felt scared. He closed his eyes and felt the roots from his shoes stretch down into the dark damp earth. Past the dead, and the Roman pots, to the whisperings.

Rain stopped, said Ginny.

When Cress and Ginny came into the pub, Ulysses looked up and said, Alys is upstairs, Gin, and she ducked under the hatch and disappeared.

Didn't expect to see you back so soon, said Ulysses. You all right, Cress?

Cress nodded and placed his empty glass on the counter. Meet me at the tree tomorrow morning, boy. Usual time. And bring Peg.

The next day, Ulysses was standing outside the pub enjoying the sunshine and waiting for Peg. He raised his hand as she came around the corner, familiar little twinge in his guts at the sway of her walk.

So what d'ya want to see me about, Tempy? she said, and before he could answer, a green ambulance, red cross and all, spluttered down the street.

Jesus Christ, she said.

He's brought it back from Swindon.

Don't they scrap their junk there anymore? she said.

Col parked the ambulance outside the pub and was about to climb out when the siren suddenly wailed.

Jesus fucking Christ, you piss bastard! screamed Col, hammering the dash.

And there's the old Col, thought Ulysses.

The siren stopped. Col closed the door gently behind him and crept over to them.

What d'ya think? he said.

Speechless, said Ulysses.

Peg?

I wouldn't be seen dead in that, Col. No offense. But what you've got there is a charisma lobotomy.

Col looked hurt but he didn't let on. He said, I'm taking Fionnula out to Epping Forest tomorrow for a night in the woods. And Peg said, You turn up at hers in that, she'll think you're taking her out there to bury her.

All right, all right, he said, I hear ya. I'll invite her over to see it later this afternoon. Bustin' my balls, he said as he stomped into the pub.

Peg slipped her arm through Ulysses's and they walked on.

Noticed how Col's dating alphabetically? he said.

That's what you wanted to see me about? said Peg, and then she stopped. Blimey, he is, she said. Denise, Elaine, Fionnula . . .

G next, he said.

They found Cress underneath the canopy of blossom and a sudden intimacy enveloped them. Cress looked troubled. He kept his voice low and said, Ginny's got a fella, and he told them about the love bite and Peg said, Christ, not again. And Ulysses said, You sure it's not kids messin', Cress? and Cress shrugged. I dunno, boy. I just know she needs a bit of mothering. And the two men looked at Peg and Peg swore because mothering wasn't her thing.

The news about Ginny sunk Peg's mood and she was a bitch to the kid all afternoon, no this and no that, and the kid kept a wide berth; well, you would, wouldn't you? That night, the kid wanted her to read a story, and she held out *The Little Prince*, the book Ulysses had given her the week before.

And how am I supposed to do that? Peg'd asked him at the time. And he'd said, It's easy, Peg. You just sit on the bed and you read out loud.

So she sat on the bed and the sound of her voice was clumsy and unconvincing, but the kid was entranced and eventually fell asleep. Peg read on. Childhood. Breaks your fucking heart.

The following evening, the ambulance set off for Epping Forest trailed by a plume of Col's aftershave. He'd made up the bed in the back, and had packed a small gas stove and two tins of soup—tomato—and tea and milk for breakfast. Breakfast was his destination and his balls were as heavy as a coal sack. It had been so long since he'd had a real woman, one who didn't feel sorry for him.

The ambulance only got as far as Cressy's tree before the siren began to wail. Cressy looked out from under the blossom and saw Col the color of puce. Fionnula stared out of the window, face blank, like a hostage.

The evening light caught the wake from a canal boat and gulls crested above the gasometers. Peg and Ginny held hands along the towpath, and to outsiders, those who didn't know, they could have been work friends, equals without a doubt. But a duck broke the illusion, and Ginny raced ahead, arms flailing, till the duck jumped back in the water. Peggy laughed. Come here, Ginny, sit with me.

Ginny sat.

How you doing, Gin?

Happy. You, Peggy?

Peggy nodded. Yeah. Happy.

She took a bag of crisps out of her pocket and Ginny opened them, shooed away a curious pigeon.

Who'd you meet down here, Ginny?

I'm not allowed to come down here.

I know that, but I know you do. And Peg leaned into her and nudged her. We all used to come down here. I had a boyfriend nobody liked, and I'd meet him down here and we'd walk all the way to Islington. It was so dark under the bridges. Just him and me. Sometimes I'd meet him at night, Ginny, and the feeling was the best feeling because I was escaping all the rules, and this fella, my boyfriend, he was older than me, and him being older made me feel older. Like I was in the world, at last. The way he looked at me.

Ginny listened.

I could make him do anything, Gin. Him all gaga over a schoolgirl. Never told me he had a wife.

Peg took one of Ginny's crisps. I know you've got a boyfriend, too, Ginny.

Ginny shook her head.

Yeah, you do. We were all told not to tell, but we've all gone through it. He nice to you, Gin? He kind?

Ginny nodded.

Is his name Travis? (Travis? Why did that name come back to her?)

No, silly, said Ginny, and she got up off the bench, waved to a passing barge. She said something that Peg didn't catch so well, and Peg said, Davy? Was that what you said? Is Davy on there? she said, pointing to the barge.

Ginny looked confused. No.

What does Davy look like, Ginny? Is he like your dad or Ulysses?

No.

Not like them at all?

She shook her head.

Different.

How different?

Stop, Peggy, too tired.

Ginny leaned down and rested in Peggy's lap. Peg stroked her hair.

No blood anymore, Peg, she said.

How long no blood, Gin?

Long time, she said.

Peg reached down and put her hand on Ginny's stomach. The bump was taut and slight under the billow of her dress.

———

That night, Peg slept over at the pub. She was there the following morning with Old Cressy and Ulysses when the ambulance turned the corner, siren wailing. Col was alone in the front.

He parked up and slammed the door. The siren died with the engine.

How was it? said Ulysses.

Fuck off, said Col as he walked into the pub.

The other three followed him inside. Col went straight to the optics. Two punches of gin straight down.

That bad? said Peg.

I don't want to talk about it, said Col.

Yeah, you do, she said.

I forgot the tin opener, he said. The IV stand fell on her when we were getting into bed—

What IV stand? said Peg.

It caught her just here, said Col, pointing to the corner of his eye. And in the middle of the night, what she thought was my toe was in fact a rat.

Christ, said Peg.

But it was the way she looked at me, Peg. That was the worst. As if I was the lowest form of life.

A phylum Porifera, said Cress.

What?

A phylum. A phylum Pori—

Stop fucking saying the word phylum!

That's the lowest form of life, said Cress. A *sponge.*

I don't think I could feel any worse, said Col.

Yeah, you could, said Peg. Ginny's pregnant.

Pub closed due to
UNFORESEEN
circumstances

———

Ulysses swept a path through the wreckage. Under his feet the crunch of broken glass and to his left a pile of splintered chairs next to the hearth.

The assault had been fast and furious and mercifully curtailed, due to Col's lack of fitness and high blood pressure. He'd fallen to his knees, panting and burping, as wave after wave of acid fell onto gastric shores. In the doorway, Ginny staring, a flash of insight into why her mother may have left.

Ulysses picked up a table and set it on its legs. Whorls of dust and blue feathers rose on a current of air. Claude had suffered another sudden molt that had left him with wing and tail feathers only. He was one of the innocents. So too was the stuffed stoat. An ashtray to the lower jaw had resulted in the mandible's hanging, literally, by a brown thread.

Ulysses lit a cigarette.

Outside, the growing murmur of voices. Mostly the old ones with an aggressive thirst on them. He looked at his watch. Pub should've been opened by now and they'd been known to riot for less.

He heard Mrs. Lovell say, Unforeseen means "unexpected." And then he heard: Unexpected? What? Death? Col wouldn't close for death. Unless Col had died. What? Col's dead?

Such was the derivation of rumor.

Suddenly, a knock at the door. It was a pianist's knock: good rhythm, light touch. Pete's long face peering through the stained glass.

Ulysses opened the door and ushered Pete in. Through the crack, he pushed Mrs. Lovell and her roast dinner back. We'll be open this evening, Mrs. Lovell, he said. I promise.

Is Col dead? she asked, relishing the role of spokesperson.

Not when I last checked, said Ulysses, and he closed the door, pulling the bolt across. Pete looked about gobsmacked. He said, I was just passing when I saw the crowds outside. Col have one of his turns?

You know how it is. You all right, Pete?

Not bad, Temps. You?

Not bad, Pete. And Pete followed him inside on tiptoe. I don't want to touch anything in case I make it worse, he said.

Ulysses carried the velvet stool back over to the piano.

I hate to ask, said Pete.

Miraculously untouched, said Ulysses. Peg put herself between him and it. He had the poker raised above his head. Don't you dare, Col! she shouted. Don't you dare! And she threw herself across the keys.

Joan of bloody Arc, said Pete. What happened next?

It was like he was hypnotized. He dropped the poker, started to blink and held his stomach.

And then what? said Pete.

He fell to the floor exhausted.

Peg kick him?

No, Pete, she didn't. She's up there with him now.

He sedated?

Like a horse.

Where's Cress?

In the cellar, looking for stock. Most of the spirits took a pounding.

Pete nodded, taking it all in. He sat down on the stool and lifted the piano lid. His fingers danced across the twelve major scales.

So? he said, cracking his knuckles. What can I do for you, Temps?

Something soothing, Pete.

Course. I know just the thing. And he lit the first of two dozen cigarettes.

Ulysses was about to turn away when he said, That's a lovely jacket, by the way, Pete.

This old thing? I've had it years.

All afternoon the public bar of the Stoat and Parot was tended to and never was there a more grateful patient. Chopin's nocturnes steered the transformation and Pete played with the same passion he'd mustered for his West End audition. Tables were hammered back into usefulness and paintings were reunited with walls. The fire gorged on splintered wood and soon a warm glow filtered into the space and took it away from death's door. Ulysses went out in search of more chairs and he did four journeys of four each time. He brought down his dad's globe and placed it on the counter for Claude to use as a perch. Cress made beef and potato stew and made enough for the evening punters too. Pete said Cress would've made a lovely life partner and everyone agreed. Cress took Peg and Ginny and the kid out and they came back with armfuls of cherry blossom. Must have hurt Cress but he didn't let on. He'd have come to an agreement with the tree. Kid and Ginny decorated the shelves with jugs of pink and white flowers and Peg bandaged the stoat's jaw and by six thirty p.m., they all stood back in awe. They'd done it. The pub was ready to open. It looked wonky but loved, and loved it had never been.

With Claude on his shoulder and the stoat recumbent in his arms, Ulysses Temper stepped forward to open the pub, five minutes late for evening opening. Mrs. Lovell was first in the doorway. She looked him up and down and assessed the situation.

We're down but not out, Mrs. Lovell, said Ulysses.

You'll do, she said, and marched in.

Through the doorway, Ulysses caught sight of Tubby Folgate's black Jaguar Mark V driving past, sniffing out trouble and weighing up the odds. Didn't take long for word to get to him, thought Ulysses.

Peg sat in Col's room, watching over him, her feelings stuck somewhere between rage and pity—but most women felt that way about Col. Thank God, in all the years she'd known him, she'd never ended up in bed with him. Small mercies.

Peg? Col stirred and pushed the blanket back.

Col.

How long have I been here?

Days, she said.

He sat up quickly.

Joke, she said, and lit him a cigarette. Pub's open. No thanks to you.

I should go down.

Not yet, you shouldn't.

(Sound from downstairs.)

I don't know what happened, he said, so Peg told him.

Ginny OK?

I dunno, Col, is she?

Peg—

Is she pregnant or is she so god-awful that you want her locked away? Or shamed—

Peg.

Or shaken? You remember that? The shaking?

Don't, said Col, covering his face with his hands.

Touch of the déjà vus, ain't it, Col? Thought we'd turned that corner.

I just wanted to know. I still do, he said.

She won't tell you.

She's frightened of him, he said.

She's frightened of *you*. Agnes all over again.

(Agnes said he destroyed everything he loved. Agnes said he'd be his own downfall. Agnes said, Agnes said . . .)

So, you tell me if she's OK, said Peg.

Col lay back down again, exhausted. She's OK, he said.

Then love her again. You're all she has.

What am I going to do, Peg?

First, you go down and you tell 'em. Just tell 'em. This you can't hide. And you calmly ask if anyone knows anything.

And if they don't?

You let it go and you don't do nothing stupid.

You slay me, Peg.

Yeah, maybe. But I'm all you've got.

Peg didn't go down into the bar straightaway but watched from the doorway. She needed a breather of sorts, a lowering of the cortisol. His pulling a pint was the balm. Him and his parrot. She'd always thought the Tempers were a daft lot with their dimples and eyebrows and ears, and their belief that life cuts you a break when you least expect it. She'd have done anything to have had a mum like Nora. Nora was all soft angles and kindness. Peg could be kind, but there wasn't enough of it to be a regular thing with her. It was like her wage. Always ran out by Thursday.

She walked up behind Ulysses and held his arms and he didn't turn around because he knew it was her. A dovetail joint they were. They simply fit. She breathed him in, and he didn't even feel the lightness of her kiss on his back. Claude saw it, though. Claude opened his beak as if to say something. Peg put her finger to her mouth. Our secret, she winked.

At eight o'clock, what they'd all been waiting for happened. Col shuffled in, part invalid, part Old Testament, with a blanket draped around his shoulders and a moth around his head. He parted the silence like an ancient sea. He downed a gin and rubbed his forehead. Walked out to the center of the room, all eyes on him. Keep to the script, Col, said Peg, and he nodded. He cleared his throat and said, Life tests us in many ways. (Pause.) Ginny's pregnant.

People looked at one another. A solitary gasp, a frown here and there, but generally it was the quiet absorption of information that filled the room. Nothing more, nothing less.

I just want to know who's been messin', said Col.

Silence.

You can tell me now or later. Face-to-face or anonymously.

Silence.

Anyone? said Col, voice rising.

Sit down now, Col, said Peg.

Col! said Peg sternly. *Sit. Down.*

Col sat down. It's like a bloody morgue in here, he said.

And whose fault's that? said Peg.

Where's Pete? said Col.

In the bog.

What about a song, Peg?

Forgive me for not quite feeling it, Col.

Temps—what about that magic trick? The one with the egg.

That wasn't me, Col.

Pete walked back in, drying his hands.

For fuck's sake, Pete, do something, said Col. We're dying in here.

What Pete didn't know about an audience wasn't worth knowing. He closed his eyes and breathed in the muse. Unity was the word she gave him. Strangely in a Northern Irish accent.

The microphone crackled. The piano surrounded by a thick haze of blue smoke.

I'd like to dedicate this song to love, said Pete. I wrote it when I was in Yugoslavia.

When was Pete in Yugoslavia? said Ulysses, leaning in to Peg.

It's about regret, said Pete. It's called "If I'd Known What I Know Now."

Hindsight, whispered Cress.

What? said Col, twitching.

Hindsight, said Cress. If I'd known then what I know now. That's hindsight.

Shut the fuck up, said Col, and Pete began to sing.

In the most unexpected way, a tincture of forgiveness bled across the dark night and entered the pub. From dusty corners looking out, ghosts of missed opportunities and held grudges and words unspoken were laid to rest. Spines straightened, joints eased, and hearts became light. Old Cress went somewhere deep inside himself, somewhere private, somewhere lush. Ulysses looked across the counter to Peg and she turned to look at him, and their eyes locked in a serendipitous embrace, slow in motion. Col had a glimpse of life on the open road and his stomach settled. Suddenly, Peg glanced toward the door and there was Ted. Mr. Insurance, Mr. Risk Averse, who may or may not have had a wife.

Peg and Ted dancing now. Claude on Ulysses's shoulder, nuzzling his ear. Cress at the counter spinning the globe like a roulette wheel. The front door opening as if caught by the wind. Tubby Folgate standing in the doorway like a Rorschach inkblot, lighting a cheroot, taking in the scene, swaying to Pete's mellow tune.

The song came to an end and how could it not have been a standing ovation? Pete had given his all. Peg was cheering, Ted modestly clapping, Col whistling, but then, like the sudden tumble of dominoes, awareness shifted to Tubby and the applause subsided, and Tubby said, Don't mind me, don't mind me. But they did mind him, and the room fell to silence.

Beautiful, said Tubby. His glottal stop sharp as a blade. Tubby limped across the floor. Lot of villain in that walk. The thick reinforced boot on his left foot was custom-made by a cousin—the cobbler strand of the family going back generations, and a rather pleasant lot in comparison. Tubby stood in front of Col's table and slipped effortlessly into Col's pain, his very presence a liberal salting. He blew out smoke and regarded Col with his good eye, the one the loading hook hadn't taken all those years before.

I heard you got a bit of troubling, Mr. Formiloe? he said. You need to talk, my man?

Not to you, you cunt.

Col, Peg and Tubby looked over to the counter. Never had there been a more unfortunate moment for a parrot to regain his voice.

Autumn brought the return of short days, early nights and endless coal fires chugging up the air. Ginny was sent away to Col's sister in Bristol to have the baby and the pub wasn't the same without her. Alys stayed over with Ulysses as Peg settled in on Ted. Every week, Tubby came by for a quiet word with Col. What you doing mixing with him? said Peg. He'll be plotting something, said Ulysses. This won't end well, said Cress.

But Col didn't listen. Col quietly on the lookout for Davy.

And then it came to pass.

A Friday. The beginning of December. Meteorologically speaking, a bit queer. There was no wind, and a layer of cold air had been trapped under a layer of warm air, and as the day progressed, a thick veil of yellow-brown fog descended and wouldn't budge. By the evening London stank of rotten eggs and the city had come to a standstill and the streets were empty.

There was no traffic on the Thames and Peg reported that conductors were walking in front of buses holding torches. Only three oldies made it into the pub, and they were wheezing from the short walk, their faces blackened like coal miners'. By eight they'd left, and the place was like the *Mary Celeste*.

Cressy and Ulysses stood outside the pub. The pavements were greasy underfoot, and Cress said, Can you see me now?

Still see you, said Ulysses.

What about now?

Just about.

Now?

Nuh.

Two yards, said Cress, walking back into sight. A remarkable phenomenon, he said.

A beam of headlights rounded the corner. Cress and Ulysses watched the dark shape of the car drive past and out of view. The car stopped in the murk. The sound of an engine ticking over. A door opening and closing. Another door. Two sets of footsteps and low chat. A distinguishable limp. Another door opening and closing and what sounded like a bag of spuds falling to the ground.

Ulysses whispered, Get going, Cress. I'll find you if I need you.

Not leaving you, son.

You have to. Go on.

Cress turned; in three steps he was a ghost.

Ulysses lay on the bed with the radio on. Big band music down low and a small Scotch in his hand. The electric heater chugging out warmth and the faint murmur of voices downstairs. When Col had seen Tubby at the door, he'd told Ulysses to call it a night, so he had. He turned off the radio and went to the door. Ears alive and a heart pumping wild to the shenanigans below.

Suddenly, the ignition of a car catching. Ulysses darted to the window and lifted it up. Streetlights nigh on useless against the sludge, and red taillights disappearing. He closed the window quick, but still the stench of sulfur got in.

Temps! (It was Col.) Temps! Down 'ere, mate!

Ulysses put on his shoes, pulled a jumper over his head and went down the stairs into an unlit bar.

Col?

Light from the fire flickering, and a cigarette pulsing in Col's mouth.

Col, mate?

It's done, Temps. Justice has been served this night of unholy nights. And Col pointed his cigarette toward the hearth and the dark shape of a body.

Bloody hell, Col! What the fuck you done?

Nothing. Pure as the driven snow I am. I'm the rubbish disposal, that's all. And that's Davy.

Or *was* Davy, because Davy was definitely dead, head poking out of a grimy tarpaulin.

Ulysses walked around the body. How d'you know it was Davy?

Because Tubby said it was Davy so Davy it bloody is. And Col poured out another drink.

Where's Claude?

He's about.

Ulysses went out into the kitchen. Not here, he shouted. Walked over to the front door and picked up a single blue feather. He held it up. Where is he, Col?

Must've followed Tubby out.

What'd ya do to him?

Nothing.

What'd ya do?

Fair is foul and foul is fair.

You what?

That's what he said to me. And then he says, Hovers through the filthy air. *Filthy air.* I mean, how does he know? That bird gives me the shits.

Suddenly at the door a face loomed large, and the two men screamed.

Only me, said Cressy through the stained glass.

Don't come in, said Ulysses.

Let him in, shouted Col.

Let me in, said Cress, and Cress came in. He stood next to Ulysses and Col and looked down on the body.

Where'd that come from? he said.

Tubby, said Ulysses. Apparently, it's Davy.

What's all this "apparently"? said Col. Apparently yourself.

He don't look like a Davy to me, said Cress.

God help me, said Col.

Suddenly, the fire went out.

Fair is foul and foul is fair, said Ulysses.

Jesus, said Col. Let's get it out of here.

Col, Ulysses and Cress sat in the front of the ambulance with the ignition running and the headlights hardly denting the soupy dark.

I'll go, said Ulysses, and he tied a handkerchief around his nose and mouth and switched on the torch. He walked in front of the vehicle, guiding it through Nichols Square, until they got to Hackney Road, where he climbed back in. The occasional car passed, a lorry too. Col waited and managed to settle in behind a trolleybus on its way to Leyton. The three men began to relax.

Cress broke the silence. He said, Death, the final frontier.

No kidding, Einstein, said Col.

You're allowed one last meal, Temps, said Cress. What would it be?

Now, that's a question, Cress. And Ulysses thought for a moment. Beef brisket, he said. Without a doubt. But when I was in Italy, a woman cooked me spaghetti and I'd never tasted anything like it. Bit spicy. Rich tomato sauce. It meant everything to me. Maybe because I did think it was the last meal I was ever going to have. I thought I was the luckiest man alive.

Col and Cress nodded. Wondered what that might feel like, to be the luckiest man alive. And they stared ahead into the unknown. Their eyes riding on two faint beams of light that went nowhere.

Col said, My last meal would be between a woman's legs.

I think you missed your turning, said Ulysses.

Col cursed. He pulled over sharply and reversed.

They got to the outskirts of Epping Forest a little after two in the morning and Mother Nature ran for cover. The trees had filtered a lot of the gunk and the fog appeared whiter, more celestial, and graced the trunks with a light spread. Col turned off the ignition and threw them into night. The sound of an owl. The sound of a ticking engine. The sound of Col's stomach.

I came here with Fionnula, he said. To this very spot. Feels like a lifetime ago.

You came here with Fionnula? said Ulysses.

Yep. This very spot. No one around for miles. Even then I thought it was the perfect place to bury a body.

Don't let anyone tell you you ain't romantic, said Cress.

Ulysses tied the handkerchief around his face again and said, Right, I'm gonna make a start, Col—show me exactly where.

And that was the cue for both Col and Cress to wrap scarves about their mouths and for all three of them to get out and fire up the torches. Col went around the back and opened the door.

Is he still dead? said Cress.

Idiot, said Col, and he pulled the bundle from the ambulance and it thumped to the forest floor. Col paced about like a prospector, felt the texture of the earth, kicked at the soil.

Here, he said to Ulysses. This is the place. And Ulysses dug out the first divot.

The soil was moist, mostly centuries of leaf mold and worms, an organic world of slow, constant motion.

My mother was afraid of beef brisket, said Col.

Sorry to hear that, said Ulysses.

She suffered from anxiety about most things. Libraries. Thunderstorms. *Beef brisket*. The world was overwhelming to her. She took her own life.

Col? said Ulysses, suddenly looking up. You know you said this was the perfect place to bury a body?

Yeah. I did.

Well, someone's beaten us to it. There's one here already.

Col shone his torch into the pit and looked down.

Well, I'll be . . . Fuck it, said Col. Just throw him in on top.

So they did.

Cress cast in a handful of earth and whispered a few words.

You're kidding me, said Col.

He was somebody's son.

Fiddled with somebody's son more like, and Col walked back toward the ambulance.

They got back to the pub at sunrise. Not that you could tell the sun had risen because the fog was even thicker, browner, stickier than before. They encountered no one as they parked up, and no one as they entered the pub.

Col poured out large whiskies all round and raised his glass and said, What happened in Epping Forest stays in Epping Forest.

And they clinked glasses and repeated the toast.

Ulysses shut himself up in his room for a couple of days afterward. He didn't want to see anyone, went a bit in on himself, that was the way Cress described it to Peg. He didn't say much, but Peg wasn't stupid, she knew what was what. You didn't do nothing sil—? No, we're clean, I promise you, Peg, said Cress. That boy's sensitive, that's all. Thought he'd left all that nonsense behind.

In February 1953, Ginny returned. She came back without a baby because she'd given it to someone else and made them happy. That's the version that came out of Ginny's mouth, and no one knew what to say about that, so mostly people hugged her and said, Good to have you back, sweetheart.

Col had a doll ready to give her, but Peg said, Don't you bloody dare, so he didn't. She looked at him as if he was the lowest form of life and the word *sponge* came back to haunt him. Tubby carried on his business in the snug and even Col wondered how he could get rid of him.

Claude didn't return to the pub and Ulysses went up the ladder and changed the sign back to *The Stoat*. Paint a tree over the bird, said Col, so Ulysses did. A large oak.

And with the first easterly of the year, the pub sign swung to and fro, in that familiar refrain of choice.

By March 1, it would be safe to say, normal had returned to the pub.

On the fifth, however, so did Claude. He flew in through Ulysses's window and landed on his chest. It was love at first sight again. Ulysses couldn't have been happier. He took Claude downstairs and Col said, Oh, for fuck's sake.

By the afternoon, Ulysses was back up the ladder painting a large Amazonian blue parrot over an English oak tree. It was when he came down that the policeman turned the corner.

There you go, Constable, said Ulysses, pushing a glass of lemonade shandy toward him.

The policeman brought a photograph out from his pocket and said, You ever see him around? Been missing three months now.

Ulysses looked at the face and could feel his heart thump.

I wouldn't give a toss, quite honestly, if he was six feet under, said the policeman. He's a bad sort.

Never seen him, said Ulysses. So who is he?

The brother of a friend of Reggie and Ronnie. That's why it's causing a bit of bother. Goes by the name of Eric Davy.

Cress walked in. Trouble? he said, and Ulysses handed him the photograph. You seen this fella, Cress?

Cress studied the photograph. Never seen him, he said.

Col walked in.

You seen this bloke, Col? said Ulysses, handing over the photograph. Eric Davy, he said. Been missing three months now, the brother of a friend of Reggie and Ronnie.

Col looked at the photo. His face blanched a bit, slight twitch at his top lip, hand to stomach.

Never seen him, said Col, unwrapping a peppermint, and before he'd finished the sentence, Tubby walked in from the snug. Col handed him the photo and said, Name of *Eric* Davy. You seen him, Tubby? *Eric* Davy.

Tubby looked at the photograph and smiled. Yeah, I know him. Brother of a friend of Reggie and Ronnie. Dirty git. Right dishonest. Owed me a ton.

Is that so? said Col.

Yeah. He dead, is he?

We don't know, said the constable, finishing his lemonade shandy.

The world won't weep, said Tubby.

Well, if you hear anything, bung it my way, said the policeman, and he picked up the photograph and left, passing Peg, who was on her way in.

Aye aye, said Tubby. Here's a woman on a mission.

But Peg ignored him and walked up to Col. Something you should know, she said.

Go on, he said.

You wanna do this here?

Why not? We're among friends.

You sure about that?

Col laughed.

Davy's back, she said.

(Freeze-frame:) Col midscream, flying toward Tubby, reaching for his neck. Tubby's grin, now a grimace. Tubby toppling back, reinforced boot waist height fending off Col's attack. Col's knee between Tubby's legs, next to his roll of cash. A jet of water spurting in from the left. Old Cress commandeering the soda siphon as if it were a mortar gun. Claude midair, wingspan impressive, no molt but a run on droppings. Ulysses on Col's back, trying to pull him off. Peg emptying an ashtray into Tubby's mouth.

Suddenly, the front door opened and a gentleman appeared.

I'm looking for a Mr. Ulysses Temper! he shouted. He picked up a chair and banged it down. A Mr. Ulysses Temper! Anyone?

The brawling stopped. Groans and panting rose from the pile of bodies, and five heads turned toward him. He said, Roland Burgess at your service, and he raised his hat.

Ulysses stood up and offered his hand. I'm Ulysses Temper, he said.

Mr. Burgess smiled and brushed a blue feather off his shoulder. Mr. Temper, he said. You don't know how happy I am to meet you.

Ulysses led Mr. Burgess up two flights of dingy stairs to his room. He closed the door behind him and motioned for Mr. Burgess to sit at the table.

Sorry about all that, Mr. Burgess, said Ulysses.

Spot of bother?

Nah. Long old story. Ulysses sat down opposite. So, what can I do for you, sir?

My card, said Mr. Burgess, opening his briefcase.

Solicitor?

You're part of a long trail that ended up at the Italian church in Clerkenwell, Mr. Temper.

I am?

Yes. I've often worked for the community around there. Especially after the war. Tricky time, as you can imagine. So they sought me for this little venture. And I found you.

Found me, Mr. Burgess?

Yes. Arturo Bernadini. Ring a bell?

Ulysses shook his head. I don't know him, sir. I don't go to the Italian church. I mean I have, during the procession, but not—

No, no, I'm confusing you. Mr. Arturo Bernadini of Santo Spirito, Florence. Not St. Peter's, Clerkenwell. Does the name—?

Hold on a minute, said Ulysses. Arturo Arturo?

I think that's probably him. Arturo Bernadini died a year ago—and Mr. Burgess pulled out a bundle of paperwork from his briefcase—yes, here we are. This, Mr. Temper, is a copy of the last will and testament of Arturo Bernadini. And he spun the document round and showed it to Ulysses.

What's this got to do with me, Mr. Burgess?

Oh, everything, Mr. Temper, everything. And he lifted the document and read: "I leave all my worldly possessions to Mr. Ulysses Temper of the British army."

Ulysses stared at him.

You are the sole beneficiary of his estate, Mr. Temper. So, you see. It was vital I found you.

Silence.

I don't know what to say, said Ulysses.

I'm not sure anyone would.

Ulysses got up, went over to a bottle of Scotch. Worldly possessions? he said.

A property and the furnishings within. An amount of money resides in a bank account, too.

Ulysses handed Mr. Burgess a glass of whiskey.

Do you believe in fate, Mr. Temper?

It's a gift, right? According to a friend of mine.

A gift? I like that. Then, let's raise a glass to fate. And before I forget, said Mr. Burgess, there's a letter too, and he rummaged around his briefcase and handed it to Ulysses.

Ulysses opened it. It's in Italian, he said.

Would you like me to translate?

Could you, sir? And Mr. Burgess took the letter and began to read out loud.

My dear Ulysses,

If you are reading this letter, then I am dead.

Nine years have passed since our brief acquaintance. And the image of you seated across the table from me has led me across them all.

Did I change my life sufficiently to reflect the kindness you showed me that strange afternoon in August? I don't know. I hope so. In my small way I think maybe I did. No single act of generosity remains in isolation. The ripples are many.

And what did the years bring you? Happiness, I hope.

In bequeathing my home to you, I give you equal opportunity and equal dilemma, I know this. But these rooms were once a good home to my mother and I, and good things happened here. You being one.

You will have been informed there's enough money to cover travel expenses, however you wish to return. There are many options. Enough money to bring a wife too, and children, of course, because I imagine your life to be a full one.

Whatever you choose, I honor.

And so, I close.

I wish you a long and fruitful life, Ulysses Temper. And I give thanks to your parents for naming you so. Had they not, I would never have found you.

[Indeed, said Mr. Burgess.]

Your friend,
Arturo
Santo Spirito, Florence

The sun was low, firing the canal with a sharp flame of pink and gold. Coots and ducks skimmed the surface and two men sat on a bench, deep in thought.

All his worldly chattels? said Cress.

Yep. Everything.

Well, I never.

Ulysses got up. He pretended to skim a stone. What am I going to do, Cress?

What do you want to do?

I don't know, I don't know. He sat back down and put his hands behind his head. I could authorize Mr. Burgess to sell everything.

That what you want? The money?

Doesn't everyone? Would be nice.

Cress lit a cigarette. Comes and goes, does money.

What you thinking? said Ulysses.

Cress pushed back his sleeves and put his hands out front. Equal opportunity, equal dilemma—that's what he said, right? You've got to see it for what it is.

And what is it?

A game of call and response. You called. You may not know it. But you did. You asked for something and you got it. Only you know what you asked for.

Ulysses stood up and kicked at an edge of grass.

It's about Peg and the kid, ain't it? said Cress.

And you, said Ulysses.

Nothing's forever, said Cress, and he blew out a stream of smoke. So, what's this place Florence like? he said.

And Ulysses said, Like that—and pointed to the colors illuminated in the canal, the shimmering peace, the iridescent light.

And the property bequeathed? said Cress.

Bedrooms. Space. A terrace.

And the two men were silenced.

What would my dad do, Cress?

That's easy, son. Everything on the black. And he flicked his cigarette away. But by God I'll miss you, he said.

Come with me, Cress.

I'm too old. Everything on the black, son.

In the days that followed, the talk of the inheritance spread and eclipsed any remnants of gossip about the pregnancy and Davy.

In the pub, Mrs. Lovell said, Two halves of stout and what you gonna do?

I don't know, Mrs. Lovell. What would you do?

Take the money and tell those Eyeties where to shove it.

Well, that's certainly an option, Mrs. Lovell. There you go. And Ulysses pushed two glasses of stout across the counter.

Peg and the kid barreled in through the door. A vein of sadness chugged through his chest.

Well, you're a sight for sore eyes, he said.

Kid smiled. Where's Ginny?

Upstairs, he said, and she ducked under the hatch and disappeared.

Peg said, You made a decision yet?

He shook his head. Can we talk?

Can't now, Temps—

No, no. Sometime. But just us.

You all right?

Ulysses shrugged.

Thanks for looking after her.

I love her.

I know you do, said Peg. What about Friday?

Friday? You not going out?

I'll get back early. And Peg finished her drink. Friday we'll talk, she said. Just you and me.

The week ran slow till Friday. It contained a lot of Col clogging up the drains.

You've got to understand, they're not like us. (Col holding forth after work.) All that foreign food.

Cress was standing at the bar with Pete, who was suffering a dose of the morose, his face longer than it had been in months.

I think you're being a bit harsh, said Pete. I buy sheet music off a lovely Pole.

We're different planets, Pete. There's us. And there's them.

Col using the globe as a prop.

Mainland Europe. And Britain. And in between, the channel. There for a reason. A God-given moat. And we pull up the drawbridge and tell 'em to fuck off. And we keep our ways. Look at the bleedin' mess they caused. You should know, Temps, you were over there. What have they ever given us except a bucket-load of heartache?

Col loved the silence that followed; he could have fucked it twice and cooked it breakfast.

Clocks, said Cress.

What? said Col.

What have they ever given us? And I'm saying mechanical clocks.

Big fucking deal.

Well, it is rather, said Pete. It's *time*.

Cognac, said Ulysses. Cellos.

Glasses, said Cress.

All right, all right. But you're missing the point.

Here's a point, said Pete. Photography, suddenly feeling emboldened by his contribution.

Don't you start, Pete.

Cinema, said Cress.

Submarines, said Ulysses.

Clarinets.

Television.

I'm going to bed. And Col stomped off.

Parachutes, said Claude.

Col came back in and eyed the parrot. What did you say to me?

Par-a-chutes, said Claude, beak to nose.

And a telescope, said Cress.

So, by the time Friday night rolled round, Ulysses breathed a sigh of relief and knocked off at nine.

Who said you could do that? said Col.

You did, said Ulysses.

He was putting the finishing touches to his room when Peg came by. At the door he saw what she saw: that he'd made an effort. Candles on the table, a bottle of fizz dripping with condensation, a bowl of crisps, daffs in a milk jug. The air was sweet and carried the scent of his cheeks. The bedclothes fresh and ironed.

But still it was a room above a pub. Where a sad old demob suit hung in full view. Where every other day the windows were blackened by soot. Where he could hear the arguments inside and those outside too. The stories of struggle. Ginny's midnight wanderings. Col's acid groans.

You've done it nice, said Peg, closing the door.

She went straight to the mirror and moved a curl away from her forehead. Thirty-three, she said. Who would've thought?

Ulysses dealt with the cork. A muffled pop.

That the real stuff? she asked.

He nodded. He was happy he'd spent the money. He handed her a glass as well as an envelope and said, Here's to thirty-three more. Happy birthday, Peg.

This my present?

Ulysses nodded.

Peg became self-conscious and shook the envelope and said, What's in here then? and Ulysses said, Open it.

Peg pulled out a map. On one side was a photograph of a river, a bridge with buildings built upon it. A rower disappearing beneath. Golden light. *Firenze* written across the sky.

Come with me, said Ulysses.

Peg placed the map carefully on the table.

Come with me, he said again.

She picked up her glass and drank.

Come with me, Peg.

Her, quietly—I can't. I'm with Ted.

You don't love him.

I don't need to.

Come with me. You, me, Alys. We could have a life there. It's so beautiful, Peg. We could start again.

Learn Italian?

Why not? People learn new languages. Mrs. Kaur had to learn English, Mr. Wassily too—they all did it. We could. We're no different.

You're dreaming.

Not dreaming. A real chance for us.

And Ulysses sat down and spread out the map. Peg—he reached out for her. He was tender and she was softening—look, this gate here, he said. This is the south side, this is where we came in during the war. Came down to this palace, and these gardens. Big, they were. Fountains and—

Her looking at his wonder, his boyhood wonder still there; bright eyes, sleeves rolled high, capable hands that could catch anything—a ball, a falling star—and she wishes she could say yes to him but her imagination won't reach that far, can't stretch that far, not since Eddie—

—they were all camped out there, he says, all the people. And along here, see? This square. A church, and here, where we'd live. High up. A terrace, too. We could grow things. And we'd look out of a morning, we'd see mountains—imagine that!—and the air, Peg. The air's clean and—

Take Alys.

What?

Take Alys, she said.

No.

Give her the life you want to give me.

She needs her mum.

She needs someone who loves her. Someone she loves.

Peg. (He said her name so sadly.)

I was her once, she said. I see how she is around you. If it's such a good life, give it her. There's nothing for her here.

And Peg reached for his hands and kissed them. I'll beg, if you—

Stop it, Peggy.

Please take her. Show her things and teach her things. That'll be my present from you. Tell me you will.

Peg lay awake, somewhere between the harsh seam of night and morning. The curve of her body against the curve of him. She'd worn him down, she knew she had. She didn't feel proud, just empty now. She unpeeled herself and rolled to the edge of the bed. In four hours, her life had changed. Like it had in '44. All the fours and the gossip to come. She smoothed down the creases in her blouse and skirt. She picked up her shoes and coat and he didn't stir, and she wouldn't wake him. He'd promised to take the kid. She felt light-headed and sick and she needed air. She closed the door and crept downstairs.

In the hallway, out of the darkness, a little nasal voice.

Ginny—what you doing up, love?

You look sad.

Peg's never sad. Come on. And she took Ginny's hand and walked her into the bar. Claude opened his eyes and Peg said, Go back to sleep, Claude, and she lifted a glass to the optics and picked up Col's fags by the till. She sat on a bench and Ginny cuddled next to her. The room felt cold, but Ginny's body was warm. Loving Ginny was easy. Loving Ginny was easier than loving her own kid. Through the window the sky was lightening at the torn edge. The faint sound of a blackbird and a horse and cart, but mostly the early hours brought silence, both reflective and confrontational. Why can't you love your own kid, eh, Peg? She shook out a cigarette and stuck it in her mouth. Because she's too much of me.

Ginny struck the match and held it up to Peg. What you drinking? she asked.

Mother's ruin.

Why's it called mother's ruin?

You don't want to know. And Peg kissed her head.

Peg crying, said Ginny.

It's just the smoke, Gin Gin.

A light mizzle of rain met Peg outside. Not cold anymore but soothing, the moonlight catching the drops in her hair. She can breathe now. She throws her head back and opens her arms out wide. She sings softly, on the breath, a smoky catch to her voice.

Peggy Temper walking tall and proud through the streets of her dominion. Dismissing pain with a whiplash flick of her wrist and casting it into the gutter to join a thousand other heart-raw tales. Right left, right left, her hips sway like a dirty dream and orange embers flare at her unpainted mouth. You could hang yourself off her every word and many a man has tried. The sound of her footsteps through the streets. The dark shape of the gasometers and always the smell of coal dust and a ripe canal rippling. These are the elements of her home. And she knows she will never leave. Just in case, you know, *Eddie.*

Drive, said Old Cress.

It was mid-April, and Ulysses and Cress were seated under the cherry tree formulating a departure plan. Mr. Burgess was dealing with the passports and legal guardianship of Alys, and it was now up to Ulysses to decide how he would get them to Italy.

Drive, said Old Cress for the second time

Knock knock, said Piano Pete outside the canopy of wonder.

Come in, Pete, said Cress, and Pete entered with three small glasses of beer. Here you go, fellas.

Nice tie, Pete.

Thanks, Temps. French silk.

I've told him to drive to Italy, said Old Cress.

Good advice, Cress. That way, your emotional state can harmonize with the landscape. Dover to Calais, Dijon, Poligny, St.-Cergue, Lyon, Geneva—maybe a turn around the lake—Milan, Bologna. Then Bob's your doo-dah.

Ulysses and Old Cress looked at him, stunned.

That's quite precise, Pete, said Ulysses.

Old girlfriend did a similar jaunt in '48. Nice scenic route. You need some wheels?

Might be useful.

I'll see if her old Betsy might be up for sale. She's become a motor-cycle enthusiast these days. Prefers the freedom.

And two weeks later, Pete pulled up outside the pub with Betsy—a Jowett Bradford utility van, in an attractive shade of blue.

Ulysses lifted the bonnet. She's a beauty. How much, Pete?

Never you mind, said Cress. It's all been sorted by Fanny. Now—I've given her a once-over and tweaked her here and there. Thirty miles to the gallon and top speed of fifty. She's five years old but she's still reli-able. She'll get you there.

And she knows the way, of course, said Pete.

And before Ulysses could say any more, Col drew up alongside in the ambulance, honking for his parking space. Move on, traitor! he shouted.

By mid-May, most people's minds had turned away from Ulysses's imminent departure to the happier occasion of the forthcoming coronation of Queen Elizabeth II. Patriotic paraphernalia adorned the outside of the pub, care of Col's new lady friend, Gwyneth. She was a florist and big on display. Ginny learned how to use the till at Mrs. Kaur's and Mrs. Kaur said she was a valuable asset to her expanding convenience shop. Peg suffered quietly the impending loss of her best friend and kid, and she hit the bottle and kept quiet the night Ted hit her too. Ulysses got the jitters and said to Cress that he didn't know how to look after a kid or how to start again. He said he hadn't started again there after the war, he'd just slipped back into a form of stasis that had held him close because that's what he'd needed. The sun rose, the sun set and the beer barrels needed changing. Cress talked him down, of course. Wish you were coming too, Cress, but Cress was too choked to say a word. And finally, a week before the off, Mr. Burgess came by with the guardianship papers and a huge pile of *lire*.

Sunday evening. Kid eating a bowl of spaghetti upstairs in Ulysses's room.

Does this mean I'm yours now? said the kid.

No. We're sort of borrowing each other, he said.

Kid thought about this.

Looking after one another, added Ulysses. Just for a time. Seeing if it works out. We can always come back, if you miss your mum.

I won't miss her.

(Hard as nails, he thought.)

Or here?

I won't miss anything.

Not even Ginny or Cress? he said.

They can visit. And Pete's coming for Christmas.

Is he now? Ulysses laughing. It'll be you and me for the time being. Think that'll be enough?

More than enough, said kid.

The morning of departure was dull and cold and a small crowd had gathered outside the pub to wave farewell.

Ulysses, dressed in his demob suit, placed the bundles of his dad's copperplate etchings carefully in the boot. He threw the sleeping bags onto the backseat.

Col? You seen Cressy?

He probably couldn't face you. Feels let down by you—

Aw Jesus, Col, give it a rest.

The last of the bags went in the van. Pete came out of the pub with Ulysses's globe, which he placed in the boot.

Cheers, Pete.

I'm not good with good-byes, Temps. Never have been—and he threw his arms about Ulysses and began to cry. He said, I'll be there at Christmas, Temps, if I don't get the Palladium gig.

Rosemary Clooney, I heard?

Yeah, big-time. I need to hold me nerve on this one.

He'll crap it as usual, said Col.

What'd you do with Claude? said Ulysses.

Don't look at me, said Col.

Well, I am looking at you. I wanted to say good-bye.

To a bleedin' bird? said Col, and he shook his head and said something indecent, and walked back into the pub.

Ulysses turned around and said, Hey hey, here they are. Ginny and the kid running toward him. Peg clack clack clack behind them, chewing her lip.

He took the suitcase from Peg and loaded it in the van.

All set? she said.

Yeah.

You seen Cress? he said.

Isn't he here?

Ulysses looked at his watch. We should get going.

Give him another minute, she said.

Thought you'd be gone by now, said Col, coming back out. I've got a delivery on its way. They'll need the space.

Col?

What?

Stop.

What?

Stop. Shake my hand. Shake it, damn it.

Col shook.

Watch your back, mate, said Ulysses. And Col said, Thanks, Temps, and he wanted to add something about friendship and distance, but the emotion and reflux got in the way, and the sound that escaped his nose was phlegmy and dreadful. He staggered back into the pub, clutching his stomach, a wordless, crumpled husk of ever-growing regret.

Ulysses looked about for Cress. He said, Peg, I gotta go. Tell Cress—

I'll tell him.

They hugged. He whispered, We said everything?

Course we have, she said.

I'll look after her.

I know you will.

Peg's fingers across his mouth.

Shh. No more now.

Come on, Ulysses! Kid tugging his jacket. Let's go.

Go on, said Peg. Now or never, eh?

Bye, Ginny!

Bye, Uly!

The slam of car doors. The intake of breath and silence. Ulysses turned to the kid. Ready?

Ready, she said, and gave him the thumbs-up. He nodded and turned the key in the ignition. The engine caught straightaway. Even the van couldn't wait to get the fuck out.

He drove around the block, stretching time to its elastic limit, in disbelief that the old fella hadn't turned up to wish them well. Peg had seemed unconcerned, said maybe he couldn't face it, you know how he is. Peg would check on him later, but still. Ulysses passed the cherry tree again, the unadorned and silent witness to the comings and goings of that small corner of earth. In years to come, it would cower as the wrecking ball swung, would face its own demise as many a tree had done before, with grace and humility at the same old same old of human disregard.

Ulysses drove away from the pub, the rusty creak of the sign, coronation bunting already loose and falling like lace from a hem. He shifted up a gear, left the terrace where his mum and dad's old place had been and headed toward the canal. A final look about for Cressy before they crossed the bridge and headed south.

There are moments in life so monumental and still that the memory can never be retrieved without a catch to the throat or an interruption to the beat of the heart. Can never be retrieved without the rumbling disquiet of how close that moment came to not having happened at all.

And when Cressy appeared in the rearview mirror, that was one such moment for Ulysses. He stepped on the brake and flung open the door.

Cressy! he shouted.

Cressy! shouted kid.

Cressy running toward them with his suitcases, desert shorts flapping. Wait! he was shouting. Wait! I changed my mind!

The Stuff
of
Dreams

1953–54

As Betsy sped toward the coast, Cress parried the whys and hows with a version of events that made Ulysses and the kid laugh. Or gasp. The truth, though, was quieter than entertainment. Carried more *sentiment*, as the old boy might have said himself.

And this version had begun three months before, when Old Cress had been sitting with Ulysses on a bench overlooking the canal. The sun had been low, firing the water with sharp flames of pink and gold. Ulysses had just expressed his fear about leaving London, and Cress had said, It's about Peg and the kid, ain't it? And Ulysses had said, And you.

And *you*.

Those two words had confused Cress because not much love had ever come his way. The deep satisfaction of hearing those words, mixed with the sorrow of never having heard them before, made for an uncomfortable alliance, and prompted him to say, Nothing's forever—a trite and clichéd response to a young man's declaration of care.

So, what's this place Florence like? he'd said.

Like that, said Ulysses, and he'd pointed to the colors illuminated in the canal, the shimmering peace, the iridescent light. And Ulysses had said, What would my dad do, Cress?

And Cress had said, That's easy, son. Everything on the black, and he'd flicked his cigarette away.

And then Ulysses said it.

Come with me, Cress.

I'm too old, said Cress.

Too much love for one day. I'm too old. End of.

The nights that had followed this conversation had brought Cress little sleep. Too many what-ifs resided on the pillow and they were niggly and hard and pushed the old boy out in search of answers.

Too old? said the cherry tree. That's a bit ripe. One of my ancestors is more than a thousand years old and they're still up for stuff. Your idea of time is obtuse.

You reckon? said Cress.

Just saying.

A breeze slipped through the branches and made the *Prunus serrulata* shudder. I love it when it does that, said tree. And another thing—I always thought you wanted a passport. You've been going on about it for years.

And it was true, Cressy had.

So, Cress filled in the application, and a couple of months later— early May, it was—he received a passport in the post, a distinct creak in the spine when he opened it.

But still the decision grumbled.

Tree said, You've got the time, and you've still got the money.

Cress nodded—it was true, he did.

And for years you've felt like a change.

I have.

It's that Peg, isn't it? said tree eventually.

And Cressy's shoulders slumped. Yeah, he said. It's her.

Cress met her by the canal a couple of days later. Clack clack clack down the stairs she came.

You decided yet? she said, and he shook his head. You want me to decide for you? she said, and he nodded.

Go, she said. You always wanted to see the world. Go look after them for me. Keep 'em safe.

And Cress held her hand and said, I'm getting on. I couldn't bear to think I'll never see you again.

It's Italy, Cress, not the bleedin' moon. And she got up, kissed his head and didn't look back.

Next day Cress went to Thomas Cook in the West End and bought his ticket. He'd written the time of Ulysses's ferry on a slip of paper and pushed it across the counter to the young woman. Dover, Calais, he said. One way, he said. One way? the young woman said, smiling. Cress nodded. There was something regal in the way life was unfolding.

So when you off? said the tree.

Day after tomorrow, said Cress.

Ooh blimey, soon.

Cress nodded and supped his stout.

You got a lot to do?

One or two things.

Tree said, Thanks for everything. It's been nice knowing you.

You too, said Cress. Will you be OK?

I'm a tree. I've done this a thousand times before.

Done what?

Good-byes.

Really?

Think about it. *Leaves.*

Dover came into sight just before lunch and the Jowett Bradford entered the Eastern Docks, where the air smelled of diesel and salt. Beyond the cranes and jetties, the open sea beckoned and there was a fair chop to the water. The day was cold. The day was doing its best impression of November.

They parked up in the customs shed and stretched their legs. Ulysses told Cress to leave the small suitcase with the rest of the luggage, but Cress insisted he keep it with him. And maybe it was Cressy's unusual attire, or the one-way ticket out of England they all held, but the cursory searches of other vehicles became a full-blown search of theirs. Kid found it exciting and shadowed the humorless customs officer, much to his annoyance.

Have you looked in here? she said. What about here? Maybe there's stuff hidden in the tires?

A final look into Cressy's large suitcase revealed nothing but a small selection of clothes—two open-neck shirts, underwear and undershirts, a flannel suit, a shaving kit, toothbrush and paste, knitting needles and wool, liniment, old boots and three books: the 1899 Baedeker *Italy: Handbook for Travelers*, *Bradshaw's Complete Anglo-Italian Phrase-book*, and a novel—a rare choice for facts-man Cress—E. M. Forster's *A Room with a View*. First edition but with the back cover missing.

Cress? said Ulysses.

Cress was still talking to the officer about his last-minute dash for the car.

Cress? said Ulysses again. It's done. You can put your stuff away, the bloke's not interested.

Cress closed the lid of his large suitcase and secured the catches. The false bottom containing several hundred pounds of the Fanny win had remained concealed. And, more important, the small suitcase in his hand had gone unchecked.

What you looking so pleased about? said Ulysses.

Cress shrugged and walked Zen-like toward the car. The kid clambered in the back and Cress sat down with the suitcase on his lap. The hours spent reading about psychophysical magic had been worth it, he thought. To render the visible invisible had been one of his greatest achievements.

Ulysses got in and started the ignition. Calais, here we come! he said, and he threw his hat in the back and looked across at Cress. He couldn't be sure, but it seemed Cress was cradling the suitcase like it was a baby.

On deck the horn blared and the wind whipped up something rotten. They waved good-bye to the white cliffs. Good-bye, England! Good-bye forever! Ulysses thought about Peg, and Cress thought about Peg, and the kid thought about lunch. They went down into the warm and ate ham sandwiches and crisps as the gray water rolled hard against the side of the ship. Kid was glued to the sight of a man vomiting in the corner, and Cress held on to his cup of English tea as if it was to be his last.

They drove onto French soil at four in the afternoon and the sky was dark and low and making rain. Unfamiliar signs rushed past and cars drove on the wrong side of the road. When Betsy was clear of the terminal, Cress asked Ulysses to stop as soon as he could, and thinking Cress had been caught short, Ulysses pulled over sharpish onto a grass verge. But Cress didn't move. Cars passed by and a whip of rain hit the windscreen. You OK, Cress? But Cress remained silent and focused like a monk. Cress flexed his fingers and breathed loudly through his mouth. He flicked the catches on the small suitcase and opened the lid. On top was an orange Shetland sweater, which he carefully lifted out. Underneath, either asleep or dead, was a large blue Amazonian parrot.

Claude! said kid.

Jeez, Cress, how—?

Shh, said Cress. We're not clear of death's door yet. And Cress felt for a pulse. Nothing, he said gravely. He lifted the parrot to his ear. It's faint but he's breathing. And he began to massage the bird's chest. You see a pipette of water in the case, Temps?

I do. Here you go, said Ulysses, and Cress slipped the pipette into Claude's beak. He's drinking, he said. That's a good sign.

But how the hell did you—?

I read a veterinary book about dosages, said Cress. Mostly about the transportation of chickens. But I figured pound for pound I was probably dealing with a similar genetic structure. I took a chance, Temps. Couldn't leave him alone with Col, could I? That bird would never've survived another molt. If I was coming, so was he. That's the reason I was so late. He wouldn't go under.

Can I hold him, Cressy? said the kid.

Course you can. And Cress wrapped the bird in his sweater and handed the bundle over the front seat.

Gently now, he said. Keep him upright and give him the water. That's it. And a gentle rub on his chest now and then. There we go.

Claude opened his eyes and blinked, bewildered. The slow dawning he was about 120 miles from the pub without having taken flight. And that, for a parrot, was a lot to take in. Are we nearly there yet? he said, and the three of them laughed, and Ulysses winked at him in the rear-view mirror. Claude felt loved up with a sudden propensity to rub. He had a flashback to the fermented seeds he and his mates used to imbibe in the Amazon. Good times, he thought. He fell back to sleep, imagining he was covered in a light pink fuzz.

They drove for three hours down through the plains of Picardy. Nearing Laon, Ulysses told Cress and the kid to keep an eye out for the village of Soutigny, a place Pete had promised wouldn't disappoint. But by the time they reached the outskirts of that nondescript French village, the rain hadn't eased, and the deserted streets were awash, and it was hard to imagine the place doing anything other than disappointing. Ulysses pulled over and peered through the windscreen as the wiper whipped back and forth.

What did Pete say verbatim? said Cress.

That he'd spent "many a happy night in a gem of a hideaway on the main square."

Cress closed his eyes and channeled. Main square main square main square. Straight on, he said, opening his eyes.

Sure?

Positive, he said.

And as the eight o'clock bells chimed, the Jowett Bradford rolled into the main—and only, it had to be said—square, and stopped in front of a bistro with rows of white lights and a red neon sign flashing *Chambres*.

We've found the gem, said Ulysses.

At the front desk, Claude pecked on the bell and out from the dusty curtain an older landlady appeared, as if she was the glamorous denouement of a magic act. *Bienvenue*, welcome! she purred. (No *willkommen*, as it was still too soon for Germans to be welcomed in the village.) She said she had one room left and would organize a camp bed for the kid and newspaper for the parrot. She flicked a switch behind the desk and the red *Chambres* sign went out. Full, she said proudly.

She led them into the dining room, hazy with smoke and chat from salesmen. The photographs that adorned the walls were of her many lovers and husbands, she explained. At least that's what they thought she said, as their ears tried to sift through the broken fragments of her English. Beef *bourguignon* and chips? she said. Yes please, they said, nodding. She seated them at a table overlooked by moribund Denis, a local boules champion with a huge mustache and an impressive trophy.

She brought out a carafe of red wine and sunflower seeds for the *perroquet* and made eyes at Cressy in a way that made him wish his shorts were longer.

When she left, Cress poured out the wine and kid held out her glass and said, Fill it up now, Cress.

Cress said, You're too young. Give it time.

And kid said, Is this how it's going to be?

How what's going be?

Because I could've got this at home. And kid sat back and scowled.

And there's Peg, thought Ulysses.

Half an hour later, kid was asleep across a plate of *frites*.

They were the last to leave the dining room. The landlady brought out brandy on the house and Ulysses told Cress that him being with them had made them whole. Cress didn't know what to do with such a declaration, all that love again. Ulysses paid the bill and lifted the kid without waking her.

On the way out, he suddenly stopped at the photograph nearest the door. Here, Cress, look at this, he said.

Cress squinted. Blimey. Is that who I think—?

Yeah. Ulysses smiled.

Well, I never.

It was Pete at a piano caught in a clinch with the landlady. He was wearing a large beret. And little else.

I've never seen him in a hat before, said Cress.

Me neither, said Ulysses. It'd look even better on his head.

The kid was put to bed and Ulysses felt an added preciousness that night, a greater need to watch over her. Cress came back from the bathroom with the front of his pajamas soaked. The hot tap's cold and the cold's hot and there's a lot of pressure in the pipes. Thought I'd better warn you, he whispered.

Thanks, Cress.

Gave me a bit of a shock—

Well, if you're not expecting it—

All this newness—

Expands the mind.

Cress took the left-hand side of the bed and settled down. When I was a kid, he said, I used to lie like this and think there was a world out there. And now I'm in it, Temps.

Feels good, right?

Feels like nothing else.

Early start tomorrow, Cress.

Don't worry, I'll be there.

Eight days, it would take.

Eight days to cross three countries and countless landscapes. A map was consulted occasionally, but there was mostly a feeling of holidaying in the air, of spontaneity, and that was because of Cress. Cress's joining them had changed everything. He looked out of the window, a quiet understanding that his life would have been less had he died without witnessing another corner of the planet. Kid only looked up from her sketchbook when the smell of farmland with its mucky fetid lilt filled the car.

They slept in sleeping bags under stars, downwind from smoldering campfires to keep mosquitoes away. Mornings came early with the rise of sun and a chill river to wash in. A crawl into the nearest village brought bread and jam and coffee and the kid got a taste for the stuff and took it milky. They chose hot meals at lunchtime but at night it was bread and cheese and wine, and lots of stone fruit because fruit was sweet and plentiful. Cress got the shits and the following day they traveled slow. Lost a bit of time while Cress dug holes across the mountainous Jura. Dark forests and fast-running silver streams and pockets of pervasive silence. Worse places to wipe an arse. That was the day they found out about Davy.

Kid was sticking a postcard in her sketchbook. Places she'd been, her mum's idea. She turned the pages and a drawing caught Ulysses's eye and he said, That's Ginny, right?

Kid nodded.

In the picture, Ginny was holding hands with a boy wearing glasses. Same smiles. Same height. Boy had shaded skin.

And that's you? said Ulysses, pointing to the smaller figure.

Yep, and that's Ginny's— Kid suddenly stopped.

I know she has a boyfriend, said Ulysses. Cress does too.

What's that? said Cress, walking back into the conversation.

Ginny's boyfriend, said Ulysses.

Oh yeah. Davy, said Cress.

Kid rolled her eyes. *Devy*, she said.

Devy? said Cress and Ulysses in unison.

Devyan. He's the same as Ginny. He's big but a kid. He lives somewhere else. Mrs. Kaur's his aunty.

Mrs. Kaur is? said Ulysses. (And there the last piece of the puzzle fell into place.)

What's the matter? said kid.

Could I have this picture? said Ulysses.

Why? said the kid.

I want to send it to Peg.

You think she'd like it?

I know she would. We'll put it in an envelope with a postcard. Show her how far we've come.

They all wrote on the postcard. All wrote wish you were here. And Ulysses wrote a little extra note with a bit of context to go with the picture. In Switzerland Ulysses posted the envelope back to Peg and kid got her first pair of sunglasses as thanks. They were too big for her but what did she care? Cress said he'd secure them with string, and kid said, Better be nice string. And they strolled the promenade and watched steamers cross back and forth across the lake. And the air smelled sharp and expensive. Mountaintops cast down piercing light and tourists in fashionable attire stopped to take their photograph.

(Click.) Two men—one in shorts—a girl and a parrot. Now, that's a story to tell.

On the ninth day, they crossed from Emilia-Romagna into Tuscany. Olive trees carried white flowers, swallows and swifts took ownership of the sky. The grass smelled scorched and poppies were abundant. An occasional whiff of rosemary or lavender seeded by the roadside was a heady accompaniment. To Ulysses every smell was a ghost.

They drove south out of a dark haze of cypress trees, and Florence suddenly appeared in the Arno valley, resplendent under golden June light. Ulysses stopped the car and got out. He raised his hat and saluted the city as Darnley had done before. Claude took flight, and the blue of his feathers against the terra-cotta rooftops was an electrifying sight.

They'd traveled more than a thousand miles, had eaten twenty plates of spaghetti, nine stews, seventeen baguettes, a crop of apricots and a wheel of cheese. They had drunk forty coffees and eight bottles of wine and seven beers and two brandies. Nights in a bed: One. The first. They had seen wild boar and falcons and stars falling across the Alps. And they'd come to rely on one another because they were all they had.

The notary, or *notaio*, they had arranged to meet was situated in the north of the city, a couple of streets behind the Piazza della Santissima Annunziata, according to the map in Cressy's Baedeker. Ulysses parked in the splendid square, underneath a large equestrian statue that Cressy said was of Ferdinand the First. Who's Ferdinand the First? said kid, and Cress said he was a man who'd had a lot of fingers in a lot of pies. They left Claude to guard the car.

The narrow streets were teeming with bikes and pedestrians, and out of nowhere trolleys would clatter past, piled high with crates of wine or vegetables. The air was a heady mix of garlic and coffee and drains. There was so much to see! To smell! To hear! This way, shouted Cress, marching ahead with his map. And by five o'clock, they were outside the offices of *il signor* Massimo Buontalenti. Kid pressed the bell on the brass plaque and the door to the modest eighteenth-century building opened immediately.

The office was on the second floor and Signor Buontalenti was waiting for them at the top of the stairs with a tray of coffee. They liked him immediately. He was a small stylish man, forty perhaps, with an affable smile and a wild sprouting of dark hair that gave the impression he'd just been electrocuted. His English, though, was terrific. Signor Temper! he said. At last! I've been expecting you! For two days now, I've been waiting.

We got held up in the Alps, *signore*—a sentence Ulysses had never in a million years expected to say.

It was a straightforward transaction, took no time for the paperwork to be signed and the deeds to the property transferred. Signor Massimo said he would go with Ulysses in the coming days to set up a bank account in which the remainder of the money could be deposited. He replaced the cap on his fountain pen—a distinct and expensive click—and returned it to his jacket pocket. He smiled and said, *Allora?*

And Cress, thinking now was as good a time as any to make a start on the lingo, said *Allora?* too.

So what else do you need to know, Signor Temper?

And Ulysses said, I made a list, *signore*, and he handed it to Massimo.

Massimo scanned the paper. *Lavanderia*—laundry, yes yes, I suggest Manfredi. (Mumble mumble.) Schools?

Who said anything about school? whispered the kid.

Shh. We'll talk about it later, said Ulysses.

I didn't come here for school, she said. I could've got that at home.

You like ice cream, *signorina*?

Who doesn't? said the kid.

Ice cream's a way of life here.

Keep talking, she said.

Two places for you: Perché No! and Vivoli.

Kid turned to Ulysses. You got that?

Got it, said Ulysses.

Massimo continued: The cemetery where Arturo is buried? I think it's up at San Miniato al Monte—he looked through some paperwork—yes, yes it is. In the family vault in the Cimitero delle Porte Sante. And what else? Ah, telephone. Easy. You need tokens—*gettoni*—for the public telephones and from the post office you can call England. You want to call England now?

Could we?

Your wish is my command. And when the coffee was finished, he took them down to an office where a young woman dialed the number and made the connection. *Un momento*, she said before handing the receiver to Ulysses.

It was Col who picked up. *Un* bloody *momento*?

Col? It's me.

I know it's you. And thank God for that. Cressy's missing. I told the cops to dredge the canal. Poor old fucker.

Cressy's with me.

What? What'd ya do? Kidnap him?

No, I didn't kidnap him.

Cress leaned into the receiver and said, I came voluntarily, Col. I'm having a lovely time.

Traitors. Both of you. You got that bloody parrot too?

(Pause.)

What makes you think I've got the parrot? said Ulysses.

I don't. That was a joke. Pete reckons Tubby ate it.

Why would anyone eat a parrot?

To show me what he's capable of.

And what's that? A varied diet?

It probably tastes like chicken, said Cress.

What's he saying? said Col.

Cress said the parrot probably tastes like chicken.

God help me, said Col.

Guinea pigs taste like duck, said Cress.

What's he saying now? said Col.

Something about guinea pigs.

Jesus Christ. Just when I started to miss the old boy. Tubby should have eaten him first. Anyway, Temps, what d'ya want? I know you didn't phone me to tell me the weather.

Hot and sunny.

Fuck off.

Tell Peg we're here.

Let me just write that down: Tell . . . Peg . . . Temps—

Yeah, funny. And look out for her for me.

Don't I always?

Ginny OK?

(Ulysses could hear a peppermint being unwrapped.)

She's fine, said Col. She's over at Mrs. Kaur's. Dunno what it is about that woman, but she makes her happy.

Col. I gotta go. Take care of yourself, right? And don't forget Peg.

I never forget Peg.

Ulysses replaced the receiver.

Massimo held up a set of keys and said, Shall we? and he ushered them out the door. You can tell me about the parrot and the guinea pig in the car, he added.

Despite Massimo's outward appearance, he was at heart an unconventional man. Always had been. And to be sitting in the front passenger seat of an English car named Betsy with a parrot on his shoulder was as good as life got. He issued clear instructions to get them to the south of the city: *Left here. Mind the tram, Signor Temper. Right here. The tram, Signor Temper!* And he nodded and smiled at pedestrians who stared at him, as if to confirm their eyes were not deceiving them, and yes, it was he, Signor Massimo Buontalenti, popular notary and all-round legal expert, revealing his closeted bohemian side.

They crossed the Arno on the cusp of evening; the water flared with color and buildings surrendered their reflections to the untroubled surface. A solitary rower passed under the bridge and the scene drew a gasp from Cressy. Look, he said. Look there, he said. Such wonder.

A maze of narrow streets brought the Jowett Bradford to a stop alongside a church at the northeastern corner of a tree-lined piazza. The last of the *contadini*, the farmers, had gone and all that remained of the daily market was straw and donkey scat, and damaged fruit that sent the flies crazy. Over the far side, people were gathered outside a café as they had been nine years before. Ulysses opened the door and climbed out. He leaned on the bonnet and took in the scene. He was careful with the memory. A bicycle traversed the stones, handlebars piled high with gilded picture frames.

It's that building over there, said Massimo, pointing to the cream and brown building that dominated the south side of the square.

All set, boy? said Cressy.

All set.

Then what are we waiting for? said kid, putting on her sunglasses. Come on! she said, and lifted out the globe and her suitcase.

They managed as much luggage as they could between them and crossed the square, unwittingly, in ascending order of height. The old women on the stone benches looked up from their knitting and watched them pass. Boys by the fountain laughed and pointed to the parrot and said *pappagallo*. A group of men came out of the café and Ulysses heard the words *soldato* and *arrivato*.

Through here, said Massimo, holding open the large wooden door with his foot. The vestibule was cool and carried the lingering smell of stone and sewage, which Massimo said were the two patron saints of Florentine stench. Behind them, an elegant glass door led out to a *cortile* crisscrossed with lines of drying washing. And this is your postbox, Signor Temper, and he indicated the one awaiting a name. And now we climb, he said.

He led them up to a bright landing of black and white tiles and a comatose potted plant. He waited for them to gather before he placed his hand against the door and said, So this is it. Your new home.

The start of our new life, said Cress.

There was a brief moment of acknowledgment—raised eyebrows, mostly—before Massimo inserted the key and disappeared into the dark and airless hallway.

They followed him like the blind of the Great War. And as their eyes began to adjust, they could make out the scattering of white sheets that covered the furniture. The faint slither of daylight creeping through an occasional broken slat. Signor Massimo clapped his hands and flicked the switches and the hallway and living room flooded with light. Cress dropped his luggage.

Bloody hell, Temps! It's huge.

Windows were opened, shutters thrown back, and sounds from the square rushed in. Ulysses looked about. So little had changed and the sequence of time reversed and there he was, young and invincible again, in front of a typewriter that had offered up his name.

Kid screamed and ran around with Claude, looking for her bedroom, and Cress still commentating on the size and elegance of the place. Look at all them books and paintings, Temps! Massimo smiling at their delight. Massimo, one of life's givers, soon to become a friend. An upright piano, too, used as a side table judging by the ornaments and candelabra strewn across its top. Signor Temper? said Massimo, nudging Ulysses out of his stupor. Shall we? And together they lifted dust sheets off two velvet sofas, the faded orange replaced since wartime by a taut vivid blue.

Terra-cotta tiles ran beneath their feet, and above them frescoes, pale pinks and blues and acanthus leaves and birds in flight and a starlit sky with constellations that really would look like night at the right hour, in the right light. Four bedrooms and not three as Ulysses had remembered, two overlooking the square at the front, two the *cortile* behind. A bathroom, which again defied Ulysses's memory by being much larger, or maybe had become much larger in the years since he'd been there.

And the kitchen.

A refrigerator! shouted Cress. Who has a refrigerator? We do! said kid, still on her run about. Two ovens, one gas and an old unused coal one, and Cressy's mind trying to take in the workings of a new system. Fuse box here, said Signor Massimo. The boiler is in the cellar. All straightforward really. Massimo turned the stopcock and the pipes and toilet cistern began to rumble. He left the room and kid ran in and said she'd found a telescope. Come see, Cressy. And Cressy went see.

And then silence.

Ulysses alone. He stood in the doorway to the kitchen and remembered holding open a book of paintings and delivering a faltering explanation about grief and a dance, things Evelyn and Darnley had so eloquently—so effortlessly—explained. If you'd asked him then if they'd all come through unscathed, he'd have bet his life on it. Would've pushed his body and soul across the green baize as the wheel spun.

He crouched under the table and felt for the raised edge of a tile. Gritty deposits caught under his nails and he tugged at the edge till it gave way. He reached into the gape of the cubbyhole, and wondered if, over time, it had become a home to mice or rats. Those thoughts fell away though as his hand landed on the smooth cold edge of a wine bottle. He lifted it into the light. Adhered to its side was the image of Pontormo's *Deposition from the Cross*, ripped from its book. You knew I'd come, he thought.

He went out to the terrace. Him and a wilting orange tree, awaiting an old man's care. Swifts squealing overhead as cypress hills became misty and grew dark. The smells of cooking rising from the kitchens below. Violet light falling onto the city, casting it into eternity. He climbed over the railing and walked down the roof. Down below, outside the café, a large man in an apron was watching him.

It wasn't as steep as he recollected, and yet he stopped midway by one of the chimneys because he knew he wasn't invincible anymore.

You OK, Signor Temper? Massimo calling out from the terrace behind him.

Ulysses nodded.

Then don't let one of the greatest adventures of my life end here. Please come back in. Now.

They gathered in the hallway as the sun dipped west and the last of the shadows cut across the floor. Ulysses held out his hand and thanked Massimo for everything. My pleasure, said Massimo. But we still have business to conclude before we say our good-byes. We still have to go downstairs.

Downstairs?

Yes. The floor below, Signor Temper. Didn't you know? That's yours too.

It was late and kid was asleep, and Cress and Ulysses sat at the kitchen table in the silence Massimo's departure had left. The two men were worn out by wealth.

If this is what rich people feel, said Cress, no wonder they're miserable.

The apartment below had been of a similar layout but with simpler décor than the top floor. It had been rented out up until a year ago and Massimo had said he would help Ulysses, should he decide to do the same. Or to sell it. I don't know what I need to do, Ulysses had said, and Massimo had laughed and slapped him on the shoulder. Call me, he'd said. The sound of his footsteps departing on the stairs.

Ulysses lit a cigarette and handed it to Cress.

We are such stuff as dreams are made on, said Claude.

They turned toward the parrot.

Where *does* he get it from? said Ulysses.

Cress shrugged. Search me.

They smoked. They listened to the run of water through the pipes, the susurration of the refrigerator. Ulysses went to check on the kid and when he came back he said, What we gonna do, Cress?

Now? Or in a month? Or—?

Now.

Cress thought for a moment. Observe and learn, I reckon. But first, you open the wine and I'll get the cheese and sausage I kept back for emergency.

Ulysses got up and looked for a bottle opener.

Cress said, We're embarking on a world of new language and new systems. A world of stares and misunderstandings and humiliations and we'll feel every single one of them, boy. But we mustn't let our inability to know what's what diminish us. Because it'll try. We have to remain curious and open. Two words for you: ley lines.

Ley lines?

Straight lines of electromagnetic energy crisscrossing the Earth at special sites, drawing men and women—and ideas—to their mysterious pulse. We were drawn here, Temps. No two ways about it. As many have been before. That Baedeker book? You know what it said?

Go on.

That "even those whose usual avocations are of the most *prosaic* nature unconsciously become admirers of poetry and art in Italy." Would that be so bad? To become an admirer of poetry and art? Until we figure it all out.

It wouldn't, Cress.

To be infused with all the city has to offer and has offered over the centuries? Our purpose revealing itself like the slow unfolding of an iris flower.

Ulysses grinned. It's started already, Cress.

What has?

The poetry.

Cress blushed and stood up. I'll get the cheese, he said.

The following morning, the square was abuzz. You seen who's back? they all said as they entered Michele's café. Clara the baker had told the butcher, who had told the priest during confession. Gloria Cardinale who sold haberdashery was lighting a candle in the church and had overheard the butcher tell the priest. She couldn't wait to tell her neighbor the tripe seller, who told Signor Malfatti who sold cheese. And of course, Signor Malfatti couldn't wait to tell me, said the elderly contessa, who was having a very public spat with the man over the contested weight of a single ball of ricotta.

So? she said, leaning over Michele's counter, drinking her first espresso of the day. A kid and no wife?

And what do you want me to do about that? said Michele.

Just saying, said the contessa, spooning out the last dregs of her coffee. And a parrot, she added. And those shorts.

The parrot was wearing shorts? said Giulia, Michele's wife.

The contessa scowled at her.

Signora Mimmi came in and before she could say anything, Giulia said, We know, *signora*—he's back!

He looks less boyish, no? said Signora Mimmi. A little more drawn here. And she ran her hand down her cheeks. But he still has his dimples. And is that his father with him? His father has a certain—

The priest rushed in. You seen who's back?

Madonna mia, said Michele quietly, knocking back his fourth espresso of the morning.

The elderly contessa was actually the first person the bleary-eyed English group met that morning. They were coming down the stairs as she was going up. Claude squawked and she stopped, mouth agape at the sight of her new neighbors.

Buongiorno, said Cress with a slight bow.

Is it? said the contessa, hurrying to get inside her first-floor apartment.

She seems nice, said Cress.

And as the nine o'clock bells chimed, they stepped out into the square and as far as entrances went, it was pretty theatrical. Sunlight dazzled, casting rays onto the pale cream stucco of the church. The sky was blue, the roofs were red, the trees green. For years they'd moved about in a palette of gray and deprivation. And now this . . .

The air was saturated with the sounds and smells of the market, and the steamy waft from the tripe seller crept around the corner and punched them in the guts. Claude flew to the white marble statue of Cosimo Ridolfi and settled on his head. He would stay there and shit on him all morning.

Eyes followed them as they traversed the stones, and Ulysses heard that word *soldato* again. Kid ran off toward a donkey and Cress exclaimed at the abundance of produce—the "cornucopia of delight" were his exact words, classic Cressy. Ulysses headed straight over to an outside table at Michele's and sat down. He lit a cigarette and wondered how he could make another man's life his own.

Over here! he shouted when coffee was on its way.

Coming! said Cress, who had just acquired a watermelon as big as his head.

It was from that outside table at Michele's that they eased into Italian life. The café was popular with locals and visitors alike; a jukebox played morning and night and photographs of cinema stars and Campari posters brought a touch of glamour to the nicotine-stained walls. Plates of food came and went under the scrutinizing gaze of Giulia—a touch of glamour in her own right—and gradually names became recognizable; things like *faraona*—guinea fowl, said Cress. And *fiori di zucca fritti*— fried courgette flowers, said the kid.

They learned that the ubiquitous back of a lorry appeared in the market after the *carabinieri* had left and shifted a whole lot of ecclesiastical reliquary and knocked-off radio sets. No different from home, then. And the basket lowered from an upstairs window was for shoes when the cobbler was shut. In the Uffizi they learned to tell the difference between a Botticelli and a Leonardo. Which one? said Cress. Botticelli, said Ulysses. Wrong, said kid. And they learned that the old women gathered on the stone benches every day to knit and broker gossip.

Kid soon clocked up 152 words of Italian and a smudge of slang and began to scowl like a native. She tried *coccoli* for the first time, balls of deep-fried bread dough, and declared it was her second-best day ever.

The *Citrus aurantium*—the ornamental orange tree wilting in the shade—was brought back to life by nothing more than a larger pot and a few kind words. On the night of the twenty-fourth, fireworks shot across the sky and no one knew why. Feast of San Giovanni, said the tree to Cress.

And one afternoon, Ulysses found a bike in the cellar and cycled from San Niccolò in the east to San Frediano in the west. He discovered workshops of every kind: antique furniture repairers, carvers, gilders, carpenters, but no one who made globes. He noticed Italian men wore shoes without socks and trousers that hung shy of an ankle. The women were beautiful but not more beautiful than Peg. And always he was followed by stares.

The stares are not malicious, explained Massimo, a month after Ulysses had acquired his Italian bank account.

They were walking down the Via dei Calzaiuoli together, and for Massimo to have the parrot again on his shoulder added an element of flair to his daily conformity. He turned heads wherever he went. In truth, he'd never felt more alive since Ulysses had entered his life.

He explained to Ulysses that he'd begun to spend time around Santo Spirito purely to eavesdrop and to assess the impact of Ulysses's arrival on the neighborhood. He said the public bathhouse on Via Sant'Agostino had become a good source of information, and he touched his hair when he said this.

They veered off the main thoroughfare and stopped at a small café with outside tables. The air was whiffy, and July's heat was multiplying the spores. They collected their espressi from the counter and sat in a sovereign corner of shade. Massimo continued his explanation.

He said, They are the San Fredianini. They are clannish.

You're not like that, said Ulysses.

No. But my family is from Emilia-Romagna. Every *quartiere* in Firenze is different, and every *quartiere* has its ways. Santa Croce is completely different from Santo Spirito and Santo Spirito is completely different from Santa Maria Novella and so on. And, he said—and stopped to drink his coffee—some resent your good fortune.

How can I change that? said Ulysses.

You can't. Time will. One day you'll wake up and it will all be different. And he clicked his fingers, but there was no sound because his hands were sweaty.

He lit a cigarette and Claude squawked.

And you have a refrigerator, he added quickly.

Is that what this is about?

Understand. At Michele's bar, there is an unofficial communal icebox. People store their milk or Sunday meat next to his *gelati*. And you—you've walked into the square and you have a refrigerator.

Arturo had a refrigerator.

Be patient, my friend. And Massimo finished his coffee and stood up. Shall we?

They turned back onto Via dei Calzaiuoli.

Have you thought about what you want to do? said Massimo.

Not yet, said Ulysses, stopping in front of a tailor's window display. I'd like to make globes again, he said, distracted by the loafers and fashionable styles.

Ah, mappamondi! Bellissimi! said Massimo. You like those trousers?

I do. And the shirt. And those shoes, said Ulysses. He turned back to Massimo. I'd need to find a workshop first. For the globes, I mean. And I'd need to source the right paper.

Too easy, my friend.

And someone to print the gores.

We'll find someone. Moon or Earth?

I've only ever made the Earth.

Palazzo Castellani, said Massimo. The Institute of the History of Science. There you will find both celestial and terrestrial globes. Of *incredibile* beauty. You want to go and see about the trousers?

Would you mind?

Mind? Shopping is my other great love.

After what?

Dancing.

Massimo cornered a street kid and had a robust conversation about

Claude. They shook hands and Massimo turned to Ulysses and said, I told him if he waits here with the *pappagallo* I'll pay him well. If he runs away, I told him you'll chase him down and kill him. *Bene.* Let's go in.

Ulysses followed Massimo up a flight of narrow stairs that smelled of leather and aromatic smoke. Waiting for them at the top was Piccolo Nico, a small (of course), wizened tailor with a tape measure around his neck, and a *sigaretto* in the corner of his mouth.

Massimo explained what Ulysses was after and in no time at all, the tailor had measured him for a suit, an extra pair of trousers and a couple of shirts. And then Nico frowned and said, *Un momento*, before disappearing into his workshop.

He came back holding a pair of cream cotton trousers described as "summer light" that had been made two months before for a young man who had died suddenly. Exact same measurements as yours, apparently, said Massimo. You can have them at a bargain price if you're not superstitious.

If they fit well, I'm not superstitious, said Ulysses, and he took the trousers into the changing room.

The trousers fitted well. He paired them with soft brown leather loafers worn without socks and he felt transformed.

Lucky for you the man had good taste and bad genes, said Massimo.

Lucky for me, said Ulysses. I'll take 'em, *signore*. Trousers and shoes both.

Twenty minutes later, he came out of the shop dressed like an Italian, his old clothing bundled up in brown paper under his arm, the suit and two shirts ready to be collected in September.

As they crossed the Ponte Vecchio, Claude flew on ahead and Ulysses said, I was thinking, Massimo. What about a telephone?

Massimo stopped and said, What about a telephone?

What if we got one installed?

Oh no no. Too soon.

Too soon?

Trust me. Too soon. Not after the refrigerator.

They entered the square in time for *aperitivo* and Claude flew from tree to tree and performed an impromptu aeronautical display for a group of American tourists coming back from the Brancacci Chapel. They took a table at Michele's and Giulia came out to greet them. She was always friendly and always elegant, dressed that day in a black and green housedress that accentuated her wide rumba hips, which Massimo said had danced two girls into the world twenty-three years before. Her hair was held up with amber combs that had once belonged to her favorite grandmother. How do you know all this? said Ulysses, but before Massimo could answer, Giulia said something that made him laugh. She took their order of two Campari sodas and turned back toward the bar.

When she'd gone, Massimo leaned across the table and said, She thinks you look very handsome in your new clothes.

Ulysses blushed and lit a cigarette. He offered his last one to Massimo.

Thank you, said Massimo. And you *do* look very handsome.

People from the neighborhood began to arrive. The elderly women took their places on the stone benches and called over the young waiter for a tray of vermouth. Massimo said, You see that woman on the left? You recognize her?

No.

That's Signora Mimmi. She recognized you straightaway. She and her husband opened the door to you during wartime. It was their kitchen you went through to get onto the roof.

I did?

Massimo nodded and raised the cigarette to his lips. Her husband died not long after, apparently. Next to her is the elderly contessa. They were all here, you know. When you were up there—Massimo pointed to the roof—Michele led the chants to release the gun. And that priest over there. He prayed. Look at these people, Ulisse. The postman. The baker. Her husband. They all knew you before you knew them. You may not feel it, but you have a place here. Let things settle. A little more time before the telephone.

When I call you, everyone listens.

Massimo laughed. That's how information is passed on. How people get to know you. It's integral to this society. I told you.

Someone asked me about your mother's kidney stones.

Did you tell them they've come out?

That's not the point, Massimo. And I have to call England. I'd like a bit of privacy.

Come to the office whenever you want.

Giulia placed their drinks on the table.

Grazie, signora, said Ulysses. He couldn't look at her.

Prego, Signor Temper.

Ulysses smiled. He liked the way she said Temper. The way she rolled her R. What? said Ulysses. Why're you looking at me like that?

Privacy is for the confessional, said Massimo.

Salute! They clinked glasses.

So, said Massimo, that brings me to the other question everyone is asking. Church.

Church? said Ulysses, laughing. No way. And he stood up and went toward the café.

Inside, he and Michele greeted one another. Ulysses asked for a pack of Camels and Michele lobbed them across the marble counter. Ulysses left a scattering of coins and turned away. He lifted his hat to wipe his forehead, the heat intense already, the overhead fan on strike again. He pushed through the stink of garlic and men and the fresh air hit him like a punch.

I'm an idiot, Ulisse! said Massimo, reaching into his jacket pocket. I'm so sorry! A letter. Arrived at the office this morning. Here . . .

Ulysses looked at the envelope, hoping it was from Peg. The writing wasn't hers, though, and the envelope carried a strong whiff of cigarettes.

Dear Temps,

I'm living in the pub after I got flooded out by my upstairs neighbor. Poor bloke died. Three times, as it happened. Col said you can't die three times and I said he's the proof: the bloke had a heart attack in the bath, reached for the ledge, got electrocuted by the heater, shot back into the water and drowned. If there's a God—and I'm by no means suggesting there is—I thought that was a bit heavy-handed. Bloke had only moved in for a new start. Big funeral, though. Nice touch with the trumpet player.

Yesterday, Col sent me up the ladder with a paintbrush and the pub's back to the Stoat. But Gwyneth threw out the stoat while she was redecorating and didn't tell Col. She bought a few bright cushions for the place, though she calls them soft furnishings. Col shouts, How can we be called the Stoat if we don't have a bloody stoat? How about we call it the Queen's Head? says Gwyneth. How about the Queen's Legs? says Col. Open all hours. You disgust me, Colin Formiloe, she says. Out! shouts Col. And take the fucking cushions. And she does, you know, Temps. Loads them into her arms one by one. Even took one out from under Mrs. Belten, and everyone knows she has that sore.

And if that wasn't enough, Peg came in that night. I could see on her face something was up. Straight over to the piano and I'm thinking, Uh-oh . . . One word, she says: Gershwin. By God, Temps. There's no one like her. Three bars in and there's not a dry eye in the house. And then Ted's wife walks in. Peg don't stop singing, she just ups the ante. You could've heard a pin drop in Luton. And the wife—get this—the wife starts to cry. And then Ted walks in. Wife turns to Ted—and here's the most extraordinary thing—the look on her face says, You win, I'm done. And out she goes. Peg finishes her song and she's all shoulders back and starlight. Peg reaches for her drink and Ted comes up to her and she says, Don't you dare. Then she turns to me and says, You ready to take me home, Pete? Course I am, I say.

It was one of them rare summer nights when England ain't so bad. Her and me down by the canal singing "My Heart Cries for You." But mine was crying for her. That Eddie bloke. He did something to her, Temps. I know it's awkward talking to you about him, but something broke in her when he didn't come back. That bridge to happiness gone.

Cressy's tree retains the dignity of the old fella. There's a soothing energy comes up from the roots like it wants to chat. I sat out there one morning and wrote a new composition—"Sorry's Just a Word." It wrote itself.

At my audition for the tour of Annie Get Your Gun *they didn't like my version of "There's No Business Like Show Business" and I guess I was a bit down that day. Bitter, was the word they used. So I'm back at the beginners' tap class. I found the stoat, by the way, out back by the bins. Back legs were missing. It's just a torso and a bandaged jaw. I reckon a rat got to it. I carried it into the bar and wedged it next to a bottle of Fernet-Branca. Hard not to see myself, sometimes, in that annexed life.*

Life's not the same since you all left, but you're better off out of it.

If I don't get the Rosemary Clooney, you know where I'll be in December. Drink a bicicletta or two for me.

Take care, Temps.
Your friend,
Pete

PS: Watch your back. August's heat's got fangs. Near took the skin off my shoulders when I was in Palermo.

August came and still no word from Peg. The heat ratcheted up as Pete said it would and brought out the unwashed tang of people. Hot nights made sleep impossible and a perpetual feeling of somnolence took hold. The sounds of lovemaking ceased because no one wanted to get that close. Ice cream melted before it got near mouths and tourists cursed that they hadn't come in May. Massimo disappeared to his family home on the island of Giglio and was missed. Claude moped and developed a wheeze from the mosquito deterrents that burned day and night. Men screamed at women and women screamed at children and children kicked dogs for no other reason than that their blood ran hot. Then every few days, clouds billowed over the hills and arms rose exultantly as violent storms rolled in. And for a brief moment there was respite.

As the month crept toward its midpoint, Ulysses grew restless. The heat was getting to him, and both Cress and the kid could see that, and every day he checked for a letter from Peg. Even sent her a postcard that said, *"Remember us?"* Cress said he shouldn't have done it, and he knew he shouldn't have, and he regretted it straightaway but what could he do? Cress said it was probably the unreliable Italian postal system. Ulysses said he was thinking about the kid and Cress said the kid was all right. She'll tell us what she needs. You reckon? I know, said Cress.

And one afternoon outside Michele's, Ulysses happened to say, I wonder if it's as hot back home as it is here. And Cress put down his Baedeker, noting the context and subtle use of the word home. This was the first chink in the boy's docile armor.

Come on, said Cress, smoothing down the crumpled legs of his shorts. Let's go for a walk. He left a handful of *lire* on the table and Ulysses called out to the kid. She was talking with a boy by the fountain.

Of course it's my parrot! she said, and spat on the ground. Claude flew down and landed on her arm.

Kid was chatty all the way to the Pitti Palace. She said Signora Giulia wanted to know what they did at night.

What did you say? said Ulysses.

I said we sang songs and played cards for money.

You told her that? said Ulysses.

And sometimes we talked about life, about good times and bad times, and we drank hard liquor.

You have all the Italian words for that? said Cress, a little envious.

Yep.

Kid was balancing on a ledge now. I said you're clean and lonely.

Cress and Ulysses stopped. Which one?

Kid pointed to Ulysses. Lonely, she said.

You told her that?

Yep. And she ran out of ledge and jumped down.

Why'd you tell her that? said Ulysses.

Because you are, she said.

A tourist passed by and threw coins at them.

Grazie! said the kid, and she bent down and picked up the *lire*.

Through the courtyard of the Pitti Palace, at the top of the stone stairs, they met the breeze. Swallows and swifts and bells on the air.

Florentines out in their droves—it's what they did in the summer months, here or in Cascine Park. To be away from the streets and the dust and smells and the niggling disputes was everything in that moment. Time moved differently, as if it, too, had buckled with the heat, and past and present shifted into one sultry indomitable dance.

They climbed the slope up to the highest point, to the Casino del Cavaliere, as storm clouds crested but didn't break. How beautiful the light! To their left, the old circuit walls carved through olive groves, and the sky was a ponderous violet gray. All around, art and life entwined. Cress held up his doorstop of a book and said, Baedeker! as if it was a new religion. And with their sight drawn across the cityscape he said, That's our home down there, Temps. Who would've believed it?

Not me, for one, said the kid. Pinch me, I'm dreaming.

See? mouthed Cress. She's OK.

Golden light edged around the dark gray clouds and Cress used the phrase "unconscionable beauty" in describing the garden. Cress was becoming poetry. On the way down, he asked for a moment by himself in the *limonaia*, just him surrounded by citrons and sentiment. A nice sentence, one of Cressy's specials. Said he'd meet them later back in the square.

He sat down on a wooden chair and Claude drank from a flowerpot nearby. From there, Cressy's roots passed deep through the labyrinthine dark, down to ancient quarry stone and the rhopography of long-gone lives. He felt the rise of those who had gone before. The poets Browning, Everly, Shelley. In time, Cress hoped to lose his fear of poetry, especially the stuff that didn't rhyme. Cress was a facts man, and facts were stone. Poetry, though, was sand. Ever compared to stars in its granular infinity. Ever shifting.

Kid dragged Ulysses away to play hide-and-seek in the cypress avenue and she stayed hidden for half an hour. A rumbling atavistic fear possessed him and he realized this fear now sat at the core of his life and would remain there evermore. He looked so hard and he couldn't find her. Right in front of him she was, but he couldn't see her. It was his worst nightmare and eventually it was her giggling that woke him from it. She'd climbed into a bush like a bird and stayed so quiet. So pleased with herself she was, he overly congratulated her just to stifle a sob.

They walked hand in sweaty hand to the *isolotto* and stood in front of the sculpture of Perseus on horseback, galloping up through the water.

I'd like to do that, she said.

Me too, he said.

And he thought they'd been so unprepared for summer and vowed it would be the last time they were. I'll find us a swimming pool, he said. Promise? she said. Promise, he said, and they sat in the shade and watched the ducks and shared a piece of chewing gum he found in his pocket.

I reckon your mum would like it here, he said.

I'm not sure she would, she said.

(Hard as nails, he thought.)

Do I look like her? she said.

Not so much. When you smile, you do.

Who do I look like then?

Eddie, I suppose.

Do you know him?

No.

I don't either, she said.

You sure you're OK?

Yep, said the kid. This is a good day.

I want them all to be good days, said Ulysses.

That's unrealistic. You don't have to make up for Peg.

He laughed. Is that what I do?

Relax into the job, I'd suggest.

Anything else?

Maybe get a girlfriend.

Really?

Someone like Signora Giulia. Or Signora Giulia herself.

She's with Michele.

He's got high blood pressure and angina. He could die any moment.

How d'you know all this?

Kid tapped her nose.

Anything else?

You're doing all right, she said.

Thanks.

And I don't want to be anywhere else.

Good to know, he said.

They left when the gates began to close. People outside cafés smelled soapy and evening fresh. In the square, they stopped to listen to a man play guitar on the steps of the church. I'm going to do that one day, said the kid.

I know, said Ulysses. You want to grow up quick.

Is that a bad thing?

Only for me.

There's Cressy! said the kid, pointing to the terrace. Cress had been watching through the telescope for their return. Kid waved.

Cress knows a lot, doesn't he, Ulysses?

Cress knows everything.

Cress never went to school.

I know. But imagine if he had.

Two days later, the *postino* cycled by Michele's and flicked a postcard onto their table. It landed picture up, revealing a view of a fortress and a walled Tuscan village. Ulysses turned it over. It was from Massimo.

The main news was that Massimo had got a haircut, which had taken three inches off his height and had plunged him into a pit of self-consciousness. It had been necessary after his nephew had infected him with lice. He said his mother's kidney stones had returned. But what can you expect? She doesn't drink water. He said he missed his new friends and told Ulysses to call him immediately and left a number at the bottom.

Giulia placed another round of coffee and *biscotti* on the table. Kid said in Italian that the postcard was from Massimo and she showed her the picture. Ah, Giglio! said Giulia, and she asked how Massimo's mother was.

The kidney stones have returned, said the kid. But she doesn't drink water so what can you expect? And kid shrugged disparagingly and sipped her coffee.

Ulysses picked up the card and went inside. The heat escaping the kitchen was already intense, and the overhead fan was out of action again. Ulysses went to the telephone and dialed the number. Massimo picked up straightaway as if he'd been waiting all morning by the telephone. Which, in fact, he had.

He spoke quickly and precisely in case the connection cut out. He said his mother had gone back to the mainland on account of her lower-body discomfort and had taken his sister and lice-infected nephew. One of his brothers had decided to go to Elba and the other brother would come in a few days. So—and this was really the crux of the matter—the house is empty. Come and visit for Ferragosto!

What? Come out to—?

Giglio. Drive down toward Grosseto, then Porto . . .

Michele handed Ulysses a pen and a scrap of paper. Porto? said Ulysses, nodding his thanks to Michele.

Porto Santo Stefano, said Massimo. Leave the car there. Get the morning ferry to Isola del Giglio.

Ulysses writing it all down.

You need to leave tomorrow because of the Ferragosto weekend.

The ferra what? said Ulysses.

Public holidays. If you don't, you'll be strand—

The line cut. The sound of the tokens being swallowed. Ulysses replaced the receiver and turned back to the room. The bar had fallen silent. Everyone was looking at him, and not all of them were pleased. Someone said, *You going to Giglio now?*

They left early the following morning, as instructed. The sun had barely lit the eastern sky when they stepped out of the building. They walked across the square, clutching rucksacks and bottles of water, and Claude flew on ahead to Betsy.

They traveled south through Tuscany as the sun rose and eventually a landscape of hilltop towns gave way to thick forests of chestnut trees and fields of sunflowers and it was quite a sight to behold. Cress leaned out of the window and kid said, First one to see the sea, but the sea had spied her long before. Stripped down to her new swimming costume she was, face pressed close to the glass, not missing a thing.

From Orbetello they crossed the lagoon and drove up into the wild Monte Argentario, a rocky promontory surrounded by the Tyrrhenian Sea. Roads were overgrown with forests and the smell was salty and herbaceous and at the base of the great cliffs, glimpses of coves and beaches could be had.

The dark green canopy thinned out as the road veered down toward the port, the aftermath of wartime bombardment still evident. Ulysses parked away from the main road and they grabbed their bags and ran toward the ferry up ahead. They were the last to board and the klaxon blared and the slow chug of the engine pushed clouds of dark smoke into a pristine sky. The water was as crystalline and turquoise as they had ever seen, and Claude flew free. A soft headwind brought the sun's rays to their noses and foreheads and kid put on her sunglasses. Kid had never been to an island before and she stood up suddenly and punched her arms in joy.

When Giglio came into sight, it reflected the long hot parchment of summer. Rocky granite crags were tufted by *macchia mediterranea* and little else. As they drew near to the harbor, the klaxon sounded, and a crescent of bright sand came into sight, and fisher cottages, and donkeys waiting to transport luggage up the steep island slopes. It was like stepping back in time, the whole scene overlaid with a sepia tint. And as the ferry moored alongside the harbor wall, they looked about for Massimo. Claude was the first to spot him, though, standing in a small boat and waving furiously.

You made it! he shouted. *Mio Dio!* You made it.

You look so well what about this heat I like your hair you still got lice no no all gone I've got a new swimming costume Cressy's spying on the stone bench *signore*.

Ready? said Massimo, catching his breath. Ready, they said, catching theirs, and Massimo pulled the cord and whatever peace had settled across the harbor and whatever conversation was still to be had was swallowed by the ugly whine of a two-stroke.

The boat hugged the curve of the island, which revealed a little more to its excited visitors—hillside vineyards and pear-laden cacti and granite steps from which to swim. Kid leaned over the side to catch every wave that slapped against the hull. Eventually, the engine steadied and the boat veered right toward a vast expanse of shingled beach. They glimpsed a house near the back, protected by native pines and eucalypts. Massimo tilted the engine and the shallow hull glided effortlessly to shore.

Cressy was the first onto the island; all he needed was a flag to plant. He looked about at the bounty of existence, full consciousness in the soles of his feet.

This way! shouted Massimo.

Across the shingle, the metronomic fall of waves overlapped with the call of doves. Massimo marched ahead, waving his arms in a manner most peculiar. He was nervous and shy and had never had anyone visit before—never invited anyone, truth be told—and he felt grateful when the shingle ran out and the house reared up in its charming incongruity. Part cottage, part shack.

This is it, he said. Go find a bedroom while I prepare lunch. And he held up a canvas bag brimming with supplies.

There was nothing now between them and three days of holiday.

Kid took off across the beach, the shingle hot on her bare feet, Ulysses not far behind. She'd never swum in the sea before, certainly nowhere where the fish were as striped as her. Waist height in the water now. Not even one bit cold! was her shout.

Kid held her nose and ducked under and came up spluttering. Again, she said.

I'll be here, he said.

Under she went.

Under he went.

They broke the surface together with a leap.

Massimo calling out that lunch was ready.

I don't need lunch, said kid.

Yeah you do, said Ulysses. Come on. And they waded through the shallows back to the towels.

Everyone look at the camera! shouted Massimo as he set the timer and ran back into position.

(Click.) Caught forever.

From left, Old Cress stands next to Massimo with Ulysses on the right. Their arms are around one another. Kid is standing in front of Massimo holding Claude. Claude has opted for the full-wingspan look. Behind them is a glimpse of the terrace. Pots of geraniums, a trestle table with the remains of *spaghetti al pomodoro* and potatoes and *baccalà*. And two bottles of the crisp white ansonica wine native to the island. One of the bottles is a good two-thirds full. Above them a grapevine casts abundant shade and clusters of grapes hang low. The kid is wearing her swimming costume and sunglasses. They are the best things she has ever owned. The costume is still damp from a swim and will chafe her bum by evening. It will be uncomfortable but worth it. Cress wears a light blue shirt and desert shorts. His feet are bare and he's conscious of the length of his toenails. Apart from that blip, he feels whole and courageous. He knows he's making up for lost time. Massimo sports an outfit of matching navy. Bermuda shorts in a cotton-linen mix in a similar shade of blue to his ironed, short-sleeved shirt. Before his friends arrived, he'd felt shy about his hair and the weight that had accumulated around his middle. But Ulysses told him he looked so distinguished— You're a good-looking fella, Mass, were the words he used—and sometimes that's all you need to restore a little height. Massimo will not grow his hair long again. Ulysses wears white shorts that stop just above his knee. His knees are good, and the fall of the hem only accentuates that fact. He wears a white vest not dissimilar to the way Marlon Brando wore his in *A Streetcar Named Desire*. Ulysses hasn't seen the film. The vest is a tight fit due to shrinkage. His smile is as disarming as ever. His eyebrows sit at an upward slant on account of the sun, and the tips of his ears are reddening.

It would be the first of many photographs taken over the years on Giglio. It would hang on the wall in the living room between two windows where white curtains billow on a salt-drenched breeze. Through the windows the eucalypts throw off a keen scent.

They have been on the island approximately twenty-six hours and thirty-seven minutes. Not long, but Cress would've broken that down and calculated a thousand moments because Cress was like that.

Nearing their last day, a little twist of Cress occurred and not a moment too soon.

Massimo had just made a pot of coffee and was asking Ulysses if he had any idea yet what he wanted to do with the downstairs flat, when Cress staggered out onto the terrace and said, I know what we're gonna do with the downstairs flat.

Extraordinary, said Massimo. Does this happen a lot?

Quite a lot, said the kid.

Cress took a sip of water and stumbled to a chair. I had a vision, he said, and proceeded to describe exactly what had happened to him only moments before.

I'd just finished my coffee—it was delicious by the way, Massimo, he said, interrupting his own story—and I'd settled down on that lovely armchair to make a start on the novel I'd brought from England. Fiction being uncharted territory for me, as you all know. (Cress took another sip of water.) He said, I opened the novel and began to read. And it was as if a large celestial index finger reached across the sky and pointed directly at me, Alfred Cresswell. Like Michelangelo's *Creation of Adam*, when God points and gives life to—in this case—an idea.

And? said Ulysses.

Cress held up his copy of *A Room with a View*. The precedent has been set, Temps. (He flicked through the pages.) And I quote, "And a cockney besides!"

(Pause.)

Besides what? said Ulysses.

A cockney landlady at the Bertolini.

What's the Bertolini?

A *pensione*, said Cress. A boardinghouse. Mostly for English people. Awful ones, mind. And, if I'm honest, the food ain't much cop, but still.

Ulysses reached for the book and scanned the pages.

A cockney landlady ran a boardinghouse in Florence fifty-odd years back and that's all we need to know. We could be that story, too, said Cress. Put the rooms to use. Get a bit of purpose.

And money, said kid.

A *pensione*! said Massimo. What a wonderful idea!

I'm in, said the kid.

Temps? What do you think?

What's to think? he said. Let's do it.

Massimo said he'd contact a colleague after Ferragosto to talk about licensing and registration and Cress channeled the god of hospitality. He couldn't write ideas down quick enough—locks on the doors, more linen, towels, soap, laundry service—maybe get a washing machine? Too soon for a washing machine, Massimo? Massimo said he'd head back and listen out for the word on the street. Back to the bathhouse with you! said the kid, and Massimo blushed and reached for his hair—which, of course, wasn't there.

They went out that afternoon, to forage for figs and apricots and caper berries, and Ulysses happened to say in passing that he always found a communal bowl of fruit welcoming.

Nice touch, said Massimo.

Cress wrote down *bowl of fruit*.

And flowers, said Massimo.

Flowers, wrote Cress.

What about a help-yourself-to-drinks trolley?

Help yourself! scoffed Claude, who was starting to sound a bit like Col.

Easy, Claude, said Ulysses. We're not like that here. And Claude apologized and felt ashamed.

And what about advertising? said Massimo.

Cress whistled at the enormity of the word. Couldn't we just wait at the railway station with a sign and meet the trains as they come in? Drive 'em back in the Jowett?

That's what I could do, said the kid. Who's gonna say no to a cute kid and a parrot?

No one, said Massimo. No one at all. And do you intend to feed them, your guests?

Cress looked daunted. Feed 'em what?

In the kitchen in a haze of steam. Massimo said, If I teach you nothing else in your lifetime, it must be this. Learning the correct ratio of boiling water to salt to pasta. When to add the salt—lots of it. When to take the pasta off the heat. Get it right and you'll always eat like a king.

Get it wrong, said the kid, and we'll end up with that mess called *pappa al pomodoro*. Right, Cress?

Massimo said, A simple addition of garlic and olive oil and chili— here, try this. You feel the resistance of the spaghetti? That is what you aim for every time.

Cress and Ulysses stood back and made notes. Kid just ate.

You two up for this? she said.

Maybe we could just give guests vouchers to use at Michele's? said Cress.

Now you're thinking, said Claude.

Night fell across the terrace. In the distance, the passenger ferry cut across the dark sea in a steady sweep of light. Us tomorrow, said the kid, still high from diving among sea urchins. Ulysses brought a candle to his face and lit a cigarette. On the table, a scattering of nutshells and empty salad plates. Massimo poured out the wine and Claude thought about saying a few words, but the moment passed.

A moon and bats and the pulse of a docile sea and friendship and the start of a new venture. Nothing more to say.

Except—

You'll need a name, said Claude, chewing on a piece of watermelon.

What about the Bertolini? said the kid. If it ain't broke?

They all laughed, and the kid felt a million bucks and a little bit tired.

So that was how the Pensione Bertolini (mark two) came to pass. Cress would eventually tell that story to every guest who wanted to listen. Bit of history for them to take away. A bit of him, really.

He went to bed fizzing that night. So bright you could've seen him from space.

They came back to the city refreshed. The island had done its best. Had grounded them and introduced them to a way of life they would aspire to and return to. Cress fixed the overhead fan in Michele's and when that strong current of air moved steadily through the bar, everybody cheered. Michele lifted Cress off the ground and to those watching, it was like the smothering of a small goat by a bear. Ulysses went to Palazzo Castellani, the Institute of the History of Science, and spent time with Coronelli's globes. They were more beautiful than he'd imagined, and he thought about the worlds his father had created, brightly colored spheres with pink for the empire. He'd paint the world differently, naturally. Green for forests, white for ice, brown for land and blue for sea. He'd readjust the borders and give countries back their names.

And then bang on the kid's birthday, three letters arrived from Peg, of all people. In the letter dated June, Peg had written her new telephone number at the bottom of the page and Ulysses and the kid ran to Massimo's office. *Un momento*, said the young woman who connected the call.

I'm eight, said the kid, pushing back her fringe. Who'd have believed it? And she told Peg that she'd gotten a guitar from Ulysses and Cress, a diving mask from Massimo, and Signora Giulia had made her *cannoli*. She's from Sicily, she said. All in all, a good haul. Kid covered the receiver and turned to Ulysses. Peg said she's sent me money. Kid looked delighted.

Ulysses heard Peg sing "Happy Birthday" and he left the room to give the kid privacy but really it was because it broke his fucking heart. He waited in the hallway till the kid called his name.

Peg wants to speak to you, she said, giving him the receiver. Kid went outside with the young woman to learn how to make an espresso.

I'm sorry, he said.

About what? said Peg.

Remember us?

If that's the worst of you, Temps, I got off lightly.

Work OK? he said.

Ted wants me to give it up.

You won't, will you?

Wants me to marry him.

Don't, he said.

What? Work or marriage?

Just don't, Peg. And Ulysses lit a cigarette.

Alys sounds happy.

She is. Come see for yourself. She tell you about the *pensione*?

What the fuck's a *pensione*?

He laughed. A small hotel.

You got that many rooms?

Daft, right? Here, Peg, you got a pen? Take this number down . . . It's a café. You can always leave a message . . . You got it?

Got it.

Here, what happened with Ginny?

Didn't you read the letter, Temps?

We came straight here. Didn't read anything.

I told Mrs. Kaur about her and Devy.

You did?

Had to. But I trust her. She reminds me of your mum. She's so kind and calm and treats Ginny like family. It's really sweet the way she is with them. The boy is, too. I'll tell Col when he's ready to listen.

We love you, Peg.

What's that?

I said—

You still there, Temps? Temps?

When September arrived, it brought cooler nights and the long good-bye of the swallows. Ulysses disappeared too, just for the day. This was something he would do year after year and eventually Cress and the kid stopped asking where he went. Kid and Cress made a colored lantern and joined the procession for the Festa della Rificolona, the celebration of the birth of the Virgin Mary. Kid said, You can't be a virgin and give birth, can you, Cress? And Cress said, No you can't. Just checking I wasn't missing anything, said the kid. In the Tuscan vineyards the grape harvest began, and in the bakeries appeared the traditional sweet flatbread *schiacciata all'uva*. Restaurants, previously closed for August, reopened with new menus heavy on the *porcini*.

And, finally, as much as the kid tried to evade all mention of it, September brought school.

The night before, she was nervous and didn't want to go to bed. She found Cressy on the terrace sitting with his tree.

What you doing, Cress?

Talking with this little fella.

Kid sat next to him and listened.

Doesn't say much, does it?

It's all going on in the roots, he said. Roots tell stuff to other trees.

Like what?

Like where to find water. Where to get a good cup of coffee.

Kid tutted.

They warn each other, too, said Cress.

About what?

Life. Problems. Dangers. They're a bit like us: social. They feel ne-glect and pain.

Do I have roots?

Strong ones. So, you ready for school tomorrow?

What if I don't make friends?

You've got us, said Cress. And Massimo. That's three. And Giulia. And Claude. There you go, you've got an orchard.

Cress reached for his beer.

Can I have a sip? she said.

Sure, he said, because he knew she hated it.

Look out there, said Cress. The solar system. Formed four point six billion years ago. And here are we. With a combined age of seventy-seven. How young we are! And the Earth spins at a thousand miles an hour and turns on its axis once every twenty-four. This is what we're governed by, Alys. Space, time and motion. Hours, days, seasons. Our lives segmented into a series of moments. You see over there, that faint patch of light? That's the Andromeda Nebula. When we look at it, we're looking back nine hundred thousand years into the past.

Big numbers, Cress.

They are big numbers, my love. That's why ten years of school will go by in no time.

I see what you did there, she said.

I thought you might.

Eight, said kid. No more than eight.

All right, said Cress. No more than eight. And he pretended to spit on his hand, and they shook.

Morning came with low clouds and cool air and kid wore the dark smock that all the kids wore, with its oversized collar and bow, and she said she looked like a clown. You do, said Ulysses. In the square she said good-bye to Cress and Giulia, and climbed onto the crossbar of Ulys-ses's bike. There's still time to change your mind, you know, she said. Yeah, yeah, he said, and pedaled with the traffic heading west to San Frediano. No veering in and out of barrows or motorbikes this time, and he kept a safe distance behind the trams. They passed the tripe seller and the swallows on washing lines waiting to depart. Bye, birds! See you next year! shouted the kid.

Up ahead children gathered at the school gates and Ulysses slowed and the kid jumped off. He wheeled the bike next to her.

You be OK? he said, handing her the satchel.

Course, she said.

A teacher came out and rang the bell and children started to head toward the door.

I'll see you here later, he said, and bent down to kiss her, but she moved away.

Don't make a scene, she said.

He walked away to a place where she couldn't see him and watched her go in. Stocky little thing with her shoulders back and a fuck-off frown. Other kids were chatting to one another but not her, she was all Peg. He'd have killed for her. He'd known that for a while. There he was skulking in a doorway, no different from Col. He took the long way back, stopping in art shops and antique shops hoping to find a globe mold.

At home, he made a coffee and opened a pack of *biscotti*. He pushed back the sofas to the edge of the living room and turned the radio on. He went into his bedroom and brought out the copperplates and laid them next to each other on the floor. There were six, approximately sixteen inches by fifty-five. Hundreds of hours of his dad's exacting work.

Before he'd left for war, Ulysses had cleaned and polished them, coated them in a light smear of petroleum jelly to protect them. He'd wrapped them in paper and card and had attached to each one a printed sheet that showed the twelve etched gores—the flattened segments of the curved surface of a globe—that ran in sequence. Finally, he'd tied old blankets around them because the plates were priceless to him.

He knelt down to the nearest one, untied the fabric and lifted out the print. He moved his finger along the steady presence of the equator line, which cut along the widest point of each gore, bisecting the meridian lines that ran from north to south. The major lines of latitude—the Arctic Circle, the Tropics of Cancer and Capricorn, and the Antarctic Circle—curved across each segment in a steady sweep. He leaned in close. Persia instead of Iran. Constantinople, not Istanbul. Russia still Russia, though. He'd date it somewhere in the early 1920s.

His dad, Wilbur, used to trace over a map of the world and that's how it would start. Names of cities, countries, mountains, rivers, oceans, whatever took his fancy. And always Nora's name somewhere. When he'd finished the trace, Wilbur would flip the paper so the world and its writing would appear in reverse. He would mark a grid system across the paper and from this template would transfer the information in each square onto a similarly gridded gore, working scrupulously across the twelve sections of the Earth. An instinctive and artistic understanding of the distortion that occurred from flat surface to curve.

All the bluster of the racetrack quietened in those moments, the thrill of the wager gone. And the old boy's hand steadied as that reverse image moved from tracing paper to copperplate.

Ulysses had completed his own trace and etching mere months before his dad died. Countries, and lines of latitude and longitude, but no names. He remembered the feeling of achievement as the printed sheet rolled free of the press. The nodding approval of his dad. The cutting out of the gores and marking their sequence. Painting the seas and landmasses. The smell of glue. Positioning the first gore—equator line matching the circumference line he'd drawn around the sphere. The feeling of heartbreak when the paper stretched too much and tore.

He sat up and reached for his coffee. It was cold but he didn't mind. He thought again about the molds and how to source them. His dad's had been Bakelite, works of art in their own right. He lit a cigarette and sat back. Aw, Jesus! he said, suddenly registering the time.

She was waiting alone by the school gates and he came to a halt in a screech of brakes.

What time d'you call this? she said, tapping her wrist.

Sorry, he said, and bent to kiss her.

Was it a woman?

A copperplate etching.

Typical.

How'd it go? he said.

I 'spect I'll get used to it.

Hungry?

What are you thinking?

They stopped at the tripe seller and had a sandwich filled with *lampredotto*. Kid swiped a sip of his wine—After the day I've had, who could blame me? she said.

When they finished eating, he lifted her onto the saddle and pushed the bike along the road.

You need a haircut, she said, flicking his ear.

Thanks, he said.

School brought structure to the kid's life in a way he hadn't foreseen. She slept when she was supposed to, and woke refreshed with the sun. She was held back a year on account of her language but that would be rectified at the end of the summer term. Her coffee intake was limited to a milky one in the morning whilst reading a book or studying Italian grammar. Being the oldest in her class brought out her care for those less able or those less fortunate, of which there were many. She was ahead in arithmetic and drawing and learning poems, and writing stories wasn't a hardship. She coasted and she knew it, but what did she care?

Her dark hair made her invisible in a coterie of other dark hair. She wanted no one to notice her, especially the boys, but sometimes they teased her to get her attention, so she learned to swear in slang and hit them back. Occasionally she was told off and occasionally she was praised. Not so bad, she would have said.

Come Friday of that first week, Ulysses, Cress and Massimo met her from school and took her straight to the cinema to watch Fellini's *I*

Vitelloni. This'll bring him to the world's attention, she declared during
the intermission.

As autumn progressed, Massimo came by with a much-appreciated
bottle of new-season olive oil. He also informed them that the paperwork was complete and the *pensione* could now open for business. A
week later, he brought a priest round to bless the venture and Ulysses
made sure a good Rosso di Montalcino was ready and waiting. The
priest stayed until the bottle was empty and blessed everyone, including
Claude. *Twice.*

The weather cooled and Cress revisited the long trouser and Ulysses
found a workshop off Via Maggio. In letters back to England, he described this time as a magic time, a settled time. *I think we've turned a
corner,* he wrote.

I'm so sorry to hear Alys's mother is dead, said the teacher.

It was late October. Outside the school gates. Incessant rain.

The shock on Ulysses's face must have registered as grief because it
brought tears to the teacher's eyes. She expressed great admiration that
he was bringing a child up by himself and handed him a chocolate
cake she'd made the night before. Flustered, he tried to refuse it, but
she'd hear none of it. He staggered over to the kid waiting by the bike,
more widower than the robust young singleton he was. You look awful, she said, and she climbed onto the crossbar and proudly took the
cake.

He cycled back with the kid, oilskins flapping, and went straight to
Michele's for tea. It was warm inside, and water pooled beneath the
coatrack. Michele nodded to Ulysses and said something about the
weather. Ulysses agreed. His Italian had become conversational. He followed the kid to the back and placed the chocolate death cake on the
table between them. Kid ordered a plate of beef *ragù* with *pappardelle*
washed down with a *chinotto.*

So? she said after a while. You look like you want to say something, sunshine.

He wasn't sure how to begin. Peg's not dead, he said. (Clumsy.)

I know that, said the kid, and she made a start on her food.

Then why are you telling people she is? Alys? Look at me, he said. Why'd you say your mum was dead?

Kid looking defiant now. Peg through and through.

Alys? We can sit here all night if—

Because it's better than the truth.

Which is?

That she gave me away.

And the kid's face suddenly flushed, and she was angry and there was shame and she began to cry because she didn't know how to explain any of it. Too young to know the depth of it. All she kept thinking about was the girl in the playground who didn't have any shoes. So, Alys told her she didn't have a mother. What's the difference? Shoes or a mother, lack is lack and it hurts.

Don't, please don't, said Ulysses, and he tried to hold her, but she ran to Giulia. And that's what I'm not, he thought. Soft edges and arms that know what to do. He lit a cigarette. How did he not know? How the fuck did he not know what went on in her head? After all this time? He caught Giulia's eye and she smiled that it was OK. OK was not what it was, he thought.

After a while, kid came back and sat next to him. Am I in trouble? she said.

Never.

Can I have some cake then?

No. We've been given it under false pretenses and we'll have to give it back tomorrow.

That'll be embarrassing.

I'll do it. (He did, and it was.)

Kid asked if she could have some *budino* instead and he said of course.

He gave her a coin for the jukebox. She ate the custard pudding whilst listening to "Here in My Heart" by Al Martino.

That night Ulysses lay next to her until she fell asleep. He looked about at her room. She'd chosen it because of the red and green wallpaper that had images of macaws and trees, a right ol' jungle. These were the decisions she, as an eight-year-old, made. The way her mind worked, what interested her. Over there, a hook on which hung her swimming costume and diving mask. The side table where she kept her sunglasses and sketchbook. The dried shell of a sea urchin on the dressing table. Her guitar at the foot of her bed. The sign they'd made together to advertise the *pensione*. These things are the sum of her life now. And she will grow up and leave, he thinks. And she will make her way and not cast her thoughts back to him. Life in all its exaltation and complexity will devour her. She will love deeply to the exclusion of all else. And he wants to know everything about her before that happens, but wonders if you can ever know anyone truly.

From down the hallway, Ulysses can hear Cress's heavy breathing and thinks he's sleeping.

But really the old boy is crying.

Cress has just finished Forster's novel and there's a lot to take in. Intellect versus feeling and Cress is all feeling and love. It's good-bye to the Baedeker, too, since it has become ridiculous through Forster's eyes. The following morning Cress will abandon it to the living room floor, where it will become a satisfactory doorstop and remain so for years. Cress stands in front of the mirror in his vest and shorts and repeats over and over, I am vital.

The next day, Cress put down his telescope and wiped his brow.

So, old fella, said the ornamental orange tree. Whatcha gonna do? It's now or never.

Is it?

Go on—put a little cologne on those smooth cheeks of yours and show 'em what they've been missing. I'll be rooting for you.

(Pause.)

That's a joke, by the way.

I know, said Cress.

Cress went to his room and did what the tree said. He positioned his new panama hat at a jaunty angle and changed his shoes. Unlike Ulysses, he was still a fan of the sock.

He walked nervously down the stairwell just as the elderly contessa was struggling up with a bag of shopping. He tried to help her with it, but she shooed him away with an invective of *idiota*, a word that, even for Cress, needed little translation.

He said *Buongiorno* to the kids hanging out by the statue and they said *Buongiorno* back to him with an additional "Signor Cress."

Signor Cress, he thought. Like a character out of literature.

Ulysses called out to him from Michele's, but Cress was in pure Zen mode. Giulia stood by Ulysses's table to watch and even the priest halted his journey across the square to cross himself.

Cress could feel the tension mount in his chest. He approached the stone bench and the old women looked up and stopped their chat. He touched the rim of his hat and delivered a florid greeting that he'd practiced well, and which took them by surprise. He sat on the end of the bench, one buttock dangling precariously off, and from his bag, brought out his knitting, a modest four rows of dark brown hem. The old women nudged one another and whispered.

Cress raised his needles and said, *Sto lavorando a maglia un maglione senza maniche*—a sentence that plunged him headfirst into the many pitfalls of Italian pronunciation, as instead of informing the women he was knitting a sleeveless sweater, he did, in fact, tell them it was a sleeveless melon. But it did the trick. A little laughter mingled with something else, and it was the something else that caused Signora Mimmi to budge up and give him extra room. The gesture priceless. He spent two hours with them that afternoon, simply listening, enjoying their smells and the effervescence of their storytelling. He even told them in faltering Italian that the Moken sea tribes didn't have words for I want, take or mine. This was met with silence. But of the wonder variety. Imagine a world like that, he said. Imagine! they said, and Signora Mimmi raised her hand and ordered a tray of vermouth from Michele's.

PENSIONE BERTOLINI
BEAUTIFUL ROOMS
GOOD PRICE
BEST LOCATION

Ulysses and the kid had been waiting three hours in the station concourse and were about to call it a day when the train from Venice pulled
in. Out sprang an older couple from Manchester (they would later learn),
looking quite at ease in the chaos of Europe. They were Mr. and Mrs.
Bambridge (Call us Des and Poppy).

Des was a businessman and had never walked away from a good
price in his life. He stood in front of the sign and said, How good?

Whatever you want, said Ulysses.

That's no way to run a business, lad.

Never run one before, said the kid.

Come on, Poppy, these two need our help. I'll telephone the Benito
and cancel.

You have a view, said Cress, opening their bedroom door ceremoniously.

The bells from Santo Spirito rang out and the divine smell of *bistecca*
wafted up from Michele's and the evening light was yellow and soft. Des
and Poppy were entranced.

Makes the Benito look like a shithouse, said Des.

Look at the *amorini* frescoes on the ceiling, Des!

And the quality of the linen! It's stunning.

Cress ran through his speech. Towels, extra blankets and pillows in
there, he said. Bathroom's down the hall. Plenty of hot water, etc., etc.
Welcome drinks in the living room at your leisure. I'll leave your keys
here, he said, bowing slightly as he departed.

Des and Poppy would stay a week.

At the end of which, the serendipitous element to this encounter became apparent.

It was as Ulysses was coming up the stairs after a day in the workshop that Des stuck his head out the front door and said, Fancy a beer, lad?

Ulysses joined him in the living room, where Cress had, only moments before, deposited a few chilled bottles onto the drinks trolley.

Des said, Poppy's in there sprucing herself up for our last night. We're having wild boar sausages at Michele's. Such a good recommendation. Cheers, lad, he said.

Cheers, Des. And thanks for staying with us.

They clinked beer bottles.

The pleasure's all ours.

And then Des said, A young man bringing up a kid by himself. Was it the war?

Yeah, sort of, said Ulysses. We do all right though.

I can see that. But I want to help. What I don't know about business you could write on a gnat's arse. A self-made millionaire by the time I was forty.

Ulysses whistled his admiration.

Plastics, said Des. Two words: jelly molds.

Ulysses's ears pricked up.

Can you mold anything, Des?

Anything. Your head. My shoe.

What about two half spheres that come together to form a perfect whole?

Consider it done. How many you want? Fifty? One hundred?

One.

A prototype. Sensible.

Thirty-six centimeters in diameter.

Inches if you please, lad.

Fourteen point one seven.

Precision. My kind of man.

———

The morning of departure, Des and Poppy handed over an envelope full of cash. Cress looked inside and said, Jesus Christ, Des.

Worth every penny, said Des. And I've made a basic business plan for you. A breakdown of what you should charge, based on that Bandini place on the corner.

Des had a snoop around yesterday, said Poppy. He was pretending to buy it.

They've got the added benefit of a dining room, of course.

We're not ready for that, Des.

I can see that, lad. So here we have it. Different rates for different rooms. Seasonal adjustments. Get to know your market. Word of mouth's a powerful tool. And I'm going to mouth off at every chance I get. The personal touch is all I've ever known. Change nothing. Get a telephone when you can—and he looked sternly at Ulysses—and a proper coffee machine. The smell alone is worth a million big ones. Then you can offer bed and breakfast. Raises the profile. Me and Poppy love a coffee and a pastry first thing of a morning.

We do, Des.

Here's my number. I'll let Michele know when the mold's ready and when you can expect it. Now, show us to the visitors' book. We've got an essay to write.

After Des and Poppy came the Willoughbys: young newlyweds from Pennsylvania. Cress went overboard with rose petals. The new year brought the two gents Mr. Rakeshaw and Mr. Crew. They were fun, everyone liked them. The Ashleys came next. Then Gwendolyn Fripworth and her niece, who came specifically for the new-season asparagus and peas.

And that would be the pattern, at least for a year or so, of how the first guests came to stay. A gradual easing into the complex world of hospitality, was how Cress described it. Till word of mouth spread and from March to October, the rooms were mostly occupied and brought in a modest income that provided all they needed. Every year the priest came by to bless the place and the length of his stay was measured by the quality of the wine at hand. Four hours for a particularly good Brunello.

Eventually, Ulysses would look forward to November, when the majority of visitors left and the weather became English for three months: a lot of rain, a little sleet and starry nights that brought a mantle of frost. The only guests, then, were loners or art enthusiasts, basically no trouble at all.

But we're ahead of ourselves.

It's 1953, still. December. The leaves are well and truly off the trees and an occasional dusting of snow flies in from the Apennines. Florentine women don their furs and the smell of white truffles mingles with that of roasting chestnuts. A *presepio*, a nativity scene, arrives outside the church and the guitar player takes his blues away. After the Feast of the Immaculate Conception, the city shifts its regard and it's all systems go go go for Christmas.

The biggest news at the Pensione Pappagallo, as it was now known, was that Des's molds had arrived. Six sets, not one, because Des was that kind of man. (Never does things by halves, said Poppy, showing her two engagement rings.) And within hours Ulysses was in his workshop up to his elbows in plaster of Paris and strips of hessian. He worked fast, sloshing the liquid up the sides of the mold, adding the hessian to strengthen, then more layers of plaster. His first attempts were crude, and he used them as practice spheres for the gores. Which glue held best on which paper. Which paper stretched too much, which held right, which absorbed watercolor paint and glue the best. The process was slow, arduous. His aesthetic instinct had grown flabby after a decade of procrastination and the floor of his workshop became a graveyard for discarded planet Earths. Two weeks later, however, two hemispheres became a near perfect one. He took a day to carve off the thick joint seam and to sandpaper the surface smooth—he couldn't stop looking at it. He should have, though. He was late again.

Sorry, Mass! Sorry, Cress! Ulysses running across the square.

Giulia came out of the café carrying a tray of coffee. She was wrapped up in a green cardigan, hair piled high and a navy scarf about her neck. She stood in front of Ulysses and placed the coffees on the table. She moved a stray curl of hair away from her forehead. She said, Six months you've been here, Signor Temper.

Already? (He still found it hard to look at her.)

It's true, said Massimo. Almost to the day.

Six months, Cress. What d'you say? Shall we do six months more?

I'm not going anywhere, son. Bury me here.

When Giulia moved out of earshot, Ulysses leaned in and said, What do you know about angina, Massimo?

Not much. My uncle had it.

He still alive?

No. A wild boar killed him.

A wild boar? said Cress.

It's more common than you think.

Nothing to do with angina, then?

It might have made him slower. You have angina, Ulisse?

No, no. I just—

It's OK. I'm teasing. I know you're talking about Michele.

How d'you know about Michele? said Ulysses.

Alys told me.

She told me, too.

No one tells me anything, said Cress.

The postman cycled past and flicked a postcard onto the table, face up. A picture of Big Ben.

London calling, said Massimo.

Ulysses turned it over.

Blimey! he said. It's Pete. Rosemary Clooney only went and bloody canceled. He's coming.

A frenzy of activity followed Pete's announcement. Cress went with the kid to buy a tree in the market and bought two on account of the *pensione*. They found a box of Arturo's decorations in the cellar and even though the effect was sparse, there was an elegance to the simple strands of silver and gold beading that draped across both floors. Downstairs, the tree had a star on top, and the one upstairs a large blue Amazonian parrot who occasionally came a cropper. Cress and the kid added a touch of the natural—sprays of holly and eucalypts—and the smell was heavenly, said Cress.

Heavenly. The word startled Ulysses. He'd never heard Cress use it before, the word having lived solely in the realm of Darnley. Ulysses couldn't shake off memories of the man all afternoon. You OK, boy? Cress kept saying. Cress knew he'd gone in on himself, as if he'd taken up residence in the far end of a telescope. I'm OK, said Ulysses, but the kid said, He wouldn't tell us even if he wasn't.

When night fell and he was alone, he went out onto the terrace. The pale unfinished façade of the church glowed like a giant monolith and he wondered what Darnley would've made of it all.

Hey, Temps, he could hear him say. It was never meant to be like this.

I know.

(Darnley pulls on his cigarette.)

This square, I mean. Not according to Brunelleschi. It should have been built on the other side, where it would have extended down to the river. You'd have arrived at church by boat. How heavenly would that have been? Like Venice.

Never been, sir.

Never been? Then we'll go. That'll be a plan. Oh, and Temps—you'll call me Alex, then.

Three days before Christmas and still no news from Pete. The weather had turned bitter and Ulysses was dozing on the sofa after a day freezing in his workshop with only a couple of small earthenware braziers to keep him warm. Claude was singing to himself on top of the tree and the medley of Christmas carols and sea shanties wasn't an unpleasant sound. Soon, though, another sound encroached, one that Ulysses had thought, indeed hoped, he'd never hear again in his lifetime, or any other come to that.

What the—?

He jumped up and went to the window just as the green 1930s English ambulance shuddered into the square, wailing like a slaughterhouse. Claude flew over and landed on his shoulder. He began to molt.

Take it easy, big fella. We don't know it's definitely him yet.

But by the time Ulysses had made it down the stairs, Col's crapwagon had already attracted the attention of his neighbors. The elderly contessa turned to him and shouted, Anything to do with you?

Maybe, said Ulysses.

Tipico, she scoffed, and turned away.

Pete stumbled out from the passenger side. His face looked paler than usual. He staggered into Ulysses's arms and said, He tied me to a chair, Temps. Wouldn't let me go till I agreed he could come. I spent a week with him in that small space.

Jesus, Pete, that's a bit bubbly.

The sound of Col's shouting and thumping the dash.

Why's he here?

Ginny won't leave Mrs. Kaur. Peg's off with Ted. He's fallen out with his sister. And I was coming here.

Who's looking after the pub?

Hayley Manners, his new woman. She used to run the Victory with an iron fist.

Nice coat, by the way.

This old thing, Temps? Had it years.

Suddenly the siren stopped. Col climbed out from the driver's side and gently closed the door.

What you doing here, Col?

Welcome to you too.

You know what I mean.

Just wanted to see what it was all about. That a crime?

Course not.

But knocking that man over in Milan was, said Pete.

You still going on about that? I hardly touched him, said Col, moving to the rear of the van. On Col's back was taped a sign: "Kick me" in three languages. Ulysses kicked him.

What the fuck'd you do that for?

Ulysses pulled off the sign and showed him.

Col turned to Pete. Don't you close your eyes tonight, he said.

Haven't closed them all week, said Pete.

Got any luggage? said Ulysses.

Pete held up his holdall. A few underpants and socks for me, he said.

Col unlocked the back of the ambulance. One suitcase, three cardboard boxes.

What's in the boxes, Col?

Spam, said Pete. He hasn't stopped eating it. It's been like lying next to something dead.

Ulysses stuck Col downstairs in the *pensione* and Pete came to live with them upstairs. It was so he could be near the piano, that was their excuse, but Pete couldn't bear to spend another minute cooped up with the man. And when Pete walked into the living room and saw Claude, he gasped and said, I never thought I'd see him again. How on earth did—?

Nothing to do with me, Pete, said Ulysses. It was all Cress's brilliance.

Got Cress written all over it, Temps.

What's got me written all over it? said Cress, coming into the room.

Put it here, Cressy, said Pete, and the two men shook hands.

Pete! shouted kid.

Hello, sweetheart.

Look what I've got! she said, and thrust her guitar his way. I want to play the blues, she said, and Pete placed her fingers along a fret—classic territory in the key of E. That's a good place to start, he said.

Claude took to the air and performed a little aeronautical magic. Fuck the Palladium! he chanted on repeat.

Look at that, said Pete.

He's a constant surprise, said Ulysses.

You'd think he was too heavy to do something like that, said Cress.

Suddenly, Col walked in. I knew it! he said. That bleedin' bird! Who'd wanna eat that?!

Claude startled and flew straight into the window. He dropped to the floor like a bag of nuts.

Claude! shouted the kid.

What you do that for? said Cress.

Do what? said Col.

No one could survive that, said Pete.

But Claude did.

And the unfortunate dip in festivities was instantly restored by the suggestion of dinner at Michele's. Kid led the way.

This is a bit of all right, said Pete, opening the door to the warmth and the smell and the Italian *ambiente*.

I still don't understand, said Col, looking down at the parrot prone in Ulysses's arms. How'd it get here?

Followed us.

Followed you?

Like a homing pigeon, said Ulysses.

Don't homing mean *home*?

Not necessarily, said Cress.

Oh, here we go, Doctor Dolittle.

Homing also refers to an ability to return to one's territory. Ergo—

Ergo? Er-bloody-go?

Ergo, said Cress. We're his territory.

Giulia led them to the table at the back and Ulysses explained that the bird had just suffered a *concussione* (he guessed at the word). She gasped and placed her hand to her chest. He wished he'd just told her that he had a *concussione*. He asked her what the specials were, and she moved close to his ear. *Tortellini in brodo*, she purred. It was as erotic a moment as he'd had in years. He felt giddy and stumbled against the chair.

Grab the bird! shouted Cress. Grab the bird, Pete!

Pete made a dive for it, caught it inches from disaster.

You're the safest pair of hands I know, said Cress.

The *tortellini in brodo* that first night was the dish they would talk about for years. Oh how it nourished them and pleased them, gave them resilience for all the unexpected moments to come!

The salty porky chickeny-ness of it, said Col in a rare moment of epicurean eloquence.

And the floating clusters of filled pasta that offer the *gentlest* of resistance, said Pete.

Al dente, said Cress.

Who's he? said Col.

"To the tooth," said Cress. *Al dente*. Means "firm to the bite." *Al dente*.

Stop saying bloody *al dente*, said Col, wiping a chunk of bread around his bowl. Just when I began to like you again.

Ulysses gave the kid a coin for the jukebox. This one's for Pete, she said. Ella Fitzgerald, "My One and Only."

Pete lit a cigarette and made them listen to the piano accompaniment. Hear that? he said. Ellis Larkins, he said, and he played note for note across make-believe keys. Michele came out from behind the counter.

Signor Temper, he said quietly. *Telefono*.

For me? said Ulysses, and he sidled out and followed Michele to the bar.

Moments later he returned.

What's up? said Cress.

That was Peg.

Peg? they said in unison.

She's coming, said Ulysses.

Comin'? Where?

Here.

Here?

Tomorrow. They're in Rome.

They?

Her and Ted.

Oh, not bleedin' Ted, said Col.

On their way to Venice.

You're gonna have to play it cool, said Pete.

Never been good at that, Pete.

Me neither, Temps. Don't know why I said it. I'll get the drinks in. And he got up and ordered a round of *biciclette*.

Kid looked worried. She leaned over to Ulysses and said, Why's Peg coming, Uly? and he said, To see you, of course! And kid smiled bright. She staying with us, Uly? No, kiddo, not this time. (He kept it light but couldn't look her in the eye.)

You staying with us, Peg?

No. Ted wants to stay in the place on the corner.

The Bandini?

That's the one. A friend of a friend of a friend stayed there.

That's some recommendation, Peg.

She laughed.

(Pause.)

Wish you were staying with us, he added.

Yeah. But you know Ted.

I don't really, said Ulysses. We had room for you, Peg.

I didn't know.

You should've asked. Kid would've loved it.

Will she be pleased to see me?

You don't know how much.

The following afternoon, the temperature dropped, and the sky tinged yellow and threatened snow. Ulysses blew on his hands and adjusted his scarf, waiting by the fountain in the fading light like a big old muggins. Col's words, of course. But he couldn't help himself. He was excited to see Peg, truth be told, and that excitement was the only thing keeping the fug of a hangover at bay. He looked at his watch. Not long now, he was sure. The front door opened, and kid came running out. Changed my mind, she said.

Frankie Lane's "I Believe" blared out from Michele's. Kid and Ulysses sang along. A car appeared in the square, the thick chug of its exhaust emphasized by the chill air. Ulysses squeezed the kid's hand, but the car wasn't a taxi and it kept on through into Via Mazzetta.

I thought that was her, she said.

Me too, he said.

Funny we thought the same thing.

Kid began to dance to keep warm. You should try it, she said.

OK, I will, he said.

Peg and Ted said little in the taxi. How could they go to Rome and Venice and not stop in Florence? Ted's little game. Look at the light, said Peg as they crossed the river. It's just light, said Ted, rereading his three-day-old newspaper.

Ten minutes later, the taxi rolled into Santo Spirito and came to a stop outside Palazzo Guadagni. Bare trees and Christmas lights and a glowing church and the perfect symmetry of buildings. And in the middle, a man and a kid dancing by a fountain in the warm pink of dusk. The man and child were laughing, heat from their breath fogging. They looked happy and that's all Peg needed to see. She could sleep now, might even be able to forgive herself. She should've left it at that, should've told the taxi driver to keep on going, but all of a sudden, the kid and the man stopped dancing and turned toward her. The man pointed and waved. Ted paid the taxi driver and said, We're not eating with them tonight. Peg opened the car door. You hear me? said Ted. Yeah, yeah, she said.

The air was sharp in her nostrils. Woodsmoke and garlic and something grubby. She smoothed her stockings and climbed out, wrapped her fur coat tight around her. She waved and the kid ran toward her and the kid was all Eddie. Those eyes, that mouth, that hair. Peg knelt down to greet her but really it was to stop herself from falling.

Clack clack clack across the square. Peggy's tune. She was coming toward him. Hips swaying, arm swinging, fag in her rouged mouth. Other hand clasping the kid. A familiar twinge in Ulysses's guts. Ted left behind on the pavement with the suitcases, pissed off that Peg had moved away (without asking his permission). Ulysses went toward her. She threw away her cigarette. The bells from the basilica began to ring.

They for me? she said.

Who else? he said. Cost me an arm and a leg to set that up. I'm still reeling from the amputation.

Peg laughed. They locked eyes, and it was familiar and there was history. Her breath felt warm on his face, slightly stale but not unattractive.

Come here, he said.

In one another's arms now. (People watching. The elderly contessa at an upstairs window. Michele and Giulia in the doorway of the café.)

You look Italian, she said.

That'll be my trousers.

Your hair's darker.

You reckon?

She ran her fingers through the top of it.

Suits you, she said.

And you look like you.

He held her hands and pulled away to take in the full effect. He whistled.

Hey! interrupted the kid. That's our building there. And that's our café. And that's Signor Michele and Signora Giulia. Wave! And that's our fountain.

Peg laughing. Ted was calling out to her.

I should go— she began.

And that's our Cressy.

Peg turned. Heart sore at the sight of him.

The old fella smiled at her; he looked red-eyed and choked.

Call the police, he said. *Qualcuno ha rubato tutta la bellezza.* Someone's stolen all the beauty.

Words as gold dust, Cress?

What else? he said. Here, have an orange.

He held out a Sicilian *tarocco*. She took it. Pierced the skin with her nail and held it to her nose. Sharp memories.

Come on, said Cress. There's a piano, a glass of fizz and an unconscious parrot waiting for you.

Sounds about right, she said.

Ted calling out to her. Peg exasperated.

Go on, said Ulysses. You three go up. I'll help Ted.

When they'd gone, Ulysses ran across the stones. All right, Ted? The two men shook hands, both polite. Ulysses said, Kid wanted to show Peg her room. I knew you wouldn't mind, and he picked up one of the cases. Good journey? he said. (Ted complaining.) Yeah, well, that's this time of year for you.

Peggy Temper walking up the stone staircase as if she was in a film. Find your light, Peg, find your light. The echo of her heels, stair after stair after stair. The bewitching line of her stocking seam, like a musical digit, da dah da dah da dah. An old woman on the first floor peeked through the door to watch. Peg smiled that smile and fuck was it catching—four years since that old bat had cracked a grin. The sweet kid up ahead, all chatty this and that with a spray of Italian loquacity. Clever little thing. All Eddie's side, her mum would've said. *Nothing* of you. The atmosphere airless, a bit like a museum. Peg out of her comfort zone but she didn't know where that ended anymore. What? she said. Cress had stopped and was looking at her. The truth, he said. Good or bad? She knew what he meant. So-so, she said. Her thighs feeling strong from the climb, her heart thumping wild. I said I'd marry Ted. Cress shook his head and went on up.

Here we are, said Alys. My home. Two words that shouldn't have affected Peg, but they did. In here, said the kid. Peg undid her coat. Heady smells of hot wine and spice and oranges and cloves. Smoke and mirrors in the hallway, doors leading off to exquisite embroidery and beds. The faint fug of coal from the kitchen. Into the living room she glided, and she shed her fur as if it was spring. Her new brassiere offered up a couple of heritage peaks. Classic Peg. Over to the tree, where her perfume mingled with its piney grip. Pete at the piano lit by candles. Col saying something about the idiot in Milan he hit with the car. Nothing changes. And yet—

Some things do. She stood at the window. The myriad of yellow lights splaying out from shutters and the bell tower and the nativity scene and the dark flit of birds across a navy and magenta marbled sky. Temps and the kid. She'd lost them to this. And in her ears came a roaring sound like waves. Cress handed her a glass of bubbles. She drank it in one and the sound disappeared. Music and laughter again. Kid handed her the parrot swaddled in a sheet. Pete saying, It's like looking at the baby Jesus and Mary. And you're the three wise men, are you? said Peg. Dopey, Grumpy, Sleepy? Claude opened his eyes. Peg, he said quietly. What is it, sweetie? And she leaned in close to him. What is it? (Her ear now at his beak.) What?

Don't marry Ted.

Anyone seen Peg? said Ulysses.

It was Christmas Eve and they were in Michele's, having a last-minute *caffè corretto* before the place shut for two days. There she is! said Cress, pointing out of the window. Ulysses noticed she was wearing sunglasses. And no Ted! said Col. There's Ted, said Ulysses. Oh, fuck it, said Col. Kid gave Giulia and Michele a present: a signed photograph of Ingrid Bergman. They were delighted. I signed it, said the kid.

A walking tour of the city had been planned, but Peg had only brought heels, so Ulysses said he'd drive everyone up to San Miniato al Monte in Betsy. Ted bowed out. Oh, that's a shame, said Col.

Ulysses took them along the *lungarno* heading east. With the river on their left, kid and Cress pointed to the sights. Uffizi, the national library, Palazzo Vecchio, Institute of the History of Science. The first chronometric devices are in there, said Cress. The first telescopes, astrolabes and maritime instruments. The first portable representations of the night sky; and, of course—Cress catching his breath—Galileo. The father of modern physics.

Peg turned to Ulysses and winked. I've missed this, she whispered.

Cress said, Galileo didn't invent the telescope as people think he did, but it was the way he used it. He experimented. He observed. He deduced. His discovery of the satellites of Jupiter proved the Copernican view that the Earth was in fact a satellite of the sun.

Heliocentrism, said Pete.

And the great bothering it unleashed, said Cress.

I wrote a song about it, said Pete. "Not All About You Anymore."

Pete hummed the chorus as Betsy carved through the undulating Viale Michelangiolo into—appropriately enough—the Viale Galileo.

From the church of San Miniato, the group looked out across the city. Peg took off her sunglasses to brush a fleck of mascara out of her eye and Ulysses was relieved to see the slight red of tears and not a bruise. Cress began to talk about Arnolfo di Cambio. Architect, sculptor, designer, city planner, he said.

But could he make a bacon sandwich? said Col.

Shut up, Col, said Peg.

Cress ignored him and pressed on. He said, It was Arnolfo's vision of 1284 that encapsulated what we see before us. The outline over there of his circuit of walls. (Do you see? We see, they said.) This new city boundary not only highlighted the importance of the river and bridges, but it brought inside the churches of the mendicant orders. Fixed points of the compass—or the cross, let's say: Santissima Annunziata in the north, Santo Spirito in the south, Santa Maria Novella over in the west, and Santa Croce in the east. And there in the center, in all its majesty, drawing the eye toward it: the cathedral. Il Duomo. Representing the glory of the city itself.

Peg found Ulysses in the cemetery.

This him? she said.

Yep. Arturo Bernadini.

She sat down next to Ulysses. You come here often?

Not often. A bit of peace now and then. He changed my life, Peg.

You saved his.

I'm not really sure I did, he said.

But you were who he remembered. You more than anyone. That's the effect you have on people, Tempy.

Aw, I don't know, he said, and lit a cigarette. Thanks for coming, he added. I know it cost you.

Peg quiet. She took the cigarette and said, You know me more than anyone.

How does that feel?

Peg didn't answer.

Christmas tomorrow, he said. I hope it snows.

Ted hates snow, she said.

She leaned down toward the grave. Make it snow, Arturo. Make it snow for this boy here.

It was Cress who drove Peg and Col back to the *pensione*. Pete wanted to walk and kid wanted to be with Pete so Ulysses led the way down the steps into San Niccolò. The city was wrapping up. Trams were packed, and the last of the shoppers were rushing by with parcels or bags of food. Kid telling Pete about La Befana, the old woman who brings presents to children. But not on Christmas Day, Pete. On Epiphany, sixth January. But I'll get mine at Christmas, won't I, Ulysses?—You will—And if the children are bad, she said, they get a lump of coal. That's a bit harsh, said Pete. A bit close to the bone, that.

They stopped along the embankment and leaned over the wall. Ponte Vecchio up ahead. The slow movement of the river below. The hills surrounding the city were dark with a scattering of lights. Somewhere, music. Ulysses lit a couple of cigarettes and handed one to Pete. He liked being with Pete. Pete had quiet junctures.

They turned in to Via de' Guicciardini and Pete said, Mind if I go in there, Temps, and light a few candles? Only time me and the Church are at peace.

Course not, said Ulysses, and they veered off toward the open door, past the sentinel Christmas tree, and into the gloom. The church felt warm from bodies, and the strong scent of frankincense lingered. Pete stuck his fingers in the font and dabbed his forehead. Can't have too many blessings, he said.

I want to do that, said the kid, and Ulysses lifted her up and she stuck her hand in the bowl. She flicked water at Ulysses and he tried to dodge her and as he did, he caught sight of a painting behind her and his heart skipped. So there it was! After all these years. Kid slid down and walked off with Pete. Ulysses dug a coin from his pocket and in no time the gated chapel flared with light and the luminosity of color. Darnley saying . . .

*Ulysses Temper, Miss Evelyn Skinner, I'd like you to meet Pontormo's Dep-*osition from the Cross.

Do you think they'd let us take it now, Captain Darnley, and save them the trouble?

Ulysses leaned against the bars. Hello again, Evelyn. Remember me?

Kid behind him. I like this painting, she said.

Me too. He smiled. I like the cloud.

Do you want to light a candle? said the kid. Pete showed me how to do it. You have to think of someone you like. Do you think you could do that?

I think I could.

They walked over to an altar.

Pete lit these, said the kid.

(There must have been at least fifty.)

Blimey, said Ulysses.

All his women, said the kid. What's an amend?

Making right something that's wrong, said Ulysses, and he picked up a candle and dropped a coin in the box.

Have you thought of someone? said the kid.

I have.

Is it a woman?

He smiled. Yeah, it is.

Good, she said. Now you light it. That's it. And you think of them really hard. Are you doing that?

I am.

Really hard?

Uh-huh.

Now you can put the candle on the stand. That's mine there. You can put it next to it if you want.

Do you think they know I was thinking of them? said Ulysses.

Pete says it's like a special telephone call and they get it even if they're not in.

Is that right?

Who am I to argue?

Night fell early. Kid and Pete went on ahead to the *pensione* whilst Ulysses veered right down Via dello Sprone toward his workshop. He walked across Piazza dei Sapiti and somewhere amidst the spray of Christmas lights, the sound of a violin spoke of loneliness. He put the key in the lock and pushed open the heavy wooden door. He switched on the light and dust roiled in the flare of the overhead bulb. Three plaster spheres, like moons, on the upper shelf. The picture was as he'd left it. He'd found a printer in San Frediano after he'd taken the kid to school and had a print made of one of his father's copperplates. Twelve gores. Early 1920s. The quality of paper not right for a globe but perfect for a painting. He'd gotten it framed locally, nice and simple. He ran a clean rag across the glass, a little bit of wax to lift the frame. He wrapped it in brown paper and tied it with string. For Massimo, he wrote.

He picked up a last-minute bottle of bubbles in Via Maggio before coming into the square. A couple of tourists were looking up at his building. The windows were open, and he caught a glimpse of Cress by the Christmas tree, Pete and Peg giving song to the night. And he thought, You'd want to be with them if you were down here looking up. You'd want to be part of them.

He ran the stairs two at a time and stopped on the first-floor landing.

He left the bottle of Spumante outside the elderly contessa's door. He rang her bell but didn't wait.

No one heard him come in. He stood in the doorway of the living room and took off his scarf. Peg singing "That's All." Pete, fag in mouth, down close to the keys, caressing them into another dimension. Col next to Cress on the sofa, their movements coordinated—hand to mouth with a cigarette, glass to mouth with the wine—and kid sitting on the floor, stroking the parrot. Ted standing by the window being Ted. Half in, half out. Awkward, stiff and rich. Bloody rum lot they were, but he cared for them. He took Massimo's package into his room and dumped his coat on the bed. Peggy's voice following him across the tiles. In the kitchen the smell of baked fish and sage. He poured out a glass of wine and came back to his position in the doorway. He couldn't take his eyes off her. He never would. Cress called it a curse and a blessing to love someone so completely and maybe that was true. Ulysses lifted the glass and drank. He'd long given up trying to fathom what Peg saw in other men. Coming to the end of the song now, she looked at him; smiled just for him. No one had what they had, he thought. Not really. He raised his glass to her. The last bars were Pete's. The soft flourish. The gulp of emotion.

The midnight bells rang out and echoed against the dark solemn hills. From the terrace they watched the congregation file out from the basilica and gather in the square. Cress explaining that the celebrations start after mass. Then comes the feasting, the opening of presents, the—

It's a big deal, Christmas, isn't it? said Pete.

And there's the announcement of the century, said Col.

I meant here in Italy.

Florence, said Ted, and then he paused to drink from his glass.

Florence what? said Col.

Nothing, said Ted. Here we are in Florence.

Col gripped his stomach and unwrapped his last peppermint.

Ulysses came out with a fresh bottle of Spumante and segments of *panforte.*

Snack, anyone?

Couldn't eat another thing, said Pete.

How is she? said Peg.

Fast asleep, said Ulysses. You wanna see?

Ted said, Of course Florence isn't Rome.

Isn't it? said Col.

Even Peg had to smile at that one.

She followed Ulysses into the kitchen. He placed a couple of coffee-pots onto the stove.

This way, he said.

Through the kitchen and along the hallway. The murmur from the terrace growing faint.

They watched the kid sleep. A pillowcase full of presents at the end of her bed. Ulysses pulled her blanket high.

Let's go to your room, said Peg.

He quietly latched the door behind him. Peg pulled up her skirt; it was a no-knickers kind of night. They fucked against the wall and it was done and dusted by the time the coffeepot was bubbling.

Peg held his face.

What? he said.

Coffee! shouted Cress.

You go in first, he said, breathing hard. But he didn't come out again that night. Left them on the terrace with the bells and booze and the bluster of Col and Ted. He got under the covers and closed his eyes. He heard Peg and Ted leave. That edge to Ted's voice, Peg's silence with men a new thing. When everyone was asleep, he went to the bathroom and washed. He knew he'd have the kid bounding in on him early.

Christmas Day found Cress drinking coffee on the terrace.

And here you are! said Massimo, appearing in the doorway.

You escaped your mother, Mass? said Cress.

She thinks I'm still in the bathroom. *Buon Natale*, my friend.

Happy Christmas, Mass!

Here, said Massimo, and he handed over a small parcel.

What's this? said Cress.

More uncharted territory for a facts man.

Cress unwrapped it. Well, I never, he said.

Poetry, said Massimo. About a love affair in this city.

Down the spine Cress read the title *Everything*. Constance Everly, he said. He flipped through the pages and stopped. He read:

> *They found a good enough place of solitude.*
> *Clambered onto the foreshore in the shadow of a bridge,*
> *Hands touched cheeks and fingers lips,*
> *And there they kissed*
> *Because the eyes of the city were not on them.*
> *Bells were faint, pronouncing the hour.*
> *But what hour? Time had ceased.*
> *Somewhere in the air the quiet cast of a lure*
> *Whipped the water and sent ripples to their feet.*

Pete, soulful and hungover, moved slowly from sofa to piano. He adjusted the stool and took a sip of grappa. He'd woken with the muse and cradled her respectfully. He leaned in close to the keys, and with his left hand crafted the soft melody, a series of repetitive chords that played themselves after a while. The right hand a gentle improvisation, wherever it took him. A song of beauty that uncovered the soul was what Pete offered that day. Named it "Cressy's Song" after it stopped the old fella in his well-worn tracks.

The music led Cress to his mum. Six kids, no money and only a view from the sink. Christmas just another day. The time he learned that she too had dreams. Hard to reconcile that pain. Has taken a lifetime and still not there yet.

Peg on the terrace with her kid, drinking in her Eddie looks. Nine years ago, thought Peg. And she's the proof those months were real.

Kid looking at Peg. So much to fathom out. I like it when you sing, she said. Peg smiled. Kid would always be looking for that smile in women.

And Pete played on.

Col at the window overlooking the square. Ginny would have loved it, but Ginny was with Mrs. Kaur and her nephew. Col knew everything now. (His stomach tightened.) But if I let her go, then where does that leave me?

Massimo unwrapping the world in twelve segments. Ulysses leaning over to show his mum's name hidden in Russia. It's beautiful, Massimo said. He never wanted to lose this friend and yet there were things still to be said. They could wait another day. Another year, even.

And Pete played on.

Ulysses moving through the hallway. He sees Col in the living room at the window. Cress in the doorway watching Pete. Ted passing him on the way to the bathroom. He opens the fridge and takes out a bottle of Spumante. He fills a glass. He goes onto the terrace. Peg and the kid, Claude flying free. He hands Peg a glass. Says quietly to her, I'll help you find Eddie. Massimo found me, and I'm sure we—

It wasn't his name, Temps. Not his real one. I tried, she said.

And Pete stopped playing.

Dusk dimmed the room, and the constellations on the ceiling, all but invisible in daylight hours, were brought to life by the fading light. Pete got up and switched on the lamps.

Hey, it's snowing, he said.

They gathered at the window.

Well, I'll be, said Ulysses.

I hate snow, said Ted.

It doesn't much like you, said Col.

Peg smiled.

Down below in the square, Signora Mimmi was waiting.

It's Signora Mimmi! said Cress. I wonder who she's waiting for.

You! they said.

But I don't have anything for her, he said.

You! they said.

He grabbed the nearest coat, which happened to be Peg's fur, and was about to run out, when—

Where's my poetry book? he said.

From the upstairs window, Ulysses and Peg side by side watched Cress enter the empty square. He and Signora Mimmi held hands and moved toward a bench. Cress brushed it free of snow and they sat down facing one another. Cress opened his poetry book and his words became mist.

Christmas 1953 was one for the visitors' book. They all wrote a version of "We'll be back!" but they wouldn't, not like that.

They left the next day, Peg and Ted as early as decency would allow, and the margins on that were close. Peg hugged the kid awkwardly and Ulysses had to look away. Ted went off and loaded the taxi. Remember what I said, said Claude. And Peg would remember, but she wouldn't adhere to it. Ted and Peg would be married in June and would become Mr. and Mrs. Holloway. They'd honeymoon in Paris. (Nowhere like it, Ted would say.)

Col was next to leave. You don't have to go, said Ulysses. Yeah I do, said Col. He missed Ginny, truth be told. And England.

I don't make sense anywhere other than that small corner of London, said Col. I'm one of them blokes who needs to know what's what. Spam on Tuesday, fish on Friday.

We do that here, said Ulysses. We're not that different.

Col offered his hand. Bye, Temps. Don't be a stranger.

See you, Col.

Cress, old fella.

Thanks for coming.

Sure I can't change your mind? said Col, turning to Pete.

No thanks, Col. I need to go it alone on this one.

Col climbed into the driver's seat. As soon as the key engaged, the scream of the ambulance filled the square. Col leaned out of the window. Spam's in the cellar, by the way!

Yeah, yeah. And then he was gone.

How you getting home, Pete? said Ulysses.

I'll hitch, Temps. I need time to think. Freedom of the open road and all that. I'll get a song out of it if nothing else.

("Freedom of the Open Road" became a hit around the clubs a year later.)

You always have a home here, Pete. We need you.

Pete collapsed in Ulysses's arms. He said, One day, Temps. You're like the brother I never had. I did have one, but we never really—

I know what you mean, Pete.

Pete lifted his holdall onto his shoulder and stuck out his thumb. A minute later he got a lift with a wine merchant heading to Bologna.

And then they were alone: two men, a kid and a parrot.

Listen, said Cress.

They listened.

Peace, said Cress.

Nice, isn't it? said Cress.

We do all right, don't we? said Ulysses. Just us?

They moved across to the lights of Michele's, which had just come on.

And so another year approaches, said Cress.

Wonder what it'll bring, said Ulysses.

More of the same, said the kid. Who's buying?

So, 1954? More of the same? No, not really.

Cress became the owner of a red Moto Guzzi Falcone complete with sidecar. His confidence with Betsy had waned. He needed something practical in which he could transport the heavier laundry to Manfredi, but also something nippy and eye-catching. He bought it with some of Fanny's winnings, off a man who'd recently lost an arm. He got a good price.

A small crowd formed in the square the afternoon Cressy pulled up on his machine. Cressy's smile shone out from under his helmet as people stopped to chat with him. He rarely had a clue what people were on about, but by the luck of the gods, he understood most of it. Bit of an oracle was Cressy.

The kid? She grew strong roots and a fury you could light a fire with. She practiced guitar and she began to sing and the voice that came out was Peg's. She made friends at school but kept to herself outside those gates. She wrote to Peg once a month but sometimes she drew a picture instead. Peg sent over a photo of Eddie. It was her only one and Peg told her to keep it safe. Kid kept it hidden from Ulysses because she didn't want to hurt him.

And Ulysses acquired many more Italian words and still spoke with an East London lilt. He couldn't roll his R's and would never be able to do so. To some, he was still known as *soldato*, something he'd have preferred not to have been called, but he stayed magnanimous.

In March, two noticeable things. He glued the last gore to a sphere and created a globe. He began to source carpenters who could make the stands. He also had sex with an American tourist in a hotel over by Piazza dei Ciompi. The experience was wonderful and long overdue. He said good-bye to her in the early hours and wandered back through an empty city. Somewhere a flower seller was setting up a stall. Twilight filled with scent, hard to beat. And as he stood in the wide expanse of Piazza Santa Croce, the first lights came on in a café, the first sound of donkey-and-carts rolling up through the streets with the new day's produce. Sunrise breaking somewhere behind the Casentino, and the moon, the beautiful satellite, shone white and full and entranced. And he became aware of the universe, that endless canopy of chance and wonder. He leaned against the statue of Dante Alighieri and lit a cigarette. He said, I was supposed to come and give you someone's best a long time ago, so I'm doing it now. Evelyn is her name. Evelyn Skinner.

The Most
Unlikely-Looking
Pair

1954–59

Evelyn Skinner, last seen in 1944 outside the modest *albergo*, was alive and well and positively thriving. Something she would put down to cold-water swimming and a daily dose of cod liver oil. She had, by 1954, long resumed her part-time teaching post at the Slade School of Fine Art and had happily swapped weekdays in Kent for her studio flat in Bloomsbury (although the county had her back most weekends). She was seventy-three years old and looked ten years younger. Her mind was agile and her curiosity as keen as ever. She was a favorite with the teaching fraternity and her students adored her. She brought them to art in a way no one else had so far done—

No, Mr. Fitzgibbon, that's not quite right. Goya picks up after Velázquez and runs with it.

Mr. Gunnerslake, Rome is the capital of all these eighteenth-century meetings. And Rubens in Rome changed everything.

I'd also like to add, Miss Shaw, that there is an immediacy to art. One finds oneself abruptly in front of a moment of ecstasy. This is where art is effective. Art captures permanently . . .

At the end of every term, she took lunch with her students at Beppe's Café, a short stroll away. Eleven of them took over the back four tables,

Evelyn positioned as centrally as such an arrangement would allow. They ate the daily special—usually a plate of pasta cooked by Beppe's mother—washed down with cups of strong tea.

Look in here, said Evelyn, dabbing her lips with a paper serviette. Look about you. It's so harmonious, she said. This could be a painting. Crimson and cream stripes and wood. Everyone dressed in monochrome attire. Good manners and joy abound. Lunch and friendship. Perfection, I say. And she raised her cup of tea.

Incipit vita nova, she said. So begins a new life.

When Evelyn had returned from war, life had been far from harmonious. She had been gripped by a startling loneliness that had propelled her to Battersea Dogs Home, from where she'd adopted an old overweight basset called Barry. Or he adopted her, wasn't that how it went? But she always liked to tell the story as if it was a limerick (There once was a basset from Battersea / Who met an old dear from Bloomsbury . . .). He was a wonderful companion for five years. Unashamedly lazy, he required little exercise to uphold his cynical nature. His modus operandi was to sit in front of the fire and drink condensed milk with whiskey in it. He used to accompany her to the odd evening of attribution and liked to break wind when he was ready to leave, behavior Evelyn told her friends she too would eventually adopt. They were good for one another. They were happy years. In her classroom at the Slade, he'd sleep on a blanket under the desk as slides of the High Renaissance sequenced above him. He died peacefully during a long and tedious talk on Giorgio Vasari. Evelyn was surprised more hadn't succumbed. It wasn't one of my best, she'd said. Midway through, even she had felt for a pulse.

An afternoon at the end of March saw Evelyn standing at the front of her class. She cut a dashing figure in pale blue linen slacks and white blouse.

Oh no no, she said. Michelangelo was an *earthquake*. He broke into Mannerism with his poses. Quite fey, really. Deeply irritating because we know so much of his personality. We still maneuver in the architecture of Vasari's *Lives*. Vasari would have been delighted, of course. That sort of man.

Her students were enraptured. Their faces lit by the slide screen behind her.

So? she said, drawing out the vowel. We were where?

She had done it again. Had veered so spectacularly away from Piero della Francesca's *The Baptism of Christ* that she glanced over to the door to make sure Bill Coldstream wasn't hovering. She looked at her watch. Curtailed, once again, by the scythe of time.

I must let you go, my dear ladies and gentlemen. But to recap. The mathematical foundations of beauty and harmony. Piero's love of geometry. His unique style within the early Renaissance. The holy moment is also the tentative moment. A very good end of term to you all. Go forth, go learn, go love!

The lights came on and Jesus disappeared, and an excited revelry rose from the class. Books were flung into bags and chairs scraped as students moved toward the door.

Good-bye, Miss Skinner! echoed into the corridor. Good-bye, said Evelyn. You too, my dear. I suggest you look up Roberto Longhi. Or Carlo Ludovico Ragghianti. Oh yes, yes, I hope so, she said. Thank you, Mr. Cornwallis, I shall try indeed. Good-bye.

And then there was quiet. And it was exquisite. She closed her eyes and acknowledged the end of term with yogic breathing. After a good five minutes, the presence of another infused the air. She opened her eyes, happy to see Jem Gunnerslake still at his desk. Him of the unruly hair and courtly manners.

Jem, she said. (First names for people she liked.)

Miss Skinner.

Are you all right?

I am, he said, and stood up. I've something for you, he said. I found it in a shop on Charing Cross Road. I know how much she meant to you.

Evelyn took the brown paper bag from his hand. Inside was a

burgundy cloth-covered book with *Niente/Nothing* in gold lettering down the spine.

First edition, he added.

Oh my! This is so wonderful, she said, and she flicked through the pages till she stopped at a poem—one about trams and lights on the Arno and sand diggers—and she became twenty-one again, about to embark on a love affair with a city that would last a lifetime. She ran her fingers across Constance Everly's fading name and said, Such was her influence on me, Jem.

As yours is on us, Miss Skinner. Jem looked at her and smiled. He didn't often smile on account of his bad teeth.

Well, I shall treasure this, said Evelyn, hugging the book to her chest. I lost my own copy on a train down to Rome. A sumptuous find for a fellow traveler, I thought then.

And now?

Careless and distracted by first love. You know how it is.

But Jem Gunnerslake didn't. First love would have to wait.

They left the classroom together, and on the stone stairs encountered a rare sighting of the artist du jour and occasional tutor.

Good evening, Lucian, said Evelyn. Are you well?

Oh, yes, Miss Skinner! And he dashed past in a fervor.

When he was out of earshot, Evelyn said, He's quite the ladies' man, I've heard. Bit of a menace.

Have you read *The Interpretation of Dreams*? asked Jem.

Indeed I have, said Evelyn. During that first trip to Florence, my friend Mr. Collins recommended that I should. We were seated in the Piazza della Signoria—I really do remember it so well—drinking vermouth—that was my drink at the time—discussing Giambologna's *Sabine Woman*, and I remember, quite distinctly, how he said that book was the way forward.

Evelyn stopped by the front door. She said, The Church does not have a language for the variations of our humanness. We need to look at Freud for that. Psychoanalysis is the way forward. That's what he said to me, Jem. And I do believe he was right. I read the first English translation.

They left behind the comforting stink of linseed oil and stepped outside. There was an herbaceous hook to the spring air, the slow roll of a lawn mower moving methodically across the quad. It was the season of blossom and leaf growth, and the bare branches appeared bewildered by the vibrancy of emerging livery.

A wolf whistle pierced the air.

Not for me, Mr. Gunnerslake. That is the call of the young.

Jem looked about. But then a rather handsome middle-aged woman emerged from behind a tree and caused Evelyn to wave.

Good God, said Jem. Is that who I think it is?

Yes, said Evelyn, it is.

Dorothy "Dotty" Cunningham, the renowned abstract artist.

The circles of art tend to overlap, as do the circles of literature, and Dotty and Evelyn had met over thirty years previously through Evelyn's painter father, H. W. Skinner, and his mistress/muse at the time, Gabriela Cortez. Old enough to be Dotty's mother, Evelyn had guided her young protégée through the fast-flowing tributaries of lesbian life. Never lovers but always friends. They said on that first meeting, I feel as if I've known you forever. A lifetime later, it was as if they had.

Dotty was leaning against the tree, cross-armed, with a cheeky tilt of the head, a pose that meant "Tell me more" or "Take your clothes off," depending on the circumstance and time of day. She was as famous for her masculine garb and short hair as she was for her painting. That afternoon, she sported worn corduroy trousers, a billowing linen shirt and the kind of rakish polka-dot neckerchief most often associated with farmworkers at harvest time. Dotty, ironically, hated the country. Hampstead Heath, for her, was the middle of nowhere.

Ready for a swim, darling? she called out to Evelyn.

Ready as ever, said Evelyn.

They embraced familiarly and when they moved apart, Jem Gunnerslake popped up between them, telling Dotty how much he admired her work. He delivered a swift and wholly competent critique of three of Dotty's most famous pieces: *Journeywoman, Maria* and *Arrested Time*.

Dotty thanked him and ran her fingers through her hair, her nail beds colored by the remnants of her latest work. I look forward to seeing you again, he said, with the confidence of a middle-aged man about to embark on his first affair.

Have a good break, Miss Skinner.

You too, Jem. And thank you, she said, holding up the brown paper bag that contained her book.

They watched him disappear out of the gates toward the underground station, toward a train to Northumberland, where he would spend a week pruning his mother's bay tree.

Dotty looked at her friend quizzically.

Jem Gunnerslake, said Evelyn. Lost soul but incredibly kind. Last-to-the-lifeboats kind of man. I like him a lot. I could imagine him veering away from art and studying medicine.

That's quite a leap. Though Leonardo was halfway there.

He also indulges my stories from the past.

We all do, darling, said Dotty, reaching for her arm. Come on, she said. Let's get wet.

They found a taxicab on Gower Street and the effusiveness of first greeting settled into a calm précis of the weeks since they'd last met.

Gunnerslake? said Dotty. Not related to that American theater critic, is he?

Who?

Jem. She's not his mother, is she?

Is who his mother?

Penelope. They look similar.

I have no idea who you're talking about.

You do. Penelope Gunnerslake. We went to see that play.

What play?

In the West End. About four years ago. Charlie took us.

Wetherall?

Yes. Charlie Wetherall took us to see that play where the frontier pianist with a drink problem stole the show.

Oh God, yes! A small but noticeable part. He was marvelous. So real.

Well, Penelope Gunnerslake was the woman we were sitting next to, said Dotty.

The redhead with pearls?

The redhead with pearls, said Dotty.

The air cooled as they drove into the shaded encampment of NW3.

Nearly there, said Evelyn.

She wore them in bed, you know. Those pearls.

The theater critic did?

I told you at the time.

You most certainly did not, said Evelyn, and she opened her bag and took out her purse. She turned to Dotty and said, Did she review you, my darling?

She was quite complimentary, actually, said Dotty.

The taxi came to a halt on Highgate West Hill. Evelyn paid and closed the door.

She didn't say, "The grand flourish at the end could little make up for a lackluster opening"? said Evelyn.

Oh, very good, laughed Dotty.

"Impetus lost in the second act"?

I'm glad you're enjoying yourself, said Dotty.

Oh, I am, said Evelyn. "Three curtain calls were two too many"?

They cut through to the edge of the heath and walked the hardened path toward the gate, the vegetation pungent beside them in the balmy afternoon heat.

I went to the Colony last night, said Dotty. Muriel says hello.

Ah, Muriel, said Evelyn fondly.

They settled their belongings in the meadow adjacent to the water and went to the hut to change. Evelyn emerged in her trusty black costume with shorts, and readjusted the strap on her shoulder. Her body had changed little over the years except for the band of padding around

her middle, an accumulation of the six o'clock cocktail, a ritual as ac-
curate at keeping time as Big Ben. Dotty's costume, in comparison, was,
well, a bit circus. It gets the job done, she said.

They walked gingerly across the wet decking and dumped their towels by the steps. Dotty limbered up before getting into the water, as she
always did. She stretched her arms across her chest and warmed up her
thighs with a good slap. Dotty nudged Evelyn to follow her gaze. A
woman was by the edge of the water showing signs of indecision. Dotty
had long believed there was a direct correlation between how one entered the ponds and how one had sex. Utter nonsense, said Evelyn. I
usually hold my nose and fall in.

Case in point, said Dotty, before performing an elegant swallow dive
with minimal splash.

The familiar cold rush hit Evelyn. Fifty-five degrees against the low
eighties of the air, the inner gasp and the letting go. She swam eye-level
to the green water, as clouds were bothered by the breeze and wavelets
crested by sunlight.

These were Evelyn's favorite days, her spring awakening. (Past the
water lilies again, and the bulrushes.) Dappled light on overhanging tree
trunks brought motion to the static monsters, and willows draped low
to meet their vivid reflection. She breathed steadily through her nose
and the ducks matched the ponderous ease of her breaststroke. A heron
took off majestically from the bank and flew low across her path. She
was in heaven.

A group of twentysomethings with sunglasses and red lips gathered
on the pontoon, looking as if they might be a synchronized swimming
team. What joy their presence brought. When Dotty caught sight of
them, Evelyn knew she would double back and swoon at their entry,
which she did. That they all dived in together caused Dotty to look over
at Evelyn and raise her eyebrows. Oh, Dotty, *plus ça change.*

Evelyn climbed out, thankful that the muscles in her arms still had
some grip. She picked up her towel and draped it across her shoulders,
walked back carefully across the dirt to the grass and let the sun dry her.

She lay down with blackbird song and wood pigeon call and bees in clover. She thought all of existence in this bucolic trance was a poem. Timeless, resolute, universal. The image would be repeated over the decades: women seeking solace, a safe place, bodies unclothed and held by nature. All the women she'd ever cared about had come with her here at some time or another. Not Livia, of course: that beautiful flyaway puffball, who'd deposited the seeds of first love across her life.

She'd first come here with Constance when the ponds had officially opened. She'd been forty-five, Constance well into her seventies; probably the same age, thought Evelyn, as she was now. By then, Constance had had mild success with her collection of poems titled *Everything*—the sequel to *Nothing*. The third collection, *Something*, would never emerge. She suffered a heart attack on the Gotthard Railway on what would have been her final trip to Florence. Crossing the Kerstelenbach Viaduct was often cited as taking one's breath away, and it did exactly that. They found her with a pen in her hand. Final thoughts on love, ultimately: "I shall remain astonished."

She had a militant following of women who wanted to put this line on her gravestone once they'd gotten permission to have her buried in the English Cemetery in Florence, as close to Barrett Browning as they could get. Of course, neither happened. Only Evelyn knew of the final wishes. Cremation. An early-morning boat ride on the Arno with one of the *renaioli*, the sand diggers. Sunlight, haze, memories. She was poured onto the sleepy reflection of a palazzo. Not a ripple. At one. At peace. Her home.

Evelyn looked up and shielded her eyes against the sun. Dotty waved as she came toward her. Dotty looked a trifle pensive. Sundowner, darling? she said.

Is it that time already? said Evelyn, reaching for her watch.

Clock's running a tad fast.

OK. I'll go and change.

———

The gods sent a chariot to Highgate West Hill, a black Austin FX3 that sped south until the green gave way to the white fringes of Bloomsbury and the red-brick mansion blocks of Fitzrovia.

Evelyn had noticed all afternoon there was something troubling Dotty. She raised Dotty's hand and kissed it. What's on your mind, my love?

Dotty sighed. My paint has turned against me again. I'm allergic.

Which one?

Titanium white. Always the troublemaker. Left me rather defeated, Lynny.

Oh, Dotty.

They crossed Oxford Street into Soho Square as the bells of St. Patrick's greeted them. Actors headed toward Shaftesbury Avenue, and prostitutes were taking an early-evening stroll before work laid them out for the night. The smell of coffee crept in through the window, and the clatter of vegetable trolleys rushing toward steamy kitchen doors. Italians and Maltese were smoking outside cafés, as music from jukeboxes brought life to their toes. Queer identity hid itself in the shadows of these dark streets and both women had, at some time, left an imprint of their body upon some unfamiliar bed; an addendum of promises, made for a lifetime but meant only for a night.

The cab turned in to Dean Street and pulled up outside Leoni's Quo Vadis. The restaurant was half an hour from opening, but the manager recognized the broad smiles of his regular patrons and opened the door and greeted them. He seated them at the best table over by the wall of paintings, where they could freely observe everyone who entered. Five minutes later, a tray of Negronis and a bowl of olives was heading their way. Evelyn stood up and said, My darling man, what a sight you are!

This'll put hairs on your chest, the barman said in his soft Celtic lilt.

Here's hoping, said Dotty, reaching for a drink as if her talent depended on it.

The women toasted one another, and before sitting back down, Dotty took out her glasses and scrutinized one of the paintings above their table. She said to Evelyn, I captured you, didn't I? Who you were, then. Who you were becoming. I count this portrait as my one true success.

Have there not been others?

Not like this, said Dotty, lifting it off the wall. Not like this.

It had been painted the summer after they first met—1924, maybe?—a forlorn study of Evelyn shipwrecked on a Roman pillow. Heartsore, facing the viewer. White dress, white sheets, glistening sun-bronzed face. Her hand shadowing her eyes against the dazzling glare. Dotty had painted sunlight straight from the tube.

Why was I so sad? asked Evelyn. Do you remember?

Livia?

Oh no. Livia was long gone. How strange the heart.

Listen to this, said Dotty.

On the back of the canvas, she had written a description of the day, which she read out loud: "Soundscape: bells, the squeal of swifts, Aunt Maria reciting the rosary. Time: midmorning. Weather: sun blazing, no respite, no cloud. Gasping."

They'd been staying with Evelyn's Italian aunt, whose chronic ill health, celibacy and wealth had guaranteed an unbroken connection with the Catholic Church. She had God's ear day and night. She also had a beautiful villa with high walls away from the gaze of the city. Because of this, Aunt Maria had long been a favored destination for both women until her slow decline and eventual death in the winter of 1943. It had been Evelyn who had closed the old woman's eyes. The villa was bequeathed, unsurprisingly, to a cloistered sect of nuns, which Dotty found highly erotic. The undervalued and wrongly attributed collection of still life paintings went to Evelyn.

At least you got the family fruit, Dotty wrote at the time.

Tell me again why you spent the duration of the war in Italy? said Dotty, finishing her Negroni. Evelyn's absence from wartime London was her go-to tease.

I was taking care of my aunt, said Evelyn. I've told you countless times, you shameless woman. I go where I'm needed. Always have. The result of being brought up by an ailing, critical mother.

You were brought up by your father.

She was a short umbilical drive away.

Spy, said Dotty, grinning.

Lot of bunkum.

Spy, spy, spy, said Dotty, pleased with herself, ordering another round of cocktails. Spy, she mouthed, and made her hand into a gun and shot the bread basket.

The two women were woefully underdressed for dinner and carried a faint whiff of pond, but their intention to leave was thwarted by Peppino, the owner, who insisted they stay by uncorking a saucy bottle of Bardolino and whispering tasty suggestions from the kitchen. When he left, Evelyn said, Do I look as tipsy as I feel?

No point asking me, dear, said Dotty, I've been talking to two of you for the last hour. Cheers, sweets.

They were eyed suspiciously, of course, by pre-theater diners until word got around who Dotty was. Her notoriety eclipsed any interest in the chef's specials and women in their elegance and pearls were the ones eager to catch Dotty's eye. Presenting themselves as the next muse, the next subject for a canvas, the next conquest. Dotty inhaled the attention, especially now that there was space.

I've left her, she said, plopping an olive in her mouth.

Ah. I *was* wondering, said Evelyn, exhaling loudly.

Caroline Beevor-Candy was the woman in question. Not her real name, obviously, because Dotty was too discreet to reveal the identities of all her paramours. But the story followed an ever-familiar pattern—that of Dotty's penchant for young married women. The subterfuge gave a much-needed energy boost to the postmenopausal hinterland of creative repetition. No matter what protestations Dotty made about the difference in age (often significant), she invariably fell in love with love and the inspiration it brought. To see a beautiful woman writhe in climax beneath her made her incredibly productive, and canvas after canvas shot through the Cork Street coffers in those early days of lust. Evelyn often wondered if the gallery itself procured prospective lovers for her friend, a guarantee against the artistic equivalent of writer's block.

It usually took six months for needy husbands and colicky children to become the inevitable reality, like the first leaf fall in September's sultry yawn. Rose tint gave way to Prussian green or blue black, and large seascapes of doom were painted over *Limbs with Summer Sweat*. Dotty looked again at the portrait of her friend. I've never painted so well, she said before replacing the painting on the wall. She downed a glass of grappa as if it was water and proceeded to deflate like a ruptured lung.

Evelyn knew what she needed to do. And she knew she was the only one who could do it. She reached across the table and grasped Dotty's hands. She said, How about Florence?

And glassy-eyed and a bit drunk, Dotty said, Would I like her?

The following day they were in Cook's travel agency in Mayfair.

C'mon, my dear Dotty, humor this ol' gal. The change of scenery will do you good.

Dotty lit a hangover cigarette and coughed. And with that, their mini-break was agreed: Train from Calais, change for the Gotthard Bahn and a journey through the Alps. Three days in Florence, three in Rome and a flight back to London Airport. What could be nicer? The cash register sang.

That night, a phone call. Evelyn climbed out of bed.

I'm taking my easel, said Dotty.

Dotty was on the mend, thought Evelyn. How exciting, she said.

Just charcoals and pencils. Back to basics. What do you think?

Marvelous idea.

You don't mind?

I would have suggested it had I thought you'd listen to me.

(Throaty laugh down the receiver.)

Dotty? It's all still there, you know. Who you were when you painted me.

Thanks, darling.

Sleep, now.

Evelyn replaced the receiver. She was wide awake again. She got back into bed and drank a glass of water. She picked up Eleanor Clark's *Rome and a Villa*. She read it whilst listening to rain on the window.

Five days later, Evelyn and Dotty set out for Europe, the most unlikely-looking pair: one sporting the workwear of a trawlerman, the other in a white cape and turban. They boarded the ferry at Folkestone and enjoyed a calm crossing of blue sky and blue water and white cresting gulls.

In Paris they changed from the Gare du Nord to the Gare de Lyon, taking a taxi on account of the easel, and then settled at a neighborhood bistro that Evelyn had known during wartime. Jules was within walking distance of the station and quite popular with wealthy families heading south. A robust wine list was its backbone, and no one got on the Pullman sleeper wide awake.

The three-hour stopover went by quickly. Late sunshine turned to dusk and eventually night, as platters of *coquilles* St. Jacques and oysters were lustily devoured with a crisp house wine that Dotty swore was Pouilly-Fumé. As Dotty swallowed the last of the bivalves, she said, Margaret someone.

And Evelyn said, Oh Lord. What about her?

Do you ever see her?

No, never, thank goodness, said Evelyn. Not since the debacle in Florence. What on earth made you think of her?

Don't turn around but there's a woman behind you who looks remarkably like her. I said don't turn around!

Oh my giddy giddy God! Look who it is! screeched Margaret someone across the terrace, a sound that made the French hate the English a little more.

Evelyn's smile turned rictus.

You look like you've had a stroke, said Dotty.

Maybe I'm having one, whispered Evelyn.

Margaret pulled out a chair and leaned across the table clumsily, putting the carafe of wine in peril. (At times like these, Dotty's reflexes were razor-sharp.)

Margaret said, Evelyn Skinner. How long has it been? Ten years? You don't look a day older.

You know Dotty, don't you? said Evelyn as if she'd just learned to speak.

Oh yes. Still up to old tricks?

Well, you know what they say about old dogs.

Naughty you for not contacting me after Florence, said Margaret, turning back to Evelyn. But I'm not one to hold a grudge. You're not heading back there, are you?

Oh no, said Evelyn and Dotty in unison. No no no.

Well, I'm on my way *back* from a little tour, said Margaret. Had a splendid time at the Verrocchio exhibition, don't you know? I've been traveling with a new (pause) *friend*.

And she turned to her table and smiled at a sweet blond demure lamb. The word "slaughter" came to Evelyn's mind.

What? said Margaret.

What? said Evelyn.

You said "slaughter," said Margaret.

I did?

Yes, you did.

Oh. I meant, that's not Meredith Slaughter, is it?

No, no. Myrtle Forbright. We share a love of ornithology. Who's Meredith Slaughter?

I don't know, said Evelyn.

But you just mentioned her.

Evelyn thinks she's having a stroke, said Dotty, nudging Evelyn under the table.

Really? said Margaret.

Evelyn nodded.

Isn't that serious? said Margaret.

Not if it's a small one, said Dotty, finishing her glass of wine and lighting a cigarette.

Should we do something? said Margaret.

Probably, said Dotty, blowing out a long plume of smoke. She turned to Evelyn and held the cigarette tantalizingly within reach. Can you . . . ? she said.

And Evelyn stretched out her arm, took the cigarette and inhaled.

She's going to be fine, said Dotty.

Phew, said Margaret. Where were we?

Well, I'm not sure where you were, said Dotty, looking at her watch. But we've got a train to catch. Cheerio, Margaret! Safe travels home.

On the dot of nine, the train inched through the dark and left the lights of Paris, heading toward Switzerland.

In the sleeper, Dotty climbed the ladder to the upper bunk and slid around in her silk pajamas. Evelyn checked her bed for fleas and was glad not to find anything with more legs than her. She poured out two measures of brandy before lights-out.

And Margaret someone? said Dotty. What on earth were you thinking? she said, turning the focus on Evelyn and her less than successful affairs for a change.

I wasn't, said Evelyn. We met not long after Gabriela died. At a dull soirée of Muscadet and attribution. I was incredibly limp that night and Margaret was—she was—well, she was—

A caliper? said Dotty.

Yes. Yes, that's the word. And she was rather vigorous in her love-making. It, sort of, woke me up.

Literally? Metaphorically?

A little of both, I think. I was in grief.

I know you were.

Such a long time ago now. She used to buy me long-lasting flowers.

Carnations?

Yes.

Well, let that be a lesson. Night, darling. See you in Switz.

Sleep came fast to Evelyn and brought with it not a dream but a vivid memory to the pillow: a dinner with her father at Quo Vadis. The atmosphere was as convivial as ever, despite a radical shift in father-daughter relations after his mistress/muse, Gabriela Cortez, had formed a passionate attachment to Evelyn. Evelyn was as willing and enthusiastic as ever in this new alliance. She had never been so happy. Father and daughter toasted one another, and at the end of the dinner, Evelyn handed her father a letter that she'd written in Florence, twenty-five years before. She couldn't explain why he was receiving it only then. She had mislaid it. And they had mislaid one another many times across the years. It was about love. He read it there and then. He was silent and thoughtful. He reached out and kissed his daughter's hand and nothing more was said.

The next day, he drove her to Gabriela's small flat with her bags.

You have my blessing, H.W. said. But please—two conditions.

The first? she said.

That you do not discuss me the man, only me the painter.

She rolled her eyes and laughed. And secondly?

That I paint you both.

Not in flagrante delicto, she said sternly.

Post? he said.

Conditions were met, and the painting was highly celebrated and bought by the National Gallery after a generous bequest by a dead Lord Somebodyorother.

Evelyn and Gabriela were together for ten years. They lived in a well-decorated nest on the edge of Bloomsbury where Evelyn still resided. In 1937, Gabriela Cortez died fighting Franco. She would be Evelyn's last great love. Not long after the funeral, one weekend in May, Evelyn stood in front of the painting in a busy National Gallery and wept. Dotty was by her side.

In the middle of the night, Evelyn awoke, aware that the train was stationary. She peeked from behind the blind and followed a lantern moving along the platform until two men found each other. She thought them to be the watchmen. She couldn't recognize the town they were in—much of a muchness, small stations at night—but that was half the thrill. The room felt chill all of a sudden, and she pulled the blanket up high, and wrapped Dotty's jumper around her head. Settled into the comfortable sound of her friend's deep slumber. She knew when she next woke up, Switzerland would be pressing itself against the window.

The train kept to schedule and, as predicted, crossed the border at six o'clock the following morning. Crisp mountain air commingled with the smell of coffee and eggs and—

Is that sausage? asked Evelyn from the lower bunk.

Definitely porky, said Dotty.

And propelled by years of lack, the two women were up, washed and dressed by the time the next round of meat hit the sizzling blackened pan.

The ever-changing sight of mountains and ravines and meadows stunned them, pulled them into an interiority they would later share in Florence, perhaps, or Rome. Silenced by the magnificent Alps, by the feat of engineering that cut through the Gotthard Pass, Dotty retreated to an empty corner of the carriage with a sketchbook and charcoals, and the hours fell away in a series of carefully sculpted lines and shading, of abstract versions of rock formations or sharp drops, the microscopic detail often appearing as a face or shell in the mastery of her craft.

Evelyn let her mind drift, fizzing, as it was, with fact and fiction because she knew the journey so well. Could anticipate every incline and shift in speed before it happened. The train clattered and entered the Gotthard tunnel. Evelyn closed her eyes and met the dark with dark. At what she imagined to be the midpoint, the name of Louis Favre came to mind, the man whose company had begun the nine-mile-long tunnel back in 1872, eight years before her birth. Two crews had bored and blasted into the rock from opposite sides of the mountain, intending to meet 4.5 miles underneath, and when they did eventually meet, were found to be only thirteen inches off. Favre was four months dead by then. Stress and bankruptcy had killed him. But at the point of connection, a canister that held his image was passed through the gap. A promise fulfilled that he would be the first person ever to have passed through the tunnel.

Evelyn was still subsumed by the keen brilliance of it all when a lurch and a clatter shook her, and sunlight fell upon her eyelids again. The train was through the tunnel. She brushed away the light dusting of smuts from her dark jumper and turned back and waved to Dotty. She opened a bottle of Evian water and drank. How excited she felt, how invigorated. Adventure, the best medicine.

At approximately five that afternoon, the train arrived at Santa Maria Novella station. Evelyn was one of the first onto the platform and exclaimed as she always did: *Firenze! Amore mio!* And the city, of course, answered her with bells.

By five fifteen p.m. the women were in a taxi heading to the demure charms of the Pensione Picci, a small guesthouse along the Lungarno Corsini, and by five forty-five p.m. they had checked into their twin room with a view, with newly installed en suite bathroom (Fancy that, said Dotty).

By six thirty p.m. they had unpacked, and by seven p.m. they had pulled up a couple of uncomfortable wicker chairs and were watching clouds pass nonchalantly over the dome of San Frediano in Cestello, listening to the roll of trams and the whine of Vespas below.

They were weary from traveling, and as the sun continued its journey west, casting shadows and drawing out colors across the water, they sipped perfectly chilled Spumante offered gratis to every returning guest.

Because we know you have a choice, said Enzo, the proprietor, in his gruff Florentine accent.

Not at this price, said Evelyn.

The next day, Evelyn woke early, flung the shutters wide and praised the light. Dotty raised her head from the pillow and said, Good God! What's that?

It's the morning, said Evelyn.

It was an unhurried start, and by the time they got downstairs they were forced to seek breakfast elsewhere after an altercation at the buffet table involving the last boiled egg. Evelyn knew of a neighborhood café in the vicinity of the Pensione Simi, although the hotel itself had long closed its doors. And with coffee beckoning, they set out along the river toward the Uffizi and Dotty's first day of sketching. The easel was lightly balanced on Dotty's shoulder, nudging the battered panama she'd found during a visit to the Alhambra. Evelyn carried the foldaway fisherman's stool against her chest. She kept complaining it smelled of carp.

In the colonnade of the Uffizi, Dotty settled her things in the corner beneath the statues of Galileo and Pier Antonio Micheli whilst Evelyn went to look for a *carabiniere* to bribe, so that Dotty's day would remain hassle-free.

By the time Evelyn returned, the easel was erected, and the large sketchbook placed upon it, and Dotty was looking thoroughly incognito with her panama pulled low. She intended to give the portraits away for free; art for art's sake, she said: an act of joy, craft and generosity.

Unsigned, obviously, though, she said.

Obviously, said Evelyn, who scribbled an explanation of the proceedings in Italian and English, to encourage the first sitters before word eventually got around about the giveaway.

Evelyn left Dotty to her first portrait, a middle-aged husband and wife from Connecticut (Hank and Gwen) who had, the day before, suffered terribly at the hands of a caricaturist.

She walked out into the sunshine, suddenly unsure what to do with the hours ahead. There was a moment's pause before she turned left. Had she turned right, however, she would have bumped into the man who had been on her mind at that very moment. For Ulysses Temper was standing in a café near the Ponte Vecchio, drinking an espresso, waiting for Cressy to come by on his Moto Guzzi Falcone.

Evelyn crossed over the Piazza dei Giudici, where once had stood a *tiratoio*, one of the vast sheds in which damp wool was stretched out to dry. Evelyn had never seen this lost capsule to Renaissance times, but Constance had as a child—Constance had written a poem about it—

before the building was destroyed in the mid-1800s to make way for the chamber of commerce. The steps were still there, though, the ones that led from the *tiratoio* to the river, where the process of washing the wool, and the rinsing and dyeing, took place. The wool industry had given Florence her wealth, a quarter of the population employed in the industry at the height of its fame. The washers, the carders, the combers, the weavers, the dyers, the spinners. All paid a pittance, of course, until the great revolt of 1378.

Evelyn turned left up Via dei Benci.

They had been packed into a notorious slum on what was once marshy, squalid land. Right here, thought Evelyn. Right where I'm walking now. Unsurprisingly, the Franciscans—one of the newly arrived mendicant orders—chose to settle there and establish a church to help the poor. And just like that, as if she was leading a walking tour, the Basilica of Santa Croce rose on her right. What timing, she thought. She veered across the piazza, through the parked cars, and made her way toward the statue of Dante. She always had the feeling he was pleased to see her.

She found the herb shop by San Simone that sold great quantities of dried sage and she bought a smallish bushel for Dotty, who liked to burn it in her studio to clear a path for the muse.

In Piazza Sant'Ambrogio, had she had more of an appetite she would have bought a midmorning snack of *lampredotto* (the long queues vouched for the quality), but she opted for a handful of Francesca apples instead, a tiny ancient variety with the most delicious perfume. Ate one straight-away in the doorway of a workshop where she watched a man carving out the body of a violin. On leaving the area, she acquired a button for her cardigan from a beggarwoman. It didn't match the other four, which were green, but it was striking.

Dotty was packing up her easel when Evelyn turned the corner.

Someone looks happy, she said.

What a morning, said Dotty. Seven studies, I tell you! And a couple of them were rather good. You?

Wandering, mostly. Happily surprised at the speed of reconstruction—the city looks gloriously intact. I bought some postcards. Choose which ones you'd like. Oh, and this . . . And Evelyn held out the bundle of sage. Dotty stopped what she was doing.

You darling! she said.

Evelyn looked about at the statues that occupied the niches and said, The *tre corone fiorentine*: the three Florentine crowns. Poets, of course. Dante here, Petrarch over there and Boccaccio. What's odd about Dante?

Is this a trick question, Lynny?

Not at all.

Go on, tell me.

Spelt his name wrong.

That's careless, said Dotty.

And the laurels about his head.

Was he never a poet laureate?

No. Boccaccio would have had him as one. Petrarch not.

Bastardo, said Dotty, handing the footstool to her friend.

They moved on through toward the Piazza della Signoria and Dotty said, You'll never guess who I saw.

Who? said Evelyn.

Hartley Ramsden and Margot Eates.

Good Lord. Did they recognize you?

No, thank goodness. Oh, and Vi Trefusis was with them, she added.

Vi? With Hartley and Margot?

Dotty nodded.

Well, I never. That's a turn-up.

Talking some piffle wiffle about Cimabue's *Crucifix*. Had I not been concentrating on the magnificent profile of the young woman from Norwich, I might have launched myself into the river.

Lunch was at a table overlooking the Loggia dei Lanzi and Palazzo Vecchio and consisted of a first-rate *spaghetti ai carciofi*, followed by tripe and potatoes and a carafe of red wine, then *gelati*—chocolate and crema—finished with the requisite espresso.

Evelyn turned her attention to the table: How the sun had cast its light and forced shadow across the debris of lunch. The jug of wine, the ashtray, the cigarette nubs with their faint ring of red lipstick. The vase of wisteria clusters, the sticky tidemark around the espresso cups, the image muted by the haze of dust falling from the makeshift trellis. A story of lunch, yes; but also a story of them.

They were the last to leave. Evelyn placed a few notes on the saucer and stood up. *Andiamo, cara!*

Oh, let's not go, said Dotty. It'll be cocktail hour soon.

All the more reason, said Evelyn. Come on, Dotty. Up up up.

Dotty picked up her easel and knocked over a couple of flower arrangements as she left.

Keep walking, said Evelyn. I left a nice tip.

They hadn't gotten far before a small child stopped in front of Evelyn and screamed, Pinocchio!

Good God, where?! said Evelyn, horrified.

He's behind you, said Dotty in pantomime mode.

Evelyn turned. The shop had a display of the puppet boy in various guises.

Not a fan? said Dotty as they moved away.

Not as a child, that's for certain, said Evelyn. I found him to be a maniac. And when he murdered the talking cricket, I was quite affected. For me it was the silencing of truth. Politically speaking, of course.

Of course, said Dotty.

And we know where that leads.

How old were you, darling?

Nine. Thereabouts.

You never were a child, were you, Lynny?

No, not really, Dotty. I was reading Vasari's *Lives of the Artists* by then.

The river came into sight. Dotty said, Sweet little film, though, right?

Evelyn stopped.

You didn't like it? said Dotty.

No, I didn't, said Evelyn. Pinocchio is a poor provincial Tuscan boy and he was forced to cast off the clothes of his identity in order to wear the same white gloves as Mickey Mouse. *White gloves*, Dotty. Sometimes I think I'm the only one who notices these things.

That's because you are, said Dotty, and she took her friend's arm and led her west toward their *pensione*.

Did you see how that woman back there looked at me? said Dotty.

I did.

I've still got it.

You never lost it.

I think I did. Just a bit.

Not for long, though.

No. Not for long.

Midnight and they'd just turned off the light. The sound of a match being struck and Dotty's face flared yellow in the darkness. She sat up and reached for an ashtray. She said, I wanted to ask you, Lynny. Earlier when I was waiting for you, I went to the Loggia to sketch the statues. In particular, the Giambologna.

Which one? said Evelyn. *Hercules* or the *Rape*?

The *Rape*—

One of the greats—

Isn't it? I felt aroused.

You're supposed to.

I did wonder. But it troubled me.

Evelyn said, Giambologna knew exactly what he was doing, Dotty. He understood the erotic dance as much as he understood the response. The struggle between idealized man versus the mortal. It's as if he's watching us looking at it. It's quite a bravura performance, really. But context is everything—and the long, heavy hand of religion was every-where. This statue, more than anything, represents the artistic freedom of the Renaissance. The *freedom* to think and feel outside of the Church.

It was only with the recuperation of the great classical tradition—subjects of classical antiquity—that artists could free themselves from the constraints of Christianity and so present narratives of Good and Evil. Bloody and exalting, thrilling and—yes—arousing.

Dotty handed the cigarette across the darkness to Evelyn. The tip glowed orange. Evelyn said, I think it's also worth noting at this point that without Giambologna, Bernini wouldn't have been Bernini.

Wouldn't he?

No. And then where would we have been?

Where indeed? said Dotty. Is there nothing you don't know, Lynny?

Oh, plenty, said Evelyn, stubbing out the cigarette. I don't know much about motor racing.

Not such a loss, though, said Dotty. Night night, sweets.

The next morning, the two women were up early. Dotty jettisoned the easel that day for a more mobile life with footstool and large drawing pad. They pocketed the last two boiled eggs on their way out, and took coffee in Via dei Neri at a bustling café full of stylish young men and women. Evelyn couldn't decide whether or not to go over to the Piazza del Carmine to see the Masaccio frescoes, but chose not to in the end. Had she listened to that quiet nudge inside her, that impulse to go south, she would have crossed into Piazza Santo Spirito at the same time as Ulysses, who was on his way to his workshop. They would have stopped and looked at one another in disbelief and she would have said, It's you, isn't it? and he would've said, Yes, it's me. She would have gone toward him and embraced him. They would have been momentarily speechless at the way fate had summoned them once again. They would have walked arm in arm toward Michele's café and would have sat down and ordered coffee, and Ulysses in faltering Italian would have explained to Michele who Evelyn was, how they'd previously met, how he'd never been happier to see anyone in his life. She would have commented on his language ability. And she would finally have said, So tell me, Ulysses—how is the good captain?

This would have been the version of events, *had* Evelyn gone south.

But what she did that morning was to go and buy a newspaper, *La Nazione*, from a nearby stand. She took the bus up to Fiesole. The almond trees were in blossom when she made the ascent to the convent of San Francesco. The roses were pink and fragrant in hedgerows, the view across the Mugnone valley exhilarating. She sat and read her newspaper overlooking an olive grove, but there was always the gnawing feeling that she should have been somewhere else, seeing someone else.

By the time she returned to the colonnade, Dotty was sketching the portraits of two handsome older men—longtime partners, obviously. It was a stunning likeness, four shades of pencil on tinted paper. They didn't demand a signature, and yet when they took the rolled picture from her, one bent low and whispered, We know who you are— thank you.

Evelyn took Dotty to lunch over by the Pitti Palace, at a small *trattoria* close to Casa Guidi, former home to the poets Browning, where they shared a *bistecca*. An afternoon walk in the Boboli Gardens proved a more sensible alternative to another carafe of red wine.

They walked slowly up through the amphitheater, the once-upon-a-time quarry that had supplied the stone for Signor Pitti's extraordinary palace. Up past Neptune's Fountain and the terraces to the top. And there, Florence revealed her splendor. Golden light, the precursor to dusk, crowned them, and they appeared exalted, happy. Evelyn sat and leaned against a wall and closed her eyes and Dotty captured her there, in that moment, in a portrait of equal tenderness and soul as the one hanging in the restaurant where the plan to visit Italy had first been devised.

They bathed and slept on their return to the *pensione*. For an hour Evelyn watched the linen curtains billow and fall and matched her breathing to the pulse of fabric. The sound of trams outside, the birds, a burst of laughter from below, and her thoughts were of people no longer living, and it wasn't an act of nostalgia but one of love of reminiscence, of the people who had made her *her*. The privilege and the freedom they had brought her. Beauty and gratitude entwined forever in a closely woven fabric of sympathetic names: Constance, Dotty, Thaddeus Collins, H.W., Gabriela, Livia, and of course her mother. Her mother was the knot that stopped the fraying. That's what she learned later, and learned it the hard way, too late to say thank you truly. A woman whose Italian lineage was a stunning counterpoint to the pale, judgmental society she at first encountered. Until the night she met H. W. Skinner, as unconventional a man as she'd ever meet, who had given his heart to countless women—gossip she really should have taken seriously, because she ended up with a husband whose artistic soul she could never own, and neither was she ever the muse. She was trapped by a form of courtly love, Church imposed, whilst her body cried out for wings. He held out a daily offering of feathers and wax, but she couldn't do it, couldn't leap. For she could only see all that she wasn't.

Her currency, in the end, was money. She gave to others the freedom she could never take for herself. She bought her daughter that first rail ticket, a gateway into her thrilling twenty-second year.

Evelyn remembered the journey from the rail station to the Pensione Simi, down dark streets teeming with life and smells and across *trecento* squares where she saw statues come to life and where the bells called the medieval dead to rise. A conspiracy of beauty everywhere. The city threw aside its cloak and introduced itself to her, and she met it with eyes wide and heart thumping and openmouthed. She stumbled clumsily from the cab into the vestibule of the hotel. She couldn't speak. It wasn't being struck dumb by beauty per se, but the acknowledgment that if such beauty existed, then so did the opposite. And in that brief moment, she'd felt the opposite.

Evelyn climbed out of bed and Dotty stirred. She said, Morning, darling, and Evelyn said, It's still evening, Dotty.

Evelyn opened the cupboard and put on a long black dress, loose fitting with three-quarter sleeves, and reached down for her Greek-style sandals. She pinned her hair and painted her mouth a vivid orange. She stood at the window, watching the city move about in dusky elegance.

The sky appeared as an ocean, the clouds as waves, and an all-pervading stillness had settled, the lowering sun an image of the rising dawn.

Less elegantly, behind her, Dotty was in her underwear with her legs up against the wall. Look at these things, said Dotty, slapping her thighs. Who could say no?

Evelyn said, We are approaching the time "when the fly yields to the mosquito." "*Come la mosca cede a la zanzara,*" and she closed the shutters, casting the room into shadow and cool.

That's rather eloquent, said Dotty.

It is. Dante's *Inferno.*

Dotty threw a glance at the clock and said, We are actually approaching the hour when water yields to the cocktail. *Come l'acqua cede a la cocktaila.* And she rolled away from the wall and unexpectedly met gravity. She fell off the bed with a thump.

Harry's Bar was tucked behind the Palazzo Corsini. It bore no relation to the more famous Harry's Bar in Venice and had been opened the year before by a man called Enrico, known as Harry or Henry to his English-speaking friends. He had tended the bar at the Hotel Excelsior during wartime and was the man who had seen Evelyn at her lowest ebb. And standing in the doorway, looking into the dark interior, Evelyn felt nervous at an encounter with her past.

She needn't have. Enrico noticed her immediately, said how she hadn't changed at all, offered his hand and kissed hers ceremoniously. How I wondered what had happened to my favorite Miss Skinner, he said, and led her and Dotty over to a corner table where they had both privacy and a view of the room. He brought them what he'd always brought Evelyn—*biciclettas!*—You are a dark horse, Lynny!

Cin cin! Clink of glass.

Evelyn told Dotty that back in '44 she'd had to wait a month before she'd been able to enter the city with the Allied Military Government, and when she had, she'd wept. The buildings that had once overhung the river were gone. The ancient quarter, the medieval towers, all gone.

She could see straight across the river to Orsanmichele and the Duomo, an uninterrupted corridor never deemed possible. What had been the heart of Dante's Florence had been reduced overnight to mountainous piles of smoking rubble. An act of destruction purely to halt the Allied advance, which of course it failed to do. There was no military justification for any of it, said Evelyn. She remembered the people stumbling about incredulous and dazed by the violence inflicted upon their gentle city.

She'd gone to work immediately at the headquarters of the Superintendency, which had relocated to the Palazzo Pitti. The Superintendency had overseen the evacuation of the artworks in the first place, and she made notes of works found, works looted, works damaged. She began the repatriation of statues and paintings to their sacred ground. Occasionally, she collaborated with the art historian Berenson and his cabal, but mostly, she kept to herself. By then, something had happened to her, to her soul. She had been eroded by war. An all-consuming weariness she could find no way back from. Nights were spent quietly drinking in the Hotel Excelsior, watched over by Enrico, who knew when to bring her another drink long before she knew she needed one herself.

Dotty lit them both a cigarette and said, That soldier you met.

Ulysses?

Yes. What was it about him?

Evelyn thought for a moment.

I don't know. I've often asked myself that. His kindness? The scar on his lip? His eyebrows, his smile?

You sound a little in love, my darling.

Hold that thought, said Evelyn, and she raised her glass and drank. She said, Two years after Gabriela died, I was in Rome looking after Aunt Maria. When Maria died, it was as if Gaby had died all over again. Ulysses's enthusiasm for life was a panacea. His optimism, his surety that he wasn't going to die. As if everything that mattered to him, he'd somehow protected from war. How was that possible? He was invincible, Dotty. Marvelously so. I wasn't. I had escaped Margaret and was waiting on the roadside for what? Death, I think. A way out, no matter how permanent. And then along came life. That priceless, life-affirming moment with a Renaissance masterpiece would have been nothing without him and the good captain. It was about the complete moment. Was I in love with him? Maybe a little. When the bombs fell overhead, and he held my hands and shouted against the tumult, Not today, Evelyn! It's not going to be us today. His faith was compelling, Dotty. I was young again. I *felt* young again. I will be forever grateful.

You could look for him, said Dotty.

Why on earth would he remember an old woman like me?

Because you're unforgettable, Evelyn Skinner.

The following day brought departure. Dotty sketched across the morning and was thoroughly worn out by twelve, so came back to the *pensione* for a nap. Evelyn left Dotty asleep in the room with a note on the dressing table weighted down by an apple. Evelyn had packed and wanted one last look at the city before the train journey down toward the sprawl of Rome and its raucous heart.

She walked out into the glinting light and slid her sunglasses onto her face. She wasn't quick to her destination, sidetracked, as always, by trails of wisteria cascading over the walls of private villas or the shy splendor of a magnolia tree on the verge of blossoming. Art and life intertwined. The predominance of blue-mauve flowers in and around the city astonished her, a compelling stream from February to May. Violets, wisteria, iris . . . not forgetting the summer cornflower, which had often been a noble bed for her and a her, in some secluded meadow, in some secluded decade. The blue against a burned umber or ochre wall, the blue against lush grass, against a white linen shirt unbuttoned and splayed, a blue of such staggering intensity, the memory too easy to find in the opaque past. Flesh and love always next to blue.

Such a precocious display of spring.

Evelyn knew where she was going. Had always known where she would end up the moment the trip had been planned—the two soldiers never far from her thoughts. She wondered at times if they were alive or dead, and always settled them firmly in life. The other was unthinkable.

In the cool dark of the church, frankincense pricked her nose, and her skin reacted to the fall in temperature. On her right, the Capponi Chapel and the painting that undid the years. The faces of the two men by her side. Darnley saying, Ulysses Temper, Miss Evelyn Skinner, I'd like you to meet Pontormo's *Deposition from*—

Do you want to go in?

Evelyn turned, surprised by the question delivered to her in English. Behind her stood a girl wearing a railwayman's cap. Nine? Ten, maybe? Dark hair, high fringe and a sweet, intense face full of questioning. Her sunglasses were hooked in the neck of her T-shirt and she was holding a scroll of tinted paper that looked ever so familiar to Evelyn.

How did you know I was English? said Evelyn.

Because you didn't cross yourself when you came in, said the girl.

Oh, well spotted!

So what do you say? I have a key.

How fortuitous, said Evelyn. And do you also have a name?

Sometimes kid, sometimes Alys. You?

Always Evelyn.

Alys looked about before unlocking the gate. Come on then, she said. Stick close. And Evelyn did as she was told. She went toward the painting and closed her eyes.

You're not even looking at it, said Alys.

No, I'm smelling it, said Evelyn. The olfactory bulb passes scent close to the amygdala and hippocampus, both areas in the brain that deal with emotion and memory.

I didn't know that, said Alys.

Evelyn stepped back from the painting and said, Do you come here often, Gatekeeper?

Sometimes. You?

Not often, no. I last saw this painting during the war.

Which one?

Touché, kid, said Evelyn.

I was born at the end of the war.

That war, then. That's when I saw it. Not here though, she added.

Not that long ago, then.

No. Not that long ago. And what do you have there? said Evelyn, knowing full well what the roll of paper would reveal.

A picture. I had it done this morning. And Alys unrolled the portrait and held it up next to her face. It's me, she said.

Oh, there's no doubt about that.

And then Evelyn noticed it. In the right-hand corner. A signature. But Dotty's *real* signature. She had given the child a valuable gift.

I made her sign it, said Alys. She wasn't going to. And then she did. It might not be her real name.

Oh, I'm sure it is.

Do you think it's worth anything?

Oh yes.

A lot?

Best keep it safe.

I'll have it framed, then.

That's the spirit, said Evelyn, and she looked down at her watch.

Do you have to be somewhere, Evelyn?

I do. I have a date with Rome.

Now?

In a while.

I'll lock up, then, said Alys, and she pulled the gate to and locked it. She placed the key on the edge of the font.

I like the cloud, said the kid.

Evelyn stopped.

That cloud. And the kid pointed back to the painting.

Do you? said Evelyn. I knew someone who liked the cloud, too, once. And she looked at the child for a resemblance to the soldier from her past. She brushed the thought from her head. Couldn't be. And she opened the heavy wooden door and stepped out into the sunlight. She put on her sunglasses and the kid did the same. They walked toward the Ponte Vecchio, stride for stride, and Evelyn said how much she liked the kid's cap.

I got it after seeing Fellini's *I Vitelloni*.

And did you enjoy the film?

Yes I did. A nice change from neorealism.

Had enough of it?

It did what it needed to do.

And what was that?

Change the rules of filmmaking forever. I think *Bicycle Thieves* will be known as one of the great films, said Alys.

I think you might be right, said Evelyn.

That end sequence in *I Vitelloni*, you know when Moraldo's on the train and the camera moves through his friends' bedrooms? It's how it is, isn't it? Saying good-bye. All the people you leave.

Have you had to say good-bye?

Just the once.

They were separated momentarily by a dawdling group of tourists on the bridge and Alys had to run around them to catch up. She said, Do you know a lot, Evelyn?

A fair amount.

You look like you do.

That'll be the white turban.

Why are all the statues men?

Evelyn laughed. Ah yes, that is problematic. Short or long answer?

When's your train?

Fair point. Short, then. Because men sculpted them, cast them, forged them. Renaissance Italy was a world of men and a world for men. A world that advocated the inferiority of women.

Gosh.

Gosh indeed. Evelyn stopped at the midpoint of the bridge. Come here, she said.

Kid went toward her and looked out across the river toward the dark hills. Evelyn pointed.

There—the Biblioteca. A showcase for men. There—the Palazzo

Vecchio, showcase for men. There—the Institute of the History of Science, a showcase for men. Over there—the Uffizi Gallery, a showcase for men. History has erased the unseen, said Evelyn. And we will never know the contribution women made to that unique time.

Where were they then? said kid.

Evelyn looked down at her young pupil. How old are you? she said.

Nearly nine. But they say I have an old head on young shoulders.

Do they? Well, they say I have the opposite.

Kid laughed. You're funny, she said.

So where were the women? Well, that depended on class. Inside, mostly, if you were wealthy and married. Considerable time in the birthing room, hoping to produce male heirs. A constant succession of pregnancies from your midteens to your forties. You'd also be expected to run the household, of course. Organizing the servants. Sewing. Making bread. Making fires. That was a woman's life, kid. Or the convent—the only available career for a woman. That was the choice.

You're not selling this life to me, Evelyn.

No. I'm not, am I? Evelyn laughed.

Didn't women paint as well?

They weren't allowed to. Actively forbidden from participating in the arts or sciences. Unless, of course, your father was a painter; then you had access to materials and a workshop. But it was only the convent, really, that provided space for self-expression. Creative women from good Florentine families often found their way there for that purpose. Here's a name for you, kid: Plautilla Nelli. She was the first female Renaissance painter and was very successful. She, in effect, ran a school for female artists. She couldn't sell her own work, but the convent could. She was a radical and defied the conventions of her time. And no one knows about her.

I do now, though.

Yes, you do now. The bridge that used to be over there? said Evelyn, pointing.

The Ponte alle Grazie?

Well, once upon a time, it had small dwelling places and oratories attached on struts that overlooked the river. Solitary hermitages for worship. Devout nuns known as Le Murate—"the walled-up ones"—used to live their entire lives in tiny rooms in these buildings without ever going outside.

Never? said the kid.

Never. And they prayed for the city. And their food was delivered through small windows that could only be accessed by ladders placed on the riverbed. Holy Communion was received every Sunday in the same manner. Their whole lives imprisoned—or cloistered, depending on your point of view. The bridge was eventually rebuilt and Le Murate transferred to a convent in 1424.

That's a lot to take in.

Isn't it? said Evelyn. And then the convent became a jail. Which it still is. Symbolic and slightly ironic.

Kid stayed silent, thinking.

Evelyn said, We'll never know the inner life lived out within those walls. The what-could-have-been. We have so much more freedom than those who went before. And you will have so much more than me.

Evelyn looked once more at her watch. My dear child, I need to get a taxi. My train's at five.

Shall we shake hands and say good-bye then? said the kid.

Let's. And Evelyn held out her hand. Oh, here's another name for you: Artemisia Gentileschi. You'd like her, she said. Full of rage. Thank you, kind Gatekeeper. It's been so much fun. Till we meet again! And she turned and walked away.

Evelyn! shouted kid.

Evelyn stopped.

Convent or marriage?

Oh, convent! said Evelyn.

Me too!

So long, kid, said Evelyn, and she threw her one last wave before heading toward a stationary taxicab.

So long, Evelyn, said kid, and she held the tube of paper to her eye and watched the taxi disappear from sight.

Ulysses looked up from his week-old English newspaper when he heard the slap slap slap of Alys's unruly run across the stones. He watched her push past a group of tourists pointing to the parrot on top of the statue of Cosimo R. She was out of breath when she got to him. He pulled her to him and kissed her head. Hair smelled of sweat and sun.

You OK? he said, and she nodded and sat down. The terrace was inching toward shade and he handed her his sweater. She brought it to her nose as she always did. One day she wouldn't. For now, he was hers and she was his. Michele came out and placed two beers on the table and asked about Cressy. Ulysses said he would be down in a minute.

The kid picked up Ulysses's beer and brought it to her lips. She still didn't like it, she just wanted to grow up fast. She tore a piece of bread in half and ate ravenously. She wanted to leave school and beat up the boys who laughed at her. She wanted to speak Italian fluently and get a job and take a train like Evelyn and look back at countless miles of late nights and adventures. She couldn't imagine herself old, but she could imagine herself no longer young.

She put down the glass and wiped her mouth. Ulysses was watching her as if he could see those thoughts.

What you got there? he said.

She held up the tube of paper and said, I'm going to wait for Cressy before I show you. It's worth waiting for, she added.

Cressy calling out across the stones. Ulysses pulled out a chair for him and Cressy reached for the beer before he sat down. Fixed it, he said.

Aw, Cressy—

Took me all afternoon, but . . .

The kid nudged him with her head. She was the one who'd found the old levered espresso machine in the flea market.

And what's this? said Cressy, tapping the paper tube on Alys's lap.

She wouldn't show me till you came down, said Ulysses.

This, she said—untying the string and rolling it out—is me. I didn't have to pay for it.

Cressy whistled. Well, that is a beauty.

Ulysses frowned. D. Cunningham?

We'll have to get that framed, said Cressy, and he took the portrait from her and carefully rerolled it.

The Dorothy Cunningham? said Ulysses.

I don't know if she's a *the*, but the signature's real, said kid. A lady told me it was—

Dorothy Cunningham was here?

Over there in the colonnade—

What lady told you? said Ulysses.

When I was in the church.

What church?

There's a mighty lot of questions going on here, said the kid, pretending to drink Cressy's beer. She wiped her mouth and said, The church where the pink and blue painting is. The one we went into with Pete. I followed an old lady inside because she looked interesting. She was dressed all in white.

Maybe she was a nun? said Cress.

She had a white turban on her head.

Maybe not then, said Cress.

And I showed her my picture. And then she said she had to go because she had a date with Rome.

A date with Rome? said Cressy. Fancy that.

Five o'clock train. I told her I liked the cloud. And then Evelyn—that was her name—she said—

Ulysses was out of the chair before she could finish. Eat without me! he shouted as he ran across the square in the direction of the river. Along the Lungarno Guicciardini people stopped to watch. He dodged cars and cyclists and came dangerously close to a tram on the Ponte alla Carraia. His lungs were bursting, and his legs burning; *Scusi, scusi*, he shouted. Through Piazza Goldoni and up Via dei Fossi. Into Piazza di

Santa Maria Novella, crossing tramlines, dodging workers, people staring, shouting.

I'm coming, Evelyn, I know it's you.

He ran up to the railway station, three steps at a time, and bent double at the departure board, a right old dog pant. He saw the platform number and raced toward it, and people were shouting and gesticulating and he's a liability in crowds. At the platform gate, he saw the train slowly moving off, and he begged to go through, and the train accelerated and he was off again and his legs were so tired, and he managed a last burst of speed and he thought he might just get there, might just—

But the platform ran out.

And the train was gone.

He sat down. A policeman stood over him as he tried to get his breath.

On the train, Dotty had been watching events out of the window. When Evelyn returned to the carriage, Dotty said to her, I've just seen something extraordinary. A young man was running for the train as if his life depended on it.

Love, said Evelyn.

What else? said Dotty.

Evelyn leaned across her friend to look out. I don't see anything, she said.

Too late, said Dotty, and she sat back and unwrapped a mortadella sandwich. Bite?

No thank you.

You look a bit forlorn, said Dotty.

I feel as if I've left something behind, said Evelyn. I feel a bit incomplete.

You'll be back.

Yes, I suppose I will.

But the knowledge of her future return didn't dispel the feelings of unease. She reached for the mortadella sandwich.

Maybe I will have a bite, she said.

Go on. Tuck in, said Dotty. There's artichoke in it.

Delicious, said Evelyn. Lifts it, doesn't it?

I meant to tell you, said Evelyn when she'd finished chewing. I met the young girl you drew.

Dotty laughed. Cap and dark fringe?

Quite a character, said Evelyn.

She rather charmed me.

But you don't like children, Dotty.

No, I know I don't. But she was more like an adult in small clothes. She said she ran a boardinghouse.

A boardinghouse?

Evelyn took another bite of the sandwich.

You signed it, Dotty, she said.

I know. But I had to. For the upkeep. Boardinghouses don't come cheap, you know.

A little under a year later, in January 1955, Evelyn planned another trip to Florence but had to cancel on account of a nasty bout of flu. She lost days to her bed and was crotchety and frustrated.

Jem Gunnerslake visited with flowers and Evelyn was happy to see him. He confirmed that his mother was Penelope the theater critic. Why? he said.

No reason, said Evelyn, who couldn't wait to tell Dotty.

He stood in front of a photograph—a rare grouping of the Three Vi's (Virginia, Violet and Vita). They looked miserable and interesting. Dotty was there that day; you can see her with a shotgun in the background. Blurred but the stance unmistakably Dotty.

Jem said, I'd like to see Miss Cunningham again.

And Evelyn smiled and thought, When she finds out who your mother is, you probably will.

That evening, Dotty came by to make soup.

This flu virus wouldn't have touched me if I'd been forty-five, said Evelyn.

That would have been the male strain, said Dotty.

Evelyn laughed and then coughed.

Dotty brought in the soup and confessed she had forgotten to put the bones in.

It's still very tasty, said Evelyn.

You must be ill, said Dotty.

I wanted to show you this, said Dotty, and she unzipped her portfolio case and pulled out painting after painting.

The light, said Evelyn.

You, said Dotty.

Your take on the city.

And you, said Dotty.

How could those men *not* have been successful back then? said Dotty. The city gave them everything, didn't it? The city was everything.

Oh yes. Had Michelangelo been born in Bologna it might all have been different, said Evelyn, suddenly on the mend.

In 1956, Evelyn did return to Florence but this time without Dotty. She took the train down from Venice, a brief respite from the Biennale, where her friend was showing the Florentine work. She spent a morning watching the reconstruction of the Santa Trìnita bridge, and from there her wanderings took her down a narrow street that led into Santo Spirito square. The market was still in progress and it was noisy and enchanting. She entered from the north side, by the church. Couldn't have known that Ulysses was driving out from the south side with the kid, although the sight of a Jowett Bradford van did register somewhat. He was delivering a globe to a villa near San Gimignano. There had been no haggling over the price and the price had remained high. It was one of his better globes. Evelyn ate an early lunch at Michele's, and from her table even noticed an old man and a parrot sitting with the elderly women on the stone benches, sharing vermouth. She cast no judgment at such a sight because Santo Spirito had always been more outré than the other quarters. Why on earth didn't she stay over this side? she thought. Colleagues stayed in the Bandini above the German Institute of Art in the Palazzo Guadagni, but it had always been too male for her. So what? she thought. When she returned, maybe she'd try it. Her espresso was brought out to her by a large man in an apron. They conversed freely about the economic changes to the area, which were considerable. Had she only thought to ask his recommendation of a nearby and affordable *pensione*. She didn't, however. He brought her the bill and she ambled back to the railway station. She took the last train to Venice and attended a party with Dotty at Peggy Guggenheim's. Peggy had a good eye. They talked about Jackson Pollock. Evelyn told her the best tinned sardines to buy and she was delighted. You're always welcome here, said Peggy.

In 1958, Evelyn and Ulysses actually passed by one another on the Ponte Vecchio. (They'd laugh about that later.) Both were in conversation, Evelyn with a young art restorer and Ulysses with Massimo. Evelyn's sight was downstream toward the Ponte Santa Trìnita, which had been completed the previous year. Oh happy day, she said, or words to that effect, even though the head of Spring would remain missing for another three years. Rumor had it that it had been stolen/kidnapped/ sold to an American billionaire. The Parker Pen Company even offered a reward of $3,000 to find it. What a palaver. A dredging crew would eventually find it on the riverbed.

As for Ulysses and Massimo, they had stopped midway and were looking upstream toward the Casentino. Massimo was saying that the person he had recently fallen in love with was actually a man. He had his hands in his pockets and was waiting either to be pitied or to lose a precious friendship, because those had generally been the two outcomes of past confessions. He'd better be good to you, was all that Ulysses said. They came off the bridge into an evening of Negronis and silliness. Relief, really. Never worry about stuff like that with me, said Ulysses. He met the boyfriend two months later. An older American academic called Phil. Quiet, dependable, interesting. Everything you'd want in a man.

Evelyn and Ulysses danced like this and would dance like this for years. Only their thoughts kept time. An elegant two-step created from a jig at the side of a Tuscan road. He went to a gallery and thought of her.

She saw a globe and thought of him. She went to a jazz club with Dotty and listened to a pianist who they thought might have been the frontier piano man from the West End play. Couldn't be, could it? He played a song he said he rarely played. "Cressy's Song," he called it.

And in December 1959, sitting in her Bloomsbury flat, Evelyn paused in front of her notebook. She was attempting to formulate an introduction to still life painting that would include the idea of female space, when she felt cold all of a sudden. She went over and put another log on the fire. She drew her cardigan tight around her shoulders and the orange button she'd gotten five years earlier in Sant'Ambrogio caught her eye. It was striking in its otherness. Just like the memory of a nine-year-old girl, who was sometimes called Alys and sometimes called kid. Evelyn reached for her glass of claret and stood in front of the fire. Some activities are exalted, others dismissed as lowly or humble or trivial, she thought. So who is it who decides? Privilege and male gaze, ultimately.

She refilled her glass and sat down.

Life of the spirit versus that of the physical, she wrote. Sacred versus the profane. The educated versus the not. A world where the outer and inner are in constant opposition.

The world of the domestic kitchen is a female world (she underlined this). It is a world of routine, of body and of bodily function. A world of blood and carcass and guts and servitude. Men may enter but they do not work there and yet work is all that women do there. Occasionally in such paintings, male items may appear on the table—pipes, watches, maps—often in the most ludicrous composition and yet, they succeed in what they intend to do—revoke the feminine space. Male triumph over the triviality of the scene.

She drank from her glass. She continued to write.

The power of still life lies precisely in this triviality. Because it is a world of reliability. Of mutuality between objects that are there, and people who are not. Paused time in ghostly absence. Who was it who prepared the food? Who gutted the fish? Who scrubbed the kitchen? These are the actions that maintain life. Objects representing ordinary life reside in this space—plates, bowls, jars, pitchers, oyster knives. The shape of these objects has remained unchanged, as has their function. They have become fixed and unremarkable in this world of habit and we have taken them for granted. Yet within these forms something powerful is retained: Continuity. Memory. Family.

She put down her pen. The child wouldn't be nine anymore, would she? Fourteen, at least. Fourteen with a new decade approaching. How wonderful.

La Dolce Vita

1960

The turn of the decade was welcomed. Farewell, the fifties—what have you ever done for us?

Quite a lot, actually, said Massimo, lighting a cigarette and preparing to deliver a well-informed speech. Let me explain, he said. The country's in the grip of an economic miracle due in no small part to the Marshall Plan—or the European Recovery Program, to give it its proper name—and there's a great sense of relief and optimism after the war and Fascism.

I can feel that, said Pete.

Me too, said Cress.

Reconstruction is at an all-time high and mass migration has shifted a demographic from the deprived rural south to the more urban affluent north. Consequently, prosperity has found its way into the working classes and a new consumer society is flourishing. Fiat, Pirelli, Alfa Romeo, Vespa—

Gucci, said Ulysses.

Gucci, repeated Massimo. Names that have put Italy on the world stage. Fashion has now become available to the masses—and he flashed the label of his new off-the-peg jacket—and washing machines and refrigerators and, more important, *tinned tomatoes* have transformed the lives of women like never before. Cars have replaced donkey and carts, and motorcycles bicycles. What else?

Televisions, said Cress.

Ah yes, televisions, Cress. Televisions everywhere! And the Pensione Bertolini even has a telephone and nobody cares. So, good times, said Massimo, exhaling a long stream of smoke. They were sitting outside Michele's, under a large awning that had been bestowed by the Campari group for consistently high drink sales. The place was packed. Ulysses watched Giulia carry out good-luck plates of lentils and *cotechino*.

A toast, said Claude, wanting to leave his mark on the evening. Hello, the sixties! More of the same, please!

The men raised their glasses. Hello, the sixties, more of the same, please!

Kid was over by the church steps, strumming a guitar. Course, she wasn't called kid anymore, she was Alys. All fourteen years and four months of her. Beatnik before she knew what it meant, in her railway-man's cap and fishing sweater and shortened jeans. She waved to Pete and Cress walking across the square, Ulysses and Massimo deep in conversation behind. She'd become distant with Ulysses and didn't know how to put it right.

Overnight things had changed. The feeling that the eyes of the world were laughing at her—well, she had that all the time now, now that she wanted to kiss girls. And she felt a bit wrong and the Church didn't help and neither did the kids at school with their gossip and jibes. She'd let Guido touch her barely formed breasts just to scotch the rumors. When she'd gotten home that night, she couldn't look at Ulysses and she went to bed and didn't eat. Maybe that was the start? Of the distance, she meant. An act of shame can never lessen another, but how could she know that, because she was fourteen years and four months old, and she was hormones and questions and no sign of a period yet. The crowd quieted and Alys smiled and the bluebirds sang.

And there's Peg, said Cress.

The first song was called "The Tower of Rotherhithe" and Alys had written it herself. Pete had helped with the music, but the words were all hers. It was the story of a woman who tried to sing a man back from war, carrying him up the Thames on words of love. "My sweet boy our river," was the refrain—"My sweet boy our river come closer come hither, come follow these words you hear on the wind, they'll guide you they'll heal you they'll feed you forever, just come back and give me the print of your hand." The soldier never returned, and the tower fell to ruin in peacetime.

It's got an Irish sensibility, whispered Pete. Ulysses knew the song was about Peg.

Peg had by then given up her job and had moved out to the eastern suburbs with Ted. They had a big house with a gothic touch and a fuck-off driveway close to the end of the Central Line. All middle-class with secrets, but that was Ted all over. No one knew why she'd done it. Cress especially. Cress thought it an act of self-sabotage and despair. Cress wanted Ulysses to go back to London and bring her home. And where's home, Cress? With us, he said. I'm not so sure she sees it that way, said Ulysses. It was their first argument and Alys said, See? She gets between everyone in the end. Sort of shut them up, that did. Not in a good way.

There were no pubs with pianos out near Peg, so she stopped singing and that barnacled lifeline slipped through her grip. Cocktail hour drew closer every day, and old Ted—Mr. Insurance and Mr. Risk Averse—he shook 'em high and made 'em dry. Olive, of course, because Peg preferred lemon. Don't be such a bastard, she'd say, and they'd kiss, and she'd bite his lip and make it bleed the way he liked it. He checked the bills and knew when she'd telephoned Italy. We have to economize, he said. Economize? Since when? Since you stopped working. You didn't want me to work. I never said that. Oh, Peg, said Claude somewhere in time.

It was Ulysses who did the calling now. That's why he'd gotten the telephone installed in the *pensione*. Whenever Peg said, Standing room only, that was the code for him to call her back another day. He hadn't spoken to her in months and the letters she sent were a tepid account of her days. *"I made a cake!"* When did Peg ever make a bleedin' cake? Pete was the last to swear, but even that got his proverbial goat.

Peg had promised to visit Florence again after that first Christmas, but she never did. Of course, she talked about it, but Peg talked about a lot of things by then. Alys went back most years, though, and even that was a fucking stretch. She came home sullen and low and eventually revealed she didn't like Ted. Why don't you like Ted? said Ulysses. I just don't, she said. You need to tell me more, he said. Has he done something to you? No, it's not that, she said. It's the things he says. What things? said Ulysses. He tells Peg I'm better than her.

Cress told Ulysses he needed to get creative and think outside the box, so he did. He arranged for Peg and Alys to have a two-week stint at Col's every summer without Ted. He knew Ted wouldn't push against Col because Col would kill him. Just give me the word, said Col.

That first summer, Col became the Col of old and lorded it around his women. Ginny and Alys were inseparable and swam in the canal when the mercury hit eighty and snarled at boys pointing hard-ons their way. But it was in Peg that change was most apparent. Ginny's presence mollified her maternal rage, and the blunt set of her jaw relaxed. Pete played piano and Peg sang her guts out. Like old times, said Mrs. Lovell over her roast dinner. Peg even mentioned Eddie at the beginning of a song, because that's what happens when a woman feels safe. Col said, What Peg loves, Peg holds close, but Alys felt confused by that because she didn't feel that close. Alys was due to go back in July but she'd lost the photo of Eddie and was frightened of what Peg might say. You had a photo of Eddie? said Ulysses. Since when? Since I was a kid, she said.

The sound of cheers from the audience brought Ulysses back to the present. Pete turned to him and said, She did good, Temps. She'll never go hungry. I have, but she won't. And he reached for Ulysses's cigarette and took a sharp drag.

Alys scanned the crowd eagerly, taking in every face till her eyes latched on to blond Romy Peller, fifteen years of fresh-faced beauty and as all-American as they come. She was the girl Alys had kissed an hour before in a darkened doorway that smelled of piss. Moonlight and mouths linked by silver strands of saliva. Alys wanted to say I love you there and then, but the night was young, and she had her whole life ahead of her.

They'd met two months before at the cinema. Sat next to one another barely moving, barely breathing. Romy had a Vespa and Alys rode on the back and she held Romy's waist tight and she leaned in close just to smell the shampoo scent of her hair. Romy's dad had taken a sabbatical from his university to write a book about Henry James and all Romy had to do was learn Italian and kiss girls and she was good at both. Everyone thought they were just good friends, but Cress noticed everything that night and followed Alys's bright gaze to a boy who stepped aside and revealed a girl.

Aye aye, he thought. Someone's in love.

But wasn't everybody by the end of the fifties? Even you, Cress?

The last six years had been the happiest of his life. His ritual courtship of Signora Mimmi had taken an intimate turn when she told him her name was Paola. They dined once a week together, either at his or at hers, and cooked out of Artusi's *Science in the Kitchen and the Art of Eating Well*. Paola had given him a copy the Christmas before, and every stain and every oil splash on a page was the equivalent of footprints along a shore. Sometimes they jumped on the Moto Guzzi and drove out into the hills and had lunch on the terrace of a modest *albergo*. Cress told Paola that she looked like a film star in her sunglasses and silk scarf, and Massimo took a photograph of her and it ended up in Michele's bar and people thought it was Anna Magnani. Sometimes Paola talked about her husband, but Cressy didn't mind. After all, a lifetime had been lived before she'd knocked him off his axis. I wonder if there's space in your heart for me, too? he said.

Alone at night, Cress couldn't believe someone so beautiful would want to spend time with him. Cress had started to let go of his mum. Or had his mum started to let go of him? Maybe it was because he was finally in good hands.

Alys shouted out, This next song was written by our friend Pete! and she pointed to Pete and people turned to look at him. For Pete that was

like being back at the Haughty Hen in '56. He'd been a minor celebrity
that summer, even had a groupie follow him back from the tube station.
The years leading up to the new decade, however, had been as unpre-
dictable and multifarious as ever. He'd gotten the part of a scream in a
West End thriller, which Col said was made for him, and in many ways
that was true. Equity contract too, so the money was OK. All Pete had
to do was to scream from the wings after every murder when the stage
went to blackout. It all went well for the first month till Pete lost con-
centration and panicked. He suddenly screamed for no apparent reason
and the leading lady fainted and ended up with a broken arm in the
front stalls. Pete was sacked immediately. Col found him busking in
Piccadilly Circus. Pretend you don't know me, said Pete. I always do,
said Col. Col told Ulysses that Pete was unemployable these days. His
reputation not only preceded him, but came with a T-shirt that said
"Fucknut" across the front.

The song's called "Freedom of the Open Road," said Alys.

There you go, the sky is low
The future's dim, but it's staying true.
'Cause . . .
Now you know the way it blows
The rise and fall of Empire scores,
It's just playing thin.
You never talked about it.
I asked but you said it's myth.
You never talked about it.
Said only the rich have bliss.
But I saw it there.
How I saw it there.
On the open road.
See—I know the way!
Oh, I know the way!
Don't you doubt my load.
Freedom of the road.

Fuck you, so wrong about time
An unwarranted sense of yours not mine,
How could you?

(I never said "Fuck you," whispered Pete.
Ulysses grinned. I know you didn't, Pete.)

How the mighty fell was used to quell
A beating heart,
A world apart, in virtue.
Don't try and you won't fail
The despot's Holy fucking Grail
Keep the people at his call
Safe against a crumbling wall
So he can shoot you.
'Cause I saw it there!
How I saw it there!

Everyone joined in the chorus. A hundred—two hundred?—voices, high on Pete's words, strung out on a new decade of peace and revolution and make love not war, man. Massimo turned to Pete and above the din he shouted, The power of your words, Pete!

You're a talent, said Ulysses. Don't ever let anyone say otherwise. Not Col, not anyone. You hear me?

I hear you, Temps. And Pete placed his hand on his chest and said, Namaste. And with that bow to the divine, the three men turned away from the ecclesiastical stage and left Alys to the evocations of youth and optimism.

Ulysses would have liked to have stayed longer, but the deal was two songs and no more. She'd become self-conscious and shy around him and he didn't know when that had crept in, but the sense of losing her was sharp. She told him less and less about her life, so whenever she sang and played guitar with other young people in the square, he took his chance. Sometimes he'd rush to the window and throw open the shutters just to learn about her—what interested her, what moved her, what made her angry. Recently there'd been a lot about love. There was so much to keep up with. He just wanted her to finish school.

Fathers and daughters, said Cress, as if reading Ulysses's thoughts. There's just so much . . .

So much what, Cress? said Ulysses.

Help me, Pete.

Help you with what?

A word. A word that describes the awkwardness between fathers and daughters.

Pete thought. Awkward's good, Cress.

Yeah, but it's not *the* word, is it, Pete?

Reticence? said Massimo.

Reticence is better. But it's not the word.

She just doesn't want you to know things about her, said Pete. There's a delight in privacy. That's adolescence for you. So much to work out.

Yeah, but it's not a word, is it, Pete? said Cress.

A delight in privacy? said Ulysses.

I don't think I ever had that, said Massimo.

She's also afraid she'll let you down, said Pete. What with Peg's crap an' all.

Don't forget I'm still after the right word, said Cress, but Cressy's word was never found, and the men separated by the stone bench. Cress waited for Paola, and Massimo headed to his office to make a telephone call to Phil, who was still in the States. Firecrackers exploded and heckled the night.

Ulysses said, What d'you say to an early night, Pete?

Thought you'd never ask, Temps.

The front door closed behind them. The tread of their footsteps, a weary heft in the stairwell.

I really like that jacket, by the way, said Ulysses.

This old thing, Temps? I got it in Warsaw.

A face peered out from the doorway to their left and looked them up and down. Happy New Year, said the elderly contessa, who had never really been that elderly, just plain grumpy.

You too, Contessa, they said.

And Alys? Her night ended where it had started. In the same dank doorway but with Romy's thumb in her mouth. She could taste the salt from the crisps they'd recently eaten. Could feel the rough edge of a fingernail. Suck me, said Romy, and Alys did and they pushed in close as the *carabinieri* drove past. Alys looked at her watch. Time had been given generously to her and she said she had to go. They separated down by the river. One went north, the other south.

At two a.m., she entered the palazzo and closed the door softly on the world. She slipped off her shoes, careful not to wake Cressy, whose bedroom door was ajar. On the way to the kitchen, a light in the living room drew her in.

You didn't have to wait up for me, she said.

I did, said Ulysses, looking up from a book. And I always will.

Even when I'm twenty?

Yep.

Fifty?

Always.

She laughed. You're hopeless.

You look so happy, he said.

I might go to bed.

OK.

When she got to the door, she said, What did you say?

I said you could never disappoint me, Alys. I'm proud of every inch of you. Every minuscule part of your being. Of your thoughts and your joy and your rage. The way you sing and navigate your way in this often godforsaken—

I love a girl.

(Pause.)

Lucky girl, I say—world.

They looked at one another and the distance halved. Ulysses said, A new year, Alys. I hope it's worthy of you.

Night, Uly.

Night, kid.

January rolled slow and revolution took a backseat. Sleet blew in from the hills and the air turned sharp with a frigid nip. The clouds stayed low and spirits dropped. Blood oranges were a staple after every meal and Alys skipped school to keep Romy warm. Cress learned how to make *gnocchi*—simple, really, he said: potatoes and flour and a nimble use of the fingers. Pete came down with a dose of the morose after Ulysses had asked him again to come and live with them. Pete stayed in his room for a whole day and Claude waited outside, working his way through a bag of sunflower seeds. Ulysses began a trace for a new set of gores. A fifty-centimeter-diameter globe, his most ambitious yet. And on January 8 at four in the afternoon, the phone rang. He picked up and there was the operator. *Sì, sì*, he said. Another pause and—

Peg? Is that you?

He put down his coffee and shook out a fag.

Temps? I didn't expect to get through.

(Pause.)

Nineteen sixty, Peg! Where you been?

Yeah, yeah. Cress OK?

Having the time of his life.

Peg lit a cigarette. Alys?

In love.

Oh fuck, Tempy. That's the worst fucking news you could've given me—

Peg, go easy—

Don't let her get fucking knocked up, please—

She won't.

How d'ya know?

I know.

Don't go all naïve on me, now. We all reckoned we—

Peg. Stoppit. It's a girl. (Pause.) She's in love with a girl.

Peg began to laugh. That's the best fucking news I've heard in years.

Easy, Peg. Be kind.

I know. I will. (The sound of Peg inhaling on the cigarette.) Well, I never, she said. That's a first for our family.

Where's Ted? said Ulysses.

Out for the count. He had a late one. I'm getting a drink. You stay on the line?

Course I will.

The sound of her footsteps moving away. Fridge door opening and shutting. The chatter of ice. Peg moving back toward the phone.

You still there? she said.

I'm here, he said.

A girl, eh?

Yep.

He tapped his cigarette onto the ashtray.

Happy New Year, Peg.

You think it will be?

You're due one, right?

Can't complain.

How's Essex?

We've got a big garden.

I never knew you wanted one.

I didn't.

Peg laughed. (It was the best thing, hearing her laugh.)

Aye aye, said Ulysses. Here he is. Our best fella's just walked in.

Pete came into the room, trailed by Claude. Ulysses covered the mouthpiece. You OK, Pete?

Much better, thanks, Temps.

It's Peg, said Ulysses, holding up the phone.

Hello, Peg! Pete called out.

Pete went over to the piano and began to play. Tell her this one's for her, he said.

Pete says this one's for you. And Ulysses held the receiver low to the keys. Peg started to sing on the other end of the line, "I'm a Fool to Want You."

Pete shouted out, You've always been a star, heavenly lady.

Peg stayed on the line the whole song. Would have cost her a fortune but worth every penny just for Peg to be Peg again. Song ended with a Pete flourish. And the chink chink of ice in an upended glass. Ulysses brought the receiver back up to his ear. His breath and her breath, that smoky catch.

No one like you, Peg.

Gotta go, she said, and they hung up.

Pete's last night at the palazzo rolled round soon enough. It was late and they were stuffed full of Cressy's *gnocchi*, which he'd served with sage and butter and cheese with a snowdrift of Parmesan on top. Alys was over at Romy's and Pete was at the piano playing his thoughts to music. Dozens of candles added an introspective dimension to the evening, which had begun with a Johnny Mathis singalong.

Pete said, You ever feel like you've been here before, Temps?

Ulysses raised his head off the sofa and said, When you say "here," Pete, d'you mean life or—

This city. Florence.

I've been here before, said Cress, who was sprawled on the floor like roadkill. I was a friar.

A friar?

Pretty sure of it, boy.

You never told me that before, Cress.

Never been sure of it till the other day. Over at San Marco, I had a strong sense of déjà vu. In one of the cells where Fra Angelico painted his *Annunciation*. It was as if I was watching him do it.

You help him, Cress?

No, I didn't, Pete. I just watched him. Light streaming in. The holiness of his heart. It was quite transcendent.

That's a nice word, Cress.

Beyond the dimension of physical human experience. Inexplicable, yet serene.

Ulysses poured out more wine.

You ever done that thing with a mirror, Temps?

What thing with a mirror, Pete?

You just stare and stare into your own eyes till nothing makes sense and your mind lets go of reality—or what little hold you had on it in the first place—and what's revealed is you in a previous life.

Ulysses stared at him. He said, No. I haven't done that, Pete.

I did once.

And? said Cress.

I was a woman.

How lovely, said Cress.

Like one of them portraits in the Uffizi. Pearls around my neck. Pale makeup. High forehead. Very dignified. An ornate red dress slipping from my shoulders. I had nice shoulders. Hair parted like this—and Pete demonstrated.

Sounds like you were wealthy, said Cress.

Makes a change.

Only the wealthy had portraits painted of themselves. The pearls would probably have been given to you by your bloke after you had a kid. They symbolize fertility, said Cress. You probably had loads of kids, Pete.

Felt like it, he said.

But you had to, said Cress. On account of the high infant mortality rate. And those you did have were whipped away and given over to a wet nurse.

That don't seem right, said Pete.

Of course it wasn't. But menstruation came back quicker if you took the kid off the breast.

How d'you know all this, Cress? said Ulysses.

Read it. The pressure to procreate was immense. Especially after the Black Death in 1348. Wiped out half of the population.

I did look a bit stressed, to be honest, said Pete. I don't think it was a good life.

It wasn't. Not for a woman, said Cress.

But it made you who you are now, said Ulysses. Sensitive. Intuitive. Profound.

Thanks, Temps. I wrote a song about it at the time: "Love Shouldn't Come with a Dowry." Melody went something like this. And his fingers moved gracefully across the keys and fag smoke vexed his bloodshot eyes.

Ulysses got up and opened another bottle of wine. He bent down and kissed Pete's head. Bless you, said Pete. Claude squawked and said, All the world's a stage. And all the men and women merely players. They have their exits, and their entrances, and one man in his time plays many parts.

Ulysses, Pete and Cress looked over at the bird.

Where does he get it from? whispered Cress.

Search me, said Ulysses.

Maybe he's Shakespeare, said Pete.

You what? said Ulysses.

Maybe. He's. Shakespeare, mouthed Pete, pointing at Claude.

That parrot? said Cress. The greatest playwright that ever lived?

Pete shrugged. I'm not saying he is, but—

Carry me, said Claude.

They turned to the bird. Claude was lying louchely on a pillow, pointing a long wing feather—like a quill—in their direction. Carry me, he said with an air of entitlement.

Pete left the next day. The sky was blue, mostly, with a sun that was firing blanks. He'd decided to hitchhike his way back to London, and Cress had packed him up with bread and cheese and a surprise jar of caper berries that would lift his spirits one lonely night to come. Pete intended to bed down in youth hostels. He said the number of hostels had doubled over the decade, as a way to encourage young people to

travel and engage with other nations. To heal the schism that war had
caused, he said. We're not so different.

They walked across the square; shouts of good-bye echoed in the air.
Cressy, Alys, Ulysses and Pete, and Claude in Ulysses's arms as had been
demanded.

They passed the recent additions to the neighborhood, the new *trat-*
toria and *tabacchi* that no one could remember never having been there.
They walked past Betsy—a loving glance her way—past the church and
up onto the *lungarno*. Pete got his sign out then. It just said *North/Nord.*
He lit a cigarette and a minute later, a Fiat Millecento stopped: an antique dealer on his way to Milan, a cheery sort of fella.

Pete lifted his holdall onto his shoulder.

Come here, said Ulysses. The men embraced.

Bye, Pete!

Bye, my love.

Come back soon, son.

Take care, Cress.

Pete striding ahead to the car with his holdall held high. The sleeve
slipping down his thin arm and a familiar trail of smoke. Pete climbing
into the passenger seat. The car driving away, heading north. And then
that airless bubble, absence.

February brought the whisper of spring. Cress got the *pensione* ready for
the new season. A bit of darning and a coat of paint on the doors, nothing taxing—and a couple of additions to the weekly menu. Three years
since the dining room had opened up. Rarely more than six guests at a
time around the communal table, so more than manageable. That's how
Des and Poppy had met the Australian couple Ray and Jane in '57. What
would become a lifelong friendship forged over a bowl of *ribollita*. What's
ribollita when it's at home? said Jane. Old stale bread, said Des. I'd never
have known, said Jane.

Ulysses grabbed Alys for a night at the movies before Romy stole her
away. Fellini's *La Dolce Vita* had just opened in town and Massimo came

too, and it was just like old times. No one dared move after the credits had rolled, and Alys declared it a masterpiece. They ended up at a table in Michele's. Cress said something about Anita Ekberg frolicking in the Trevi Fountain and everyone laughed because frolicking wasn't a word Cress would normally use. Giulia said she wanted to see the film, but Michele didn't, and Ulysses—so high on the night—said, I'll take you, and he and Giulia blushed because it was the closest they'd ever gotten to going out on a date. It would never happen, of course, but it felt good to imagine. The perfect end to a moony old night.

Alys saw the film a second time with Romy. She told Romy that this was the trajectory she'd always imagined for Fellini after seeing *I Vitelloni*. Romy wasn't that interested actually. A little chink in love's bright armor. Alys pasted over the crack and sketched Romy naked one afternoon after school. She used charcoal and white chalk on black paper and made Romy look like a statue.

In March, the swallows returned.

Alys was the first to see them around the *campanile* and Cress said, They're early this year, and Alys said, That's what I thought. March also saw the return of the guests. First through the door was Mrs. Shields from Sunderland. She was a Michelangelo enthusiast and spent hours gazing at David's allure. She also had a soft spot for the hostess trolley and, come an evening, made a considerable dent in a bottle of Campari. An art appreciation class from Boston took three rooms for two weeks and appreciated everything, which isn't always the case. Anyway, it was a solid start to the tourist season and an effortless way to bolster the coffers. And even Des turned up. Just for the night, but still. He came down from Milan after an industry seminar on the future of plastics.

You're looking at it. That's what I told 'em, said Des.

Business good then, Des?

One word: telephones. I shit money, Temps. You want a red one?

I'm OK, Des.

Sticking with the classic black. I like it. Man of style.

Des and Ulysses were sitting on a bench in Piazza dei Sapiti, drinking coffee. Des said, So, this is where you come to be alone, eh? You got yourself a woman yet?

Not really.

No one special?

They're all special, Des. Visitors, mainly.

That suit you?

I think it does. What with the kid and Peg, you know, and—

You're allowed happiness, lad. I'm sure there's a woman—or a man, let's be modern—who'd like you at their side. I learned how to embrace my true masculinity from my wife.

You told her that?

Not in so many words. I buy her things instead. You need any money? said Des.

No, we're good. Cress won a fortune during the London Olympics. We're still working our way through that.

What he bet on?

Fanny Blankers-Koen.

Not the four golds?

Ulysses nodded.

Man of vision, said Des.

Des took a slurp of cappuccino. A pigeon flew past and dumped a load of scat.

Now show me them globes, he said.

Ulysses pushed open the door and the smell of damp and paint and glue found the nose. The floor was covered in discarded paper and plaster of Paris offcuts. Drying on lines across the room were the painted gores.

So this is it? said Des. Where the magic happens.

Back here, said Ulysses, and he went on ahead and lit a cluster of candles and set the scene.

Six thirty-six-centimeter-diameter terrestrial globes, slowly spinning on an axis, each one mounted on a walnut-and-brass base. All painted differently. Some carrying the ancient look of age. He'd given depth to the oceans and lightness to the shallows and the land various shades of ochre and brown.

Stunning, said Des. And these came from my molds?

Wouldn't have happened without you, said Ulysses.

From an artificial compound of highly toxic resin comes beauty. Who would've believed it? said Des. I'll take four.

Des, you don't—

Four. One for each of my boys and me. I'll let you choose.

Take a look at what I'm working on now, said Ulysses, and he led Des back to his desk by the front window, where a globe still in the process of being painted rested on a pile of stained rags.

So far I've been working from my dad's old copperplates. All thirty-sixers, all dated. This one here, though, was from my etching. First one I ever did. Outlines of countries only, and longitude and latitude lines.

No names.

Not yet. But look: I'm putting in the names by hand. Pen and ink. Also, a drawing here and there.

A sea monster, Des chuckled. And mountains. A kangaroo. I like it.

Yep. And these globes will always be up to date, Des. Right names for countries, correct boundaries.

I'll take two.

Des—

I'll sell 'em for you. Get you in galleries. You don't want some little bleeder in school grubbing them up. This is art, lad. Needs to be priced right. I'll do the pricing.

I'm tracing for a fifty-centimeter—nineteen-inch—globe right now. This is it here. This is the map I'm using.

That how you do it? With a grid?

Yeah.

And back to front too?

Almost complete now. I'll make two versions. One with names and one without. Then I transfer the trace to the plate.

That's dedication for you. And time-consuming. Nothing quicker?

Lithography one day. But for now, an artist fella, in San Niccolò—
he's a master at intaglio. He's got an acid bath large enough to etch the
plate and a press bed that can print that size.

You need the molds?

I do, Des.

Consider it done. Can you go bigger than fifty?

Sixty-five, maybe?

I'll chuck in a couple of them too. In case you get bored. Now,
what's on the menu tonight?

Bistecca and cannellini beans and spinach.

Des stopped. *Bistecca*? You can't be serving nosh like *bistecca*, lad. I
didn't draw up a business plan for the margins on food to be so narrow.
Feed 'em cheap, we agreed. *Brodo, brodo* and more bloody *brodo*. And
don't skimp on the tomatoes. Steak's for the Excelsior!

Ulysses laughed. It's for you, Des. You're the only one in tonight.

I am?

We're eating together. You, me, Cress and the kid.

And Massimo?

He'll be along later with Phil.

They doing all right?

So–so. Distance and . . .

Wanting different things?

That's it.

Me and Poppy were like that for a while. I wanted a Bentley and she
wanted a Jag.

What happened?

Compromised. Got one each. We need any cheese for tonight?

And before Ulysses could answer, Des disappeared into the *pizzi-
cagnolo*, greeting the owner as if she was a long-lost friend.

Des left and April arrived. Brought with it sun and flowering wisteria
and Cressy's shorts. Officially the first day of spring when those shapely
legs appeared to the world. The stone bench *signore* whistled whenever

he passed. He pretended to be shy, but he liked it really. Felt a bit of a catch, something he didn't expect to be at the age of seventy-six. And just to see that admiring sidelong glance from Paola as he strutted across the stones to fill his canvas bag with lemons and artichokes. Was that a little dance move there, Cressy? It sure was!

Cress settled on the terrace next to his *Citrus aurantium*. Clusters of dense white blossom fragranced the air with neroli, and Easter fireworks from the Duomo carried faint across the river.

What you reading? said the tree.

Cress held up his book. Elizabeth Barrett Browning. *Aurora Leigh*, he said.

Any good?

All the associations are a bit off my radar but it's quite magnificent in parts. Not as accessible for me as the Constance Everly—

But she's your go-to, isn't she?

She is. But listen to this—and Cress scanned the pages—here, he said. "I felt a mother-want about the world, / And still went seeking, like a bleating lamb . . ." A mother-want, he repeated. Now, there's an image.

Is that how you feel, old fella?

No, not me, said Cress. Though I worry it might be Alys.

One afternoon, the air warm and polleny, Alys and Romy were in Romy's bedroom, listening to music. They were down to their under-wear, arms draped about one another's necks, moving slowly in time to the beat. The shutters were open, and the view was of the river, on which a fisherman was struggling to land a catfish the size of a small boar. The door was locked from the inside and the music was loud but not so loud as to make Romy's father complain about the shallow head-way he was making on his book. He lit a cigarette and gazed out of the window at the green river. The location was what had persuaded him to hand over a hefty deposit all those months ago. He'd intended to come alone but had somehow been saddled with wife and daughter. He pulled the sheet of paper out of the typewriter and screamed silently. He began again. Tap tap tap. *I hate my wife.* He stared at the words. He'd meant to write *life.*

His wife, Patty, was drinking on the terrace. She could hear the faint sound of music, but she didn't care; she thought the girls were probably smoking and talking about boys like she'd done at their age. She settled down on the sun lounger and thought about Marcello Mastroianni. If she'd been alone, she'd have run an ice cube up the inside of her thigh and popped it in.

The music came to an end and Romy lifted the needle back to the beginning. Alys stood awkwardly in the middle of the room.

Lift up, said Romy, and Alys raised her arms and her vest was pulled over her head. She felt the breeze on her skin. She didn't need a bra but wished she had one. Romy led her to the bed and Alys wanted to say I love you, but events moved at a considerable pace. Romy slipped her hand in Alys's knickers and she was all nerve endings and came quickly and it felt extraordinary. Alys was about to reciprocate but Romy's mum, half cut and in need of company, knocked on the door and asked if they'd like a little something to eat.

What you got? shouted Romy.

Ricotta. Oh, and ham.

So, they ate ricotta and ham with Romy's mum on the terrace as dusk laid out its colors. Romy's mum talked nonstop through the splendor. Alys thought Peg would probably have done the same.

Alys left shortly after. She and Romy tongued one another in the rickety old lift going down and that's when Alys said I love you. Romy smiled. Alys walked back along the embankment, crotch wet and whiffy from the exertions of before. She suddenly wished Romy had said I love you back, and wondered why she hadn't. Claude was the first to see her enter the square. He flew off the statue of Cosimo R. and landed on her arm. I love you, Claude, she said. I love you too, he said. See? she thought. How hard can it be?

She got her period two days later and hid her introversion behind packs of sanitary products. Her body had a life of its own and all she

could do was to hang on and try to enjoy the ride. Ulysses asked if
she wanted a hot-water bottle. She just wished she had someone to
talk to.

A week later, the plan to escape to Fiesole was hatched. They were in
Vivoli having ice cream and Romy had just finished talking about a
villa that was owned by friends of her father. He had the key because he
was supposed to check on it, but never did.

So what d'ya think? said Romy.

Think about what? said Alys.

You really are dumb sometimes.

Am I?

The key. It's ours for the taking, said Romy. I'll say I'm with you and
you'll say you're with me and we'll go on the Vespa. Two nights away
from that nuthouse I live in. You and me, kiddo. How about it? Love's
bright dream.

It was as poetic as Romy ever got. How could Alys say no?

She waved good-bye to Cress and Ulysses on Friday after school. She
had a small backpack with a swimsuit and a clean top and a bottle of
wine she'd taken from the cellar. Her guitar was strapped across her
shoulders and a jumper around her waist. She left them the telephone
number of Romy's mum and dad. See you Sunday! she shouted. She met
Romy along the *lungarno* by the bridge. A buzz at the sight of her on the
Vespa. Alys climbed on behind and smelled sunlight in Romy's hair.

It took little time to get up to Fiesole. The air was fresh in comparison
to the city and Romy stopped in the square and they picked up supplies
at a market stall. Romy didn't know if there was gas in the villa, so they
bought bread and doughnuts and cheese because they were often hungry
after kissing. And from the main square, meandering dirt roads took
them away from civilization and cast them into ancient olive groves and
tall grasses. Eventually, Romy stopped and looked at a hand-drawn map.
She cut the engine. This is it, she said. They grabbed the bags and walked
toward a stone villa surrounded by cypress trees.

Inside was cool and dingy, the furnishings modest and Florentine. Heavy wooden chairs much too uncomfortable to spend time on
were dotted about the periphery of the room. They walked through to
the kitchen, opened doors and threw back shutters and raised windows
and the light that sabered in was hazy and ravishing.

Alys walked out into the garden and continued across the lawn to the
periphery of the property. She thought the view might have been of
Florence, but it wasn't, it was countryside—rolling hills, vineyards, umbrella pines and the odd private villa—extending forever. All this space,
she thought. There was freedom being so high above the city, the claus-
trophobia of the streets all gone. She felt emboldened and kicked off her
plimsolls, the grass dewy underfoot. She took off her jeans and the sun
cast warmth on her legs. Romy called out her name. She turned. A terrace on the upper floor. Romy waving. Up here, she shouted. Coming,
said Alys.

They lay naked on the warm stones of the terrace and ate oranges
and drank water. They shifted their bodies close and closer still. Alys
moved on top, her leg between Romy's, and the stone rubbed hard
against her elbow, but she thought that a small price to pay. Her sweet-
smelling mouth enclosed Romy's nipple and her hand moved between
Romy's legs. They didn't have to be quiet out there in the wild. And
they laughed at the sounds they made and pretended to howl like wolves.

Night fell cold. The villa was dark. The electricity had been turned
off and Romy couldn't find a torch. They had two candles between
them and rationed light. They kept warm by drinking wine and smoking cigarettes and the stars were out in their billions and pinpricks of
light punctuated the black hills. Darting specks hovered in their peripheral vision and Alys said they were *pipistrelli*, bats.

Disgusting, said Romy.

Alys laughed. They're sweet. They eat the insects that want to eat us.

You know a lot, don't you?

Alys shrugged. I just pick things up as I go along.

I bet you could build a fire from scratch.

Do you want me to?

No. But I knew you could. You're like a boy.

I'm not a boy.

Alys and Romy didn't say much after that. Alys picked up her guitar and began to play. She'd started to put words of a poem to music and Pete said the melody was super fine. Romy suddenly leaned over and kissed her. Alys thought it might have been an apology, but she didn't know why.

They went to bed when the candle burned down. The beds were damp, and they kept their clothes on. They slept long and deep and Alys awoke to the coruscation of dawn. She went out onto the terrace and saw the sky ablaze. Nothing else mattered and she finished her song.

They headed into Fiesole for an early lunch and parked up in the main piazza. Romy was all dressed up and looked at least twenty-one. Alys, though, wore the same clothes as she had the day before, but now had red upon her lips. She'd asked Romy to apply it for her and Romy did and told her she looked hot. Alys asked Romy where they were going and Romy said to one of her mother's favorite restaurants. This way, she said. The steps led down to a tree-strewn terrace and a waiter seated them at a table that gave a view of Florence. Do we have enough money for this? asked Alys, and Romy said, We wouldn't be here if we didn't. We'll get the works, she said. Pasta, fish, salad, dessert and coffee. Romy had wine but Alys didn't.

Romy got chatting to the American family behind them. The son was called Chad and he was at college and Romy said yeah yeah yeah and flicked her hair. Alys felt uncomfortable but she thought it was because of the price of the food.

Suddenly, space in the conversation opened up for her and she took it and said, Monte Ceceri.

Everyone turned to look at her.

Are you sure? said Chad.

Quite sure. It's over there. And Alys pointed. Where Leonardo da Vinci tested the theory of flight. He sketched his ideas in notebooks, although none of the machines were ever built in his lifetime and even if they had been, they wouldn't have been successful. Most of them were modeled on the anatomy of birds. They had pulleys and rods to imitate the flapping of wings—

She knows everything, said Romy, cutting her off and laughing.

Not everything, said Alys, and she felt awkward and ran her hand over her mouth and took off what little lipstick was left.

Romy paid the bill and Alys said she was going to the amphitheater to draw. Wanna come?

Romy didn't move. I'll meet you there, she said.

Alys had the place to herself. She sat on the steps and took out a small notebook and pencil from the back pocket of her jeans. At her feet, flowering weeds were breaking through the Roman stone. She put her pencil on the page and let the line become an intricate flower head. It felt strange not to like Romy. She liked what they did together, but Alys was happier in bed with Romy than talking with her across a table. Or going to a gallery with her. Or even the cinema these days. She wondered if most people felt that way about the person they were with. Peg certainly did. Peg and Ted were physical but their words were unkind. These were Alys's thoughts by the time Romy came down the steps. Romy bent down and kissed her; fuck was she confusing. They climbed up the stones together to the Vespa in the square. Romy told her to hold on tight.

That evening, they lay in bed smelling of one another and Romy turned toward Alys and said, Did you think he was cute?

Who? said Alys.

Chad.

I don't know.

Really? You don't think he's, like, the perfect man?

And Alys shrugged because she didn't know what Romy meant by "the perfect man."

I'm going to marry someone like him, said Romy.

In seven words Alys's life changed.

And back in Florence, someone else's life was about to change too, with inevitable consequences for the young lovers. Romy's father had just inserted a fresh sheet of paper into the typewriter when the overhead chandelier fell on him. He had no time even to cry out. It was a simple equation of rotten roof beams plus gravity equaled accident waiting to happen.

Patty Peller was on the terrace, drinking. She heard a crash and thought it was an incident down below on the *lungarno*. She even leaned over the railing to check. She only went into her husband's study to see if he wanted a sandwich, and by the time the police and ambulance arrived, Reade Peller had been pinioned beneath the ornate light fixture for at least an hour. It took three men to lift it off his back. When his face was finally freed from the portable Empire Aristocrat, the type bars had dug so far into his skin, his cheek was an incongruous mess of letters and numbers. His wife was about to follow the stretcher into the ambulance when she suddenly remembered she had a daughter. She clambered out and spent the next half hour looking for the telephone number Romy had scribbled down. She lit a cigarette and dialed.

What? said Ulysses. I thought they were with you, Mrs. Peller.

And I thought they were with you, Mr. Temper.

The conversation, as you can imagine, was brief.

It was the first time in Ulysses's life that he didn't know where Alys was. It was hide-and-seek in the cypress avenue all over again and he wanted to howl. Cress said, Just because you can't see her it doesn't mean that she ain't close or safe.

Cress got him onto the sofa and said, We need to think this through. She's in love. She's gone willingly. A delight in privacy, remember what Pete said? Nipped off to a hotel—

A hotel?

That's what I reckon.

What about money?

Probably nicked some from my drawer.

Cress, she—

What did you want to do at that age, eh? Be alone. With Peg. You got up to all sorts.

Ulysses stood up. I'm gonna go and look.

Where?

Anywhere, Cress.

You go. I'll stay and get the guests fed.

Ulysses left and Cress carried on with dinner. He wasn't as calm as he imagined, because the pasta was overcooked and the *salsa al pomodoro* underseasoned.

Night fell.

Patty Peller sat in the hallway of the apartment with a large drink in one hand and the telephone in the other. She thanked the doctor and replaced the receiver. The prognosis for her husband was good because he had an exceptionally thick skull. She could have told them that herself. She stared at the telephone, at the ugly console table cluttered with photographs and museum ticket stubs and keys for this, that and the other. Her daughter was missing, and she had the feeling that something obvious was staring her in the face—which, of course, it was. It would take another Negroni for her to work it out.

Alys couldn't sleep. She'd never lain next to someone before and cried silently. For a whole hour she'd done it. Shame for thinking that Romy would want to spend her life with her when really what she wanted was a boy like Chad.

She got out of bed and dressed. She picked up her backpack and guitar and crept down the stairs. She swiped a box of matches and Romy's hand-drawn map. A soft click as the door closed behind her.

The air was night-pungent and carried the sound of owls. She didn't know which way to go and the roiling sway of panic made her queasy. But once her eyes had adjusted, she could see the night was blistered with stars and the dirt road glowed as pale as bread crumbs through the trees. She carried her guitar like a club and walked on ahead.

In the darkness, the fear lessened, and she was left with the quiet spill of sadness. She didn't understand how their love could end with a boy. Was this how it would always be? She felt all wrong again and she'd missed a turning and ended up in front of a gate. She lit a match and held it by the map. That was when Peg rose in her, defiant and clear. Back that way and fuck anyone who says otherwise. Peg led the way for the rest of the night, head up and switchblade sharp. And fuck that Romy fucking Peller, said Peg. You're better than ten of her. Keep to the left now. There you go. You're almost there.

Five minutes later the piazza opened out before her. Streetlights still on and the Villa Aurora hotel lit. Alys went inside and blagged a phone call. It was hard to keep it together now that she knew she was safe.

The phone rang in the *pensione* and Cress picked up.

Slow down, Mrs. Peller, he said. What missing keys? Where? A villa in Fiesole? Cress scribbled directions onto a notepad.

No, no I'll go. You keep the home fires burning. No, not literally, Mrs. Peller, and Cress hung up.

He wrote a note to Ulysses and grabbed his crash helmet. Claude said, I'm coming too, old man. And Cress said, Appreciate it.

Cress had just gotten to the door when the phone rang again. He ran back and picked up. Mrs. Peller, I'm— Alys? That you, sweetheart? Cress listened. Stay where you are and don't move. I'm coming.

Cress climbed on the motorbike and fired up the engine. He pulled down his goggles and Claude hopped into the sidecar. Cress sped off along Via Mazzetta, took a sharp left onto Via Maggio and another onto the Lungarno Guicciardini. He missed a red light and gunned it across the bridge. Along Borgo Ognissanti he leaned low into the handlebars, his body streamlined, shorts billowing, man and machine moving as one. Suddenly, the wail of a police siren settled in behind him. Claude popped up from the sidecar to see what was happening. Oh bugger, he said. Cress was in no mood for police interference and he told Claude to hang on tight whilst he tried to shake off the cop. Top speed now and a few blue feathers were launched into the slip-stream. Cress managed to get to Via il Prato before he was forced to slow down and finally stop. Cress, giddy from the chase, watched the policeman in his rearview mirror. The flare of lights pulsed across the road. What we gonna do? said Claude. Leave the talking to me, said Cress.

The policeman stood in front of Cress and asked for his documentation, and when Cress removed his goggles and helmet, this wasn't the man the police officer had expected to see at the controls of a Moto Guzzi Falcone. And certainly not with a blue parrot in the sidecar.

Before the policeman could say anything further, Cress held up his hand impatiently and explained in Italian that if the policeman was going to give him a ticket could he please issue it quickly, because he was in a hurry.

Why in a hurry? said the policeman.

An *emergenza*, said Cress.

What type of *emergenza*?

Cress stayed silent.

Signore?

Tell him! shouted Claude.

My granddaughter. She ran away to experience the nascent stirrings of love (*le nascenti agitazioni dell'amore*—Cress remembered the words from a poem) and now love has run away from her. She's somewhere up there—and he pointed to the black hills—cradling a broken heart, attempting to understand the complexity of human emotion. Why it's left her diminished when not long ago she felt like a conqueror. And here am I thinking what words can give the experience value. How to explain to her that the improbability of love, which she feels will last forever, will one day shine its light again. What words of consolation can be offered? What words of reassurance can I give her that a life lived without the object of her love is still worthwhile and hers for the taking?

And? said the policeman.

Claude turned expectantly to Cress.

There are no words, officer. Just me turning up and telling her how loved she is. And always will be.

The policeman blew his nose. Where we headed? he said.

We?

The policeman nodded.

Piazza Mino. Fiesole, said Cress.

Follow me, said the policeman.

When Cress entered the square, Alys thought the police escort a bit much, but from then on events happened fast. She got up from the pavement and ran toward Cress, and the policeman stumbled out of his car and ran toward her. Told her about his first love, Giulietta, and for a while it became all about him. Unburdened, he drove off with a wave and *Ciao*, Cressy!

Cressy gave Alys his handkerchief and said, You're safe now, my love. But we have to go and get Romy, you know that. We need to tell her about her dad.

I'm not talking to her, said Alys, clambering into the sidecar. You don't have to, said Cress, and Claude said, The course of true love never did run smooth. Shut up, Claude, said Alys.

Romy was awake when Cressy knocked. He explained what had happened to her father and she said, Guess that's the end of the book then. The world won't weep.

Romy drove close to the Moto Guzzi and Cress dropped her at the Ospedale Santa Maria Nuova, where her mother was waiting. Romy waved but Alys didn't. I don't know what I ever saw in her, said Alys.

Whatever she had or hadn't seen in Romy Peller, Alys still managed to cry for hours in her room. Midnight. One o'clock. Two. The clock ticked over and just when Cress and Ulysses thought the tears had ceased, a fresh tidal surge carried her out to an ocean of despair. Ulysses went in with a bowl of *brodo di pollo* and Alys asked if she could just have a small glass of wine to go with it. No, he said. Cress went in later with a hot chocolate and Alys asked if she could have a cigarette to go with it. No, said Cress. Alys eventually fell asleep fully clothed and Cress covered her with blankets.

Ulysses watched her sleep. He tried to stifle the rise of emotion, but it got the better of him and he turned away. It's just relief, that's all, he said. I know, I know, said Cress. But they both knew it was something more. Together they saw the sunrise that morning. There was no tiredness left in them as the day drew color. On the terrace Ulysses said, I couldn't have done any of this without you, Cress.

It was one of those moments I was made for, he said.

No, Cress, I mean any of *this*—and he gestured to his surroundings—and of Alys.

Cress didn't know what to say. All that love again. Paola came out on her terrace and waved to him. He waved to her.

I'll make the coffee today, said Ulysses. And dinner. You go brighten someone else's life.

Repercussions there had to be, and they came fast. The *pensione* took away any free time from the kid; afternoons and evenings were spent washing up, or cleaning rooms or stripping beds.

Romy came by the *pensione* a week later when she knew Alys was at school.

Can you give her this letter please, Mr. Temper?

Sure, said Ulysses. And, Romy? How's your father doing?

Good, I suppose, considering. We'll be leaving as soon as he gets used to the industrial brace. It's tricky on a plane, apparently.

Alys read the letter that night.

It was tender and eloquent, but mostly it was a letter of thanks. That's what surprised Alys. The things Romy had remembered. Alys brilliant at billiards in the Gambrinus basement. The pet shop behind Palazzo Vecchio, the plan to buy the songbirds and set them free. Alys's comments about the statue of David—that it was a statue of character first and foremost, and not of ideal physical proportion, not like the Donatello. I have the sketch you did on the paper serviette, she wrote. I'll keep it because I think it will be worth something one day.

I don't know why you left in the night, wrote Romy. I don't blame you. I'm sure it was something to do with me. On a good note, my parents are getting a divorce. I might go and live on a commune. So long, Alys. And Romy signed off with love.

Romy and her parents left for the States a day or two after the letter was delivered.

Cress said to Ulysses, I don't think that's the last we'll hear of Romy Peller, and Ulysses said, Oh Jesus, Cress, don't say that, I'm bloody exhausted.

I know, son, I know.

Summer arrived in a fanfare of heat. Tourists sweltered and the *pensione* was busting its guts. The photo of Eddie that Alys had lost was found in Claude's cage next to the mirror. Ulysses thought Eddie was good-looking, but Claude said, He's not so hot. Des's molds arrived and Ulysses began work on the larger globes. Alys went to London and when she came back, all she said about Peg was that she seemed smaller. Col was happy to have Peg, Alys and Ginny back under one roof again. He'd been under a bit of stress lately since the area including the pub had been placed under a compulsory purchase order. "*The council want to demolish it to make room for a new estate. Even Nichols Square,*" wrote Col. Col's new lady friend Ingrid had a pug called Lesley and Col didn't see it when he reverse-parked, and all hell had broken loose. Ingrid said it wasn't something she could ever get over, so she left. Col didn't mind being single again, not now that he had his women back. Col loved having Peg around. All that scorn, all the derision. Peg loved being around Col too, truth be told—not that she would have said so. Pete had an unexpected stroke of luck when he got a part in a new West End musical called *Oliver!* Pete said it was based on a novel by Charles Dickens and Col said, It'll never catch on. Pete brought the musical score into the pub and that was the night Ted turned up. Sat by the door with a pint he never drank and watched Peg come and go. Like the bleedin' Stasi, said Pete. No one saw Ted leave, of course. Later, Peg sang "As Long as He Needs Me" and there wasn't a dry eye in the house. Usually, Peg held the booze reins tight whenever Alys was around, but that night she unraveled. Full-on goad mode, with nothing and no one off-limits. Said to Alys, Loosen up, kid, and find yourself a boy. Alys went to bed ashamed that night. But of herself and not of Peg.

Early the following morning Alys found her mum sprawled out in the snug. Pissed her pants she had, something Alys would never share with anyone.

Alys? Anything else? said Ulysses.

Oh, said Alys, suddenly remembering. Mrs. Lovell died.

Mrs. Lovell died? said Cress. How?

Old age. Facedown in her roast.

But she's younger than me, said Cress. He stayed quiet for the rest of the day.

Ulysses said, When you said Peg seemed smaller . . . ?

Oh, you know. Just older.

Mid-August and Giglio couldn't come quick enough.

They set out early across the square as they always did and Claude flew on ahead to Betsy, although he struggled to gain height on account of the paunch. (You've got to stop carrying him, said Cress.) Betsy fired up straightaway and Ulysses bent down and kissed the steering wheel. To Porto Santo Stefano, Betsy!

Glimpses of sunflowers and a turquoise sea, and the air piqued with salt and that herbaceous tang. Windows were wide and Alys's hair blew free. Now and then she held it back with her hand and her smile was wide and Peg's. Ulysses watched her in the rearview mirror. Nowhere else was the passage of time so evident as in her face. Seven years gone like that. From child to young woman. You gotta let her go, the constant refrain.

They were the last to the ferry. The klaxon blared and the ship moved into open water and the soft, cool head-breeze. Claude took flight and tourists raised their cameras. Click! Click! Click! Cressy adjusted his shorts and let the sun get to his upper thigh. Alys drank from a bottle of water and let it dribble down her chin. Ulysses quiet and at peace, the tips of his ears already red.

Ulysses stood alone in the *salotto*. He could hear Massimo in the kitchen at the stove making coffee. The afternoon light was hazy; insects hovered with plant spores in a soporific trance. The linen curtains billowed and abated, billowed and abated, a slow rhythm in sync with the sea. The tiles were cool under his feet and he could feel grains of sand between his toes. Through the windows the familiar rustle of the eucalypts and the sound of cicadas.

On the walls, the photographs were as good an account of their life as ever there was. Seven years of salt and wine and friendship. Of laughter and tantrums. Of possibility and pain. Saved it up each year, they did, till they were on that ferry and then—

Ulysses turned. Massimo handed him an espresso cup. Massimo was no longer with Phil and although the decision had been his, he'd gone in on himself a bit, according to Cress. Massimo leaned his chin on Ulysses's shoulder and said, Look how slim I was there, Ulisse. Only a year ago.

But you're wearing stripes, Mass.

You're kind.

You know what Cress told me?

Go on.

That we weigh less at the equator than at either one of the poles.

So I move to Ecuador?

Just one option.

Massimo laughed. How's Alys?

A bit bruised. You?

Same. But better now that you're here. And Massimo kissed his back.

Will you talk to her, Mass?

Alys was days away from being fifteen. She should have been sleeping in or moping and yet the sun lifted her from that bed docilely and sent her into the hinterland to watch its fiery rise from that eastern line. She clambered down granite rocks and swam as a new day took hold.

On the ferry over, Ulysses had said to her, We need to know what the heart's capable of, Alys.

Do you know what it's capable of?

I think so, he said.

Why aren't you with anyone, Uly? she'd said.

I can't answer that. Not even for myself.

Is it Peg?

Not anymore. We had our moment and moments pass. Learn to seize them, Alys.

He'd never spoken like that before. As if he knew what she was feeling and his silences, his calm veneer, weren't passivity at all, but quiet reflection, the hidden pain of something unmentionable.

Alys held her breath and dipped her head under the water. Below her, the dark splodges of sea urchins. The distortion of her legs as they kicked to keep her afloat. They looked so pale in dawn's skylight.

Hey, Alys! (It was Massimo.)

How is it? he said.

Delectable, Massi.

(A middle-aged man briefly in flight.)

Massimo surfaced. There's a world out there, Alys, he said. Of people like us. Get out of this country and find them.

Mid-August lunch. Eighty-two degrees Fahrenheit in the shade and a slow economy of movement.

Everyone look at the camera! shouted Massimo as he set the timer and ran back into position.

(Click.) Caught forever.

From left, Alys next to Massimo with Ulysses on the right. Their arms are draped around one another in simple familiarity. Cress stands in front of Ulysses, holding Claude. Claude is lying prone, his face alluringly turned to face the camera. Behind them, the terrace is flush with color. Geraniums of course, but lavender too, and dahlias of vivid orange and red. The glimpse of a trestle table with the remains of fried fresh anchovies and tomatoes galore and *fagioli* with clams, the menu devised and cooked by Ulysses. Two bottles of the crisp white ansonica wine native to the island can just be seen over Massimo's shoulder. One of the bottles is half full. Above them, the grapevine is thick and established and the grapes hang low. It is Claude's favorite place to rest. He no longer dreams of the Amazon, only of Giglio. He wants to live here forever but hasn't yet voiced the prospect. A lizard scampers out for a close-up. Alys is wearing cut-off shorts and an old shirt of Ulysses's. She wears sunglasses and her face is bronzed and she looks older than her years. Just by a year or two, but that is enough to secure the tentative beginning of adulthood. Whilst swimming in those crystal waters, a seed has been planted: She will leave home in two years' time. She will go to art school. Live in London. She will love again many times. And each time will be as exhilarating as the last, and each person will be the one because she will love deeply and be loved deeply back. Her smile is wide because she senses something is germinating. She's only thought of Romy eleven times since she's been there. Cress wears the desert shorts that Paola made him to accentuate the shapely profile of his legs. His collared T-shirt is Aertex, a versatile fabric he swears by. His feet are bare, and his toenails clipped. Every day is a new beginning, and Paola told him that she began again with him and Cress walked tall that day. Picked figs without needing a box to stand on. Massimo feels attractive and funny and interesting with his friends and dresses accordingly: a red Hawaiian shirt and white tennis shorts very similar to the ones worn by the great Nicola Pietrangeli. His thighs have lost their comfort padding since the breakup with Phil and have become muscular and lean. Heartbreak suits me, he thinks. He might even use it as a way of controlling his weight. This makes him laugh. A guttural and spontaneous delight of a laugh, a rare sound for him. That's what prompts Ulysses to turn the moment the shutter clicks. Ulysses is wearing long white shorts and a white shirt over a vest after his shoulders were burned on an afternoon fishing trip. He's barefoot. His feet are brown. Caught in profile means the dimple in his cheek is pronounced and his hair has flopped across his forehead. Oh, the way he looks at Massimo! Big old story in that look. The laughter, you see—reminded Ulysses of Darnley.

Hey, Temps, he could hear him say. I was thinking. After the war, we could . . .

We could what, sir?

(Darnley lights a cigarette.)

We could just sit here. And look at the sea. That'd be enough, right?

More than enough, sir.

In October, Ulysses turned forty. Peg sent a telegram that said, FUCK. FORTY. OLD. Ulysses bought himself some heavy horn-rimmed glasses, now that he needed them for reading and close-up work on the globes. It would be fair to say that he was turning into a fairly handsome middle-aged man.

That night, the gang went to see *Ben-Hur* at the Odeon. Came out all agog at the CinemaScope spectacle. Never seen anything like it. And the costumes! I don't usually like Charlton Heston. Was that Charlton Heston? Get on with you, Cressy! But that chariot race. I couldn't watch, said Massimo.

Dinner was at Michele's afterward. A nocturnal stroll from Piazza della Repubblica across the river and Giulia did them proud. Brought them *penne* and rabbit, and *bracioline* with green bean sauce and a liter of Sangiovese. Ulysses's birthday cake was *castagnaccio*, his favorite chestnut tart. Even Michele came from behind his counter to shake his hand. What followed a little later could have been awkward, and yet neither he nor Giulia could truly say how it happened, it was simply that a private shadowed space opened up around them, where no one else stood, and they kissed. No guilt. No lamenting the moment of madness, simple joy across both of their faces. And it would remain what it was—a kiss—and nothing more. But sighting one another after such a tender act of intimacy added a certain flush to the cheeks from then on. Her whisperings of the daily specials made his pants tighten in a way they hadn't for years.

———

And suddenly, 1960 came to its upright end. Ulysses was on the terrace with Massimo, waiting for a new year to start. Pete had to stay put in London because of *Oliver!* but he didn't mind because the money was good, and he was putting the cash away. Alys, all fifteen years and four months of her, was singing on the church steps surrounded by crowds of young people. Had a microphone this time; piercing feedback but it did the job. And Cress and Paola? They were sitting arm in arm on the bench with a glass of something warm. Just them, their world, their love.

Alys strummed the opening bars and the crowd hushed. She leaned in close to the mic and said, This song's called "Grace and Fury."

It's Just
the Way
of Things

1962 – 66

In 1962, the summer she turned seventeen, Alys left Florence. She put Ketty Lester's "Love Letters" on the jukebox, picked up her guitar and backpack and said, Adieu. Ulysses took the train with her to Milan. Slipped an envelope of cash and a packed lunch from Giulia into her bag. Not so hard to let her go.

She went to live at Col's. Worked in the pub even though she wasn't really allowed, but everyone knew her, including the coppers who hung out in the snug. She got her portfolio together and saved for art school, the only fixed point on the horizon. Some evenings she sang with Pete and something new happened then, something she'd never had to confront before: comparisons with her mother. People said she didn't have Peg's looks, but she did have her voice. It did something to her, it did. Little bit of rage, little bit of ugly.

Alys was there when the first stage of demolition began. Standing with Col and Gin Gin as the wrecking ball swung. The gothic villas in the square went first. *"They call it slum clearance, but we were never a slum, were we?"* she wrote to Ulysses and Cress in her first letter home. *"Col said he's not selling the pub and they'll have to drag him out in a coffin. Ginny cries when the walls fall because she doesn't understand and thinks it's war all over again. Devy came to visit her yesterday and Col didn't say anything. He's got too much on his plate to fight that battle too. Devy brought a cake and put candles on it to make Col happy. It wasn't Col's birthday, but it did make him happy. I miss you both. Love as always."*

In the January term of 1963, Alys went to Wimbledon School of Art. She lived partly at Col's and partly on a sofa nearby. She lived in a state of uncertainty but came to realize she probably always had. She struggled, initially, in the way she saw things and how this was expressed as marks on a page. But she turned up every day and she practiced her craft and that was significant. Until she saw people achieve what she hoped to achieve and she wanted to be generous and yet, at times, feared that their success would mean no success for her. She was so impatient for her work to be affirmed. She'd walked into art school hoping to be discovered as the NEXT BIG THING, only to live in the shadows of disregard. Her mother-want became a mother-please and crushes on teachers became evening tutorials of charcoal and perfume. And she read wise words over and over and yet when she closed the book it was still her, unchanged, and the disappointment could send her to bed for days.

But then one night in spring, she was invited by friends to a lecture hall in Holborn. Too much dope and the wrong bus had her clattering through the doors and racing up the stairs. Suddenly halted by the unmistakable voice of Evelyn Skinner coming from the main hall. She began to laugh.

Oh no no, I totally disagree, said Evelyn. If women's lives are not documented, then how on earth can we say we have the full picture? We have framed the narrative. Or I should say you and your predecessors have, Mr. Dixon. And wherever there is framing, there is exclusion.

The women in the audience cheered. Alys hurried on up to the balcony, where she saw the magnificent Evelyn Skinner onstage. Eighty-two years old and thriving, by the looks of things. Looking ten years younger due to cod liver oil and cold-water swimming, and frequent dinners at Quo Vadis with Dotty Cunningham. Not that Alys knew that then. All Alys saw was the woman who had left such a lasting impression on her.

The balcony was smoky and packed with art students. Alys looked about for her friends and saw Martha in the front row leaning attentively on the rail. Alys walked down toward her. Sorry, sorry, she said as she inched along the row. Alys sat down and she and Martha kissed French style.

(Alys would put all this down in a letter to Cress and Ulysses. How Evelyn looked: elegant and imposing. Linen slacks and blouse and a bright scarf. *"Oh, she was marvelous!"*)

Evelyn continued. She said, Let's take as an example Gentileschi's *Susanna and the Elders*. On the screen behind me now. Take a good look. It's a biblical story in which a young woman bathing is spied upon by old men who are trying unsuccessfully to blackmail her into sexual relations. A popular theme in Renaissance and Baroque painting, mainly because of the opportunity it afforded to paint naked female flesh.

The audience laughed.

You may well laugh, said Evelyn. And yet these are the choices we are talking about. In Gentileschi's version behind me, we get a woman's point of view. And it is an uncomfortable one. Susanna is centered in the painting and her anxiety and distress are central to the piece. This is no jocular flirtation. These men are lecherous, scheming and threatening whilst she is vulnerable and naked. Her body is twisted. They are abusing her. And the painter knows this because this is *her* experience.

Outside Conway Hall, the night had turned chill, a slight mist hovering in headlights and streetlamps, and even in the flare of a match. Alys was standing on the pavement, smoking a cigarette. Her friends were milling about, jumping on scooters, heading into Soho. Coming? In a bit, said Alys.

An hour passed, and the cold had gotten in and Evelyn had been secreted away through another exit. Alys turned around and headed to Soho. Along New Oxford Street she was gripped by a rare moment of actual mother-want and found a phone box down a side street and filled it with coins.

Ted? It's Alys. Peg there? No, I—I just want to talk to Peg, please. (Fuck, just get her, will you?) Peg? Yeah, I'm fine. You? (Peg slightly slurring but sweet.)

Alys leaned against the glass and told Peg about her evening. About the talk and about Evelyn and how she'd waited. Peg was good on the subject of waiting, Peg was reassuring. Told her to go and buy some chips and find her friends. Peg was kind before the money ran out.

Ulysses folded the letter and said, Well, well, well. Evelyn Skinner was back in their life. He said, Today's a good day, Cress, and put the letter back in its envelope.

I'll get the coffees in, said Cress.

In May, something significant happened. Something unforeseen. Something that shook the foundations of that small Florentine world.

The Iris Garden, up by the Piazzale Michelangelo, had not long opened for the season, and Cress and Paola were first through the gates that day. A rare cream and peach variety had caught Paola's eye and she'd knelt down to view it better. When Cress turned round he saw a crowd of people where she had not long been, and they were looking down.

It was Cressy who telephoned Michele, who telephoned the best friend in Lazio, who notified the sister and brother, and after that Paola's death was taken away from him. Her body interred with her husband outside Prato, as he knew it would be. But he sat on a stone bench every day and Giulia brought him coffee and Michele brought him *La Nazione* to read and people came to him, spoke words of consolation to him because they knew. Cressy and Paola, they were something, weren't they? That the people of the square understood was enough for Cress. And he had the Iris Garden, of course. That it was open for a mere four weeks a year made it the most private, the most perfect of resting places.

Cress got old quick that summer, but that's grief for you—that's what

Ulysses said in a call to Col and Pete and Peg. All three huddled around the telephone in the pub late one night in July. What can we do for the old Romeo? said Col, and Ulysses said, Be gentle. And that shut Col up quick. Col even apologized in case he was out of line.

I'll keep you posted, said Ulysses.

And we'll think up something too, said Peg. Tell him he's my rock. Tell him, you know—

I will. Words as gold dust, Peg?

You got it.

She said that? said Cress.

She did.

Cress drank his coffee that morning. Even had a pastry, too. Peg's words, you see—the old fella simply loved her. It would be wrong to say Cress wouldn't be the same again because he would, but he needed time. So, Ulysses took over the running of the *pensione*. Coffee dripping into espresso cups by the eight a.m. bells. Pastries on the plates and a tray outside every door. A little knock, a walk away, the door opened, the sound of delight. Ulysses did the changeovers too, drove the heavy linens over to Manfredi's. Alys even wrote a telegram to see if Ulysses wanted her home. STAY PUT, MY SWEET, AND THRIVE. He'd never written anything so poetic in his life. She'd keep that telegram all her life.

Cress stayed on the terrace with his citrus tree, surrounded by scent and blossom. Tree said few words and together they watched the pungent flare of dawn, the glare of the midday trope, the drift of dusk. Cress slept a lot. Cress kept dreaming of butterflies.

The scene: Late August. An eerie, soporific trance of a day. Heat settling across the city like a fucking furnace—Col's words. Shutters bolted firmly against the scorching haze and the square lifeless 'cept for a couple of malnourished pigeons and the odd tourist at Michele's forking strands of spaghetti into their parched mouth, wishing they'd ordered a salad instead. When all of a sudden:

An ambulance siren, wailing and screaming, bansheelike. A sound Ulysses hadn't heard in ten years.

What the—? he said, waking up from a nap. He got off the sofa and threw open the shutters. Well, I bloody never, he said to Claude. Claude flew to the window and had a run on droppings.

Ulysses slung on a shirt and raced down the stairs. The elderly contessa was waiting for him at the bottom.

You need new friends, she said.

Sì sì, I know, I know, Contessa, he said.

Out of the door now and into the sunshine, tucking in his shirt and protecting his eyes from the glare. He watched the green ambulance appear at the side of the basilica. Col shouting and swearing and hammering the dash and Pete barely holding on to the remaining back door as it jolted across the uneven stones. Shutters on all sides of the square were flung open to witness the commotion. Suddenly, the van came to a halt, and Pete was thrown out headfirst. The wailing stopped and the thick silence was broken only by the sound of two hubcaps rolling menacingly into the gutter.

Pete crawled toward Ulysses and said, Never again.

What happened, Pete?

We lost one of the back doors the other side of Parma. Caused a pileup on a major road. Col took off and only Peg's quick thinking stopped me from ending up under an Alfa Romeo.

Peg?

Yeah, said Pete. She held on to my legs till Col could pull over and help drag me back in.

Peg's here?

Yeah. Hey, Peg!

Not quite the introduction she'd hoped for, but there you have it. Peg slunk out, bare legs and heels first, followed by a belted midi short-sleeved dress in emerald green. Sunglasses hid the ten years older and the sun highlighted the ten years blonder. Oh my God, said Ulysses.

Clack clack clack across the stones she went. Hips swaying, arms swinging. Peg's tune, right? And there it was again, that little churn in Ulysses's guts.

Peg? What the—?

Worst fucking days of my life, Temps. Don't ask. Don't *ever, ever* ask.

Ulysses opened his arms and held her. I've missed you, he whispered.

Oi! No one ever interested in me? said Col. What am I? Chopped fucking liver?

Pete began to retch.

Keep your mouth shut, Col, said Peg.

Oh, that's nice.

Mouth. And Peg pointed to it.

Col blew into his hands and recoiled. Anyone got a mint? he said.

Come here, said Ulysses, pulling him into a tight clasp.

That's more like it, said Col.

The sound of a door latch made them turn. It was Cressy. A bit sleepy and dazed. He looked from one to the other and said, Peg. Col. Pete.

Hasn't lost his memory then, said Col.

Shuttup, Col, said Peg.

What you all doing here? said Cress.

We're here for you, Cress, said Pete. Make sure you're OK.

Course I'm OK. (Cress choked now. Oh, those watery eyes.) Course I am.

Come here, said Peg.

Cress did as he was told because Peg's arms were a good place to be. Cress had shrunk. It's OK, said Peg. It's OK.

They clattered up the stairs, carried on with the same old yacking and joshing from where they'd left off. They passed the entrance to the *pensione*, which had been taken over by an art history group from Leamington Spa, and Cress said they were a fractious lot due to differing views on Leonardo and Raphael. By the time Cress put his key in the door and led them into the hallway, rooms had been divvied up and it was decided that Peg would be in Alys's room, Pete in with Ulysses, and no one wanted to room with Col. Oh, that's really nice, that is, said Col.

It was strange for Peg to be standing in her daughter's room after so many years. A bed shoved up in the corner, an easel and a drawing desk the only furniture. Disused tomato cans full of pencils, empty wine bottle with a candle in the top, and a paint-splattered terra-cotta floor that looked more terrazzo in style now. The photo of Eddie was stuck to the wall with tape. Still that yearning between Peg's legs, oh where the fuck did the time go? Peg old enough to be his mother now, sort of twists the story of their love to something odd. Twenty years of loving and hoping had broken her and allowed Ted to slip in through the cracks and there was no turning back. I sold my soul, Eddie, and I feel that vacancy every single day. And now our kid, all grown up. At art school! All your talent, you'd be so proud, and she looks like you too, Eddie. Got my smile, they say, but I only see you. And sometimes it hurts to look at her, at her smooth skin and the years she has ahead, and I want to slap her, Eddie, and that's why I have to keep her at arm's length, because sometimes she makes me bitter and I don't want to be bitter because it unseats the love and I just don't know what to do. So that's me, Eddie. Who I've become. My mother, after all.

She moved away. Stood in front of a portrait of Alys, a proper drawing, white pencil capturing the light in her eyes, so fierce and intense, and Peg suddenly realized how little the kid was when she'd let her go. She felt an ache in her guts, but she hadn't eaten so maybe that was it? She lowered her face to the few clothes hanging on a rail. She didn't know her daughter's smell, but it was the closest she'd ever felt to her.

Peg sat on the bed and looked out through the doorway. Some kind of commotion. Col was trying to stem the blood from his nose, Pete holding Claude protectively, Cress telling Col, Well, what d'you expect? Making a parrot feel diminished like that.

Old Cressy. How she'd missed him. How he knew her, how he could soothe her. Coming here had been *her* idea. She let Col take the credit, but it was her because she knew what happened when the waves hit—that lurching shift when the ballast slides into empty space and you tilt so far over you think you're gonna capsize, think you're gonna drown.

Temps has come into her room. That smile of his, same as when he was a boy. Bit awkward, bit sweet. He sits on the bed next to her. He holds her hand and she doesn't pull away. She could say anything to him, and he'd forgive her and never judge her. But what do you want to say, Peg? Eh, Peg? That you're tired of life and out of your depth? But you won't say a thing. Still swagger on with a belly full of bluster and a blah di blah who's up for another?

I know this was your idea, he says.

Col's the hero.

I know it was you.

What's going on out there?

Col was rude to Claude, so Claude flew into his face.

How is he?

Col or Cress?

Cress.

Better now that you're here. How long you staying, Peg?

Till we take the stabilizers off.

Thanks.

You look good. (She runs her hand over his cheek and chin.) Grown into you, haven't you? What? You looking at me like you wanna know something.

How'd you get away from him?

Let's not, Temps.

I worry for you.

And I worry for you. It's what we do, right?

He hit you?

Wash your mouth out. This is supposed to be a happy day. Now change the bloody record.

Here. And he reaches into his pocket and puts on his glasses self-consciously. I have to wear them now, he says. When I work or read.

They suit you.

You reckon?

You wear 'em in bed?

He blushes and takes them off. Her hand on his leg.

Not here, Peg. This is—

I know, I know.

That evening, Peg joined Ulysses in the kitchen and helped prepare dinner for the guests. Col, Pete and Cress went on ahead to Michele's, and Peg could hear them in the stairwell. Col saying something about running over Lesley and Cress said, Not Lesley Greenaway? And Col said, No, Lesley the pug. Ingrid's pug. What pug? said Cress. Jesus Christ, said Col. Just when I'd started to feel sorry for you.

Peg was laughing now.

What? said Ulysses.

Just them, she said.

As if they'd all never been apart.

Peg took instruction easily. Her first time using a pestle and mortar, first time making pesto, too, and she said she found it soothing. Afterward, she became a waitress for the night, turned a few heads when she interrupted a conversation about Carrara marble. She'd even end up as a comment in the visitors' book, although the page would have to be torn out. What's wrong with people? Cress would say. Writing something like that for all the world to see.

Just before ten, however, Ulysses blew out the candles and turned off the lights. He thought they were heading down to Michele's, but Peg took his hand and led him back upstairs to his room.

Peg?

She pushed him down on the bed.

Through the window, a black and blue marbled sky, a now-you-see-me-now-you-don't moon and stars and household lights and Col's laugh rising outside Michele's.

Put these on, she said, reaching into his trouser pocket and pulling out his glasses. She unzipped him, pulled up her dress and straddled him. They didn't move for a while. A slow pelvic rock till it became unbearable. She pressed both hands onto his mouth to stop his groans.

At ten thirty they went down to the square. Peg called out to Cress and the old fella's face lit up at the sight of her. Peg sat down next to him and held his hand and Ulysses grabbed a stool from the neighboring table and sat next to Pete. He poured out the remainder of the wine and said, What we interrupt, Cress?

Well, I was just about to tell them about my new vision, said Cress.

What's it this time? said Col.

England to win the World Cup in 1966, said Cress.

You're dreaming, said Col. They're crap. Always have been, always will be.

But there's more, said Ulysses, lifting his glass. This is the genius twist.

Col turned to Cress. Well, Mr. Genius? he said.

Geoff Hurst hat trick.

Mr. Two Left Feet? said Col. Mr. Geoff "I've never played for England" Hurst?

He will in February, said Cress. And he'll be picked for the squad. That's what came to me and that's the bet. England to win but with a Geoff Hurst hat trick. Everything on the black.

I'm in, said Pete.

You'll have to put the bet on in London for me, Pete, because they don't like that sort of thing here. I'll give you a specially adapted false-bottomed suitcase to take the money back in.

Pete tapped his nose. Thanks, Cress.

You ain't going near Tubs, I hope? said Col.

I was thinking Soho Sid.

Soho Sid? scoffed Col. He still got a patch?

Quite a big one, said Pete. Holed up next to the Mandrake.

I like Sid, said Peg.

I'm after at least ten to one, said Cress.

Ten to one! said Col. He thinks it's Blankers-Koen all over again. Lightning don't strike twice, Signor Cresswell!

But it does though, don't it? said Pete. Alan Beantree.

Alan—?

Beantree, said Pete. You remember him. Out walking his dog. Struck by lightning in August 1939. When he recovered he showed everyone his foot.

His foot?

Where the lightning came out. A year later, out walking his dog and it happened again.

Dead?

I hope so, said Ulysses. 'Cause they buried him next to me mum and dad.

But what's this all about? said Col.

About lightning not striking twice, said Pete. I'm saying it does. Because it did.

But in all fairness, Pete, said Cress, the two strikes were different.

Fucking hell, said Col.

The first strike that afflicted Alan Beantree was a side flash. When the current jumps from a tall object—in this case a tree—to the victim. Alan Beantree acted as a short circuit for some of the energy in the lightning discharge.

What happened to the dog? said Peg.

Cinders.

Dead?

No, the dog was *called* Cinders.

Jesus help me, Temps, said Col.

It ran off, said Pete. Found a new family in Bow.

And the second strike, said Cress, was a direct strike. In the open air. Alan Beantree hadn't even got to the tree. Struck down in his prime, he was.

Cress, he was seventy! said Peg.

A direct strike it was, the deadliest strike of all, said Cress. From which there's no coming back. Who's for another carafe of red?

I'm in, they all said.

Peg winked at Ulysses. "Cress'll be all right" was what that wink said. He pushed his leg against hers under the table, their own little energy discharge. Giulia noticed it when she brought over the wine; so much static it nearly lifted her hair combs. Someone's happy, she said in dialect before walking off.

As the days passed, Cressy's spirit raised its head above the ramparts again and it was a glorious sight to behold. Ulysses told him to take everyone out so he could get on with the cleaning, and Peg wanted to help Ulysses, but of course it was Peg whom Cress wanted by his side. Pete wanted to wander by himself and compose a song or two. I can feel the muse right here right now, he said.

That's just someone walking on your grave, said Col.

So, with Col riding pillion, and Peg in the sidecar, Cress pulled out all the stops. And all those experiences he'd had with Paola, no longer dormant but alive. He gunned it out to Piazzale Donatello and the English Cemetery: a green hillock surrounded by choking traffic, but Cress called the place a mirage.

Under a September sun, the great cypresses threw down geometrical shadows across the dead, and tight red fists of rose stood out against the white marble monuments. With his hand resting on her tomb, Cress recited Elizabeth Barrett Browning's "How Do I Love Thee." Little catch to the back of the throat by the word-perfect end. Classic Cressy. He waited for Col to ridicule him, but Col didn't. Col said it was a deeply moving rendition. Col never used words like that, and even Peg's eyebrows thought it worth a raise.

Walking along a shaded pathway, Col said he was worried about the demolition's blighting the terraces. Everyone knew that Col was his pub and without the pub . . . well, it wasn't worth thinking about. And then Cress said, What'll happen to my cherry tree, Col? And Col said, I'll tie myself to it, if needs be, Cress. I can be that kind of man.

———

Now, the following day, Cress had planned a trip to Chianti but had forgotten to tell anyone about it. He'd hoped Ulysses would drive them out to the vineyards in Betsy but when morning came, Ulysses had gone. Peg was sunning herself on the terrace. You see anything, Col? she said.

Col was scanning the square with the telescope. Nothing, he said. He's scarpered.

You seen him? said Peg to Pete, who had just come in from his walk.

No, I haven't, Peg. Betsy's gone, though.

Betsy's gone? said Cress. That'll be it then. Happens every year, same sort of time. He's gone for the day.

Gone where? said Col.

Cress shrugged. Disappears, sometimes overnight.

Well, I never, said Col. He's got a woman. About bloody time. And he lit a cigarette.

Peg stayed quiet.

I'm not sure it is a woman, said Cress.

I'd like to think it is, said Pete. Every year, you say, Cress?

Cress nodded.

I don't think I've heard anything more committed, said Pete, and he even wrote a song about it later that day. "364 Days and Counting," it was called. He wrote it fast and completed it by the time Ulysses walked through the door later that night.

Hey, Temps, listen to this!

Ulysses put his hat on the stand and walked into the living room. A soft melody, with a soft chorus about a lifetime lived in a day. Pete ditched the obvious reference to a mayfly.

Peg said, And where'd you go, sunshine? She said it all nudge nudge, wink wink, but Ulysses wasn't in the mood. He went to bed early that night. Contemplative, was the word Cressy used to describe him.

Peg called Pete into the kitchen and asked him to swap rooms with her, and Pete all amenable said, Of course. He's a lovely fella to sleep with.

Peg tiptoed into Ulysses's room, slipped out of her dress and got into bed with him. Ulysses said, I really just want to be quiet, Peg. And with arms around one another, they listened to voices give way to bells and bells give way to oblivion. Peg said, You got a woman, Temps? and Ulysses said, I don't have a woman. They rolled away from one another to sleep, but the soles of their feet touched all night.

Peg, Col and Pete left the following day. In spite of the protestations, they all took up their allotted positions in the van. Cress had fixed a solid sheet of wood to the back as a replacement door and Col had promised Pete they'd stop in Soutigny on the way back. What the fuck's in Soutigny? he said. Claude flew down from the statue and shat on the windscreen and Pete held up the specially adapted suitcase and tapped it knowingly. No one could bear to watch Ulysses and Peg say good-bye.

All set? shouted Col.

Get on with it, said Peg.

The ambulance jolted back to life and wailed.

Bye, Temps!

Bye, Peg!

Good riddance! shouted the contessa.

And then they were gone.

Cress would never forget their turning up for him for as long as he lived. All that love again. Cress thought he'd had more than his fair share, and that, for Cress, was as bad as having none at all. But the tree said, That can't happen. Love's the way. And its leaves quivered as the breeze came in from the southern hills. Tree said, They're starting the grape harvest somewhere.

That so? said Cress.

And the swallows are lining up to leave.

I'll miss them, said Cress.

It's just the way of things.

———

Sergio Leone rode into the Odeon in 1964. It was the start of the *Trilogia del Dollaro*. Walking out of *A Fistful of Dollars*, Massimo said, For me, Ennio Morricone has completely redefined the cinematic soundtrack.

And Cress and Ulysses wholeheartedly agreed.

Massimo said the same thing a year later after watching *For a Few Dollars More*.

Col sent regular updates on Geoff Hurst and spied on him at the training ground. Col got a bit of a reputation, and not a good one, and Peg told him to lose the binoculars. Col said Hurst was no match for Jimmy Greaves and his acid reflux returned. He blamed it all on Cress and his gambling ways. In October, Alys and Pete were arrested outside the US embassy in Grosvenor Square during protests against the Vietnam War. Alys made the banners that said MILITARISM IS THE SAME AS RACISM. They were released that night without charge because Col knew the station sergeant. Col was waiting for them outside. He said, This is a new low, even for you, Pete. Bless you, said Pete.

Geoff Hurst did make the England World Cup squad, but Col said he'd remain on the bench unless something bad happened to Greavesy.

Something bad happened to Greavesy. A leg injury put him out of the quarterfinals.

Why'd you doubt? said Cress.

I feel ill, said Col.

Go to bed then, said Cress.

Till when?

Till the final, and Cress hung up.

July 30, 1966, was the final, and the day history was made.

Outside Michele's, the sun blazed down on the Campari canopy now faded to an attractive shade of pink. A crowd had gathered in front of a small black and white screen that had been precariously rigged outside. The atmosphere was electric. Literally. One spilled drink away from disaster.

It was from this vantage point that Cress, Massimo and Ulysses calmly saw England win the World Cup and, more important, Geoff Hurst get his hat trick. They celebrated quietly and modestly on the terrace that night. A slightly better class of wine was had.

There's only one Geoff Hurst! sang an aging and topless overweight man in a pub somewhere in East London. Only one Geoff Hurst! There's only one!

Soho Sid paid out with grace. He'd already made a mint, so what did he care? They found out later that he'd been so intrigued by the bet, he'd placed the same one with Tubby Folgate, of all people, so Sid was quids in and Tubby back to his smarting ways.

Took Col an hour to get a telephone connection to Italy that night.

How much we win? said Ulysses.

A bloody fortune, said Col, unwrapping a mint.

The gang had pooled their bet money and three days later Pete shared out the winnings accordingly and everyone did very nicely for themselves, thank you very much. Col looked after Peg's share on account of Ted. Peg had her ticket out of there, finally, but she just needed to know where to go.

Alys came back to Florence that summer. The summer she turned twenty-one.

She may not have had Peg's looks, but she had something more. She read esoteric works and communed with nature the way Cress had been doing for years. She had taken acid once but never again. She had seen Bob Dylan play at the Albert Hall and thought he was something else. She'd had many lovers, including men, although her preference would always be women, because kissing women undid her soul. Her art school career had been unsuccessful, but it had given her time to inquire and try. She came back from painting and settled on drawing and technically she was brilliant, she just didn't know what she wanted to say.

She walked through the concourse of Santa Maria Novella station with a porter following behind with her luggage. She wore her fringe high and her hair tied back, and denim flares and a white cheesecloth shirt, and she had the requisite beads around her neck and a love bite on her shoulder from the woman she'd shared the sleeper with. A guitar in her left hand and the false-bottomed suitcase stashed with cash in her right. She saw Ulysses up ahead and her heart surged. Uly! she shouted. He turned. How she'd missed him!

Mud Angels

1966–67

Autumn rolled round again and brought shorter days and early nights and six weeks of continuous rain due to a cyclone over the Mediterranean. Northern Italy was awash.

Beginning of November, and Ulysses looked out from his workshop at the deluge. He could feel the damp rising up from the ground. It was nearly dusk, and the square was bleak and torn of life. The following day was a holiday, when the city celebrated the country's victory over Austria in the First World War. People had already left for the weekend and Alys had driven Cress to Rome on account of the old fella's keen interest in the Romantic poets. There were no guests in the *pensione*, so Ulysses was alone for the first time in years—a queasy proposition. He'd arranged to meet Massimo later that evening, a British industry gathering, something to do with the swinging sixties and London. The rain was making the prospect of a night out unappealing.

The fifty-centimeter-diameter globe in front of him was his best yet. It was sold already to a family whose lineage went back a few centuries, not an uncommon occurrence in a city such as this. He was adding minor details, that was all now, brush in one hand, rag in the other. Paint dab paint dab, careful not to overwork it. The stand was being made by a carpenter nearby, a freestanding base made of oak with a brass meridian. It would break his heart to let it go.

He stubbed out his cigarette and decided to call it a day. He opened the door and emptied the hot coals from the *scaldini* into the gutter, then put on his hat and mac and turned off the lights. The sound was of rain only.

Coming out onto Via Maggio the smells and luster of the *alimentari* drew him in. He loaded himself up with cheese and meat and pasta and two special bottles of wine and by the time he got to the square, he was soaked.

He showered long. Lay on the bed and listened to the drum of rain against the shutters. The red neon sign from Michele's pulsed across the dark and the Beach Boys sang "Don't Worry Baby" faintly from the jukebox. If it was anyone but Massimo, he would've canceled. It was the kind of night to settle on the sofa with a grappa and a large parrot for company.

He put on a suit, loosely knotted a dark tie and discarded shoes in favor of Wellington boots. He grabbed an umbrella and headed out into the storm-lashed night. Along Lungarno Guicciardini, thunder rumbled across the hills. The streets were inundated and cascades of water were thrown up by passing taxis and packed buses. Black umbrellas clogged the narrow pavements, and the green, white and red bunting, hastily erected for the following day's holiday, was drenched.

But it was the river whose transformation was most startling. The grassy flatlands where the fishermen stood had been swallowed by the swollen current. Crossing Santa Trìnita bridge, the water raged through the stone arches only a few feet below. How could such a softly spoken green stream have turned into this?

Massimo was waiting for him outside Palazzo Strozzi, and after commenting on his sartorial elegance—and why not Wellington boots, Ulisse?—he said that he'd already been up to the gathering and it was incredibly dull although the wine, as you'd expect, was good. So I suggest we go eat.

The suggestion was Zia Chiara, tucked behind Piazza Santa Croce.

It was a small restaurant that was really a domestic front room, with three tables of two only and no menu. You ate whatever Zia Chiara had made that evening for her family upstairs. Ulysses knew the food to be superb. The evening, finally, on an upswing.

The wind had subsided, and the journey east was made at a fair trot. They arrived at Zia Chiara's door relatively dry and in good spirits. The walls carried photographs, some sepia, some faded, of farm life before the family's move to the urban north. A crucifix too, of course, and a signed photograph from a beloved film star: *"Zia Chiara. Nobody does it better. Sophia Loren x"*

They sat next to a cat, who, seemingly indifferent to the nightly incursion on its home, washed itself thoroughly before settling on Massimo's lap. A jug of red wine and a basket of *pane casalingo* were placed on the table and for an hour Chiara forgot about them.

The conversation turned immediately to Alys and Cressy's pilgrimage to Rome. Ulysses said that Cress wanted to see where the poet Keats had died, said it would help him get a sense of the city through a twenty-five-year-old's eyes.

I was engaged when I was twenty-five, said Massimo.

You were?

To Annunziata Berlingo. After I broke it off, she married a Frescobaldi.

That's quite a rebound.

He wasn't the main branch. A mere twig. You think they'll get to the Cinecittà Studios?

If Alys has her way.

Any souvenir would be appreciated.

Ulysses laughed. She knows that.

Massimo poured out the wine and said, My mother has an admirer, by the way.

Your mother does?

I know, I know. We placed her in the home for safety. She's like a teenager. Very amorous. But what can you do?

By the time the beef came out, the men had made good progress on the wine, and the bad weather outside, a thing of the past. Rain? What rain? said Massimo. At some point, Ulysses thought to mention the height and force of the river.

Massimo said it was probably the snowmelt from Monte Falterona. Or maybe they opened the gates on the dams to release the pressure? Massimo stood up. Talking of releasing the pressure, he said, and the *signora* pointed to the back.

They paid the bill and wished one another a happy *festa* and the two men left the old woman in a chair resting her eyes, the older brother shuffling down the stairs in search of a sliver of cheese.

Piazza Santa Croce was quiet, a few parked cars, but no wanderers that night. At the corner of Via dei Benci, they clasped one another and arranged to meet on Saturday for a rerun of *8¹/₂* at the Rex. Massimo went north, Ulysses south, the river loud as he approached.

He crossed at the Ponte Vecchio. The bridge was shaking beneath his feet, the Arno grinding against the old stones that Taddeo Gaddi had laid in 1345, throwing up water against the parapet. The moon waning gibbous, cloaked by clouds among a starless night.

By the Palazzo Pitti, the city was empty. Ulysses cut through Via dello Sprone into Piazza dei Sapiti and noticed water bubbling out from the narrow slits along the gutters. He threw a glance at his workshop, at the globe suspended in the darkness, vulnerable and pure. Cress said he'd captured the essence of the planet itself.

As he entered Piazza Santo Spirito, all was calm. The shutters on the buildings were closed, as you'd expect; the odd light or two, but he knew who the insomniacs were. Water was coming up from the gutters here too. He entered his building but didn't go up straightaway. It was that niggle in his guts that made him head for the cellar.

He stepped down the stone stairs into ankle-deep water, and a strong stink of drains was no surprise. The overhead light flickered but didn't go out.

The topmost bags of coal were still dry, and they were the first to come up. And the boxes the elderly contessa had asked him to store. Crates of cheese and wine for the *pensione* came next, jars of homemade *passata*, bottles of oil, bottles of San Pellegrino mineral water, anything unadulterated, anything he could wipe free of water, all brought up to the ground floor. And every time he went back down, he had a sense the water was rising. The bike came up last, wheels dripping. He was wired and exhausted and his best suit was drenched. And at two a.m. he went over to Michele's.

Michele out of the top-floor window: Hey, *soldato!* What time you call this?

It's the cellars, Michele.

It's always the fucking cellars! But Michele came down. His night would be long.

Ulysses put on a pot of coffee and changed his clothes. He moved about with a sense of dread and thought, at first, that it was about Alys and Cressy. He went out onto the terrace for air. The rain had softened to a drizzle and the city was trapped under a haze, both torpid and eerie. Dawn was still five hours away. What is it? he wondered. The restlessness felt like wartime, the unseen enemy in wait. He wouldn't sleep, he knew that. He finished the last of the coffee and decided to set about the task of bringing up the coal and the crates and sacks; it seemed the most sensible thing to do. He grabbed a torch and went out into the stairwell.

At four thirty a.m. the elderly contessa opened her door. You stealing my things now, Signor Temper?

The cellar's flooded, Contessa. And he placed the last of the boxes at her feet. Take them or leave them, he said. (He was in no mood for her rancor.)

Grazie, graz— But he was gone.

He closed the wooden door quietly behind him and stepped out into the night. Lights were on in Michele's and he could see the big man at the counter having an espresso. He turned left into Via Maggio, torchlight leading him down to the river.

He heard it before he'd even gotten close: the sound was deafening. A terrifying black torrent, almost level with the top of the parapets, was frothing and howling and pitching foam into the wind. Suddenly, a mighty oak dragged down from the Casentino slammed against the wall in front of him, sending up clouds of spindrift. He stumbled to the ground, heart pounding at this mad confrontation with nature. The torch went out.

He stood up. The river was now cascading over the top of the embankment wall and black waves were eddying and turning back on themselves. He hit the torch against his leg and a beam of light shot out against the bricks. Small cracks had begun to appear, spurting water.

He turned and ran, Borgo San Jacopo already inundated as he passed. The wail of a siren ominous in the distance.

Michele was in the bar, talking to a group of men, and before Ulysses could tell them what he'd seen, Michele called out to him. Everything's going down, *soldato*! Electricity, phones—you need to collect as much water as possible before the pressure gives out.

Ulysses entered the hallway and ran the stairs two at a time.

He knocked on the contessa's door.

You again, she said.

Contessa. Fill every container you have with water. The bath. Bowls. Anything.

You frighten me, Signor Temper.

Don't be frightened. Just do it, Contessa.

What's happening?

I don't know.

Back inside, he lifted the phone to warn Massimo, but the line was dead. Bath, pots, saucepans, anything capable of containing water was filled and he went down and did the same in the *pensione*.

Back down the stairs once more, but this time, out of the front door. A helicopter swooped overhead. His torchlight cutting a path through the inundated streets. By the time he got to Piazza dei Sapiti it was already two feet underwater. A beam of light through the window showed sheets of paper and plastic molds shimmering on the undulating black surface. The wooden door had swollen, and it took his shoulder to get it open. Inside, the smell of paint and sewers and water rising by the minute. The rain had stalled, and he needed to take the globe now. He stuck the torch in his pocket, lifted the giant sphere and began to back out of the doorway. Only then did he notice the three bundles of his father's copperplates on an upper shelf. Fuck. It was simply too late.

Darkness all about him. An occasional whisper of moon. His boots were waterlogged, heavy as stone, legs fighting against the current, water waist height now. He lifted the globe higher still, grateful for the halt in rain, which would have destroyed it. Out onto Via Maggio and the water pulled like mud.

Flash!

He turned. (Click.) Caught forever.

The photographer raised his hand and waded off toward the Palazzo Pitti.

Ulysses turned right. The street drew color from the lightening hour and the undulation of the ground made the water shallower and his footing felt firmer. He was in the square, he was almost there, and his arms burned from the carry but home was up ahead. The globe achingly beautiful in the violet light of morning. Michele shouting to him from the top window. Ulysses looked up and nodded. Suddenly, a fierce brown surge rose behind him and threw him into the deluge. He felt the moment the globe was ripped from his hands, the impact as he was slammed into the fountain, the roaring in his ears. He gripped the ledge with the last of his strength as the water rushed past him into Via Sant'Agostino. But it was too much, and eventually he had to let go. Carried across the square to the statue, where he came to rest. When the water settled and shallowed out, he stood up. He looked about but the globe was gone. He just about had time to get into his building and close the door before another frothing surge rolled across the square. He sat on the stairs, dazed, breathless, shaking. The contessa above, calling out to him. The slow climb up.

By noon, Mayor Bargellini had gotten to a radio mic and announced to the city that the water had arrived in Piazza del Duomo. And in some neighborhoods, it had reached the second floor of buildings. He told everyone to remain calm and told those with boats and canoes to bring them to the Palazzo Vecchio.

Shortly after Ulysses had changed clothes, there was a knock at the door. The elderly contessa must have listened to the radio announcement too because she stood in the doorway and said, Signor Temper, I have no electricity. No lights. I have no gas. I am cold and I have no water, and now the *idiota* talks of floods. Why didn't he stop it?

Ulysses invited her inside and sat her beside the coal stove.

I had coal once, she said, but they made me have gas and now I have nothing.

It was a simple lunch of spaghetti and *passata* and she followed his every move about the kitchen. He threw in a couple of leftover sausages and a handful of black olives, a pinch of chili. He opened one of the good bottles of wine and she said, Very nice indeed. From the transistor radio a broadcast warned that the city water was polluted. For how long now? said the contessa. He drained the pasta but kept the salted water for the toilet.

Why the toilet? said the contessa.

Because you can't flush them, he said.

O mio Dio. Just like the war.

They ate and said little after that. When she'd finished, the contessa complimented him on his cooking. A little more salt maybe, she said.

Maybe, he said.

He put the coffeepot on the stove. The contessa said, That's the best type of coffeepot. It never lets you down. Not like the mayor, she said.

Ulysses took his coffee onto the terrace with Claude. The fountain had become its own island and you'd need a boat to get to church now. Before light faded, the water ran putrid with a shimmering yellow scum and there was a high stench of oil. Red gasoline cans bobbed on the surface, such an incongruous trespass of color. A car swept into the square and clattered against the metal shutters of the *tabacchi*. All about, the narrow streets were awash, the *cortile* below immersed.

All those workshops, all those livelihoods, all those ground-floor magicians who made shoes wearable and mended chairs and carved wonder and made frames of gold. Paintings began to float in on the tide, an antique shop or gallery broken into by the onslaught. A quick glimpse of cherubim before the canvas sank.

By five p.m. the city was in blackout. Ulysses and the contessa sat by the stove and listened to the Italian news broadcast by candlelight. All Tuscany had suffered flooding. Florence was cut off by road, rail and telephone from Rome in the south to Bologna in the north.

Someone needs to go down and check on the place, said the contessa. But I have the wrong shoes.

Ulysses switched on the torch and went down through the stairwell. He entered the *pensione* and opened the dresser where Cress kept boxes of candles. He didn't go back up straightaway, kept going down the stairs till he hit the waterline. Three, four feet maybe; far below the contessa's landing, he could at least give her that reassurance. He sat on the stone. The heady smell of petroleum and sewage, the sound of debris battering against the front doors like the heaving clang of a ship slowly sinking. He thought about Massimo but knew Massimo lived up high. Wondered when Cress and Alys would get back home. He needed to know everyone was safe because without them he was nothing. The torch flickered. He banged it against his hand and a faint beam skimmed the surface. A carp darted away from the intrusion. And the water rose.

Night stayed black. No stars but faint spirals of smoke. Helicopters cast light across darkened rooftops, the rhythmic chug of rotor blades against the air. Ulysses held the umbrella above the contessa whilst she looked through the telescope. She said she was scared during the war. Scared like this, she said. She said not many people had liked Arturo Bernadini, but she had. She said he was a man worth saving. She said she'd watched Ulysses climb onto the roof all those years ago. She thought he was brave. Strange, but brave. And you were so young. I think the helicopters are rescuing people from the rooftops, she added. Maybe they need you over there too.

They camped out in the *salotto*. A candelabra, a bottle of grappa close to an elderly woman's hand and a parrot singing show tunes.

Does he often do that? said the contessa.

Ulysses shrugged.

What's that noise? said the contessa.

Where?

Out there, she said, pointing.

Ulysses got up and opened the shutters. Michele at his window with a candle. Names were being shouted across the square. Signor, Signora Bruni? he called out. Signor Carrai?

The flicker of lights appeared in the darkness. *Sì. Qui!*

Are you all right, Signora Buonarroti? *Sì sì.*

Signor Conti? *Sì. Qui!* Another candle.

Signora Moretti?

One by one candles appeared at the windows, human stars across a watery night.

And then Ulysses heard it. Not *soldato* this time, nor Signor Temper, but Ulisse. He raised his candle and shouted, I'm here, I'm well! He said that the contessa was with him. That she too was well.

A sudden cry across the square: I'm Signor Lami and I have no candles!

Where are you, *signore?*

West side. Top floor. Five along from Michele.

Wave something white, shouted Ulysses, and he waited.

I see you! shouted Ulysses. Open both windows, *signore*, and keep waving!

Ulysses turned to Claude. Here, Claudie, and he picked him up. Over there, he said. You see the white in the window? Follow my finger, Claude. Just there?

Claude squawked.

Good boy.

Ulysses grabbed a candle from the box and held it in front of him. This needs to go over there, he said. Think you can do it, Claude?

By now the contessa was following events avidly. *Che straordinario!* she kept saying. *Che straordinario!*

Think you can, Claude?

Claude squawked.

Ulysses placed the candle carefully in the parrot's beak and positioned him out of the window. Over there, he whispered. Straight over.

Keep waving, Signor Lami! he shouted. And stand back when you see the parrot!

Go, Claude, go!

Whoosh!

A flash of blue and yellow in the gloom and what a sight he was! The weight of the candle caused a sudden drop in altitude and there was a sharp intake of breath from the contessa as Claude's chest feathers skimmed the black lake, but then he rose. Oh, how magnificently he rose! He circled the square twice until the flight path had been worked out and the landing zone calculated: ten feet . . . nine feet . . . Straighten, straighten . . . Decrease speed.

You can do it, whispered Ulysses.

You can do it, whispered the contessa.

Ulysses shouted to Signor Lami to stand back and suddenly Claude disappeared through the open window. There was a sound of broken glass. Anxious seconds passed.

You sure the man opened the window? said the contessa.

(He had. It was simply that he was so surprised by the appearance of so large a parrot that he dropped a wine bottle.)

Look! shouted the elderly contessa. He did it!

And he had. Where previously darkness had reigned was now light.

Claude launched back out into the sky. He flew high, as high as the *campanile*, and he glided on the still point, the rush of air a silent and ancient sound, heard first inside his egg. The calling to break free. The splintering of the shell. That first indescribable gulp of air. Oh, what it was to fly! He perched on the head of Cosimo R. adrift in the Arno sea, where he would remain witness to the night, watching over his people till land appeared again out of the primordial vortex that once had birthed life itself. They may even erect a statue of him. Now, wouldn't that be something?

———

Ten p.m. news broadcast:

Florence is a lake. Ten feet of water in the Piazza del Duomo. Families calling out from second-floor windows. All afternoon helicopters have been rescuing stranded people from rooftops. Women and children only. Men left on the roofs. Pisa has taken the full force of the deluge across its plain and has asked Florence for help. Florence can't even help herself.

Ulysses turned off the radio. The contessa said, We have a long night ahead of us.

(At this point Ulysses realized the woman had no intention of going home.)

He said, You can stay here if you wish, Contessa.

I'd like that, Signor Temper. Guest room, of course.

And before she fell asleep, she said someone needed to stay awake just in case. Ulysses promised he'd stand guard all night.

At midnight, he left the door on the latch and went down the stairs. Torchlight showed the water was lowering, and he knew they'd gotten off lightly. Ten feet in the Duomo square.

In his bedroom he opened the shutters. The rain had stopped. He lay down and fell asleep immediately.

Seven a.m. brought a flaming sunrise. The beautiful sound of the swoosh of car tires. He got up and looked out at the devastation. A Madonna stood muddied in the middle of the square. Her broken hand pointed to the sky.

One by one, on the morning of November 5, people emerged from doorways dazed by the horror that awaited them. The water had gone, but had left behind the unimaginable: a thick layer of black stinking mud that coated everything. A slick composition of heating oil, soil and sewage, a wafty waft that marked buildings at the highest point of the river's reach, an inconsistent line that would rise and fall throughout the city streets. Metal shutters on shops and restaurants had either buckled or been ripped away, and the interiors destroyed. Two cars had overturned near the fountain, and at the doors of the basilica, Cressy's Moto Guzzi Falcone was lying on its side. The stone benches, holders of memory, had become holders of muck. Flagstones had been torn up, windows smashed, and out into the mire had been sucked the intimate and the everyday. Shoes from the cobbler were strewn about the black landscape, giving the impression that scattered corpses lay not far beneath. This was not life that would ever return to normal.

Anything that could not be salvaged from ground-floor homes or shops or cafés began to appear in the square: a pram, an accordion, cushions, a toy car, tins of food, chairs, clothing, radios, a television set, suitcases, paintings, letters. It broke your heart, but you had to do it, you had to place it on the pile with all the rest. Even if it was a jukebox.

Michele was trying unsuccessfully to maneuver the machine out of the bar. He looked up at Ulysses's approach. *Che disastro*, he said. Ulysses grabbed a corner and helped shift the machine into the square. Inside the bar, the watermark stood at just over a meter. Bottles of alcohol on the higher shelves, the public telephone, and the ancient coffee machine that had traveled up from the south were the only things untouched by the mud.

Ulysses picked up chairs and carried them out and placed them on the pile. Giulia hovered by the kitchen. I will do this only once, Ulisse, she said, tears falling. He followed her down into the kitchen, where the tidemark rose. Everything covered by shit, the smell noxious and potent.

Where do we start? she cried. Tell me where? No water even to clean the— And Ulysses wanted to hold her but Michele moved past and said something harsh about her tears. Ulisse, he said. Help me. We take it all out. Icebox first.

Massimo found Ulysses in the square. The two men held one another till a hundred silent words had passed between them.

How's it your side? said Ulysses.

So bad. And Massimo recounted what he'd seen and heard:

Embankments had been washed away. The Biblioteca Nazionale was still completely cut off by water and inundated. Santa Croce no one can get inside. Street after street of overturned cars, and dead cattle. The Baptistery doors have been ripped from their frames—the mayor and a film crew are over there now—and panels from the Gates of Paradise are missing.

Madonna mia, whispered Giulia, and went back inside the bar.

No one knows how many are dead, he said.

The men looked up at a helicopter.

You hear they released all the prisoners from the Murate? said Michele. And now the looting starts!

Ulysses went across to help Giulia carry out a table.

You been to your workshop, Ulisse?

Not yet.

Michele turned. You do this but you haven't been there? Take him now, Signor Buontalenti.

The pavements were slippery with stinking mud—the *fango*—and each step was slow and perilous. People were out in the streets, starting the clear-up. Worse than the war, they said. Faces hardened, the swish of brooms, the scrape of wooden rakes, an impossible task without detergents and water, but we have to do something, they said. The cheese seller, fishmonger, butcher, all gone. The contents festering in the road. Haberdashery shop, toy shop, bike shop, gone gone gone.

When they got to Piazza dei Sapiti, the narrow streets had funneled the water with such velocity that the small square had taken the full force. The door to Ulysses's workshop was ajar and inside, the walls were blackened. Globes, once the prize of the upper shelves, had been sucked into the eddy; old map books that he'd collected since arriving in the city; Des's molds; tools; his father's plates—

Outside, a woman wailing, I've lost everything. I've lost everything.

Ulysses felt dizzy. The place stank. The woman's voice rising with panic.

Ulisse? said Massimo.

Ulysses felt Massimo's hand on his back. He reached into his jacket for cigarettes.

Not here, said Massimo gently. It's all oil, Ulisse.

Ulysses staggered out and threw up.

Down by the river, they walked with silent groups of Florentines. The water had dropped fifteen feet but still raced toward the sea. On the Ponte Vecchio, tree trunks stuck out in all directions, great swathes of leaves and branches clung like giant nests. The goldsmith and jewelry shops had been ransacked, and the owners left scavenging in the mud for a glint of anything worthwhile. The waterfront outside the library had been torn away and vast banks of mud blocked the entrance.

On the north side came the first sighting of boats and canoes being poled along, buckets lowered from upper windows to collect food, water, anything to make the hours ahead bearable. The two men were forced to backtrack. Another street revealed blackened mattresses and clothing drying and hardening in the sun and wind. A pet shop full of caged, drowned songbirds. *La fine del mondo*, said a man. The end of the world.

In Santa Croce square, they stood where they'd been only two nights before. Cars were stacked on top of one another, half in water, half in mud, and the tidemark was clear on Dante's statue. Twenty feet, was it? Unthinkable. Here mostly the poor and elderly were housed, in basements or ground floors. Come on, said Massimo, and they slipped and clambered across the stinking wasteland, holding on to each other for balance, but every attempt to get close to Zia Chiara's restaurant failed. Street after street underwater and the *carabinieri* forced them back, saying foundations were unsafe and walls were about to come down. Massimo shouted to a man to ask if he knew where Zia Chiara and her brothers had gone, but the man shrugged. No one knew anything, it seemed. No one knew even how they would eat that day.

Light faded by four and the cleanup stopped. Ulysses and Massimo dumped boots and muddied clothing on the upper-floor landing. They washed on the terrace with a bowl of rainwater and left the dregs by the toilet cistern. A little after six, a knock at the door. Not too early, am I? said the elderly contessa.

They ate the last of the cold meats and spaghetti with oil and garlic and chili. The contessa complimented Massimo on the balance of flavor he'd achieved. A little more *pepperoncino*, perhaps?

Perhaps, he said.

Ulysses got up and put the coffeepot on the stove.

The night air was frosty and carried the wail of fire crews and the ambulances of the Misericordia. The contessa said that Rome had washed its hands of the city and in a remarkable volte-face said that Mayor Bargellini was the only one who cared.

And the Casa del Popolo, said Ulysses.

What do you know about those Communists? she said.

I know they're giving out food and medicine.

And don't forget the bakers in Fiesole, said Massimo. They've been getting bread to the poor.

Yes, well, bakers are good people, she said. A baker I'd trust with my kidneys. But where are the bulldozers? Where's the army? Rome thinks we can clear a landslide with a spoon.

The contessa finished her coffee and declared she was tired. She took Ulysses's arm and he led her down to her apartment. In the short time it took for Ulysses to return, Massimo had fallen asleep on the sofa. A dogged exhaustion clung to everything. He covered Massimo with blankets and closed the shutters.

Ulysses lay in bed. His tiredness had now passed. Slow hours ahead listening to the despair of a city, cold and forsaken and entombed in mud. Maybe people don't know, he thought. Maybe no one really knows how much help we need.

But they did. The world *was* listening, and long before his thoughts had settled, volunteers from around the world were mobilizing. Experts in art restoration, and hundreds of students with the intrinsic belief they could change the world. Even a man from Manchester whose memories of lovemaking in a Renaissance palazzo made him tingle.

Des leaned across the table and turned off the radio. I need to do something, Poppy.

I know you do, Des. You're that kind of man.

I'm going to drive down to Tuscany in a Land Rover. Take a few essentials, show I care. You coming?

Not this time, Des. (They were awaiting their first grandchild.) But why not go to London and take Piano Pete? You've been longing to meet him.

Great idea, said Des. I reckon I could start out in a couple of days.

You need a Land Rover, Des.

I'll buy one.

And in Bristol, Jem Gunnerslake, now thirty and studying medicine as Evelyn Skinner had once predicted, put down his copy of the *Observer* and phoned his university to say he needed ten days off to deal with a family crisis. He jumped on the train with galoshes, a K-Way rain jacket and one change of clothing. He looked out from the ferry as England pulled away. He was going to Florence to save art. He was a sixties man through and through, and peace and love pulsed through his pulmonic and aortic valves. And he smiled wide now that his teeth were fixed.

Ulysses woke to a day of firsts: First trucks brought water into the city, for cleaning and not for drinking, but that was something. And the first wave of young people gathered outside the Biblioteca and formed a human chain to clear the mud from the entrance. And the first of the telegrams started to get through and Ulysses received one from Rome. It had been sent the day before, and was handed to him as he was shoveling mud out of the *cortile*.

ROADS IMPASSABLE WILL TRY AGAIN TOMORROW HOME SOON LOVE YOU

The tears came then. He turned away from the group because he couldn't stop.

That afternoon, having kept close behind a bus chartered by the Grottaferrata monks, Betsy rolled into Santo Spirito square, muddied and worse for wear. Alys, close to the windscreen, tried to absorb the broken lives in front of her. Ulysses saw them first and oh, the look on his face—the look on hers. (Click.) Caught forever. He'd been standing outside the café with Michele and Giulia and the elderly contessa, who said, About time. I hope they've brought food.

Of course they had. Wine and water too, and it would be the first time in days that anyone would eat eggs or bread or drink milk. Alys climbed out of the van and Ulysses went toward her. Arms around him, she said, If anything had happened to you . . .

What's that jukebox doing over there, Michele? said Cress. You bring it in from the cold and I'll have it cleaned up and fixed in no time. Giulia said, Can you do the same for my heart, Signor Cress?

Alys was waiting at the rail station. She was muddied from head to toe and wearing jeans, jumper, smock. Hair up, sunglasses and a cigarette in her mouth. Massimo called her the epitome of cool. Elongating the double vowel, of course.

It was the third time in as many days that she'd been there, and despite the afternoon cold she liked it. Direct connection to the outside world, what with trains coming and going, and newspapers, and a chance to stock up on cigarettes. Standing above the height of the flood, the place retained an air of normalcy. If you could ignore the mud-streaked floors, that is, and the posters telling people to BOIL ALL WATER due to the latent danger of typhoid and cholera. A stink of diesel streamed out from the generator keeping the telegram office alight. Alys lit a cigarette and watched a train pull in.

Hundreds of students were arriving daily, and the city was finding it hard to house them. Youth hostels and dormitories were overflowing and the empty sleeping cars and coaches in the railyard had now been commandeered. Cress and Ulysses had agreed to open up the *pensione* for whoever needed a place to stay and so far it was working well. Some of the kids had even taken it upon themselves to help Michele and Giulia clean out the bar. Alys watched a young woman pass in front of her.

Made it quite obvious she couldn't take her eyes off her. It was easy to flirt when you had rooms to offer. The woman ran on ahead, though, and put her arm around a man. Ah well, win some lose some, and Alys inhaled on her cigarette. And then she noticed him. A bit lost, a bit older than the rest. Nice smile.

'Scuse me! she said, running up to him.

He stopped. Me?

Have you come to clean up?

I have, actually.

D'you need somewhere to stay?

Yes. I s'pose I do, really.

I'm Alys. And she offered her hand.

Jem. Jem Gunnerslake.

Follow me, Jem.

And they left the station concourse, went down the steps to the mud-covered square. Tarred cars and huge piles of detritus gathering outside. The watermark at six feet.

Jesus, said Jem.

Careful where you tread, said Alys. You can't see, but a lot of the paving stones are up.

Was it worse than this?

Hard to say. Down by the river it's as bad as ever. In Santa Croce. Gavinana, San Niccolò. Cellars are still flooded because there's not enough pumps, and you'll see thousands of cars like that. They've got the army shoveling this shit but apart from that, there's not much that will make a difference right now.

Jem rubbed his nose.

Chlorine. I'm getting used to it. They've covered the city with it.

I saw the posters.

Vaccination centers are open now. You need one, Jem?

I'm fine. And he patted his arm.

Walking across Santa Maria Novella square, Alys said—and she pointed to the church—If you need candles, you can buy them off a priest over there for a hundred *lire* apiece.

Do I need some?

Not for now, we have plenty. But they're always welcome.

And if I want to make a telephone call?

No chance. Telegrams are OK. International go through the central post office. Be prepared to queue for hours, though. We have no lights, no heating, no water at the moment. We flush the toilet with a bucket twice a day—when we all leave for work and when we go to sleep. Unless it's really necessary. You know.

Righto.

You'll get a towel and a bowl of cold water, morning and night, to wash in. All muddy clothes and boots left outside on the landings. Bread and jam for breakfast. Tea mostly, sometimes coffee if we can get it. Milk sometimes—

If you can get it.

She smiled. A bowl of pasta at night. There's also a canteen in the Accademia if you'd prefer to eat there. Just let us know in the morning, though. You may have a room to yourself one night, or you may have to bunk in with others. That make you squeamish?

Autopsies make me squeamish.

Alys laughed. Left here, she said. I'm giving you the tourist walking tour.

How much? said Jem.

For the tour?

For the room, he said.

Nothing, Jem Gunnerslake. This is the city's gift to you. In lieu of the hundreds of backbreaking hours you'll do.

How does it work? he said—and he slipped trying to catch up with her—I mean, how do I start work? Do I just turn up?

You could. But there's an office at the Uffizi that sends you where you're needed.

And where's that, usually?

Depends. Could be a hospital—Duomo straight ahead, Jem Gunnerslake!—or getting food to the elderly. Mostly it's the Biblioteca right now, though. It's pretty gruesome inside. Twenty-two feet of mud in the lower floors and waist-deep water. That's where the books are. No generators, just torchlight and candles to work by. There're hundreds of us in there, Jem. Passing buckets of mud or books to each other. Mud goes outside, books upstairs to rinse off and dry out.

And then what?

Then they're taken to the Forte Belvedere. For the start of restoration.

Right.

Sculpture goes to Palazzo Davanzati, canvas paintings to the Accademia, and panel paintings are sent to the *limonaia* in the Palazzo Pitti. To date, eighteen churches and fifteen museums devastated.

You know a lot.

You get to know a lot. Everyone you work with has been somewhere else. I actually spent my first day at the Uffizi.

Cleaning masterpieces?

No. Those had been moved, thank God. They trusted us only with the ones deemed insignificant.

How insignificant?

Woman next to me uncovered a Velázquez.

No way!

Gallery didn't even know it was in the basement. That's the trouble with this city, Jem. No one knows where anything is.

That night in the *pensione*, the upper landings and handrails were strewn with mud-caked clothes and boots. Inside, the hallway was a jumble of coats and jumpers and scarves, the bedrooms like dorms: double beds were separated into single beds and camp beds made three. The bathroom floor was streaked with mud and someone had left the radio on and it crackled with static and occasionally a tune.

On the upper floor, the coal stove cranked out heat and steam and the dining table was set.

This is Jem, everyone! That's Alicia, Tom, Aldo, James, Carole . . . Jem nodding, Hello, hello, he said, but he'd never remember their names. (Too nervous.) Alys said, You sit by me, Jem. Thanks, said Jem.

At seven, Ulysses and Cress carried in bowls of pasta and bread and salad. Always a cheer when they entered, and you should have seen the look on Cressy's face! Big fuss of Cressy every time. Five minutes later a knock at the door: Not too early, am I? The elderly contessa entered and added, You're all still here then.

Nice fur, said a young woman called Niamh.

I killed it myself, said the contessa.

By ten o'clock, the candles had burned low among the debris of dinner. Students, tired and blush-cheeked, sprawled on chairs and sofas and floors, wrapping scarves tighter around their necks. Cigarettes smoldered in ashtrays, raised to mouths during the telling of tales. The last of the wine was drunk.

On the terrace, a kerosene lamp flickered. A clothesline pegged with towels and cloths and rags, and Ulysses, Cress and the elderly contessa huddled against the freeze. The conversation from inside drifted out into the untroubled air. Cress said, The young have brought something intrinsic to the city.

Crabs, said the elderly contessa.

I was thinking energy and hope, said Cress.

(Overheard):

What do you do, Jem? Studying. Medicine. Will you take a look at my foot? (Laughter.) What? It's been hurting for days! I bet you get asked that all the time, Jem. Not all the time, and I'd be happy to have a look. Although I'm specializing in gynecology. (Laughter.) Alys strummed her guitar and the conversation stopped. Familiar opening bars to what would become the anthem of that time. "God Only Knows" sung over and over, voices parading across the star-packed night. And don't tell me that didn't bring a little catch to the throat of those listening. Soldiers patrolling the streets, the insomniacs and restless hearts tossing prayers in the air. A pure melody lifted by the haunting glare of a kerosene lamp. Pete would've said, Life don't get much better.

The next morning was bitterly cold. The kids left early for the waterfront and Ulysses and Cress made a start on the stone benches. So far, so normal. Then all of a sudden, into this routine sped a spanking-new Land Rover packed to the hilt.

Well, I'll be, said Cress. And even Claude flew down from the statue of Cosimo R. to have a peek.

The Land Rover skidded to a halt. Des clambered out from behind the wheel and adjusted his driving gloves.

Des! said Ulysses and Cress.

Hello, lad. Hello, my old friend Cress. Must have done a hundred all the way.

And Pete! How on earth did you two—?

Long story, said Des.

Pete fell into Ulysses's arms. Oh, it was a lovely journey, Temps. No drama at all.

What are you both doing here? said Ulysses.

We're the coordinated disaster relief team, said Des. You can't rely on that president in Rome—

Des met him at a conference once, interrupted Pete.

Right tosser, said Des. So here we are.

And he moved to the back of the vehicle and flung open the doors.

I've got manual bilge pumps, gas masks, wet-weather gear, Wellington boots, waders, kerosene lamps, candles, blankets, woolen socks, transistor radios and batteries, moisturizer for the ladies, powdered milk, cream for foot rot, bleach, sponges, shovels, brooms—what else, Pete?

TCP, he said.

Gallons of TCP, said Des. First-aid kits, and as much food and mineral water as we could get our hands on. Right, Pete?

Pete gave him a thumbs-up. Pete had never looked happier.

I feel bad we couldn't have got the vaccines, though, said Des quietly.

What vaccines? said Ulysses.

Typhoid and tetanus, whispered Des. Contact was arrested at the border.

Sorry to hear that, Des.

Right then, Ulysses, lad. Any chance of a—?

Coffee with a touch of grappa?

My kind of man, said Des. Lead the way, comrade.

Pete bunked in with Ulysses and Des got the guest room to himself. I like the new touches, he said to Cress. Ceramics are definitely the way to go.

Afterward, they each took it in turns to pump out the cellar—These waders have already paid for themselves, said Des—and Cress made a start on the jukebox now that he had proper industrial cleaning fluid.

And across the river, Alys and Jem descended the stairs of the library, down into the murky underworld where the air was poisonous and gas masks were worn. The water had gone but the mud about them was still boot height and frozen. They stopped at their allocated positions and Alys gave Jem a thumbs-up. The first bucket came through and then the next and the next at a cracking pace. A book now blackened by sludge. Book after book after book, the written patrimony of Western civilization. And sometimes through the mud, a glimmer of gold or a glimmer of blue stilled their breath. Made them humble, that shy glimpse of ancient holy.

Bloody hell! said Des.

Jesus, Temps, said Pete. It was two days later, and the men were in Piazza dei Sapiti, where the rotting debris from the flood stood five feet high. A stinking oily mass of furniture, broken globes, books, clothing.

I managed to save a couple of molds, said Ulysses.

Well, that's plastic for you, said Des. Indestructible.

It's calamitous, said Pete. They clear the mud and more appears.

Sisyphean, said Des. But people are tenacious. If evolution has taught us anything—

Thousands of homeless already, said Ulysses. Many of them old.

The keepers of history, said Pete.

All those craftsmen gone.

Changes things, doesn't it? said Des. Soul of the community goes. You boys need any money?

Nah, we're good, thanks, Des. Cress had another little moment.

What was it this time?

World Cup, said Pete. Not only to win but—

The Geoff Hurst hat trick? said Des.

The two men nodded.

Man of vision, said Des.

And at that moment, the man of vision himself appeared. Brand-new waders up to his armpits. Bright eyes, mouth quivering with anticipation. Clearly Cress had something important to say.

I've got something important to say, he said. We can flush the toilets again.

A small mercy, said Pete.

And . . . , said Cress.

And he gestured for them to follow.

They stood on the bank of the river, back to its normal level but full of crap—a right old junkyard in which people had tossed wrecked cars and mattresses. But that wasn't what Cress wanted them to see. Look, he said. Over there!

A long procession of heavy trucks entering the city, each one loaded with a crane or a tractor or a generator, and cheers went up around them. The rumbling sound and heavy clank as the first of the wrecked cars was towed away.

Night rolled in cold and sharp. Cress sitting at the dining table, surrounded by candles and students, holding court.

I would actually call it a small *miracolo*, he said. The Moto Guzzi was thrown clear of the tumult by the first surge of water, landed on the steps, ergo it was protected from the onslaught of oil and muck that was to follow. Now, you tell me why.

God's a motorcycle enthusiast? said Ulysses, collecting the plates.

Massimo was by the window, watching Cress and the students. He said, Alys, who's the young man in the green jumper?

That's Jem. He arrived a few days ago. He's lovely. I've been working with him at the library. You want me to introduce you?

No. Go on then. Yes. No, Alys, no. I—

Jem?

Jem looked up from the table and smiled. Alys waved him over. This is Massimo. Massimo, Jem.

On the sofa the elderly contessa was staring at Claude and Claude was staring at her. First one to blink.

In the doorway, Pete and Des. Des was heading back the following day for a conference on the sustainability of plastic, and was even taking one of the tar-soaked molds with him. Pete, though, had decided to stay.

D'you mind, Des? said Pete.

Do I mind? Course I don't. If I wasn't a keynote speaker I'd be staying on myself. But I'll miss your company in the cockpit, I can tell you that for nothing.

Temps!

Ulysses came out of the kitchen. You OK, Pete?

I've been thinking, Temps. I'm not going home. Not with Des. Not ever. How does that sound?

Sounds really good to me, Pete. How's it sound to you?

Bit daft, if I'm totally honest. I've no idea what I'm gonna do.

You'll do what you've always done, said Ulysses, glancing at the piano.

Pete huddled low, fingers dexterous across the keys, fag smoke bothering his bloodshot eyes. This song's called "Angeli del Fango," he said. Mud angels.

It was a ballad, about the young men and women who'd come to the city. About good rising out of need, about love in all its forms, about kindness and looking out for one another, and only the third verse was about art, but even that was about the paradox of meaning. It was classic Pete. Took you one way, took you back, then delivered the punch. He leaned away from the keys and cracked his knuckles. The soft waft of dope inched in from the terrace. 'Ello 'ello. Marrakesh all over again, he said.

So that was it. Early to bed. The students switched on their torches and went down the stairs to the *pensione* to sleep. Des called it a night too, handed Ulysses an envelope and asked him to give it to Michele and Giulia. Is this what I think it is? said Ulysses. You think right, said Des. Money for a new kitchen and anything else they need. Note inside explains it all. If I can't do it for people in need, what's the point of being rich? Night, lad.

See you in the morning, Des.

That left only Jem by the bookshelf, head down, reading. In his hands a burgundy cloth-covered book. He looked up and quoted:

Old women light the porte cochères
Shut the grilles with thorough care
And with that same maternal light
They close the city for the night.
But like a child, un-keen to sleep,
The city rises from the deep . . .

Massimo clapped—a little too enthusiastically.

"Everything" by Constance Everly, said Cress.

Yes, said Jem, and he held up the poetry collection. I bought the book *Nothing* for my old art teacher, Evelyn Skinner. She and Constance were great friends. That's one of the reasons why I'm here, I suppose. Because of Evelyn. Anyway, he said. It's late. And I'm talking too—

Oh no, said Alys. Stay where you are, Jem Gunnerslake.

Constance Everly? said Cress.

Evelyn Skinner? said Ulysses.

Yes, said Jem.

I think you need to sit back down and tell us all you know, said Cress.

Massimo fetched a bottle of *amaro* and Jem duly did.

Now—

A thousand miles away, Evelyn Skinner was sitting in her flat in Bloomsbury, leg up on a stool, with her right ankle wrapped in ice. Her ears had been burning for the last twenty-four hours, although she didn't think the two afflictions were linked. She'd been following stories of the flood avidly, maybe a little too avidly, because it made her distracted and a few days ago, climbing out of the Kenwood Ladies' Pond in Hampstead, she'd slipped. It was a silly sprain, that's all, and had caused huge merriment at the time, on account of her suddenly finding out at the age of eighty-six she could do the splits. The prescription was to rest up and follow the medical advice.

Sunday afternoon and Dotty handed her a large G&T. To be taken with a painkiller, said Dotty. Oh, and here, she added, suddenly remembering the newspaper. Florence floods are on page five, she said, handing the *Observer* to Evelyn.

Evelyn read out loud. "Florence struggles to save its past." Well, it's always done that. Oh God no! Cimabue's *Crucifix* unsalvageable, they say.

Is that significant?

Oh gosh yes. It really is, Dotty. A salutary link between the Byzantine and the Renaissance. Without Cimabue there wouldn't have been Giotto.

And without Giotto? said Dotty.

We may as well have called it a day. Evelyn looked down and continued to read out loud. She said, Army are using flamethrowers to dispose of horse carcasses, del Sarto's *Last Supper* in San Salvi has succumbed. Prisoners from the Murate were released temporarily and now they've escaped.

Well, you would, wouldn't you? said Dotty. Hardly news.

And frogmen have gone into the sewers to clear them.

Deserve a king's ransom for that, said Dotty.

Professor Carlo Ragghianti—and I quote, said Evelyn—"believes help from abroad for stricken Florence will do more than anything to revive the spirit of its citizens for the long struggle which lies ahead."

Dotty stood up and said, Fancy some olives?

Why not, said Evelyn, and she turned the page. And as soon as she had, she cried out Dotty's name.

Dotty rushed back in. What is it, darling?

Evelyn handed the newspaper to Dotty: a photograph of a man, waist height in the floodwaters of Florence, holding aloft a large globe. The caption read: *Atlas rising from the flood.*

It's not Atlas, said Evelyn, shaking. It's—

Your soldier, isn't it?

Evelyn nodded. I've found him, Dotty.

Five days later, they were marching through the Rome airport. The lovely woman at Cook's travel agency had suggested they take a flight, on account of the flood-damaged railway system, and then a bus to Florence. Bus? said Dotty, as if she'd never been on one. She hadn't.

Dotty was dressed for a month at sea, but Evelyn was definitely dressed for mud. She was wearing galoshes and a riding mac that had seen better days and never a horse. Dotty said she smelled strongly of rubber. Which was not wholly unappealing, she added.

A taxi took them to the bus station, where a kind and helpful luggage porter led them to a spot of lunch in Giuseppe Verdi's, an Italian equivalent of a transport caff. It was packed, which was a good sign, with just one table available.

As soon as Evelyn opened her mouth, she became an Italian again. Her charm offensive opened the door of a surly waiter, behind which was a host of homemade specials, none of which were chalked on the board. Eventually, both Evelyn and Dotty agreed on the *spaghetti alla carbonara*, bread and a carafe of house wine: white.

Evelyn looked about and sighed.

You're home, said Dotty.

We're home. All those years we spent with Aunt Maria.

We were rather naughty, said Dotty. D'you think she knew?

Of course she knew! She told me as much—*Ah, grazie,* said Evelyn as the wine arrived—told me as much before she died. She said, I pray you find the right one. She used the feminine for "the right one."

Oh, classy Maria, said Dotty, and she poured out the wine. Here—

And the women raised their glasses. To finding Ulysses, they said.

The wine was crisp and reviving, the *carbonara* delicious. Wholly authentic, said Evelyn. In what way? said Dotty. No cream whatsoever. No cream? But it's so creamy! The creaminess, said Evelyn, is purely yolk with the faintest hint of egg white. With the addition of cheese, both Parmesan and pec—

I thought it was pecorino! said Dotty. And is the bacon bacon or another sleight of hand?

Not bacon, my darling. But *guanciale.* Pig jowl.

Guanciale, repeated Dotty. How I've missed Italy! A delicate crunch, and then your mouth floods with an oily saltiness—

The only seasoning, said Evelyn, is a grind, perhaps, of pepper. And the whole ensemble brought together with a soupçon of pasta water.

Well, I never.

They struggled through the terminus with their luggage until a young American woman brought help their way.

In the queue to board, Dotty said, Well, this is an adventure! And the young woman said, Have you not been to Florence before, Miss Cunningham? And Evelyn said, She's talking about going on a bus.

A quarter of an hour later, Dotty said, Never again.

The bus hadn't even left Rome.

They pulled into Santa Maria Novella rail station just before the five o'clock bells rang out, and dusk was a solid accompaniment. Evelyn and Dotty climbed down the steps and collected their luggage. The smell of diesel and sewage cut through the air and set a somber tone to this encounter.

Oh my, said Evelyn. What's happened to you, *Firenze, amore mio?*

There's a medieval feeling in the air, said Dotty. Brutal, violent and yes, suspicious.

They moved carefully down the incline into a bleak square lit glaringly by arc lights. They said good-bye to the young American woman and watched as she almost came a cropper on the oil.

I don't fancy our chances on that stuff, said Dotty.

And by a stroke of luck, one of the only remaining taxis that had a special permit to enter the city happened to pass at that moment. Dotty raised her hand.

Oh, well spotted! said Evelyn. She gave the address and they clambered in.

The taxi took the long way round to the river due to the unpassable nature of many roads. No streetlights, no neon advertising, only the sweep of headlights caught the undulating wave of destruction. An occasional lit brazier around which soldiers and the homeless warmed themselves.

At five thirty p.m., Evelyn and Dotty arrived outside Pensione Picci, only noticing then that the guesthouse had been built on a slightly elevated part of the *lungarno*, which had ultimately spared it. Enzo was waiting for them outside, holding a kerosene lamp.

My dear Enzo! You got the telegram! said Evelyn, and Enzo said it was the highlight of his week. You're my only guests, he said in his gruff Florentine accent. He took their luggage and led them inside. As they climbed the stairs, he explained the small miracles that had happened every day, the progress the city had made. Electricity and running water had now been restored. And although dinner will be a little basic, I will not let you starve, he said.

And how are the people coping? said Evelyn.

(One more flight of stairs to go.)

Ah, the people! (A deep sigh.) Resilient and suffering. Thousands of businesses in ruin. Thousands of families living in barracks. Twenty thousand on the relief roll. But we keep going, we always have. We keep cleaning and when we remember to, we keep singing. And one day, we will triumph once more. Here we are, he said. Your room, *signore*. Just as you left it.

Inside, a small electric heater in the corner glowed orange. Enzo placed the cases on racks. One last thing, he said, and he disappeared. Five minutes later, he knocked on the door and handed Evelyn a bottle of perfectly chilled Spumante. Because I know you have a choice, he said.

When he closed the door, Dotty threw herself on the bed, inconsolable. These people, Lynny.

I know, my darling.

The next morning, the two women set out carefully under a low gray sky. Although the worst of the debris had been dragged away—into the river by the looks of things, said Dotty—a new wave of mud and oil had appeared after the cellars were pumped clean. The city, once again, sat under a thick brown layer of precarious stinking rot.

Red Cross tents had sprung up in squares, and trestle tables and benches too. Braziers and the wail of the ambulances or the fire service were a constant reckoning.

Along the Arno, the embankments and parapets were being rebuilt, and the earth shook with the rumble of tractors and diggers. Away from the river, shops had begun to reappear, albeit timidly and with little stock. A *fruttivendolo* sold them clementines and pears.

They stopped at a café that had only reopened that morning, and the owner showed them the waterline: six feet. He sat them beneath it ominously and brought them cappuccini and pastries and Evelyn had a glance at *La Nazione*. Thirteen thousand artworks injured or lost. No hope at all for the Cimabue *Crucifix*. Millions of books still under mud. And my dear church of San Firenze has suffered terribly, she said.

Anything good at all? said Dotty.

Evelyn scanned the pages. Oh yes, here's something. Masaccio frescoes in Cappella Brancacci unharmed. Giotto's frescoes in Santa Croce also safe for now, although the water's coming up through the walls and the salt is threatening to unseat the paint. Do you think we might head over there, Dotty?

If we take it slow, I think we might just have a chance, Dotty replied.

It took them two hours to get to Santa Croce. Trying mostly to walk in tracks laid down by cars or other people's feet, Evelyn especially was exhausted by the effort. Her heart was dealt a double blow at the sight of narrow streets still full of water, and unstable building fronts held up by timber scaffold. When they got to the square, apart from the removal of cars, it seemed little headway had been made in fourteen days. The square was still a rotten bog.

Only the flood of 1333 could be compared to this tragedy, she said.

She stood back as a bulldozer rolled past. She leaned against the wall and wondered what on earth she was doing. What use was this eighty-six-year-old woman in a city that needed energy and strong arms, and yes, good balance? You silly, silly woman.

Chin up, Lynny, said Dotty, as if reading her thoughts. Still early days.

And they turned back, Dotty leading the way to the Uffizi. Outside, in the piazza, sprawled on the ground, were dozens of young people caked in mud. Some wore beads, all had tired, glazed eyes and faces streaked with dirt. Evelyn lit up at the sight of them. Long-haired, short-haired, beards, hippies, women in skirts or shorts or trousers, an air of soporific exhaustion and a little love, warmed by a brazier, passing bottles of wine donated by a grateful Florentine and the songs of the Beatles, Beach Boys, Bob and Baez tripping out from a frail transistor radio that had seen better, cleaner days. Most of the men look like Allen Ginsberg, said Dotty.

They're the future, said Evelyn.

God help us, said Dotty.

But those students who were studying art recognized Dotty immediately and made room for her and Evelyn at a makeshift dining table.

The women shared their clementines and pears, and the students shared their wine. A young woman asked if they were there to help with the restoration and Dotty said, Oh yes. And also for this—and she nudged Evelyn to show the newspaper photograph of Ulysses. There were many comments about the force of the water and the effort on the man's face and the beauty of the globe, but no. No one knew who he was or had seen him around.

Worth a try, whispered Dotty.

If only they'd known that six hundred meters away underground, Jem Gunnerslake was passing books to a young woman who was once called kid but was now called Alys. But these revelations would have to wait. For now, an air of contentment hung over the scene.

Days passed. Frost, mist, gloom, blue sky, sun.

Evelyn showed the photograph of Ulysses to shopkeepers, passing students; she even showed it to a group of *carabinieri* outside the Duomo. One man thought he'd heard of a globe maker in San Frediano and Evelyn headed there but to no avail. That trip wore her out and her ankle flared from overuse. She needed two days with her leg up at the *pensione*. We're so close, I can feel it, said Dotty, jollying her along.

But Evelyn wasn't so sure. She slept a lot, which wasn't like her at all.

International funds started to pour into the city to rescue the damaged art, and Dotty got the volunteer bug and donated a piece of work to Artists for Florence. She sent a telegram to gallery owner Joyce to see if a large work titled *It's Only Ever the Start* was still available. (The return telegram revealed it was.) Evelyn persuaded Dotty to do what she herself would have liked to do, which was to head back to Santa Croce and make herself useful.

Dotty joined a line of students into the basilica and there recognized Mr. Hempel from the V&A, who recognized her at the same time.

They'd met at a fundraiser for somethingorother. He was a sculpture conservator, and he put her to work immediately on the marble monuments. Layers of solvent followed by layers of talcum powder to get the oil out of the stone. Tedious to the hilt, and a day felt like a month to Dotty, but not only had she been tasked with Dante's memorial—couldn't wait to tell Evelyn!—she was also working alongside a very lovely young woman from Stockholm.

Could you hold this please, Dotty?

I most certainly can, Inga.

And then . . .

One morning when December was within reach, when the sky was sharply blue and a brittle frost brought clarity of mind, Evelyn held on to the wall in her bedroom, stood on one leg and put her full weight on her ankle. A little hop and no pain. She was revived. Onward, my darling.

She was back in the newly reopened café, seated under the waterline with a double espresso. The caffeine was hammering away in her chest like a woodpecker. On the table in front of her was the picture of Ulysses. She felt something was staring her in the face, something so brutishly familiar, and yet it remained elusive; she couldn't put a finger on it. A shadow fell across the image and she looked up at the owner.

Chi è? the man said.

A friend, said Evelyn. But I don't know where he is. I know he's here, in Florence. Somewhere. But where? That is the question.

The man picked up the newspaper clipping. After a beat, he said, Il Palazzo di Bianca Cappello.

What? said Evelyn.

Via Maggio. You see? he said. Just see here—this corner. The pattern is so distinct.

Oh my goodness, that's it! That's where I recognized it from! Thank you, thank you, my dear man.

And Evelyn retied her scarf, downed her coffee and left.

She crossed over Santa Trìnita bridge, pausing momentarily to watch the engineers below clear the riverbed of its debris. The sad sight of a gutted piano hauled into the air, the death song of its strings sharply plangent.

The other side now, careful to look left and right. Past Borgo San Jacopo, and into Via Maggio. She slowed down. Took her time to look at faces, to look into small alleyways, because she knew she was close. She stood outside Bianca Cappello's *palazzo* and looked at the photograph and it was no mistake that it had been taken right there, that fateful hour.

A woman cleaning out her cheese shop stands next to her and points to the photograph and says, Signor Temper.

Sì, Signor Temper, says Evelyn. *Dove?*

The woman points. Santo Spirito, she says.

Of course, Santo Spirito! thinks Evelyn.

Onward she goes. Takes a right, past the basilica, and is careful across the stones, always pausing, always looking. She is so close now she can feel it. She sees an old man scrubbing a jukebox, a large blue parrot atop a statue. And then—

Him. Cleaning a stone bench.

She moves closer. Ulysses? she says.

He looks up. He smiles.

It is you, isn't it? she says.

Hello, Evelyn.

Twenty-two years and where do you start?

Some might say where you left off.

So tell me, Ulysses, how is the good captain? And it was the silence that alerted her. That long, steady intake of breath.

And around the kitchen table in an old palazzo, Ulysses told his story. First time Cress had heard some of it and it made him a bit choked, truth be told. Darnley, Arturo, Peg, the kid called Alys, the inheritance, the move to Italy, the *pensione*, Dotty's portrait of Alys, a wild dash for a train. So that was you? said Evelyn. Yes. But how do *you* know that was me? Evelyn laughing now. She said, Dotty Cunningham saw you from the train. Dotty Cunningham? said Ulysses. She's my oldest friend, said Evelyn. She's here with me now. And they couldn't believe how so many roads had either led to him or led to her. And for Evelyn, there was equal sadness as there was delight at hearing how close they'd been to one another, how touchable, if only—the *preciousness* of time, you see.

They heard the front door open. In here, Alys! said Ulysses. Oh my God, said Alys. Hello, kid, said Evelyn. Miss Skinner? said Jem. Jem Gunnerslake? said Evelyn. Fair to say there was more than a touch of farce to the reunion.

Two days later, Evelyn and Dotty moved into the guest room. It was the best room and still smelled of Des. Amber, isn't it? said Evelyn. With a touch of citron, said Dotty. Expensive, they added.

Dotty and Evelyn's first night turned into a double celebration on account of tap water's finally being declared drinkable in the city. That meant unlimited baths and showers, albeit in cold water. The students glistened and Pete said they smelled lovely and fresh like summer linen. He was head down at the piano as he always was, a medley of show tunes to get the evening warmed up. Jem, Alys and Massimo sang along, and Claude performed a spot of asymmetric hovering.

Dotty turned to Evelyn and said, I might be wrong, but d'you think Pete's the man who played a frontier pianist with a drink problem all those years ago in the West End? A small but noticeable part.

I think you're right, said Evelyn.

I feel as if I've imbibed a hallucinogen, Lynny.

How lovely, said Evelyn.

Suddenly a knock at the door. I'll get it! shouted Ulysses.

Not too early, am I? said the elderly contessa, barging in. Ulysses had bought her an electric stove, but she'd found every conceivable thing wrong with it and ultimately shunned it in favor of food and company at the *pensione*. But who could blame her?

We've sat you at your usual place, Contessa, said Ulysses. And we have two more guests.

Two more? You giving Saint Francis a run for his money?

Sixteen sat down for dinner that night. The wine kept flowing, bowls of *tagliatelle al tartufo* kept flowing, bread and conversation flowing. Pete telling Cress about Col's new girlfriend June. Not June Woeful? That's her, said Pete. Won't last, said Cress. He needs someone older, said Ulysses. Older than Woeful? Older than him, said Ulysses. I always prefer someone older, said Pete. What's he saying? said the elderly contessa. Pete says he prefers an older woman, said Alys, translating. I'm not on the market, said the elderly contessa. Massimo talking to Jem about Ernest Hemingway and Dotty said she'd met him in a bar once. Kept going on about a six-word story, she said. Such a bore. So male. Jem said his mother still talked so fondly of the weekend Dotty taught her to paint. Ah, the divine Penelope, said Dotty. Do you think she might enjoy a follow-up? Incorrigible, whispered Evelyn.

A knife tapped against a spoon. The conversation hushed and Ulysses stood up. He delivered an invocation of thanks, mostly. That they were all gathered at that moment in time. How that meant something, would continue to mean something over the years. True worth, he said.

So there they were, young and old and some in the middle, shadows and candlelight, freeze-framed, with glasses raised.

To this moment, he said, looking at Evelyn. She smiled.

To this moment, they all said.

At the approach of Christmas, the students began to depart. Jem was on his way to the station with Alys when he caught sight of Massimo on the concourse. Massimo wasn't there to say good-bye but to persuade Jem to stay. Till term restarted, that's all. Not much persuasion needed. Jem thought Massimo handsome and the easiest man in the world to talk to. (He really said that? He really did, said Alys.)

The three of them walking back across the square.

Well, I'll be . . . , said Cress, looking through his telescope on the terrace. Jem's come back, he said.

Not surprised, said Evelyn. We all came back.

You staying with us for Christmas, Dotty? said Ulysses.

I'll be here, Temps. Scrubbing Dante next to my Swedish muse.

Music drifted in from the other room. It was Pete and his "Lament for Vietnam." People quieted to listen to Pete.

Christmas Eve saw the Pope giving midnight mass at the Duomo but the gang from the *pensione* weren't there. They were coming out of the cinema. Last episode of the *Trilogia del Dollaro. The Good, the Bad and the Ugly.*

That Ennio Morricone, said Massimo.

I think he's completely redefined the cinematic soundtrack, said Jem.

Ulysses and Pete laughing. Made for each other, whispered Cress.

A slow nocturnal wander across the river. The water black and tame and the lights of the city pulsing quietly on the glassy surface.

Happy, Lynny?

Evelyn nodded. You?

Nowhere I'd rather be.

A late supper at the newly reopened Michele's. Nina Simone on the jukebox and a photograph of Des pride of place on the wall above the coffee machine. *Biciclette* all round and eight for *spaghetti alle vongole*, if you please. The basilica emptied out and crowds gathered in the square for the Christmas hour. Alys walking back across the stones with her guitar. Like old times, said Giulia, and her hand brushed against Ulysses's. Faint, but still that flicker.

The first anniversary of the flood brought everyone back as promised. Even Des returned with Poppy. Some of the best days of my life, he said. And wouldn't they all say that in time? The shared loss became the shared bond. Thousands walked down from the church of San Miniato al Monte to the Ponte alle Grazie in a candlelit procession. That was something, that was. By then it was known that in Florence, thirty-three people had lost their lives, fifty thousand families their homes, fifteen thousand cars had been destroyed, six thousand businesses lost, and the mighty shift of the working artisanal class had begun. The floodwater had traveled at forty miles an hour and had left behind six hundred thousand tons of mud—a ton for every citizen. Fifteen hundred works of art had been destroyed or wrecked beyond repair and a third of the National Library's collection damaged. It would take twenty years before restoration work on many of these items would be completed. Some would take longer. And the cause? Investigations into the massive release of water by both the Levane and La Penna dams resulted in shifting blame and would be a bone of contention for years. Lots of conspiracy sprang up in that unaccountable schism.

But everybody was questioning everything by then. Strikes and protests flared up across the country and students occupied the universities. Good-bye authoritarianism, hello civil rights. A new ideology was taking hold and the young left no stone unturned: family, Church, Communism, Fascism. You name it, they challenged it. Divorce and abortion were back on the agenda and the Catholic right balked.

On a lighter note, Michele's acquired a piano. It used up the last of Des's money, but it was that or a billiard table and Giulia put her foot down, especially when she knew that Pete was staying for good.

I Do Love Nothing in the World So Well As You

1968–79

Pete began his new working life at Michele's at the beginning of '68. Massimo photographed him for his publicity pictures and those early posters reflected a brooding presence of genius. Slightly soft focus due to the fag smoke, but they did the trick. He picked up gigs at basement clubs and the odd hotel, no shortage of older women queueing up to be on Pete's arm. They're the future, he said.

Massimo took a sabbatical in London to be with Jem, who was now a junior doctor at UCH. He was still worried about the age difference, but the elderly contessa reassured him, saying, As long as there's still grass on the pitch . . . Col stayed on the lookout for the demolition teams and got to know Cressy's cherry tree and tree said, What took you so long?—something a woman would say to him in the not-too-distant future. Ted got a new car and Ted got a mistress and Peg learned to drive when he was away. But that's a story for another day. Alys began an apprenticeship making globes and she was a natural and Ulysses was stoked. Him and her having coffee together in Piazza dei Sapiti. Life couldn't have been sweeter. By March, Cress was back in his shorts, which was regarded with the same enthusiasm as the return of the swallows—something you could rely on in an ever-tumultuous world.

He was gearing up for Apollo's first orbit around the moon and was thinking big thoughts the day Martin Luther King was assassinated. Cress howled and birds flew out from the *campanile*.

As the world burned and raged and mourned, a moment of calm was taking place at the Folkestone ferry terminal.

The day was warm and settled, the sky azure blue and quite atypical for April. Gulls swooped and the air was salty and auspicious. Dotty closed the boot of her Sunbeam Alpine. Evelyn picked up her suitcase and tested the weight of it.

Not too heavy? said Dotty.

Not at all, said Evelyn. I think I could manage that myself if there happens to be a dearth of porters.

So you've got everything?

I have.

I can send on anything you need.

Thank you, Dotty.

Quick ciggie?

Come on then, said Evelyn, and they leaned against the bonnet of the car. Dotty flicked her lighter.

The decision to move to Florence was not as wrenching for Evelyn as she'd imagined. Her visits to the city had become more frequent and the duration longer. Dotty was thriving in a proper relationship with an available(ish) older(ish) lesbian(ish) and she seemed happy. Her allergy to certain paints had miraculously subsided and she was reunited with titanium white. In fact, it was Dotty who had persuaded Evelyn to leave London in the end. Dotty who could see the draw of Florence, the ready-made family, the care, the memories.

I'm going to miss you, said Dotty.

Well, don't, said Evelyn. Come and visit instead. Bring Hannah.

Helena.

Oh God. Yes. Helena. I can't keep up, she said.

It's like the war all over again, said Dotty. Back to your life of espionage and intrigue.

Nonsense, said Evelyn.

I wish you'd flown. Seems such a long way.

I know. But it's the last time I'll probably ever take that train, Dotty—

The lure of the railway—

So much to reflect on. So much to remember.

Only way to travel, really.

Oh it is. Dotty, the keys! said Evelyn.

Got them. And Dotty waved them in front of her.

I told Jem to get in touch if ever he and Massimo need a place in London. And there's nothing for you to do with the Badleys in Kent, they're good as gold. They'll keep renting it till they drop. So everything's in order. You have nothing to do except paint. And be brilliant.

Righto, said Dotty.

And don't die before me, added Evelyn. I'm not sure I could handle that.

I won't then, said Dotty. And you know I love you the most. Out of them all. Always have. Always will.

I know.

Dotty looked at her watch.

Is it time? said Evelyn.

'Fraid so.

Shall we say good-bye here?

Probably best, said Dotty.

And then I'll follow those people down there. And I won't look back—

Oh no, don't look back.

Dotty suddenly fell into her arms.

Don't cry, said Evelyn.

Don't you cry, said Dotty.

I said it first.

———

And so began the last chapter of Evelyn Skinner's multifarious life. Eighty-seven years old and looking at least ten years younger, she stood on deck and watched England recede. No tug, no regret, the slate wiped clean. She opened her arms out wide and shouted, *Incipit vita nova!*

She'd given herself ample time between Gare du Nord and Gare de Lyon, and the taxi delivered her to the neighborhood bistro Jules with two hours to spare. A perfect spot under the canopy and a late lunch of *coquilles* St. Jacques, bread, salad, dash of wine was exactly what was required before the long night ahead. She wrote a postcard to Dotty as a subtle shift of sunlight caused refraction through her wineglass. She drew what she'd had to eat. A sweet little sketch. Dotty would place it in her kitchen by the coffeepot.

Nightfall was uneventful and Evelyn slept soundly as she always did on a train, vaguely aware of her upstairs companion, tossing and turning and complaining about a man named Antoine. She awoke only when daylight broke through the shutters. A quick peek at the mountains and the years rolled back.

It was one thing to fly, but quite another to pass through the inviolable majesty of the Alps. She caught her reflection in the window and realized she was older now than her mother had been when she'd died; older than her father, too. She had out-aged them all. What a strange phenomenon. As if there'd only been her, Evelyn Skinner, born from a shell.

She stepped off the train at Santa Maria Novella station wearing a pale rust trouser ensemble, a vivid silk scarf (early Hermès) and large tortoiseshell sunglasses. She stood in a shaft of sunlight that was both hazy and soporific. The type of image that would have sent Dotty racing for the easel. And she exclaimed, as she always did, *Firenze! Amore mio!*

Evelyn! shouted Ulysses, racing through the concourse.

My darling boy.

You're home, he said.

———

Evelyn immediately joined Cressy in the *pensione* kitchen and what would once have been considered an unusual friendship became a golden one. Cress said that being with Evelyn was like being with Pellegrino Artusi himself. Ravioli straight from the pages of the book. Cress talked about Paola and Evelyn said she sounded like the most formidable woman and Cress said, She was, she was. For a while I was the happiest man on earth.

Cress and Evelyn were on the stone bench together the day they learned Bobby Kennedy had been shot. Cress said he feared for mankind, and hand in hand they walked silently back home.

Cress took to his bed and Evelyn settled on the sofa and started a letter to Dotty about the end of goodness. Such violence for June. We had the best and I'm not sure we'll see the like again. How cruel that glimpse of what might have been, she wrote.

The front door opened. Evelyn! Evelyn!

It was Alys. The same sweet intense look on her face as the day they'd met.

Did you hear? she said.

I heard, said Evelyn. Come. And she lifted her arm and Alys sat under it.

Pete came in next. I'm not one to swear, Evelyn, but fuck it all, he said.

Come here, said Evelyn, and she lifted her other arm.

At the age of eighty-seven Evelyn Skinner became an unexpected mother. A role she was far more suited to than she had ever imagined.

Turbulence and heartbreak overshadowed everything that year and man's first orbit around the moon failed to lift Cressy's spirits to the dizzying heights that science and achievement often did.

Despite the somber lilt to the air, Christmas Eve at Michele's went ahead. A feast of togetherness, no more no less—that's how Ulysses described it. He stood at the window overlooking the square and

Giulia came up to him and said, How long's Cressy going to stay out there, Ulisse? and Ulysses shrugged. Till he finds what he's looking for.

An old man standing on a bench with a telescope pointed at the moon. In the very gesture of his defiant, unmoving stance was a prayer for the world.

And as he looked up, so a man looked down.

From a small window in Apollo 8, 250,000 miles away from the Earth, William Anders loaded his Hasselblad camera with color film and took a photograph.

(Click.)

Here would be the hope, Cressy.

(Click.)

Here would be your answered prayer. A simple image of what the moon sees:

Us.

A blue marbled sphere, amplified by the lunar horizon, precious and beautiful and vulnerable, floating in the eternal darkness we all shall face. That's how Evelyn described it whilst gazing at the cover of Cressy's *Life* magazine. Cress thought Evelyn had something of the poets about her, but didn't everyone that year, Cress? Loss and love. The only ingredients required.

So, 1969 was under way. Last year of the decade. You'd better have something good up your sleeve or— Yeah, right.

In London, January was sleeting its guts up and Col was woken by the ringing of a telephone. He got out of bed complaining.

What the fu—?

It was the hospital. Acid reflux began to spurt like Vesuvius.

He phoned Mrs. Kaur and was outside her shop in half an hour, handing over Ginny. Thank you, he said. Really, thank you.

Mrs. Kaur had a calming presence. I'll bring Ginny back home tomorrow, she said. And I'll offer up prayers for Peg. And be careful on the road, Mr. Formiloe.

Col pulled into Whipps Cross Hospital siren screeching, hammering the dash and causing confusion with the bona fide ambulance drivers waiting outside, smoking.

Along the corridors, he could feel his emotions churn. So mixed it was, all his fear and pain, as boy and man. Peg had told the doctor he was her next of kin. No one had ever done that for him, not even Agnes in them early days.

At the desk he asked for Peggy Temper. I mean Peggy Holloway, he said.

(He'd never gotten used to the name change like he'd never gotten used to the marriage.)

This way, said matron.

Legs like jelly now.

Second on the left, said matron. Go on, Mr. Formiloe. Go on in, be brave.

Col took a deep breath and pulled back the curtain. Oh, Peg, he said, and sat down. He took hold of her hand, but she didn't wake. Gently pushed back her hair. Bruised and concussed but all in one piece, thank God. Matron said she was a walking miracle. Tell me something I don't know, he said.

Mr. Holloway? A policeman peered round the curtain.

No. I'm Mr. Formiloe. Friend. Old friend. Long before the cunt she married came along.

Policeman tried not to smile.

So, booze, was it? said Col.

No.

No? (How wretched did Col feel in that moment. His easy dismissal of her and her good-time ways.)

No alcohol present at all, said the policeman. Black ice and bad luck. Car's a write-off.

Where's the car?

Leyton. She was heading west.

She was heading to me, thought Col.

Looked like she was going away, said the policeman. She had suit-cases in the back.

You got 'em?

In the squad car.

I'll come down now, he said.

Col put the last of the cases in the back of the ambulance and closed the door. He shook hands and gave the policeman his details. Emergency si-rens cleaved the air and a rush of vehicles came to a halt. Blue lights flashed across Col's face. Col lit a cigarette. So you did it, Peg. You made a bloody run for it. I'll get you wherever you need to get. And he flicked the ciga-rette away and headed back to the ward. Wasn't quick enough to grasp the look on the young nurse's face, though, as he pulled back the curtain and—

All right, Col?

It was Ted.

Col could feel the acid roil and his hand reached for his guts.

You look a bit pale, Col. You should see a doctor (Ted laughed). Now, you tell me what the chances of this were, eh? That a bloke I know was visiting his old mum. Actually walking out the same time Peg was going in. Well, you'd phone the husband, wouldn't you? At least to find out what was what. Husband didn't know what was what, but that call made him feel like God was on his side.

Col feeling woozy.

Anyway, as you can see—and Ted sat on the bed—I'm here now. Your assistance no longer required.

Col feeling his hand tingle. Getting breathless now, all that blood rushing. And as swift as Col had ever moved in his life, he pulled Ted into a headlock and held something sharp against his throat. He said, I swear to God, the only thing stopping me sticking these scissors in is that you'd get immediate medical attention. Now fuck off. (A little nip to Ted's ear before Col let him go.)

Ow, yelped Ted, and he reached up and saw blood. You don't know who you're messing with, he said. I know people.

You know people, do you, Ted? People who need people? Piss off, said Col. And stay away.

Col kept vigil for the rest of the night. And when he was moved on by the matron, he kept vigil somewhere else. Stayed like that all night. Moved on. Vigil. Moved on. Vigil. Fags and tea. He overheard a nurse tell another nurse that he was the boyfriend. Slight giggle afterward. Would've loved to have heard that once. Now it was about something else.

In the early hours, a nurse found him and told him Peg was awake.

Col looked through the curtain. All right, love? he said.

Peg turned away.

She said nothing in the ambulance on the way home. She leaned against the window with a faraway look in those Peggy blues. Unresponsive when Col squeezed her hand. Not far now, he said.

He led her into the pub. Straight past the optics she walked, didn't even register. Up the stairs, kicked off her shoes and sat on the bed.

You want a hot chocolate?

Col waiting for the ridicule. What am I, Col? Nine? But it didn't come. Peg needed help taking off her cardigan. Slipped out of her skirt and got under the covers. Said nothing and looked away.

He heard the back door open downstairs. The voice of Mrs. Kaur and Ginny running up the stairs. Col up quick to the door to hold Gin back.

Peg's hurt her face, love. Peg's sad.

I make Peg better, said Ginny. I made Claude better. I make people better.

Ginny tiptoed into the room. She sat on the bed and rubbed Peg's back. I love you, Peggy. I love you so much, Peggy. And that's the way it'll always be, Peggy.

Peg's face crumpled. Peg pulled a pillow over her head and sobbed.

Col left the room.

The kitchen smelled of curry.

At the stove stood Mrs. Kaur in an apron brought from home. She said, I thought you would be in need of sustenance after such a long night, Mr. Formiloe.

Col had never eaten curry before. Smelled it on Ginny plenty of times, though.

Sarson ka saag, said Mrs. Kaur. *Dal makhana*. And this is *roti*.

Col repeated the words.

As he ate, Col said something about the profusion of flavors. And no meat?

No meat, Mr. Formiloe.

Well, I never. Is that to do with—you know, your—?

Life as a Sikh?

Col nodded.

No. We have the choice. I choose not to.

When they'd finished eating, Col offered Mrs. Kaur a cigarette. Offered her a whiskey, too.

I don't smoke or drink, Mr. Formiloe.

Why?

She laughed at that. He did too, even though he was being serious.

D'you mind if—?

No, no. You go ahead, she said.

He was aware how comfortable he felt with her and told her what he'd done to Ted on the ward.

Nonviolent action is the only way, said Mrs. Kaur.

I'm a long way from that, he said. My wife was frightened of me.

Did you give her reason to be?

I never hit her.

That's not what I asked.

Yeah, she had reason to be.

I'm not frightened of you, Mr. Formiloe. So, there at least is progress.

Col drank his whiskey. He said, I need to get Peg to Cress and Temps for a bit. Reckon you could look after Ginny again, Mrs. Kaur?

Always my pleasure—

And I'll find someone to manage the pub.

I can manage the pub, said Mrs. Kaur.

You?

The pub and Ginny, both, yes.

You could handle that?

Mrs. Kaur stared at him. She said, I was widowed twenty-five years ago, Mr. Formiloe. In a place not my home. I have a thriving convenience store. I also have one in Leeds and I'm looking to open one in Southall. I support my family in the Punjab. I pray. I give shelter to people like me who came to this country to help people like you. In the tradition of *langar*, I often feed thirty people a night. I do not drink alcohol but neither do I judge those that do. A pub, Mr. Formiloe, I can handle.

Col thought she was magnificent. He gave her the spare set of keys and went to the telephone.

God knows how Col managed it, but he got to Italy in a matter of days. Foot down all the way, the ambulance became a right old bone shaker, straining at the sixty-mile-per-hour leash. Peg was mostly quiet, head buffered by a pillow against the window, looking at the landscape. The movement of the sun and clouds and birds transfixed her and sometimes she sighed deeply and Col said, You OK, Peg? And Peg said, Yeah, I'm OK, Col.

And at about four p.m., the 1930s ambulance spluttered into the square for the last time, screaming and wailing with the bonnet steaming. Col cut the engine and the van rolled to a deathly stop. Here we are, said Col.

Through the windscreen, Peg could see Cress and Temps waiting for her. Formally posed with hands clasped in front and heads at a slight tilt. Like they were waiting for a hearse. And there, standing behind them, Alys. A brief collision of eyes before Peg looked away.

You ready? said Col.

Give me a minute, said Peg.

Course, and he climbed out and stretched. Peg heard Ulysses say, All right, Col? and she watched the two men embrace.

She could have stayed in that van for the rest of the day, just her watching the world pass by. Not participating, not commentating, not caring, just removed. Cress always said she'd end up with them eventually. Cress and his ley lines. Peg took out her compact and looked in the mirror. She began to powder the bruising, get herself ready to bring the curtain up on the Peggy show, but she suddenly noticed that Alys had gone back inside and she put the compact away. No-show due to unforeseen circumstances. She opened the door and climbed out shakily.

She stood blinking in the brittle light of a February afternoon. Ulysses's arms were open to her, and his sweet sorrowful eyes, and there was no clack clack clack of Peggy's tune, just heels in hand and stockings on stone, and a swing of those hips because that's just the way it was. Oh, he smelled so sweet, so kind. Cress was choked and he moved toward her, but Peg cut him off at the pass and said, Don't you dare go soft on me, old fella. I don't have the strength for you and me both right now.

That gave Cress a shot of the masterfuls.

You lean on me, Peg, and I'll lead the way, he said.

Col and Ulysses fetched the suitcases.

You look good, Col, last thing Peg heard as she climbed the stairs.

Peg went straight to her room. Lay in bed and listened to them all outside, the tiptoeing and the hush-hush as they passed by her door. Hours governed by bells and the shift of light and she slept.

One time, she was briefly aware of Alys standing in the doorway. But she didn't move, too ashamed she was to acknowledge her. That seesaw tug in their guts that would never let them go. And the men stayed away. Kept a wide berth and she wondered what bright spark had set that in motion. Temps, of course. Could almost hear him saying, Peg needs women now and not us. Even you, Pete, he added.

In and out, in and out she faded, and it was the out she sought. No more pills and yet the pain ran deep. Ted the game she thought she knew the rules of. She got tired and he got meaner. She got small and he got richer. Looked about one day and he was the only one in the room. Sleep, Peg, sleep.

Alys sat on the floor of her mother's room with a sketchbook on her lap. Her scrutiny was not loud and the sound of a pencil moving across the page was soft. Peg wouldn't have agreed to this in waking life, but this was what Alys needed, not Peg, because in the space between artist and sitter could be found understanding and forgiveness and maybe love.

Peg heard the door open. It was the old woman. Imposing and practical. Reassuring and kind. Brought her food, sat with her, even washed her. Just arms and face and feet but it felt so pure and generous and Peg's tears ran, and the old woman said good words that rang as true as those ancient bells.

On the fifth day, Peg went out. Before-the-market early. She ran down the stairs and moved about the city as a ghost. She took as her fixed point the river, as she always had, and she walked east.

The walk revealed the pain of solitude that had lain central not only in her lifetime but in her mother's and her mother's mother's, too. No education, no money, only men. A cycle of repetition so ridiculous that it needed only organ music and a scattering of plastic horses to be that predictable fairground ride.

Her beauty had been her currency. Always had been. No one talked about when the bank ran dry as it inevitably would. All those books she never read. All those museums she'd rubbished as brain-box boring. Cressy said it took effort to turn a page. Takes patience and care, Peg. Takes a leap of grace to say I don't know.

Sex, though, was what she was good at. She could turn a twenty-year-old boy into a man, and a middle-aged man into a twice-a-night. Mother was a drinker who couldn't stop. Mother had boyfriends who couldn't stop. Thought her dad was Bill but found out too late it was George. That was a hard one to live down. The street found her out by the canal, stony-eyed with a mouth full of bluster and a fag between her lips that she'd cadged from a decent bargeman. Take me away, she'd asked him. When you're old enough, he'd said. See? Decent. Men who wait.

And Eddie? As the clouds gathered overhead and the morning turned dark, she realized London in wartime had been the star of that fateful show. Love and sex came fast and danced with the nearness of death and my God did it make life golden. Made it giddy and immediate. They clung to one another because the essence of life itself had been revealed to them, and it was as simple as a Californian orange grove with the sound of bees, and blossom, and heat as heady as existence itself. Eddie always looked at her as if the future was ripe. Ted looked at her as if the fruit had fallen.

Peg sat and took off her shoes. Her feet were tinged mauve. She rubbed them and they didn't look like hers anymore. And in the mud on the foreshore as the rain began to fall, she grieved it all. Mother, Ted, Eddie, Alys. The uncompromising inevitability of it all. That one-way ticket to this. How she cried.

It was Evelyn who found her. With hair plastered across her forehead and mouth open in silent pain. Evelyn said, We will find your soul, Peg, and bring it back to you. And she wrapped Peg up in a mac that smelled of rubber, that had clementines in the pockets.

Col's last night was spent in Michele's, and no one expected Peg to turn up. But in she walked, holding tight to Evelyn's arm. Lippy in place and a touch of the swagger and there was a roar of greeting. Took Peg back a bit and she did look surprised, but it was like an infusion of blood straight to the heart. All that love, Cress would have said. Can't fake that, Peg. Alys organized the budge-up and Peg settled between Cress and Ulysses and both men took a hand each and kissed it. Nothing more said after that. Peg was treated like the Peg of old and the night stayed forward-looking.

Col lobbed Peg a fag and Ulysses poured out the wine and Pete got up to the piano because he felt an impromptu rendition of "Bewitched, Bothered and Bewildered" coming on. Silenced the restaurant, that did, and by the last verse everyone was humming. One of those nights, Evelyn wrote to Dotty. The haunting aspect of devotion. Hard to describe.

Time to order and Giulia stood in front of Ulysses, pencil poised and smiling.

Polpettone all round? said Ulysses.

Yes! they all said.

What's *polpettone*? said Col.

Meatloaf, said Cress.

No meat for me, said Col, and they all laughed.

No, I'm being serious, he said. No meat.

You ill? said Pete.

Why do I have to be ill to stop eating meat?

'Cause you only eat meat, said Ulysses.

Sometimes straight from the wrapper, said Cress.

Once. That was only once. Anyway, I've seen the light, said Col.

What's her name?

Don't you start, Temps.

I knew a man who stopped eating meat, said Cress.

Oh, here we go, said Col.

Benny Fedora, said Cress.

Weren't he that whistler down the market?

The very same, but hold that thought, Pete. Benny Fedora was a big carnivore. Benny Fedora—

We know his bleedin' name, Cress! said Col. Benny Fedora Benny Fedora . . .

Well, he stopped eating meat after a dream, said Cress.

What dream? said Alys.

That he ate his own leg. He said it was so real he woke up and vomited.

We're about to eat! said Col. Who wants to know about vomiting and eating your own leg?

I'm just saying what he told me, said Cress.

Col finished his wine and poured out more. Ulysses turned to Peg and winked. So good to see her laughing.

So he gave up meat, said Pete. And?

And his teeth fell out.

Jesus Christ, said Col.

Because he didn't need them anymore.

So that's why he could whistle, said Pete.

When he had teeth, not a note, said Cress. Afterward, like a songbird.

Fucking hell, said Col.

Giulia said in broken English, You like the *sformato ai carciofi* instead, Signor Formiloe?

Yeah, I would. *Sformato* sounds lovely, said Col. *Grazie, signora.*

You don't even know what it is, said Cress.

If it's not a leg, I'm happy.

The next morning, Col watched his ambulance get towed away to a junkyard outside Prato.

Worse places to end up, said Ulysses.

Out with all those memories, eh? said Col. Nonviolence is the only way, Temps.

I'm with you on that.

Come on, I'd kill for a coffee.

Peg had paid for Col's flight home. Course, they all had their Geoff Hurst money, but it was the gesture for Peg. To show him how important he was to her. How he'd been there when she'd needed him. She tried to say something to Col, but he cut her off; No need, he said. Next of kin meant everything to Col.

Ulysses drove Col to Rome in Betsy. On the way he turned to Col and said, Mrs. Kaur?

Who else knows?

Just me and Peg.

Keep it that way, said Col. This one's important. Like my life depends on it.

Spring saw the return of guests to the *pensione*. Capacity was down to two rooms on account of Pete and Peg, but Cress liked that, he found it manageable. A Miss Banderhorn turned up with her friend Miss

Coleridge—they were from Kansas—and a father and son duo, the Sweephills, came in from Exeter. Both pairs requested nothing spicy for dinner.

Alys was alone in Ulysses's workshop, pen in hand, radio on. She was putting the finishing touches to a globe that featured only cities more than a thousand years old: ancient names that became the ancient trade routes. Her globes were solely objects of art and Dotty had already alerted gallery owner Joyce. The globe before that had been luminous with pilgrimage walks and from that study had come intricate sketches of a bridge, seen from all angles. And on this bridge, attached by struts overlooking the river, the solitary hermitages for worship—the world Evelyn had long ago described. Wooden slats. Abutments. A ladder. Closing in on a window and the woman inside. And Alys came to understand why women would seek refuge on a bridge and she drew their youth, their pain, their aging. Their existence and worth given shape by a virgin who birthed a child. She drew the lives they'd given up in the microscopic study of a flower, a vase, a cup, a plate, a piece of fabric—lace intricate and fine—darned sheets on a bed, a sketchbook in the corner, a fine lock of baby hair hidden between two pages. On and on and on, she drew the details of undetailed lives. Of forgotten women who once may have wanted so much more.

She put down the pen and stretched out her neck. She was taken aback to see Peg staring at her through the window. Alys opened the door.

Peg said, You looked so peaceful. Didn't want to disturb you. I came to see if you wanted a coffee and Temps said they do nice ones round here. (Peg nervous and saying too much.) It must be weird having me around. And I don't want to get in your way. That's mainly what I wanted to say.

For twenty years I've wanted you to get in my way, said Alys.

Peg didn't know what to say to that. Peg didn't know if Alys was being kind or hurtful and she nodded and left. Ulysses said Alys was being kind. Peg went back and apologized. They had coffee together and there were awkward silences, but it was a start.

———

July brought heat and plenty of it. Mosquito deterrents burned incessantly and the English group sought respite at a swimming pool in Poggetto. (You need a new swimming costume, Pete. Thanks, Peg, it is rather itchy.) July also saw man walking on the moon. Twenty-seven hours of continual television coverage at Michele's sent Pete and Cress doolally. They fell asleep by the flickering black and white light and Claude kept guard. Cress attempted to walk as if there was zero gravity and Peg said he looked like his nuts were twisted.

Come the evening, Michele's was fully booked. Lots of Americans in town drinking up a patriotic fervor. Pete became Master Commander of the atmosphere and shifted over to that velveteen stool and pulled out all the musical stops.

"Fly Me to the Moon," "Old Devil Moon," "Blue Moon," "It's Only a Paper Moon," and then of course . . .

"Moon River."

He played a long introduction, kept looking over at Peg as if to say, Come on, Peg, for old times' sake if nothing else. Eventually, Peg stood up. Slightly bashful, slightly unsure. Long time since she'd stood by a piano, and you could see it on her face, certainly those who knew her could. And you felt for her and loved her in that moment like never before. Pete squinted up at her, a fag-clamped smile, his admiration for all to see. Peg winked and there it was. You could see it. Peg the Performer, just like that. In her DNA it was, that's what Cress said.

And back in London, as Neil Armstrong's foot touched the lunar surface for the first time, Col took a giant leap of his own when he asked Mrs. Kamya Kaur out on a formal date. What took you so long? she said.

Autumn in Italy, and the north of the country was rocked by further strikes in factories and industrial centers. Students continued to demonstrate and clashes with police were frequent. Communism, Marxism,

Fascism all fighting for a place at the political table and Massimo wrote that it was bubbling up to something darkly ominous, this unholy alliance of civil despondency and unrest. Ulysses missed his friend and didn't hesitate to tell him so. He wrote to him of life in the square. *"Chestnuts, truffles, chicken livers and pockets of mellow fruitfulness drift in on the season's warm and fragrant breath. The grape harvest is under way and the schiacciata all'uva back in the bakery. Some things never change, thank God."*

The second week of September, Ulysses disappeared for the day as he always did. Peg said they should follow him and Evelyn said she wasn't sure that was a good idea and Peg said, It's only a bleedin' joke! First time Evelyn had a glimpse of Peg's sharp elbow.

By mid-October the swallows still hadn't left. But why would you? said Cress.

Pasta alla Genovese using *trenette*. It was a Cress special. Peg made the pesto and followed Cressy's every move. The windows were open, and Peg liked the radio on, though she turned it down low. She sang English words over Italian lyrics—just made them up, she did—and jigged from stove to sink, housedress unbuttoned and feet bare. What? she said.

Just looking, said Cress.

You look like you wanna say something, old man, she said.

You're beautiful, said Cress.

Don't start. And Peg turned away to cut the bread.

We've had fun, haven't we, Peg? And you're OK now, aren't you? In yourself. And being here.

I'm OK, Cress. And Peg held his face and kissed him on the nose. You're my rock, she said. Always have been, always will be.

And later, when the guests had retired, when they'd washed up and put the crockery away, Peg and Cress ate ice cream on the terrace, just the two of them standing up, as the sun set red and gold, and Gianni Morandi sang "Scende la Pioggia" on the radio. They danced and when night turned black and one by one the lights on the hills expired, Peg went to bed. Cress gave her Constance Everly's poetry book for company. I've never read poetry before, she said. What if I don't understand it?

You will, he said. You will.

Knock knock.

Alys looked up from her worktable. You going out for your walk, Cressy? You need company?

Not tonight, my love. Just wanted to say good night in case you're asleep when I get back.

Alys got up and kissed him. What is it?

Here—and he gave her his torn-off cover of *Life* magazine, showing William Anders's portrait of the Earth. Most problems can be solved by gazing at this, he said.

Alys smiled. You reckon?

You wait.

Cress hovered in the doorway of the *salotto* and said, I was thinking, Evelyn. What about us going to Assisi?

Oh yes, let's. Next month. Assisi is a spectacle that can never be forgotten.

You and me on the Moto Guzzi—

Now, won't that make Dotty jealous!

Night, Evelyn.

Night, my darling Cressy. Don't stay out too late.

In the hallway, Cress put on his hat and corrected the angle in the mirror. See you later, squawked Claude.

The soft sound of the door closing behind him. Cress outside in the night air with its accompanying lilt of drains. How he loved that smell! He walked toward the stone benches, the neon from Michele's in his peripheral vision, the sound of Pete on the piano, the gentle murmur of the last of the diners, the chink chink of cutlery, his ears alive to it all.

Cressy! Ulysses running across the square. Where you off to? he said, catching his breath.

Nowhere and everywhere, said Cress.

Fancy company?

Not tonight, son. Oh, by the way: Peg's in bed with Constance Everly.

Nothing would surprise me anymore, Cress.

It was dark under the trees and the ghosts rode wild across the square and brought a sardonic eyebrow-lift to Cressy's soft, accepting features. A Fellini-esque quality saturated the nocturnal tableau—to his left a drunk carrying a big fish, to his right a nun with a strange-looking habit, and straight ahead a glowing church of shapely perfection.

Cress didn't feel tired anymore. He was traveling the highway of memory. How about we throw in a little ecstasy for good measure, Cress? What a life!

Three in the morning, Ulysses awoke with his heart thumping and a strong ominous feeling like the first creeping awareness of smoke. He threw on a T-shirt and a pair of trousers and walked barefoot through the apartment. A flash of blue in the gloom. Shh, he said to Claude, who settled on his shoulder. He checked the kitchen, the *salotto*, and all seemed well. He listened at Alys's door and could hear her steady breath. He moved along to Evelyn's and listened for the same easy, sleepy drawl. Cressy's door was ajar. A gentle push revealed the room was empty and the bed unslept in.

In the square, the Moto Guzzi was where Cress had left it and Ulysses wished the old boy had taken off on a whim. He launched Claude into the night—Go find Cress, he said, and the bird took flight.

Ulysses walked down Via Maggio and turned in to Piazza dei Sapiti. He went past the Pitti Palace, down to the Ponte Vecchio, and headed east along the river. Could almost see the old fella's footprints glowing in the dark. He called out Cressy's name, shone the torch into dark corners but the city was pretty empty 'cept for a dog bark and the clandestine clinch of lovers, nothing unusual. The river was still and lit by streetlamps and the faint edge of lightening sky. He began to run.

All the way to San Niccolò, he could feel it, and his legs weakened and his breath shallowed, and yet he needed to hold it all together for all that was to come. He lit a cigarette and doubled back.

He called out for Cress again and it sounded more like a lament, and then suddenly, along Lungarno Torrigiani, he heard it: a faint squawk.

He stopped. Claude? He approached the Lutheran church, a splay of torchlight cast out in front of him. Shadows and bushes and there against the wall by the portico, the crumpled shape of a body with a parrot standing guard. Ulysses ran toward Cress and felt for a pulse. The heat had gone, though, and the face was at peace. Ulysses sat next to him and leaned into him one last time. He lifted Claude onto his lap and could feel straightaway that something was wrong.

Hey, little fella, what's going on?

Claude struggling to breathe.

What is it? said Ulysses.

Claude's voice was faint. Out, out, brief candle, he whispered.

You wanna go with Cress?

Claude blinked.

Life's but a walking shadow, Ulysses.

I know, said Ulysses, holding him close to his chest. I know, I know.

And I do love nothing in the world . . . so well . . . as you.

Ulysses watched the sun rise and the river turn gold and he didn't remember much after that. Pete found him, though. Pete had a sense, too. Pete went back and made known what needed to be made known.

The women rallied. A seamless tide of knowing exactly what to do. An English send-off, that's what Cress got. No funeral mass, no open casket, but a crematorium and a gathering at Michele's after. A death notice attached to the building informed the square of the arrangements but mostly it was the elderly contessa who delivered the news. She delivered it tenderly because she had feelings for the old boy that she'd always kept hidden. It was the elderly contessa who took Ulysses to buy chrysanthemums in the market. Watched him decorate the doorway of the *pensione*, watched him fill the sidecar of the Moto Guzzi with orange blooms. Nice touch, she said. And in English she added, Classic Cressy.

Massimo raced back, of course. He took the first plane out and was surprised to see Ulysses waiting at the airport for him. I'm OK, I'm OK, said Ulysses, and Massimo said, No you're not, Ulisse, now stop. Sort of did Ulysses in, that did, and he had to pull over and let Massimo drive. Des and Poppy came back, too. Des said, I thought Old Cress'd live forever. I thought he was plastic. And Pete played "Cressy's Song" and would never play it again. Afterward he disappeared with a bottle of whiskey and Alys found him in the cellar. I feel safe down here, he said.

Col didn't come back because Col couldn't face it. Had a memorial at the pub for Cress and the turnout was huge. Spilled out onto the pavement despite the rain. Col learned by heart the poem Cress had recited in the English Cemetery and Col got hammered and ended up a blubbering mess. If not now, then when? said Mrs. Kaur.

And what of Peg?

Peg didn't have a drink at all. Peg sang "Someone to Watch Over Me" and afterward sat out in the square and wrote a letter. Evelyn's idea. "*Dear Cress*," it began. All those memories, all those thanks. When she'd finished, she walked back into Michele's, and using Cressy's phrasebook, she ordered a glass of bubbles and a plate of ham. She sat alone and drank and ate. She looked at the phrases he'd underlined in the book. Those early days of what had been important to him. "A stamp for a letter to England, please."

Winter arrived and brought emptiness.

Ulysses could barely lift his head off the pillow, such was the weight of loss. He went in on himself as far as he could go. Nineteen seventy and the turn of the decade. So long, the sixties! What have you ever done for us?

Hello? Anyone?

He lay still and let it wash over him. Evelyn sat with him and read out loud until he fell asleep.

And then March came to pass. Warmth crested the air and the shift of nature was felt on the wind and it was uplifting and that couldn't be denied. Rooms splayed yellow and the first guests arrived downstairs. Alys's voice saying, Hello, hello, you're very welcome.

Ulysses was lying on the bed with his mind drifting, when all of a sudden the flit of wings and a sharp chirp caught his attention. He opened his eyes and took a moment to focus. Two swallows flying in and out of the shutters with mud and twigs in their beaks. In the corner of the room was the start of a nest. He watched transfixed and could hear Cressy say, And here endeth an epic journey of trials and tribulations we know not of. These two came up from the Nile Valley, I reckon. Do you, Cress? I do. It's just a feeling and I may be wrong but— two hundred miles a day they've covered, Temps. Superb navigation. Flying at up to twenty, twenty-two miles per hour, although thirty-five miles per hour has also been known. They've survived starvation, storms and sheer exhaustion for the sole purpose of being here. And making a home. Sounds familiar, eh?

Ulysses called out to Peg. Peg stood in the doorway and smiled like a kid. Rare to see Peg like that. She kicked off her shoes and lay pressed against his back. And together they watched the swallows.

When Ulysses returned to the globes, which he did at the beginning of April, he put Cressy in the heart of Italy. Gave him an "i" at the end of his name instead of a "y," and this would be the marker of the post-1970 editions. There was something noticeable about these globes. How sorrow ran tributary to beauty. There was a majesty to them, something delicate and precious and startling. Like the image William Anders took from space. They would be Ulysses's finest.

They set off on a beautiful June afternoon. Big old palaver about what to wear on their feet—something comfortable and practical and with grip, said Pete. Massimo and Ulysses took the rucksacks and Pete—"the safest pair of hands"—carried the urn. Peg and Alys had the blankets and Evelyn's sole focus was to not die of overexertion. If I don't make it, she said, don't resuscitate me, just roll me over the edge like a boulder.

And in a convoy of Betsy and the Moto Guzzi, they drove up to

Settignano and parked in the main square. As the afternoon leaned into the evening, they walked down toward the *cimitero*, down past the fluttering olive grove, and from there they stepped onto the ancient way of the stonecutters. Evelyn had been tasked with finding the right place for facts-man Cress and she'd done him proud. Every step they took was history. Every step was for him. Following in the tracks of those who'd carved out the *pietra serena* in Renaissance times. How he would have loved that! And, of course, the heavily wooded walk took them up to Monte Ceceri, where Leonard da Vinci had dreamed and had pondered the idea of flight.

This is it, said Ulysses.

The forest had become a cathedral. Beneath columns of sunlight, Evelyn and Peg and Alys lay on the blanket head to head to head in a three-pointed star. Pete felt for a pulse and declared he didn't have one. Is that possible, Temps? I don't think so, Pete.

Massimo and Ulysses sat side by side and uncorked the wine and handed around glasses. The wine was still cool, deliciously so, and revived them. Pete opened the urn and as Evelyn recited Constance Everly, they each took it in turns to scatter Cressy's ashes across the forest floor.

They drank the wine and felt grateful he had walked among them. How lucky we were! said Ulysses. He and Alys told the story of Fanny Blankers-Koen again and how Cress had smuggled the money and Claude onto the ferry, back in '53. And what followed was an impromptu homage from Evelyn, a little nudge to Claude and his Shakespearean leanings:

> *But thy eternal summer shall not fade,*
> *Nor lose possession of that fair thou ow'st,*
> *Nor shall death brag thou wand'rest in his shade,*
> *When in eternal lines to time thou grow'st.*
> *So long as men [and women, she added] can breathe or eyes can see,*
> *So long lives this, and this gives life to thee.*

Evelyn raised her glass to the forest, and everyone raised theirs. Pete swore there was a hush of appreciation through the leaves, and Ulysses said he heard it too.

The walk back was slow and uneventful and for a brief moment they all held hands. That was Alys's idea and she held Peg's.

And there they left Cress to become a tree.

The years 1971 to '74 were a mixed bag, all in all, and Cressy's absence was sharply felt. Right- and left-wing political extremists were trying to transform the country according to their own utopian vision, and assassinations and bombings hit the headlines. The gentle people of the *pensione* were quietly shaken, Ulysses especially. Evelyn said, We're still living in the footprints of the French Revolution, of Hitler and Mussolini. Scratch the surface of the varnish and it raises its head again. Evil was defeated but it never went away. This is something we must live with, Ulysses.

Against this backdrop of insurrection, Peg began her professional singing career. That it coincided with her divorce from Ted was lost on no one. She joined Pete in the hotels and clubs, and they became an instant hit with a repertoire honed across the decades. They were a couple of pros who could match one another's musical instinct. They were called Temper Fine—nothing more than their surnames tagged together; Pete, low into the mic, said, Ladies and gentlemen, I give you Peggy Temper. Dotty and Evelyn stood at the back and applauded loudly. The slow fade to the first number as the orange sun set across the flaming Arno. Dotty leaned across to Evelyn and whispered, In another lifetime, Lynny, her and me— Oh don't be fooled, said Evelyn. She'd eat you for breakfast. If only, said Dotty.

'Seventy-two saw Fellini's *Roma* come to Florence. Evelyn was ecstatic at the director's homage to a city she knew so well, and Pete declared he'd give his left foot and an ear to be in a Fellini film. You've really thought about this, haven't you, Pete? said Massimo, and Pete said he had. And in the most peculiar turn of events, which had Cressy written all over it, Pete's headshot ended up on the casting desk for *Amarcord* and he was whisked away to Stage 5 of the Cinecittà Studios. Massimo begged Pete to take him along too, but Pete wasn't allowed to bring a friend—although he did ask, God love him. Pete's part was small but noticeable, and the cinematic experience in its entirety changed him. He was treated like a star for the day. Sometimes that's all it takes.

That's a lovely jacket, said Ulysses.

One of Marcello Mastroianni's, said Pete.

Really suits you.

Thanks, Temps.

That was also the year that Massimo moved into the *pensione* after his mum died. There was money for a flat, but he didn't want the scrutiny when Jem came to stay, so . . .

You really want to? said Ulysses. Here with us?

Do you mind? Do I mind? Are you serious? Are you? (The conversation continued like that for a while.) Massimo took over dinner service on occasion and his cooking even got a mention in the visitors' book: *Those rice-stuffed tomatoes were heaven scent.* (There was a spelling mistake, but quite an apt and charming one.)

And in London, Col tied himself to the cherry tree when the bulldozers rolled in. The *Hackney Gazette* was all over the story and reported Col as saying: "Nonviolent action is the only way." The demolition crew cut Col free, the cherry tree ended up in the back of a skip, and Col had a night in the slammer after punching a policeman. Mrs. Kaur and Ginny were waiting for him when he came out. Mrs. Kaur said she was proud of him and Col walked like a king that day.

So there they were: a cold afternoon in Santo Spirito square at the beginning of '73.

Ulysses, Massimo and Evelyn were outside Michele's, drinking coffee and grappa. The market had cleared away early and Evelyn was telling the men about the summer she'd met Katharine Hepburn at the Kenwood Ladies' Pond in Hampstead, when into this reverie ran Pete. He'd been with Peg and Alys at a demonstration for abortion rights and his hand-painted T-shirt extolling women's choice was pulled tight over his sheepskin coat.

He stood in front of them, trying to catch his breath.

You won't believe who we just saw, he said, panting.

Go on, said Ulysses.

Romy Peller.

Never!

Pete said that he, Peg and Alys were walking back through the Piazzale degli Uffizi when they witnessed an accident.

What kind of accident? said Massimo.

A Vespa drove into a living statue. What are the chances of that? he said.

High, if you don't like mime, said Evelyn.

Ulysses laughing.

The living statue didn't even cry out, said Pete. Such was the focus and dedication to the craft.

Romy was driving the Vespa? said Ulysses.

No, Temps. Romy's the living statue.

Romy's a living statue? I don't believe it.

Alys couldn't either. There she was, bending down to administer first aid to this white-faced Jean Seberg lookalike, when suddenly— Hello, Alys, it's Romy—Alys almost shit herself. Sorry, Evelyn.

We've all done it, Pete.

She studied at Lecoq, said Pete.

How d'you know all this?

She told us.

I thought she'd just been run over? said Evelyn.

Yeah, but not badly. Mostly shock. The Vespa driver came off worse. Apparently, he had to choose between taking out a group of tourists or a statue. So he took out the statue. Well, you would, wouldn't you? The surprise he got when the statue spoke. Fell back and slammed his head against the stone. Ouch, said Pete.

And here they come now, said Massimo.

Alys and Peg appeared at the side of the church, arms tight around a limping, white-faced sheet.

Evelyn couldn't wait to explain all this to Dotty.

From the moment Romy sat down in the *salotto*, she was her charming and animated self. Albeit no longer an adolescent but a woman in her late twenties, just as Alys was. Peg said she thought Romy talked a lot for a mime artist.

How's your mum and dad, Romy? said Ulysses.

Oh my goodness, Mr. Temper. How their lives changed after Florence. My father didn't write his book on Henry James, but he did eventually write a bestseller under the pseudonym of Dante Pelloni. A romance/thriller about a man who went to Italy in search of love, but whose wife tried to murder him with the help of a local builder.

I read it! said Evelyn. How I laughed when the chandelier fell on him!

It's been optioned for a film, said Romy. Ali MacGraw's penciled to play my mother.

And how is your mother? said Ulysses.

Really good. She's head of marketing for a drinks company. Dating a friend of Onassis.

Romy Peller was the breath of *aria fresca* they all needed: a joyous and slightly barking counterpoint to the grief that had beset the previous two years. She taught Pete the stuck-in-a-glass-box mime routine and Pete spent the following week trying to escape from something he couldn't see, which Col said was the story of his life anyway, so what was new?

And in a delightful twist of events, Romy Peller fell head over heels in love with Alys. They jumped into bed together in a lodging house near the Accademia. They had history, they had ease and the sex was great. So what d'you say? said Romy. (She had just asked Alys if they should give it another go.)

You and me, kiddo. Love's bright dream? said Alys.

Oh God, said Romy. Please don't say I ever said that to you.

You said that.

Romy squirmed and lit a cigarette. She blew out a long stream of smoke. And in answer to my question?

Yes, OK, said Alys. But let's take it slow.

Romy laughed because Romy didn't know the meaning of the word slow. But she did encourage Alys to pick up her guitar and sing from the church steps that night.

Alys sang "Freedom of the Open Road" and Massimo pointed to Pete and everyone cheered. She also sang "The Tower of Rotherhithe," a song Peg had never heard before. And walking back across the square, Peg asked Ulysses when Alys had written it and he said when she was fourteen. That threw Peg. That the kid had understood the depth of her pain all those years ago. Peg thought it the most beautiful song she'd ever heard. She wrote a note saying just that and slipped it under Alys's bedroom door. Neither woman would talk about it for years.

A week or so later, Ulysses said to Alys that Romy was more than welcome to move into the *pensione*, but Alys said no fucking way.

Oh, said Ulysses. He rather liked Romy.

I mean, not yet, said Alys. For the first time in my life, Uly, everything's good and stable. I want to keep it that way.

When *Amarcord* finally opened at the old Rex later in '73, the rough edge of grief had been planed smooth and everyone was up for the occasion. Peg wasn't dressed up to just the nines but the tens as well. Pete had his head held high, which was an anatomically rare occurrence, and that brief moment when he appeared on-screen—oh God, how proud they were!—face looming out of the black, full of intention, full of yearning. He said he'd had a line but they'd cut it and Alys said, What's a line when you can convey everything in a look? Ask Romy. And Pete turned to Romy and Romy nodded and Pete seemed happy with that. He even started getting fan mail again. God knows how they knew where he lived, but that's show business for you. Nothing's sacred.

June 1975 and the late-afternoon sun poured into the room. The record player was up at full volume. Extended play of Van McCoy and the Soul City Symphony doing "The Hustle" whilst Ulysses and Peg fucked— for old times' sake—against the wall in her room. The slap slap of sweaty flesh complemented the disco beats whilst the soaring trumpet lifted the melody to epic and euphoric proportions. Peg came loudly, Ulysses close on her tail. He carried her over to the bed and they fell down onto the mattress.

Christ you're good, Temps, said Peg, breathing hard.

The alarm clock went off. And on time, too, she said. Thanks for that. (Still as romantic as she ever got.)

A cab took her and Pete over to the Hotel Excelsior bar. Always a decent crowd; they enjoyed their evenings there. Gucci kaftans and orange lipstick and sports jackets and men's sandals and the money chink chinked into the till. The staples for the night would be:

"Someone to Watch Over Me" / "But Not for Me" / "Stormy Weather"/ "I've Never Been in Love Before" / "You Don't Know What Love Is" / "Time After Time" / "That's All" / "Everything Must Change" / "Always on My Mind" / "Being Alive."

The musical bread and butter, as Pete called it. They could perform it with their eyes closed and he often did. Peg set a rule that any drinks sent their way would only appear during the second half. The second half was often show tunes; that's when Pete went up a notch and his theatrical history shone through and song after song brought a standing ovation.

So, that night they were halfway in and Peg had never been better.

One of those evenings people remember. She'd noticed a fella at the bar watching her, but that wasn't unusual in itself. And yet this one wasn't doe-eyed or hiding his wedding band, and he wasn't hanging the fantasy of his youth on her as they so often did. He looked interested in her talent, genuinely so, and there was an intensity to the man that could have been unnerving.

He didn't send over a drink and Peg was surprised by that. In between numbers Peg said, See that bloke at the bar, Pete? Melancholic aura? said Pete. Yeah, that's him, said Peg. You know him? said Pete. Never seen him before, said Peg. Well, he seems to know you.

(Last song.)

Thank you so much, everybody, and good night.

Peg and Pete took a bow together and the man only got up and went out. Strange, thought Peg.

After they'd packed away, her and Pete were having a quiet drink together with the city illuminated behind them. Sometimes they commented on the set and what they could've done better, and sometimes they looked out across the river and commented on how far they'd come.

Peg?

Peggy turned. It was the man from the bar.

Pete downed his drink and got up. I'll go, he said.

No, stay, said Peg.

Pete sat down and wished he hadn't finished his drink so quickly.

Peggy Temper? The man obviously American. Yeah, that's me. Peg saw an uncanny resemblance to Eddie in the man. Of course he had gray hair, but Christ, so did she under the blond, but there was something about him . . .

Have we met before? she said.

Thirty years ago.

(Just like that he said it.)

Peg was a teenager then, said Pete.

Shut up, Pete. Peg laughing.

I'm Glen. Glen Mollan.

Peg stretched out her hand. Nice to meet you, Glen.

And then the man paused as if he didn't know how to proceed. He said, Eddie was my best friend.

The air was sucked right out of the room as a vortex spun them back to August 1944. The night Peg and Eddie had met in the Soho dance club, Glen Mollan had been there too. He'd had a charm of his own; he certainly didn't go home alone that night. He and Eddie were often mistaken for brothers. It was Glen who'd noticed Peg first. Nudged Eddie and said, Look at her, and both men whistled quietly. But Glen had already bought a drink for a young woman at the bar, so what could he do? All yours, Eddie. Eddie cupped his hands around his mouth and smelled his breath.

Eddie and Peg locked eyes. Stars colliding forever and forever and forever.

Peg went to the bathroom. Pete knocking on the cubicle door.

Peggy? You all right in there?

I'm OK, Pete. It's my stomach, that's all.

I'll wait for you. I won't let you out of my sight.

The shits, Pete. Bit of privacy, love.

Oh yeah. Sorry, Peg.

The sound of a toilet flushing.

Peg opened the door and Pete rushed at her and put his arms around her.

Glen was waiting for them at the table and he stood up as they entered. Pete was relieved to see three drinks on the table. He sat furthest away from Glen.

How much do you want to know? Glen said.

All of it, said Peg.

Eddie Clayton, Peg's American Boy, had died in France six months after they met. His official name wasn't Eddie Clayton but Henry Edward Claydon. Known as Eddie. And he was married young but unhappily so. He had planned to divorce and marry Peg and take her back to the States, that much was true. Had even told his parents this intention. They were a gentle family. They would support whatever their son needed to do. Peg wasn't a secret, Peg was real.

So he did love me. Those were the first words out of Peg's mouth.

Glen answered, He was crazy about you.

How'd he die? said Peg.

Two jeeps racing. Eddie's hit a tree stump and flipped.

Peg felt dizzy. All those years. All those years of waiting. All those years of waiting to be set free. Pete reached for her hand and she didn't pull away.

Glen said, I'm sorry to . . .

No, I . . .

But words dissolved. The chink of ice. The loud swallow. The flare of a match. Pete offered his cigarettes. And the three of them sat in silence.

I wasn't supposed to be here, said Glen. Should have flown out from Milan yesterday. Meetings were changed, though, and I didn't want to stay there for the weekend, so I came—

Eddie has a kid, said Peg. Her name's Alys and she looks like him. And she's smart and talented and fierce. Tell them.

I'll tell them.

Here, she said, and she opened her handbag. Fag in mouth, blinking, rummaging around till she found her purse. Hands shaking, she took out a photo of her daughter and handed it over.

Give 'em this, she said.

Glen nodded and looked at the picture.

Jeez. She really is all Eddie, he said.

Peg and Pete walked back home along the *lungarno*. Peg, shoes in hand, leaned on Pete and Pete was solid. Streetlamps softened the pitch of night and Peg led them onto Santa Trìnita bridge. They stood against the parapet and looked across the water. A lantern took their sight. A whole world on that grassy shore as a man poured liquid from a flask and checked his fishing lines.

I don't know what to say, Peg. And Pete began to cry.

Hey, she said, and pulled him to her. Hey, it's OK. I'm OK, Pete. Look at me.

Pete looked at her.

Come on, dry those tears, you silly sod.

Pete blew his nose and wiped his face.

Peg said, He was coming back to get me, Pete. I think that's all I ever wanted to know.

One in the morning and Pete opened the front door of the *pensione*. Peg went on inside and Pete said, I'll go get Temps. OK, she said. She sat on the sofa and looked at her hands. Running her thumb across the creases, inspecting that little glitch across her lifeline—

Peg?

Ulysses in the doorway, sleepy and disheveled from bed. She reached out for him and he came and sat next to her. Put his arm around her. You all right? he said, and she nodded. I really am, she said, and he drew her close.

Evelyn helped Pete bring in the cocoa and Massimo appeared with blankets and those old walls whispered, Here's your family, Peg. Ulysses woke Alys up and she came and lay on the floor while Peg told her everything Glen had said. Alys, stoic as ever, took it in like a weather report. Peg cried, but not for herself. If you'd asked her who for, she couldn't have said. Maybe simply for a young man who never grew old, that same old same old tale of war. Alys went over to her mother and held her. First time ever, it was. S'pose you could say that's what Eddie gave them that night.

And there, as the sun broke through the shutters, the ghost of Eddie Clayton was finally laid to rest.

The air was September warm and Evelyn had taken up her early-evening position on the stone bench. She wore a white short-sleeved shirt, navy linen slacks and the requisite sunglasses. Her eau de cologne was fresh and citrusy and was frequently the recipient of many a compliment. She wished the stick was not a necessity, but it was useful, too, as a pointer of interesting things. Like that flower by her foot.

Evelyn?

She looked up. It was Ulysses.

Sit, she said, and tapped the bench beside her. Look, she said, pointing to the small yellow flower by her shoe. She said, Imagine the effort involved in pushing up between these fifteenth-century stones and saying, Here I am! Look at me! When everybody wants to look at the church or the palazzo over there or the statue. Nature is an ample gift, Ulysses. With art, my mind interacts in a very different way. It is often taxed by the history or by the analysis. And yet here—this tiny yellow flower asks for nothing more than to be appreciated.

(How he adored her!)

Clack clack clack! across the stones she came. Pale gray shirt and purple bell-bottoms, sunglasses, orange lippy and unlit cigarette swinging in her hand.

Peg sat down with a thump.

You look absolutely divine, said Evelyn.

Thanks, Evelyn, said Peg, and she lit her cigarette. Look at them all looking at us, Temps.

Ulysses turned.

Peering out from Michele's were the elderly contessa, Giulia, the priest, Clara the baker, Gloria Cardinale who sold haberdashery, and of course Signor Malfatti, holding a roundel of cheese. All wondering if Peg and Ulysses would become a couple again now that there was space.

But Peg and Ulysses knew their time had passed. Had known it since Cressy's death, since they'd lain on the bed together and watched the swallows. Everything had changed then. That they'd brought each other safely to the other side was everything and everlasting.

You can't blame people for wanting a happy ending, said Evelyn.

We are a happy ending, said Ulysses. Right, Peg?

Right, Tempy.

The blare of a taxi horn and Pete waving and calling across the square.

Peg stood up and brushed ash off her trousers. Gotta go, she said. You'll both be there at the Excelsior later?

Wouldn't miss it, said Evelyn.

What time you meeting Glen Mollan? said Ulysses.

In an hour. Quick coffee before the set.

Nervous?

A bit.

It'll be fine, said Ulysses. And you look lovely, Peg.

And remember, said Evelyn. It's only coffee. You don't have to fall in love with the man.

Ha! said Peg. She's funny.

A year later, Peg and Glen Mollan fell in love.

So, let me get this straight, said Des. Eddie was dead all this time. His best mate, Glen—in a serendipitous turn of events—met Peg at the Excelsior and now Peg and Glen are an item.

That's about it, said Ulysses.

Des shook his head in disbelief. You couldn't write it, could you?

It was All Souls' Day, and the two men were up on Monte Ceceri, sitting next to a fine-looking sapling with a bunch of flowers propped up against its trunk.

Ulysses smiled. Pete says it's got a twist of Cress all over it, he said.

Pete might be onto something, said Des. What's this Glen bloke like, then?

Really nice. Met him a few times. He's one of us, Des.

(Glen Mollan literally was. A curious mix of Col, Pete and Ulysses, said the elderly contessa—*but* with matinee idol looks, she added disparagingly.)

That's all I need to know, lad. That our Peg's in good, safe, respectful hands.

That's what we all want, Des.

Des pulled out a paper bag from his pocket and began to chuck sunflower seeds on the ground.

Claude's not here, Des.

Is he not?

No. Giglio.

I just presumed he was with Cress.

We scattered him under the grapevine where he always sat. Pete said he'd seen more ash from a pack of twenty. But we were all there. Even Dotty came back.

With Helena?

No. With Penelope.

Jem's mother?

The same.

Well, I never, said Des. People have been busy.

Ulysses lit a cigarette. You like being a granddad, Des?

Hate it. When your kids marry, it opens up a whole 'nother gene pool. Lot of little bleeders, they are. Here, he said. Two words for you: hypo-allergenic. My plastic is revolutionizing the medical world. Who knew England was so ill? You need any money yet?

No, I'm OK, but thanks.

Well, you let me know.

And as dusk whispered its intent, the men stood up and Des brushed leaves from his new red corduroy trousers. He said, Evelyn a hundred yet, lad?

Three years off. But she reckons she's bowing out at ninety-nine. We'll do a big party then. Doesn't want a telegram from the queen. Quite adamant about it actually, so she's cutting it short.

Not a royalist, then?

I think she thinks a bottle of champagne is more in keeping. Or a knighthood.

Such a clear-eyed appraisal of life, said Des. What a woman! When I call it a day, I'm going to be in my Land Rover with Poppy by my side and I'm going to drive straight off a cliff.

Poppy know about this?

Not yet, said Des.

Best tell her.

Maybe you're right.

Nineteen seventy-eight and abortion was finally made legal in Italy. A milestone in women's bodies' becoming their own. Alys was more circumspect; she called it a start. In London, Col stood at the front of a large crowd with Ginny and Mrs. Kaur and watched the demolition of his pub. Mrs. Kaur had helped him to surrender to a situation over which he had little control. Consequently, there was no acid reflux when the first wrecking ball struck. Great laughter, though, when the pub sign went flying and took out a councilman. Dickhead! shouted Col. Col bought a pub the other side of Kingsland Road, which he said was like Timbuktu to him. Mrs. Kaur said he was being overly dramatic. Ginny said he was too. Devy agreed. Col bought a VW camper van and immersed himself in Seva—what he called selfless service for purely altruistic purposes for the betterment of the community. *"You giving away drinks, then, Col?"* wrote Ulysses. *"Ha bloody ha!"* Col wrote back. And after a business meeting in Milan, Glen Mollan traveled down to Florence and asked Peg to marry him.

What did you say? asked Alys.

I said not yet. And Peg poured out the wine. The evening was warm, the air fumy, and night was yet a few hours off. They were outside Michele's, surrounded by tourists. Pete was at the piano inside, and at a nearby table, Ulysses and Massimo and the elderly contessa were discussing the best age for Parmigiano-Reggiano. On the stone bench, Evelyn was writing a letter to Dotty, and over by the statue was Romy—being a statue.

I'm not sure I want to go anywhere, said Peg. I'm not sure I want my life to change more than it has. And I'm not sure I want to leave you. And she lit a cigarette.

I'm not a kid anymore, said Alys.

But you were. And I wasn't here. So for now I'm staying put. And Glen can visit.

That'll keep it fresh.

That's what I thought, said Peg.

Alys grinned. And therein spoke a thousand words.

Here, said Peg. Before I forget. Thought I'd lost this. And she handed over the cameo brooch that Eddie had given her all those years ago. The one that had cost her a hotel room and had propelled her under a railway arch where Alys may or may not have been conceived. Strange how things work out.

Alys started laughing. Really? That's how it happened?

Yeah. What a fucking legacy I've given you. Be kind to Romy, Alys. I know how she looks at you. It's powerful, that kind of thing. Careful what you do with it.

It was October 1979. Evelyn Skinner was looking out of the window, watching time in the shift of light and shadow. Daylight beautifies and moonlight mystifies; that was day one for every new consignment of students. She had, moments before, turned ninety-nine but she looked ten years younger, something she would put down to cod liver oil and cold-water swimming and being loved. Despite the years' having taken inches from her height, her seated posture was taut and upright. She heard Ulysses knock and enter her room and her face lit up at the sight of him. He handed her one of the glasses of *frizzantino* in his hand.

This would have been enough, you know, she said.

I know.

You, me, this—and she indicated the dusk-drenched square outside. "How beautiful is sunset, when the glow / Of heaven descends upon a land like thee, / Thou paradise of exiles, Italy!"

Dante?

Shelley, she said, and they clinked glasses.

Happy birthday, he said. To your long and extraordinary life.

She took a sip and said, You grew into your name after all. Took you a long time to get back from war, but you did it, Ulysses. I've left you the flat in Bloomsbury, by the way.

That's not necessary.

London may beckon once again. Or give it to Alys. Dotty's got Kent. She hates the countryside, but she'll see the joke. And she'll cherish it in the end. Everything else is by the by. And I want my ashes scattered on the Arno like Constance.

OK, he said. Anything else?

I think that's all you need to know.

Righto.

You look like you want to ask me something.

It's something Dotty—

Oh, don't listen to her!

Were you a spy?

Of course I was. She'll find out when the National Archives release the papers. Hopefully she won't be driving or operating heavy machinery at the time.

He looked at his watch.

You're going to tell me they're all upstairs waiting, said Evelyn.

Not all, he laughed. Jem's on his way. And Des, Poppy and Col got in an hour ago. They're the surprise.

And Dotty and Penelope? said Evelyn.

But before Ulysses could answer, a wolf whistle pierced the air. Evelyn turned and there was Dotty leaning against the doorway, crossarmed, with a cheeky tilt of the head.

Evelyn squealed.

Hello, my darling Lynny. And Dotty rushed to kiss her. She took Ulysses's glass and said, Sorry, Temps. Don't mind, do you?

Go ahead, he said, and Dotty downed it in one. She handed him the empty glass.

Me and Pen, said Dotty, we've just had our first argument in the taxi.

Good Lord! What about? said Evelyn.

You'll never guess—Dotty suddenly turned to Ulysses.

OK, OK, he said. I'm leaving.

Surprise! they all shouted.

Evelyn gasped theatrically in the *salotto*. Des. Poppy. Col! What are you all doing here? she said.

You told her, said Col.

I did, said Ulysses, and everyone laughed.

Massimo and Jem came in with plates of *crostini*—chicken livers, anchovy, tomato—and placed them in the middle of the table between the candles. More bubbles were poured and Ulysses opened the wine for those whose craving was red. He held a bottle in front of Evelyn and she read the label: *Carruades de Lafite. Pauillac.*

Was that Captain Darnley's—?

Yeah, said Ulysses. Des got hold of a case. Not the 1902 because the 1929 was better. That right, Des?

What, lad?

The wine. The 1929 better than the 1902?

Heaps better. Five hundred quid a bottle.

Everyone stopped what they were doing.

Des, you've done it again, said Poppy.

What, love? said Des.

The money thing.

Two words, said Des. Disposable syringes.

Ah, they all said, and Pete asked Massimo to stick a bottle aside so he could sell it later.

The doorbell rang and Alys went out. Moments later the elderly contessa shuffled in and said, I found this man wandering about outside.

At which point—

Glen Mollan! they all said when he appeared.

What the bloody 'ell you doing here? said Peg (still as romantic as ever).

I've never met anyone who's ninety-nine before, Peg! How could I miss this?

Nice jacket, Glen, said Ulysses, and Glen said, This old thing, Temps? I got it in New Orleans.

And there they sat. For hours. Across chestnut-and-ricotta-filled ravioli. Across *peposo* for the carnivores and Massimo's famous rice-stuffed tomatoes for Col.

You a vegetarian, Col? said Des.

Ten years and counting, said Col.

What made you change? said Penelope.

Bowels? said Des.

The most incredible woman, said Ulysses.

And the intricate flavors of Indian cuisine, said Col. Nothing like onions caramelizing in ghee, green chilies, ginger, garlic and turmeric to make my mouth and eyes water every time.

Massimo came up behind him and kissed his head. You're cooking for us tomorrow night, my friend, he said.

He'll be doing yoga next, said Romy.

Already am, said Col.

Me too, said Pete. Helps my moods.

And that was the cue for Pete to get up and play his new song called "Ninety-Nine Is the New Hundred." It was upbeat and funny for Pete, and had more than a touch of the Beach Boys about it.

Suddenly, Romy leaned down and reached into her bag. She pulled out Cressy's copy of *A Room with a View* and said, I'm reading this, Evelyn.

Good God! said Dotty. What is it about that bloody book?

It's terrific, said Jem.

But the people are quite unlikable, said Dotty. Ask her. And she pointed to Evelyn. She was *there*.

You were—? began Glen Mollan, but he was cut off by Dotty.

Small-minded snobs, she said. An endemic English quality, believing only the educated middle class know the secrets of art.

But they come to love in the end, said Jem.

But is that enough? said Dotty.

Yes! they all said.

Go on, Lynny, said Dotty. Tell them everything.

Yes, tell us! they all said.

Do we have time? said Evelyn.

We have all the time in the world, said Ulysses, and he went around the table and refilled the glasses.

Evelyn sat back and took a sip of wine. She closed her eyes and the thunderous weight of age gave way to the lightness of youth. Well, she said . . .

All About Evelyn

It was October. And the year was 1901.

Evelyn was days shy of her twenty-first birthday when she came out of Santa Maria Novella station for the first time and exclaimed, *Firenze! Amore mio!*

The slow journey down from Lake Como had been made under an unrepentant, overcast sky but here, the sun was exceptionally bright. There was a strong smell of horse in the air. Omnibuses were waiting to transport tourists to hotels, and now the sound of bells!

To look at her, she was dressed as any young modern English woman of the time might have been. She had shunned the corset in favor of a naturalistic silhouette. Long dark linen skirt complemented a tonally matching blouse. Her bonnet she carried. She had developed an ungainly gait due to a sudden growth spurt, but it would disappear by the time she was twenty-four. On the plus side, though, she had the air of good breeding (mother's side) and bohemian outlook (father's side) to excuse whatever indiscretions might befall her throughout her life. Of which there would be many.

She looked back to check that the railway porter still had hold of her trunk. Hurrying after her were the newly married couple she'd met on the train. They were the Luggs, Hugh and Miranda, and it was their first time in Italy. Hugh was moving up the ranks in a private bank and he was a shining example of a certain type of Englishman abroad who hated everything foreign. He was dragging along his new wife as if she was a wet blanket. Her pale face and large haunted eyes were symptomatic of a lymphatic temperament unsuited to a European diet. They had been traveling for ten days already, and tripe had been the last straw. Even the word propelled Miranda Lugg toward an open window. In her arms she clutched a small portable medicine case, prepared and stocked with tabloid drugs by Messrs. Burroughs, Wellcome & Co, Holborn Viaduct, London. On her breath was the faint whiff of camphor and indigestion.

A tram rattled past and Evelyn turned to watch it. Children were squealing and hanging off the platform at the back.

You couldn't have heard me, Miss Skinner, said Mr. Lugg. Shall we travel to the Simi together?

Oh, let's, said Evelyn, and she handed a generous gratuity to the porter (Far too much, said Hugh Lugg) and strode toward a bored cabman. In unconfident but charming Italian, she said:

We would like to go to the Pensione Simi, two Lungarno delle Grazie, if you please.

They wound down tight streets that echoed with the cries of men selling wares. Handcarts were laden with sacks, and baskets from windows were being lowered to hawkers. Wine, vegetables, fruit, live chickens—look, a chicken!—but Mrs. Lugg didn't want to look at a squawking chicken, she was huddled over her handkerchief and having quite a turn because of the smell. It was of both human civilization and lack of it. So different from Kent, thought Evelyn.

The horse turned left, and suddenly the Arno and bridges came into sight. Oh my, said Evelyn as they clattered alongside the green water. A young man on a bicycle rode next to them, weaving in and out, laughing.

Make him go away, said Mrs. Lugg.

Shoo shoo, *niente*, *niente*, said Mr. Lugg, having consigned to memory Baedeker's advice on how to deal with importunate beggars.

Evelyn said, He's not a beggar, Mr. Lugg.

What is he then, Miss Skinner?

Evelyn turned back toward the cyclist and smiled. He's *alive*.

When the cab eventually pulled up outside the Simi, the horse released a torrent of hot fumy scat, which sent Mr. and Mrs. Lugg running toward the entrance of the building. Trunks were carried in next and Evelyn could hear the impatient ring of the desk bell. She followed swiftly behind the luggage, eager to acquaint herself with what would be her home for the next twenty-eight days.

Evelyn veered off to the drawing room, where her sight was arrested by Empire mahogany furniture and an ugly chandelier. Queen Victoria was still on the wall, sandwiched between two stained Hogarthian prints. A couple of silent elderly women and a white-whiskered clergyman looked up from the chesterfield without acknowledging her. It was a room of melancholy, she thought. More like a funeral parlor than the authentic Italian boardinghouse full of *conversazione* that she had been expecting. The piano in the corner had acquired a thick layer of dust as insulation.

Evelyn got to the reception desk just as the landlady bustled down the stairs.

Scusi, scusi, she said. Me 'Enery's 'ed got stuck in the back ov a chair.

(And a cockney landlady at that!)

Welcome, dearie, she said.

Evelyn heard "dreary" and said, Yes, it is a bit.

Her bedroom was a lot more agreeable—a lot more Italian, come to think of it—than the rooms downstairs and after running her hand across the exquisite bedcover, she went to the window and threw open the shutters. The late-afternoon light journeyed across the red tiled floor and rested warmly on her feet. Below, trams rattled along the *lungarno* and the river slapped against the stone walls. The cypress trees appeared black against the golden haze of the sky. I have a view, she sighed.

When Evelyn entered the drawing room later that evening, she was not surprised to find the drink *du soir* was sherry, and not a quina-vermouth or the bright red bitters associated with *aperitivo* time.

The silent women whom she had noticed when she had first arrived were sitting side by side on the same sofa, tête-à-tête with the same clergyman. On closer inspection, Evelyn realized that the two women were twins, quite elderly, with an outlook of similar bewilderment.

They are the Brown sisters, said a stout middle-aged woman suddenly at her side. Their wardrobe seldom veers away from their name, so you can't forget them. The one on the left is Bernadette. The other is Blythe. We may presume someone in their family had a sense of humor. The clergyman is Reverend Hyndesight. Take from that what you will. He is a Protestant. The man in heated discussion with the Russian is Mr. Collins. He will fight any cause. He's a socialist. And I am Miss Constance Everly. I noticed you when you first walked in and I said to myself, this young woman may yet be our savior. As you can see—and she turned to the room—not the liveliest bunch ever encountered at the Simi. Death hovers above the chintz, Miss . . .

Oh. Skinner. Evelyn Skinner. They shook hands.

You are welcome, Miss Skinner. So lovely to have you on board.

And with that, the first rule of *pensione* life—that of scrutinizing a guest for a day or two before conversing—was swiftly abandoned.

Suddenly, the creeping waft of overcooked brassicas corralled everyone to dinner. Massacre of the Innocents, intoned Miss Everly, as she raised her arm aloft and directed the troops toward the battlefield next door.

At the dining table, Evelyn could see that trenches had been invisibly drawn and she was glad to find herself opposite Miss Everly and next to the socialist. The reverend placed himself at the head of the table (of course) and Evelyn was grateful that whatever grace he said was said silently. The Brown sisters made a fuss of sitting opposite the Luggs and the Luggs were simply happy to be at a table with only English people. Evelyn looked over at the other table and couldn't work out if the four still waiting for their soup were sleeping or dead.

The reverend did the honors with the wine, and after the soup had been cleared, Evelyn dabbed her mouth with the linen and answered the question at hand.

I have a *view*, she said most emphatically.

I don't, said Mr. Collins. I have the *cortile*.

I, too, have a view, said Miss Everly. As befits my status.

Miss Everly is a poet, said Mr. Collins.

Are you really? said Evelyn.

For my sins.

Which are countless—

Mr. Collins!

According to your *verse*, that is, Miss Everly.

You've read me, Mr. Collins? said Miss Everly.

How could I not?

Miss Skinner? said Miss Everly. Do me the honor of telling me what you saw when you looked out of your window for the first time. Be robust and adventurous. Hold nothing back. And Miss Everly closed her eyes, ready to receive the descriptive benediction (her words).

Mr. Collins leaned in close to Evelyn and said, She asks the same of everyone when they arrive. Make it good.

Evelyn cleared her throat. She said, I saw a lone rower carving across the Arno. The foothills were darkening, and the cypress trees around San Miniato were topped by a ghostly mist. Ochre walls appeared more golden as the sun softened. Lights appeared throughout the city and took their place on the surface of the river. The rower slipped through this spectacle of light. Water dripped off the blades of his oars, and momentarily, I was in that drip. Falling into the green twilight depths of history.

You have silenced the room, said the reverend.

The elderly twins applauded.

The lady poet laughed, She is smitten already! You have caught the fever of Firenze! Oh, my dear Miss Skinner, there is no turning back. You shall die with those lights in your eyes. Miss Skinner has turned looking into loving! The first rule of art. Looking into loving! Oh welcome, my dear! Welcome!

Mr. Collins stood up and replenished the wineglasses. He said, Reverend Hyndesight? What delights await you the other side of the shutter? Vista or *cortile*?

Cortile, said the reverend, wishing to move away from this subject.

Washing lines and dripping undergarments for us, isn't it, Reverend? said Mr. Collins.

Really, Mr. Collins, said the elderly twin sisters in unison.

He does it on purpose, said Miss Everly. He likes to shock.

I like to reposition.

Bravo word, said Miss Everly.

And what on earth does that mean? said the reverend.

It's a changing world, was all Mr. Collins said. Evelyn caught him looking over at the painting of Queen Victoria. Out with the old, he mouthed to Evelyn, and raised his eyebrows.

Mr. Collins is a philosopher, said Miss Everly.

Soi-disant, said the reverend to the newly married couple, whom he planned to take under his large vestal wing.

Humanist, said Mr. Collins.

Humorist, said Miss Everly.

Evelyn looked back and forth, following the conversations and consigning to memory who said what and how they said it. English through and through, they were, and they expressed an excess of bonhomie like those without life belts on a sinking ship.

She liked Miss Everly immensely, and she liked Mr. Collins too, as he reminded her of her father—when he was younger, of course. And yet she was most intrigued by the maid waiting in the corner of the room, staring at her. She didn't know what it was that made her heart thump so furiously, and at first thought it might have been the soup.

Miss Skinner, you're positively red! said Miss Everly indiscreetly. Are you hot?

No. I—

It's the wine—

Maybe a slight fever—?

All the traveling—?

No, said Miss Skinner, I'm . . . I'm decidedly happy. That's all. To meet you all. And to be here in this moment in time.

Reciprocal sentiments were scattered like sugar beads and in the midst of it all, Reverend Hyndesight made an ill-timed proclamation. He said, I shall be delivering a sermon at St. Mark's English Church this Sunday if anyone is interested? Anyone? he said again. Luckily the stew was carried in by the maid at that moment, saving anyone from answering.

Beef stew again, said Mr. Collins.

We presume it's beef, said Miss Everly. But I, for one, haven't seen the elderly concierge for a while.

Miss Everly, really! said the reverend.

Once more unto the breach, dear friends, said Mr. Collins, picking up his spoon—or did he need his fork? A knife, perhaps? And he rallied the other guests by example. All except the new wife whom Evelyn had met on the train. The cockney *signora* had prepared for her a bespoke meal of boiled egg and crumpets. Something recognizable and, more important, *binding*.

The next day, Evelyn slept in late and missed the breakfast prunes.

Outside the Simi, she was greeted by a medley of sun and cloud; the temperature, though, was still warm. She didn't rush off to join the reverend and his band of merry men; instead she stood back and watched life pass. The jingle of bells as horses and carts rattled by with laundry sacks from hotels. The one leaving the Simi had a young man balanced precariously on a mountainous pile. He waved, she waved.

That's Matteo, said Mr. Collins, standing behind her.

Evelyn turned and smiled. How lovely that Mr. Collins knew the young man's name. But, of course, he was a socialist.

And where are you off to today, Mr. Collins?

I'm going for a shave. You can't beat an Italian barber, Miss Skinner. See you at dinner!

And she watched him race after the laundry cart.

She crossed the road and leaned against the embankment. The river was low, and the *renaioli* were on a break. From dusk till dawn the men shoveled sediment from the riverbed into carts or waiting boats. Four of them were sitting smoking now. Hats tilted back, shirtsleeves rolled high. Miss Everly said the gravel had been caused by the erosion of stone buildings along the riverbank in times of flood, and would be used again in future construction. Nothing was ever wasted, she said. The Arno was like the Ganges, the source of life. Both giver and taker. Sewer and fishmonger. Miss Everly knew everything about the city.

Midway along the Ponte Vecchio, Evelyn's eye was drawn to the dark mass of the Casentino valley, partly enveloped by mist. It was a thick forest land of black trees and swine and myths and hidden hermits, and had once been home to an exiled Dante. From its highest peak at Monte Falterona, the origins of the Arno bubbled forth. Evelyn thought about the holy place of La Verna, the desolate mountain given to St. Francis of Assisi, where he had received his stigmata and the grace of God. There were things she didn't believe in and things she did. Saints she believed in.

She continued north to the Piazza del Duomo and when she arrived, the sun burst out between dark clouds and bells tolled from Giotto's marble *campanile*. She held on to her bonnet and looked up at the cupola, that unfailing landmark, glimpsed perpetually throughout the city. Ever since she was six and had first opened the pages of her father's sketch-book, she—

Suddenly, a small chestnut mare, head concealed in a large bag of oats, shat loudly. Two English ladies, passing by at the time, were unconscionably splashed. Their screams were piercing, and Evelyn's moment of homage ruined.

Undeterred, she wandered the vicinity and came across a delightful secondhand bookshop and picked up a copy of Elizabeth Barrett Browning's *Casa Guidi Windows*. Miss Everly had said she would take Evelyn to visit Casa Guidi the following week. And just as Evelyn was handing over her money, she spotted a slim volume in burgundy cloth by one Constance Everly. Down the spine, in faded gilt, its Italian title: *Niente/ Nothing*. All roads really do lead to poetry!

Evelyn settled outside at a café in the Piazza Vittorio Emanuele and couldn't decide which book to open first, so embraced the European pastime of watching people instead. Women, mostly, it has to be said. And the obvious comparisons issued forth—better hair, better shape, better smile—but there was something else, too, something to do with the maid who had trespassed continually on her day. It hadn't been an uncomfortable intrusion, and in truth, she couldn't wait for dinner.

That night, the reverend was complaining about having paid half a *lira* to see vast quantities of bad art in a palazzo he couldn't remember the name of. Baroque! he said, tutting loudly. The art of bad taste.

The reverend believes Florentine art stopped at the end of the sixteenth century, said Mr. Collins.

What's that you're saying? said the reverend.

You believe no good art came after the sixteenth century, said Mr. Collins, voice elevated.

It had reached its zenith, that's all I'm saying. The city had changed.

So no Rubens, no Velázquez, no Artemisia—

No listening, Mr. Collins.

My father is the painter H. W. Skinner, said Evelyn.

Oh, I knew it! said Miss Everly. I could see the likeness. I saw his recent show at the Royal Academy.

I did too, said Mr. Collins.

Would I know his work? asked Reverend Hyndesight.

I doubt it, Reverend. Lots of nudes. And not all *pudica*.

He did landscapes, too, said Evelyn.

And nudes in landscapes.

What was that one?

After Titian.

He was heavily influenced by the post-impressionists, I read, said Mr. Lugg proudly.

Yes, said Evelyn. Cézanne especially. I met him.

Sleeping Venus. That's the one, said Miss Everly.

Did you really? asked Mrs. Lugg.

And how was he? asked Mr. Collins.

Titian? asked the reverend, confused.

Cézanne, clarified Mr. Collins.

French, said Evelyn, and everyone said, Ah, as if that was description enough.

Evelyn sat back and thought, What a lively table we are.

She looked at the other guests and they were silent and still struggling with their soup. She wondered how they would cope, should they have to chew.

When dinner came to its natural conclusion, the maid began to clear. She maneuvered herself behind Evelyn and Evelyn could feel the nudge of her body and the faint whiff of sweat as she bent over her shoulder. Evelyn couldn't take her eyes off her. And as the maid's hand moved to collect the furthest plates, a shaft of candlelight lit the dark hairs on her arm and Evelyn felt a little light-headed. An empty glass was knocked over and Evelyn instinctively reached for it and so did the maid and their hands touched briefly, and they looked at one another. *Vi chiedo scusa,* said the maid, and she threw a surreptitious wink Evelyn's way. Evelyn tried to hide her smile but failed.

Share your thoughts, Miss Skinner, said the reverend.

Um, said Evelyn, playing for time. It's my birthday next week. Am I allowed to say that, or was it—?

Indeed you are, said Miss Everly.

I'm going to be twenty-one, said Evelyn.

Twenty-one!

Maybe the *signora* could rustle up a roast, said the reverend.

A roast? said Evelyn. I was hoping for something a little more authentic. Maybe a visit to a *trattoria* full of locals.

The rumble of a delicate Home Counties stomach voiced its protest.

I know the perfect place, said Mr. Collins. On Tornabuoni. Open kitchen, charcoal stove stoked by hand. Sparks flying everywhere.

Mr. Lugg said that he and his wife wouldn't be able to join her, should the dubious charms of an illegible Italian menu prevail over the safety of English fare.

We must stay close to home on account of my wife's condition, he said.

Evelyn said she understood.

(The phrase, however, went around the room as swiftly as a cholera outbreak, and Mrs. Lugg's condition was, of course, understood as pregnancy.)

In the days to come, the comments came quietly on the breath: How are you doing, Mrs. Lugg? A little sickness?

A little, said the unwitting new bride.

But you must be so pleased?

(This confused her.)

First time?

No, I had a little bout in Venice.

Later, lying in her room, Evelyn was left swooning and breathless by the events of the evening. The attraction she had to the maid, the attraction the maid had to her. Life was unfolding at an extraordinary pace. She could still hear voices in the drawing room below. A faint murmur and a burst of laughter. She knew that at some point in the evening, after she'd left the table, the conversation would have turned inevitably to her father's mistresses and the so-called arrangement in her parents' marriage. And sure enough, she heard footsteps on the landing, the word "mistress" and "money's on the mother's side." She rolled over and attempted sleep.

The next day. Rain. The smell of woodsmoke crept under Evelyn's bedroom door as the first hearth fires were lit in the salon below.

In a letter to her father, Evelyn wrote:

My dearest father,

I was awoken by a very dramatic storm last night. Lightning splintered the sky and by morning the Arno was a raging torrent. The sand diggers cannot work this morning, I fear. I shall miss them. My thoughts turn to the great flood of 1333 . . .

Evelyn put down her pencil. She had little to say on the great flood of 1333. She stood up from the desk. The sky was marbled violet gray, though the sun was trying to break through. She opened the window and stuck out her hand. The rain had ceased and there wasn't a moment to lose. She put on her bonnet and hoisted up her skirt. Full pelt down the stairs straight into the arms of the maid. Linen broke their fall, and laughter their embarrassment. They were so close, it would have been rude not to kiss, but—

Perdonatemi—

No, it's me, I'm the one who's sorry—

Woss goin on 'ere? said the cockney *signora*, marching across the landing.

It was all my fault, *signora*, said Evelyn. I didn't look where I was going—

Bit of decorum, dearie, said the *signora*, who moved swiftly over to the linen closet.

The two young women were silent. They watched the *signora* depart and shifted gracefully into her absence. They acknowledged their hand-holding with further pressure. They swapped names (Livia, Evelyn) and they said good-bye. Evelyn stopped by the door and looked back. She said good-bye again. She rushed out. She felt light-headed and giddy and the most intense happiness she'd ever felt in her life. She turned

toward the Uffizi, knowing she was on the threshold of the most thrilling adventure *ever*.

Miss Skinner!

(It was Miss Everly.)

Hello there, said Evelyn.

You look positively radiant. The city is infusing us with all sorts of—

Oh my, said Evelyn, covering her nose.

Ah yes, said Miss Everly. The smell of Florence. Waste and deteriora-
tion. It's the *pozzi neri*, agitated by the rain. Vast containers of the stuff
spilling beneath us. Suddenly its presence rises up. But one doesn't come
to Italy for niceness, one comes for life. For passion! And where are you
off to, Miss Skinner, this fine day?

To here. The Uffizi.

Oh goodness! So am I. Would you like company? And a very enthusiastic guide?

I'd be delighted, said Evelyn.

As they approached the entrance to the gallery, the corner of a damp
loincloth was lifted by the breeze, alerting them to the presence of a
half-naked living statue.

I really did think it was a statue, said Evelyn. Who's it supposed to
be? she whispered.

Michelangelo.

How can you tell?

The pose. Rather fey. And also, the tondo at his feet. A poor imita-
tion of the Holy Family. I would have thought a tin cup more appropri-
ate to collect coinage.

Shall I give him a *lira*, Miss Everly?

You will certainly not! Stick to the coppers, Miss Skinner. A couple
of *centesimi*, at most. It's not as if he's doing anything. And they bustled
past him into the building.

At the bottom of the stairs, Miss Everly said, You'll see lots of An-
nunciations, Miss Skinner. Many Adorations of the Magi, Depositions
from the Cross, and oh yes, let's not forget Flagellations of Christ. And

we'll see a lot of ecstasy today and not all of it spiritual. But I can see you are a woman of the world.

I am, I am, said Evelyn.

Good, said Miss Everly, and she held up her skirt and said, I hope you have good knees, Miss Skinner?

Oh, I do, said Evelyn, taking off her bonnet. They're my mother's. Sturdy and Italian. Hers found every saint's day.

Marvelous. *Avanti*, then! Let's proceed to climb.

There was little conversation until they'd reached the upper floor, where Miss Everly suggested they head straight to the Tribuna.

Along the corridor, they passed countless Apollos and Cereses and Tiberiases and various other Roman antiquities, only for Miss Everly to point out a facial anomaly or expression—"Full of indecision, that face. Couldn't order a *bistecca*, let alone an army"—and when they came across *Hercules Slaying the Centaur Nessus*, Miss Everly said that the Giovanni da Bologna in the Loggia dei Lanzi was *far, far* superior.

Through here! said Miss Everly. Ah, Masaccio's *Madonna and Child*. Such fragility. Such—ooh. The Filippo Lippi. *Madonna and Child* again. But this time with two angels for variation. Botticelli was his pupil, Miss Skinner. Can you see the influence?

I—

(But it was a rhetorical question.)

Come on, then! said Miss Everly. There's some lovely hair in the Botticelli room.

And to the Botticelli room they went.

They stood back, scrutinizing a painting.

Well?

She looks bored, said Evelyn. It must be hard being a Madonna.

Utterly thankless, said Miss Everly. And yet, she is the prototype for all Italian women. Now—the pomegranate, Miss Skinner, is the symbol of . . . ?

Eternal life? Resurrection?

Correct. It is also the fruit of many legends. And Miss Everly looked about and lowered her voice. She said, Greek mythology says that the pomegranate grew out of the blood from Acdestis's wounded . . .

Evelyn leaned in closer. From his wounded what, Miss Everly?

Miss Everly looked about her again and said, Penis, Miss Skinner.

(Gasps from a nearby tour group.)

Acdestis was a lustful young god. Violent and rather unlikable, whose genitals were tied up by good old Bacchus. A peckish nymph came by, ate the fruit, and became pregnant as a result. Ergo, symbol of fertility. And you won't get that from a Baedeker. This way, my dear! And she marched ahead. Not going too fast for you, am I?

Oh, not at all, said Evelyn.

Another *Annunciazione!* said Miss Everly. Hello, Gabriel; hello, Mary. Ah, and here we are. La Tribuna. *Scusate, Americani, scusate.* (They do hog the space somewhat.) The most important jewels of the Medici collection, Miss Skinner. A dome of wonder encrusted with thousands of precious shells, whispering of distant shores, of trade and commerce. A marble floor, the red velvet cloak of walls. How many poems, how many declarations of love, how many promises to better one's soul, has such a room elicited? Where beauty and gratitude go together. This is how we become enriched, Miss Skinner.

The confinement of the room sent them in opposite directions, and Evelyn felt glad to have a moment to herself. The sight of so much female flesh was having a very positive effect on her body, although a dizzying one on her mind. There were two Venuses here to inflame her heart: the sloping back of Carracci's *Venus*, the top of two pert buttocks emerging from a fallen robe. Although the satyr exposing his tongue made her feel slightly self-conscious and she moved away.

Miss Everly came back to her side to view Titian's *Venus of Urbino*. She said, It used to be covered by a sliding panel to conceal her nudity. Such a waste.

Evelyn was glad it wasn't now.

In the *orientale* corridor, they happened across a painting class. Nothing to see here but childish enthusiasm, said Miss Everly as she waved

Evelyn past a Rubens at a brisk pace. They overtook a dawdling group of Americans murmuring about Cara-vag-eeo and Miss Everly whispered, Pro-nunc-iation, as she sidled past them. Ever since Henry James, they think they own the place, she said. And then she led Evelyn into a room and with a grand flourish said, Caravaggio. As if she had discovered the artist herself.

What do you *feel*, Miss Skinner?

Evelyn wondered if there was a right answer.

Horror. Beauty, she said.

Indeed. And here, look—follow the narrative of light to this scene beyond. Oh no, oh no, said Miss Everly, suddenly interrupted by an American to the far left of her. What that man's saying is not right at all. Caravaggio came out of Mannerism and stepped right back into reformed classicism, full of rage and drama. He was a slap in the face to his peers. See here—

Shadows, pain, dark, light. Repeat, Miss Skinner.

Shadows, pain, dark, light.

Correct, said Miss Everly, and they marched to the next room, the mantra startling a nearby tourist, who looked for the reference in their well-thumbed Baedeker.

When weariness and lunch had overtaken them, they took rest by an open window and let their eyes fall uncritically across the city.

Could only be Florence, couldn't it? said Miss Everly. Burned umber, ochre, cream. Brown, gray shutters. The Arno always green. Such is the palette of Florence.

It's my first time in this city, Miss Everly. There's so much to see and I wonder if I have enough time and—

Miss Everly raised her hand. You will be back, my dear. We all come back.

Do you remember your first time?

Do I indeed! Like Saul falling from his horse and becoming Paul. It changed me. The city spoke to me in a language I didn't understand, and yet in here—she clasped her chest—I knew exactly what it was saying to me.

Which was?

Miss Everly held up four fingers. She said, I. Will. Astonish. You. (With the "you," she gently pressed her finger against Evelyn's heart.) Open up. Things happen here, if you let them. Wonderful things, Miss Skinner. When you least expect it. Are you ready, my dear, for things to happen?

Oh yes, said Evelyn. I've never been more ready.

"Cherish the body, and the soul *will* follow."

Did you write that?

Alas no. The Greeks, probably. Sounds like the Greeks.

Their last port of call was a sculpture room. No one of quality here, said Miss Everly.

True, it was an exit room, but it was in this room that Evelyn became overcome. Miss Skinner's voice in the background. Maybe Cleopatra, she said. Ariadne, perhaps? It might even be Sappho . . . Odd arm, though.

But Evelyn didn't care about the arm or who sculpted it or who the subject was. It was the most beautiful woman, prostrate and naked, and that was all it needed to be. The whoosh of the sea crashed inside her ears. Breasts peeking from the folds of marble—the nipples so real—for the sole tantalizing effect of making Evelyn feel alive. Awake. Vital. And true.

Miss Skinner! You've gone quite pale. Make way, make way! *Scusate, Americano*, please *scusate!* Out of the way immediately, if you please. Come, take my arm, Miss Skinner. Follow me. It's the beauty. It's all this beauty. We English are at the mercy of the muse. I took to my bed for days when I first set eyes on the del Sarto.

And she led Evelyn away to a seat and a restorative glass of water. Neither spoke. The moment was too momentous.

That night, Evelyn avoided dinner. Little notes from Miss Everly were slipped under her door, and she enjoyed reading about the Luggs' amusing faux pas with the pronunciation of a German count.

And then, as she was about to sleep, there was a knock at her door, which she answered, and which brought her face-to-face with Livia the maid. A fresh bowl of water in her hands. Livia walked past her and placed the bowl on the dresser. She turned and smiled at Evelyn. Iss ya berfday soon, she said.

(Broken English with an unexpected cockney accent.)

Yes, said Evelyn. It is.

The night of Evelyn's birthday, and vermouth was the drink *du soir*. Vermouth! Imagine! Miss Everly offered a toast about being twenty-one—all in verse, of course—before she led Evelyn into the dining room, into an exquisite setting of candlelight and scent. Sprigs of rosemary, slightly crushed, were draped over picture frames and woven into the backs of chairs, the small blue heads a perfect complement to the pots of violets running centrally down the table. The aroma was heady and majestic.

Evelyn sat down and Livia came out from the kitchen and smiled. She moved behind Evelyn, flapped out her napkin and placed it on her lap, somewhat slowly and sensuously. She did the same for Miss Everly but without the added tactile delight. Other guests entered and gasped at their evening of Italian authenticity and *bellezza*. Reverend Hyndesight was overcome and said grace before he sat down and Mr. Collins bellowed, Well, this is more like it! and took his position opposite Evelyn. He lifted the bottle of wine and filled the glasses around him.

By the time the rabbit, white beans and bitter greens were on the plates, two conversations played out either side of Evelyn and she found it hard to follow either.

To her left, Miss Everly was enjoying a heated disagreement with an American who was studying Henry James: the effect he had on the city of Florence and the effect the city of Florence had on him. Miss Everly loathed him from the start.

Oh no! said Miss Everly. I totally disagree. The factionalism of the Guelphs and Ghibellines, at its heart, was a struggle between Pope and emperor. And in Florence, a permissible interfamilial war for power. Totally unnecessary and led to the exiling of my dear heart Dante. He never got over it. And frankly, neither have I.

And to her right, the reverend had just asked her a question.

Miss Skinner? he said. Can you think of one? An element of transformation?

Evelyn thought for a moment. Livia brushed past, which prompted her neural pathways to spark and caused a momentary flicker of the candles. *Il calore è un elemento di trasformazione*, said Evelyn, looking at Livia, who had begun to clear the table. Heat is an element of transformation, she said.

Heat? How interesting. You make it sound so positive, said Mr. Lugg. Heat rather transforms me into a heaving blob. Ergo we travel in the autumn and winter months. I had to turn down a position in India because of the heat.

Not just because of the heat, darling, said Mrs. Lugg.

No, no, no. Not just because of the heat.

And they looked eagerly about at their fellow diners, seeking a reflection of their own prejudice and bigotry.

Oh, that's rather lovely, said Miss Everly suddenly, ignoring the new guest and joining in the discussion. Simply put, Miss Skinner, you are advocating the need to wear fewer clothes?

I am, said Evelyn. The fewer the better. What might that do to a body? The shifting of weight. The lightness on the soul, you might say—the ease of movement. To rid oneself of an encumbrance: that to me is transformational.

We remember the rigid corset, said the Brown sisters. When we stopped wearing them, our spines had no strength and we toppled over.

Bone turned to aspic, said Mr. Collins.

Miss Everly said, It is a startling fact how the heat of a European sun encourages us travelers to slough off the English tweed and embrace the linens of fairer climes. Lighter clothes, lighter the impulse, lighter the body, lighter the mind. I also feel a need to wear trousers here, she added.

Good Lord! said the identical twins. *Trousers?*

Indeed trousers, Miss and Miss Brown. The sturdy feel of enclosure around the most intimate part of my anatomy would bring great freedom.

Evelyn noticed that the other table had stopped slurping soup and were looking over at them.

Why the need for trousers, Miss Everly? asked Mr. Lugg.

I have a need to stride out, Mr. Lugg. To walk as a man might walk. With all the benefits. I do not need to be a woman here. I wish to repel the male gaze. To move through the city with the ease of a man. I want to view the city through the eyes of a man. A poet, you see, is a shape-shifter.

A what? said Blythe Brown.

A selkie, said Miss Everly. One moment a seal, one moment a man. I am there to probe the hidden depths of the ocean—the raging tides of emotions—and then to surface in all my humanness, in all my humility, to recount in a handful of lines the myriad of tales I have encountered, the worlds in which I have traveled, the battles fought like Odysseus.

Didn't she say she was a seal? said one of the Brown twins.

Not a real seal, said Evelyn.

Then why did she say it?

Luckily, the conversation came to an abrupt end when an overweight gentleman at the next table choked on a piece of rabbit. Mr. Collins was up first.

Make way, make way.

He stood behind the gentleman—who was now blue—gripped both hands below his breastbone and forcefully pushed against the diaphragm. The offending meat shot out of his mouth and hit Queen Victoria between the eyes.

The dining room became silent. Morbidly so. Evelyn wondered if her birthday would end there. Miranda Lugg, misreading the incident as she so often did, said quite loudly to the gentleman: You disgust me.

It was fair to say, the near fatality took the edge off what had been, up till then, a very jolly evening. But in the small fissure that had opened

up, the Brown sisters took their chance and suggested a musical inter-
lude. They offered to play a duet they'd written together when the First
Opium War was in its ascendancy.

Cheery, said Mr. Collins.

I have known the Brown twins for many years, Mr. Collins, and I
can confidently say that there is no finer duet playing, said the reverend.
We are incredibly fortunate. Miss Everly? After you.

Miss Everly groaned and downed a full glass of wine.

Evelyn waited for the dining room to clear.

Are you not coming, Miss Skinner? said Mr. Collins.

In a minute, Mr. Collins. I—

Say no more, Miss Skinner. And he smiled that smile he'd recently
adopted around her and left the room.

Evelyn stood awkwardly by the table, a bit hot, a bit tipsy, a sprig of
rosemary coiled around her fingers. She had just decided to go into the
kitchen and present herself when Livia exited. They stood unmoving,
gazing into each other's eyes. A lustful note undeniably felt. Evelyn
hesitated. I—she began. Io—she began again in Italian. I've never been
given such a gift. Thank you, Livia. (Oh, how good it felt to say her
name!) For all this. Which I will never forget. Which I will talk about
till I'm old and decrepit.

Livia laughed.

I will, you know. Remember it forever, said Evelyn. Because when I
like something, I like it very much and never want to let it go. I don't
want this to end, she said, and she stepped closer. Closer still.

Livia laughed. Livia said, Nothing has to end, and she leaned over
the table and picked a violet and handed it to Evelyn. For you, she said.

Evelyn rushed into the drawing room and saw that a space had been
left between Mr. Collins and Miss Everly.

You look radiant, said Miss Everly.

Just a little hot, said Evelyn.

But heat is an element of transformation, is it not? said Mr. Collins,
raising both eyebrows.

Midnight. Evelyn twenty-one and one minute old. Lights from a tram flickered briefly in her bedroom. She unwrapped her handkerchief and there, in the middle of the white linen square, was the violet flower. She opened her Baedeker and pressed it between the pages. She bent down and kissed it. Little did she know that two days was all it would take for that kiss to progress from Baedeker to lips.

It was the afternoon. Evelyn in her room, sluggish from lunch. Drawn to the window by the sound of a violin. And there was Livia out walking. Evelyn ran down the stairs. Bonnet loose, buttons undone, hair askew.

Can't stop, Miss Everly!

Fly free, my sweet thing!

Out into the street now, running alongside the Arno, hands holding up her skirt, weaving around handcarts and laundry boys and working girls and dogs and priests and nuns and washerwomen and tourists and all the while calling out her name—

Livia stopped. Turned. And smiled.

They walked the river east and left behind the sand diggers until they found a good-enough place of solitude. They clambered down onto the foreshore in the shadow of a bridge and shyly faced one another. Hands touched cheeks and fingers lips, and there they kissed because the eyes of the city were not on them. It was their first kiss. Evelyn held her bonnet as the breeze tried to lift it. Bells were faint, pronouncing the hour. But which hour? Time had ceased. Somewhere in the air, the quiet cast of a lure whipped the water and sent ripples to their feet.

In the time it took for them to return to the *pensione*, the most extraordinary shift had taken place within those tired, judgmental walls: that of love preceding them. It had crept ahead, scattering benevolence and joy. The heavy mahogany furniture acquired an Italian flair, and the cockney *signora*'s aitches, as rare as a Marian apparition, made an unexpected appearance. Stew had been taken off the evening menu once again, and even Reverend Hyndesight practiced compassion by including Mr. Collins in an upcoming visit to the opera. And Miss

Everly? Simply put, she wrote her best poem in years. The weather, too, was affected by the tenderness of that sweet embrace. The sun was reenergized, and the warmth of its long arm encroached upon autumn's flimsy grasp; stars shone brighter, and even a full moon declared itself a honey.

Love was resplendent that day. And when the light was angled right across Piazza Santa Croce, one could almost believe that Dante smiled when he heard a young woman called Evelyn whisper to one called Livia, *You are my teacher and my author.*

The rapid progression from kissing to something more happened the night the reverend arranged a visit to the Teatro Verdi to watch a production of Spontini's *La Vestale.*

I've heard it's as good as Covent Garden, he declared at breakfast one morning.

Evelyn knew the outing would fall on Livia's night off, so both women agreed that Evelyn would leave at the end of the second act and Livia would be waiting somewhere nearby. In the dark. The subterfuge was dramatic enough. Who needed opera?

The orchestra tuned up, and Evelyn sidled along the third-tier row toward Miss Everly's enthusiastic waving. Mr. Collins hadn't arrived yet either, and his empty seat inflamed the reverend's ire. He was seated in the first tier, along with the Luggs and the Browns and an American couple he'd saved in San Lorenzo, after they'd been cornered by a pack of feral cats. The audience was quite boisterous, and not like Covent Garden at all. And here came Mr. Collins all flustered and surprisingly handsome. Sorry, sorry, sorry, he said as he made his way to his seat. You're late, said Reverend Hyndesight. The sharpness of the last consonant was the cue for the gaslights to dim, and the overture began. Miss Everly clasped Evelyn's hand and the women succumbed to the music.

After the first act, Evelyn and Miss Everly followed the crowds to the café and accepted a glass of champagne from a portly German who spoke good English. Miss Everly thought the soprano was jolly good and Evelyn agreed and then Evelyn leaned in close to her ear and said, I'm going to feign a headache and leave at the end of act two, Miss Everly.

How marvelous! said Miss Everly. A romantic assignation?

Evelyn smiled.

Leave it to me, said Miss Everly. I shall take care of this.

So, when act 2 came to an end and Evelyn got up to leave, Miss Everly could be heard saying, She has an awful headache. A right old thumper. We might not see her for days, Reverend.

The night air was fresh and Evelyn, head down, pushed through the waiting cabmen and their lascivious comments and raced toward her rendezvous. She hadn't gotten very far before the rendezvous came to her and pulled her into a dark alleyway.

A warm mouth on hers, a broad wall at her back. Footsteps, some-where, pressed them further into the shadows. A dog barked. A man singing from an upstairs window. Warm breath on her neck, in her ear; the recklessness of the situation made her brave. She slid her hand into Livia's blouse and onto her breast. Livia clasped the hem of Evelyn's skirt and drew it up. Livia's hand slipped into her drawers and soon Evelyn felt the smooth glide of fingers inside her. The sound of a horse and cart going past. And then only the sensation of pleasure, as her mouth was smothered by a hand and her body turned liquid.

Undeterred by the Church, class and convention, sex between the young lovers favorably won out. They decided they'd need a protective cloak under which to hide their love, and they found one sharpish and called it "Italian lessons."

Whatever afternoon or morning Livia had free became the frame-work for this study. Beyond that, brushed shoulders and looks of long-ing were the flint spark to this tentative bed of passion. Evelyn became quite the linguist.

Isn't she a delicious little thing? said Miss Everly as Livia passed by one morning with an armful of linen.

Evelyn blushed. An hour before, they'd just fingered one another in the closet.

She's a jolly good teacher, said Evelyn. She's already got me on the modals. Could and should.

And let's not forget would, said Miss Everly.

Between silent kisses, verb declension could often be heard coming from Evelyn's room. Sometimes the cockney *signora* would stop to listen, recalling her own intrepid years of learning. The reverend passed by her door full of admiration at "Miss Skinner's enthusiasm and diligence." And Mr. Collins? All he could do was shake his head and smile. As if he was party to a private joke he had no intention of sharing.

Back in the room, Evelyn's notebook had been cast aside next to blouses and stockings and undergarments. The young women facing one another on the bed, topless, kissing, a light breeze through the shutters texturing their skin. All the while, Evelyn remembering to say out loud: The omnibus is due at ten. The omnibus was due at ten. The omnibus had been due at ten . . .

A few days later, Evelyn bought postcards at Alinari's, intending to return to the *pensione* to write them. However, the morning suddenly shed its dull cloak, revealing an ensemble of bright wonder, and instantly energized, she took off into the city, which was becoming more and more familiar every day. She would stop to smell an orange, or a bunch of basil, or to converse with whoever manned the till. In Piazza della Signoria, tourists had gathered at an outside bar and she immediately decided to do the same. A quick tour of the statuary and then back to a table to write her postcards. A horse and cart passed in front of her and she was careful not to follow too close behind.

The light was beautiful. Faint shadows whispering. Sunlight caught the trefoils above: Fortitude. Temperance. Justice and Prudence. The four cardinal virtues.

A breeze followed her into the Loggia dei Lanzi like a spectral presence and led her to Giovanni da Bologna's *Rape of the Sabine Woman*.

The statue startled her. Bewitched her. Coaxed from her equal feelings of shame and exhilaration.

Her gaze rested on the foot, the curve, the rounded heel, the hand pressing onto the woman's buttocks, the flesh yielding. But it wasn't flesh, was it? It was marble. She took out her notebook and drew a simple sketch. No shading needed, just lines that traced the liquidity of movement, mapping the erotic to the horror. This execution of genius.

She was shown to a table where she ordered a quina-vermouth. She felt great freedom sitting outside. She rolled up the sleeves of her blouse, her skin olive like her mother's. She was about to begin a postcard to her father but thought it better to practice in her notebook first, before committing words to the back of the Duomo. She looked across once again to the statue of the Sabine woman.

Miss Skinner?

Evelyn turned. The flare of sun caught her eyes. She raised her hand.

Oh, Mr. Collins.

May I?

Please do.

Mr. Collins sat and gestured to the waiter for the same drink as Evelyn.

I've just been to the Uffizi with Miss Everly. She's quite the guide. I'll never look at a pomegranate in the same way again.

Evelyn laughed.

She said you came over faint in one of the sculpture rooms?

Has she told everyone?

No. Just me, said Mr. Collins.

Grazie, signore, said Mr. Collins as his drink was placed in front of him.

Was Miss Everly worried? said Evelyn.

Not at all. I think she thought something quite marvelous had happened to you.

Like what?

She didn't say. You know how she is. She gets that look upon her face as if—oh, you know. As if a secret has been unearthed, said Mr. Collins, and he looked at her intently. *Has* something happened to you, Miss Skinner?

I'm not sure, she said.

Good Lord! It's not love, is it?

Of course not, said Evelyn crossly. Crossly enough for Mr. Collins to reach for his drink, smile, and change the subject.

A toast, he said.

They raised their glasses.

Incipit vita nova, he said.

So begins a new life, said Evelyn.

Clink.

Do people think Miss Everly's a good poet? asked Evelyn.

A line appeared between Mr. Collins's eyebrows. He said, I think people at the Simi think she's faintly ridiculous.

I think she's clever.

I do too. And I think she's thoughtful and thought-provoking. And funny, too. Is she a good poet? Yes. There is humanity in her work. And nonconformity. But she will remain without glory.

Why?

Because the world doesn't know what to do with her.

But I want the world to know!

You are a romantic, Miss Skinner.

I'll shout her name from the highest peaks!

Mr. Collins picked up his glass and drank. (The sound of ice hitting the side.) He said, "The worthiest poets have remained uncrowned / Till death has bleached their foreheads to the bone." Not everyone can be Elizabeth Barrett Browning. Constance knows that. And the fact she's not doesn't render her efforts unimportant. Forty, fifty years hence, she may be garlanded. But I, for one, enjoy her mind.

Evelyn watched the softness in his face as he spoke. The cleverness, the cynicism of the dining room had been replaced by admiration. She liked this man more than the evening version.

Mr. Collins looked down at the postcards.

H.W.?

My fa—

Of course, of course, your father.

He likes me to call him H. W., rather than Father, because Father makes him feel old. He has quite a young mistress at the moment. Please don't tell anyone, Mr. Collins. We are an unconventional family. And Evelyn reached for her drink.

David. Ponte Vecchio. Il Duomo. And apart from your father, who will the lucky recipients be?

I'm not sure yet. What I want to say won't fit on a postcard.

What do you want to say?

Oh, so much. Is it wrong to admire beauty when it is the subject of such horror?

The Sabine woman?

Yes.

Mr. Collins thought for a moment. He said, It's calculated and erotic in equal measure. The male is enjoying her terror. The artist our discomfort. (The sound of ice as he swirled his drink.) Imagine, Miss Skinner, imagine Giovanni da Bologna is with us at this table. What do you think he's doing?

Drinking?

What else?

Listening to us. Enjoying being the center of attention.

Most certainly. What else?

You tell me, Mr. Collins.

Smiling, I would say. Because he understands the response. This statue was seen by *everyone*, Miss Skinner. Butcher, baker, candlestick maker and the grand dukes of Tuscany. Maybe it would have been less shocking, more acceptable, had it been placed in a museum. But it was commissioned for a civic square. This man knew what he was doing. A sculpture with no fixed viewpoint so we can walk around it, be part of the horror, part of the action, part of the dance. He knows the great dilemma he is presenting, Miss Skinner. He's showing us what's in *us*.

Mr. Collins lit a cigarette and beckoned the waiter for two more drinks. Evelyn didn't protest.

He said, The Church doesn't have a language for the variations of our humanness. We need to look at Freud for that. Psychoanalysis is the way forward, Miss Skinner. Have you read *The Interpretation of Dreams*?

I have not, Mr. Collins.

I think you would find it fascinating. One day, the Church will lose its hold on society and what a society we shall be. He looked at Evelyn and cocked his head. I think maybe you and I are rather similar, Miss Skinner.

Evelyn drank her vermouth and wondered if he meant socialist.

May I? said Evelyn, reaching for a cigarette.

You certainly may. And Mr. Collins struck a match.

It was her first cigarette and it made her light-headed and full of insights.

Today a cigarette and tomorrow the vote! she said.

How very daring of you, said Mr. Collins. He lifted his glass. And what does life hold for Miss Skinner on her return to England?

She shall continue to work for her aunt at the gallery in Cork Street.

It seems to me, said Mr. Collins, looking down at her sketch of the statue, that her father passed on a good deal of talent. Maybe there's another avenue to walk down?

I am mediocre, Mr. Collins. My father has been and continues to be my greatest supporter but the talent, the resilience, isn't with me. And I don't grieve that loss because it has freed me. I've seen my father parry the blows—

But your father's successful!

Not in his eyes. He's not Cézanne. All artists are tortured by all they're not and by art that's not theirs. It's lonely, Mr. Collins. But I think I could be a memorable teacher.

Memorable? You're giving yourself away.

Who doesn't want to be remembered?

I, for one.

Evelyn finished her drink. I don't believe you, she said.

They walked across to Neptune's Fountain and stopped behind the white god.

Mr. Collins said, Marvelous *chiappe*.

Evelyn raised her eyebrows in query.

Buttocks, Miss Skinner.

They are quite the engine!

Mr. Collins laughed. Evelyn blushed. The vermouth had made her witty.

Across the square, cabs maneuvered back and forth. Horses ate in repose, freed from the bright red blankets they wore on their backs. The usual movement of English tourists, oblivious to life around them, looking for answers in their guidebooks.

They wandered back through the Piazzale degli Uffizi, along the *lungarno* to the *pensione*. The light was yellow—a late-summer burst—and a sleepy vigil crowned the air. Mr. Collins offered his arm and Evelyn took it.

You seem so sure of your life, he said.

I am.

Marriage? Children?

Just because one can, doesn't mean one should, Mr. Collins.

He nodded.

She had never made a truer statement in her life. She felt she was wearing Miss Everly's metaphorical trousers.

They stopped as the *pensione* came into sight.

Shall we go into the Simi strategically? asked Mr. Collins. Me then you? In case of gossip.

Let's go in together and cause a little, shall we? said Evelyn, and they took the stairs, and passed reception and walked through the sudden turn of heads.

A couple of evenings later, English stew was back on the dinner menu, much to the delight of the Luggs.

God brought us all together at this table, said Reverend Hyndesight, practicing his pulpit voice.

And the Gotthard Railway, said Mr. Collins quietly. Mr. Collins was attacking a gray piece of meat that he suspected was horse.

Dominicans or Franciscans, Miss Skinner? said the reverend.

Oh, Franciscans, without a doubt, said Evelyn. Saint Francis was a gentle soul. Full of anguish, so sincere. The Franciscans fought heresy with love and I, for one, am an admirer of love.

(Livia was in her sight line.)

Hear hear, said the reverend.

And of all the Catholic saints in the Middle Ages, he was the one who suggested the idea of nature as God. *La Creazione*, she said, and she drank her wine. *Domini canes* also means "hounds of the Lord." That's where they get their name from. I always found it rather unsettling.

Goodness, does it really? said one of the Brown sisters. I won't sleep at all tonight.

The very thought makes me shiver, said the other.

They always were a militant bunch, said Mr. Collins. Seeking out the heretic with a lit torch. I'd have been the first to the flame.

If only, said the reverend quietly.

And they took against Dante of all people, said Miss Everly. They set the conditions of authoritative literature, no vernacular texts for them. And that Savonarola. Encouraging the burning of nudes and portraits of women because of the temptation conveyed. Can men not control themselves, Reverend?

Don't look at me, said the reverend.

We once had a gardener who used to chase us with shears, said one of the Brown sisters.

Good God! said Miss Everly.

And which church belongs to the hounds? asked Mrs. Lugg.

Santa Maria Novella is one, said Evelyn. It has rather a solemn atmosphere. I heard someone suggest it would be called stony-faced if it was a person.

One to avoid, then, said the sisters.

But you must not avoid it! said Miss Everly. You must go! You must see the chapels of Rucellai, Gondi and Strozzi!

Indeed you must, said Mr. Collins.

Then we shall, said Blythe.

Just don't yawn.

Yawn?

And Mr. Collins performed a silly mime about ghost dogs entering an open mouth.

Mr. Collins! said the reverend, a smile breaking through his admonishment.

We're going to Santa Croce tomorrow morning, said Blythe.

Oh, the grace and humanity of Giotto's—began the lady poet.

Morning light is the best time to see the frescoes, said the reverend, cutting her off. May I suggest you take your opera glasses too. To the right of the high altar is the Bardi Chapel and there you will discover the fresco cycle of St. Francis.

Unless you understand the relations of Giotto to St. Francis and of St. Francis to humanity, it will be of little interest, said Mr. Lugg, reading from Ruskin's *Mornings in Florence*. Could you clarify the relation, Reverend?

Indeed I can, Mr. Lugg. And I can do it in one word: *devotion*.

The Brown sisters sighed.

That sweet delectable saint preached work without money and embrace poverty. Work without pleasure and embrace chastity. Work according to instruction and embrace obedience.

Sounds ghastly, said Mr. Collins, giving up on the meat. And what does tomorrow hold for you, Miss Skinner?

My day shall revolve around an Italian lesson, said Evelyn.

You are eager, said Mr. Collins.

Possessive pronouns, said Evelyn.

What's mine is yours and what's yours is mine? said Mr. Collins.

Something like that.

However, when the lesson came the following morning, it was more: I am yours and you are mine.

The two women lay on the bed fully clothed, gazing into one another's eyes. They had little time together because Livia had a crate of chickens to pluck, and Evelyn, between sighs, could hear every grain fall inside that wretched hourglass. When Livia got up to leave, Evelyn felt tormented and left the room shortly after.

Had you been looking for her, you would have found her the other side of the Ponte Vecchio, seated outside a café close to the church of Santa Felicità. The south side of the river was another world, just as Miss Everly had said it was. A medieval quarter of narrow streets and soaring towers, the defensive architecture of the time for the rich and powerful. She could be alone here, she thought. Anonymous among the cabinet-makers and saddlers and hatters.

Her drink arrived and the clink of ice snapped her out of her musing. She picked up her pencil and wrote.

> *Dear H.W.—may I call you Father today? Do you mind? I feel in need of a fatherly ear right now.*
>
> *You once talked to me of an affliction. I was quite young, I remember, but felt grown-up at the fact that you had taken me into your confidence, outlining the complexity and paradox of the human heart, before explaining the separation that was to occur between you and Mother. Looking back, I see how advanced I was for a nine-year-old.*

Evelyn raised her glass and drank the vermouth. The sunlight making her squint.

> *"I have become afflicted too"* (she wrote).
>
> *When I see her walk through the doorway, or come about the corner, or appear on the stairwell, the muscles in my legs are subjected to a form of atrophy, and it takes all my willpower to remain upright. This makes me sound as if I'm ill; I am not, I have never felt better.*
>
> *The world is sharp. So sharply in focus that my eyes see everything— in fact, beyond everything, if one can suspend the logic of that sentence. If you show me a painting of a bowl with citrons and figs and plums and*

pears, I can describe the woman who picked that fruit off the tree, and can describe her with such tenderness that I can see myself reflected in her iris, like a candle, the sole source of light. Show me a painting of a ray fish, dripping sea off a kitchen table, and I'll tell you about the man who caught it.

That brace of pheasants? I can tell you the farmer's journey from bed to field to a shotgun ready to fire. Half a scallop shell? The hand that opened it.

Is this imagination? Is this what spurs you to paint? Is this my inheritance from you?

It's always been quite hard to know—to pinpoint, let's say—where one's unique story really begins. Does it really start at the moment of birth, or with those who came before? Instilling, distilling, in one's veins the lived life, the unlived life, the regrets, the joys, as effortlessly, as dubiously one might say, as they hand down a certain walk (you to me), or a frown (you to me) or limp, mousy hair (Mother to me). If this is so, then my story starts with you.

What I want to say is, you have handed me your affliction and its accompanying power. What I'm writing about of course is—

Love, said Miss Everly.

A shadow fell across Evelyn's page.

What? said Evelyn, covering her writing and looking up.

Only in the experience of *love*, do we know what it is to be human. I've been thinking about that sentence as I walked around San Frediano today, said Miss Everly. The poverty is acute. A life of hardship, mostly, and yet—may I?

Oh, please do, Miss Everly. I'm so delighted to see you.

Miss Everly sat down opposite Evelyn and took out her cigarette case.

Evelyn closed her notebook.

Miss Everly placed a cigarette in her mouth and said, I came back through Piazza Santo Spirito and entered the basilica. Shafts of light divided the nave. I witnessed a young woman throwing herself down in front of the altar. The scene was as dramatic as any Caravaggio. What could have caused such despair? What are we without love?

Waiting, said Evelyn.

Miss Everly smiled. She rested her chin in her hand. Her eyes set firmly on Evelyn's face, scrutinizing. Waiting, she repeated. And are you waiting, my dear?

No, said Evelyn. Not anymore.

Miss Everly suggested a walk east and a climb to San Miniato al Monte and the finest views of the city. She said a shift in outlook—physical, of course—would bring a sense of proportion to the onslaught of insight and passionate regard both women were experiencing. She said they could also call in to a wonderful *forno* and stock up on some pastries.

Cypresses stood tall on either side of the path, and the cool, damp air offset the heart-pumping warmth of the ascent. Miss Everly's face was red and shiny, and she stopped against the mossy wall and took deep breaths in the shade of umbrella pines.

She said, I knew someone who did this on their knees, and he wasn't even a Catholic.

Gosh, said Evelyn.

Actually, we're quite close to the spot where he died. Come on.

They eschewed Piazzale Michelangelo and the gathering of tourists and continued climbing toward the monastery and church. We will be changed by this experience, said Miss Everly. This is godliness in its highest. Small *g*, of course.

Of course, said Evelyn, smiling, who already felt changed.

The view was as beautiful as Miss Everly had said it would be. Evelyn thought Miss Everly was still catching her breath, but the timbre of her inhalation was far more emotional; she might even have been crying. Evelyn looked away discreetly.

Miss Everly unexpectedly and rather tenderly took hold of Evelyn's arm and said: You can still see it—the layout. Arnolfo di Cambio's final communal circuit of walls to enclose the city. Follow my finger, Miss Skinner. Over there, over there, down . . . An enclosed city was his dream. His *insieme*. What the Italians call a togetherness. Of course, it *was* a masterpiece of defense, and yet, so much more. It *shaped* the city. Made it a direct descendant of Rome, and that made people believe its destiny was golden. He created a knowable city, Miss Skinner. And knowable it remains. It's how the city becomes part of us forever. Never lets us go. Pulls us back time after time.

And then silence. The wind through the cypresses. The song of birds. Evelyn unwrapping bakery delicacies.

Would you like a *sfoglia* now? she said, offering Miss Everly one of the *crema*-filled puff pastries bought especially for the climb.

What a splendid idea. Let's go to the graveyard and sweeten death a little.

They walked past the church, past a friar heading toward the *campanile*, and they entered the cemetery.

Come, said Miss Everly, let's go and sit next to those *amorini* over there. They look in need of some mortal company and a touch of gossip.

They sat on a low wall at the end of an ornate crypt.

Would you like a photograph on your grave too, Miss Everly?

Me? Oh no. Ashes in the Arno if you please. Fish food. And please do call me Constance.

Evelyn agreed. But only if Constance called her Evelyn.

Evelyn dabbed her mouth with a handkerchief and said, The other night, I heard you talking to Mrs. Lugg about a nun who was an artist.

Ah yes. Suor Plautilla.

That's her.

Vasari wrote about her. She must have been important for him to do that.

Mrs. Lugg seemed rather dismissive of her, said Evelyn.

Well, follow the river to its source and you'll find the husband.

Evelyn smiled. You said Suor Plautilla was prolific.

Oh, she was. Fell into oblivion because of her gender. It's a tired old story, that one, I'm afraid, my dear. I am one of the few who have ever seen her painting of the Last Supper, which was a first. For a woman, I mean. Largest painting in the world by an early female artist. Nearly as big as Leonardo's. Top left-hand corner her signature and also the words: *Orate pro pictora*—"pray for the paintress." A simple acknowledgment of who she was.

Where can I see it, Constance?

You can't. Rumor has it it's still somewhere in the monastery at Santa Maria Novella. In the refectory, perhaps? Other than that, I really don't know.

That's awful.

Isn't it? If we don't know where all her works are, what hope for the others?

Were there others?

Oh yes. The choice for the educated woman was clear and stark. Marriage and no creative expression. Or convent and creative expression. So, women entered the convent in order to paint. Such was the sacrifice. But when have women not sacrificed to live as they feel? Not all of us will embrace men, marriage, motherhood. Nor should we. We have one life, my dear Evelyn, one life and we must use it well.

Nighttime at the Simi, and it was the last dinner together for the English group. Or as Miss Everly liked to call it, "our Ultima Cena."

There were two conversations happening as usual across the table, and when the evening had moved on to the safer tectonic plates of cheese, Miss Everly leaned across to Mrs. Lugg and said, Are you feeling better, my dear?

Indeed, I am, Miss Everly.

Not to everyone's taste is the European cuisine. One must gird oneself for an adventure.

So I've been told, said Mrs. Lugg.

I thought of you when I penned this little ode, said Miss Everly.

Let me hear too, Miss Everly, said Evelyn, leaning in.

Miss Everly said:

To eat parts that we'd consign to waste
Takes courage and great faith.
A trotter to one
Un zampone to another.
A feast by any other name.
But even I draw the line at brain.

Mrs. Lugg felt something rise in her throat. She held her stomach.

Bravo, Miss Everly! said Evelyn. Such fun.

Just a little silliness. Goat! said Miss Everly, holding up a stinking plate of blue *formaggio di capra.* Anyone for goat?

Culture and decency, said the reverend, refilling the wineglasses.

Culture and decency do not begin and end at the white cliffs of Dover, said Mr. Collins.

You are not a patriot, obviously, said the reverend.

Nothing to do with patriotism. I believe in the unity of the world. I believe in the power of people working together.

Piffle, said the reverend, and he muttered, Socialist, quietly to the elderly twins, who were morphing into one another in front of Evelyn's eyes.

We shall be at war one day with your European brothers, as you call them, Mr. Collins. It's inevitable, said Mr. Lugg. They're not like us. But they want what we have.

And do we not want what they have, Mr. Lugg? Michelangelo? Dante? Beauty? Wine on a sun-drenched terrace? Villas nestled in the hills going for a song?

Mr. Lugg ignored Mr. Collins and reached for a plate of stinking goat's cheese.

Yes, but will you fight? said the reverend, bringing the conversation back to British imperialism. It's a simple question.

For what cause? said Mr. Collins.

Cause is irrelevant.

Cause is not irrelevant.

To teach another nation a lesson, then, said the reverend.

A nation is not a person. And so I will not.

Humph, said the reverend.

The sound of a teaspoon against a glass and Mr. Lugg rose from the table.

Our last night with you all, said Mr. Lugg. You've all been so kind to us—

Nonsense!

Especially to my wife. Thank you one and all. And he raised his glass. And yet, we've seen so little of the city during this trying time. For our last day tomorrow, what would you recommend, Reverend?

The reverend thought about the question at hand. He milked the silence and the attention.

I think you should take your wife up the Duomo, he said.

Evelyn reached for her napkin and covered her mouth. Mr. Collins began to snigger. Miss Everly busied herself with the cheese.

Do you think she'd like it up the Duomo? asked the reverend.

Everyone likes it up the Duomo, said Mr. Collins. In *my* experience.

Finally, something we both agree on, said the reverend. Excellent!

Evelyn stood up. Excuse me, she said, and left the room.

Did you know that whenever Ghirlandaio left Florence he complained of Duomo sickness? said the reverend to Mr. Lugg.

Did he really? How touching.

Evelyn made for the drawing room and fell onto a chesterfield. A cloud of dust rose. Opposite, she noticed that a picture of King Edward had surreptitiously appeared in a face-off with the former queen. A loud cough. She looked over to the door. Mr. Collins was standing there, holding two wineglasses and smirking.

Miss Skinner?

Don't say a word, Mr. Collins.

I—

Don't.

I've brought you your wine, he said. May I? And he sat down next to her.

Stop looking at me please, Mr. Collins.

How can you tell?

I can.

She suddenly turned toward him. I have something important to say to you, she said.

Mr. Collins leaned in close. Tell me, he said.

Forgive my forwardness, but—and Evelyn shifted position—I like you, Mr. Collins.

And I like you too.

But I'm not in love with you.

I know you're not.

You do?

You're in love with Livia the maid.

I beg your—?

It's all right, Miss Skinner, nobody else knows.

But how—

Because I'm in love with Matteo the laundry man. You see, Miss Skinner, whilst you've been looking at the breast, I've been looking at the *chiappe*.

Oh, Mr. Collins!

Thaddeus, please. And he kissed her hand. Write to me, Evelyn, he said. Else I'll hold it against you forever.

They're in here! bellowed Miss Everly, leading the group into the drawing room. Oh no, Mrs. Lugg, she said. Time is what it's all about. The ephemeral seed of time. The heavy thud of the pendulum swing, the noose of time. Mmm, the *noose of time*.

She reached into her pocket and took out a notebook and scribbled furiously.

There was much talk about what should happen next and Mr. Collins skillfully headed off the suggestion of another duet by the elderly twins. Instead he proposed that Miss Everly should read some poetry. Hers, preferably, he said.

Really, Mr. Collins! said Miss Everly, but she was, of course, delighted.

However . . .

The insecurity that stalks the artist was never far behind, and in a swift lunge, Miss Everly was mugged of all confidence and acclaim. Rather than read her own work, she decided to culminate her stay with a rendition of Elizabeth Barrett Browning's "Casa Guidi Windows." (We had a loose friendship once. How loose? I was ten.)

All 1,999 lines, Miss Everly?

Would that be a problem, Reverend?

I was thinking of the Brown sisters.

Will they not make it till the end?

Miss Everly didn't chance it. She read for an hour, plenty of time to elicit rapturous applause. The grandfather clock struck midnight with eleven gongs, and people said good-byes and good nights and bon voyages and climbed the stairs to bed. Evelyn looked about her and thought she would miss them all. Even the Reverend Hyndesight, in hindsight.

Dust hovered in the wake of departure. Just her and Miss Everly left now, facing one another and holding hands.

Constance.

My dear Evelyn.

I shall miss you.

I shall miss you too.

I want to cry, said Evelyn.

So cry, my dear. This room needs the outpouring of emotion. The stiff upper lip is woven into the haberdashery.

I've never had so much fun with anyone, said Evelyn. At which point Livia entered and caught their eye.

Except . . . ? said Miss Everly.

Evelyn blushed and both women laughed.

Cherish it, said Miss Everly. I did at your age. Love is the most wonderful discovery in the pantheon of human existence.

The next day, the reverend left with the elderly sisters for Arezzo, the Luggs made an early start for the Duomo so as to avoid the beggars, and they all left in a convoy of cabs.

Miss Everly was heading south to Naples in search of squalor and inspiration. And Mr. Collins north to Venice in search of romance and a gondolier. (He would find both and would live out a short but ecstatic life overlooking the Grand Canal.)

Evelyn waved them off from the steps.

Good luck, Thaddeus! she shouted.

Good luck to you too! he shouted back.

Write well, Constance! she cried.

I shall! And don't forget to write to me too, my dear, shouted Miss Everly from her cab.

The sound of horses' hooves on stones, the turn of wheels. Good-bye, good-bye!

And then they were gone. And she was alone.

And the Simi returned to what it was: a dreary haven for the English middle class who complained about everything foreign. She watched the next intake arrive. An American commercial traveler, a large German with gout, and a touchy-feely Italian cheese seller. We're the start of a joke, she thought.

By the time the young man and his mother arrived at reception, Evelyn had been in Florence for fourteen days. A lifetime if you were a fruit fly. She'd noticed them as she came down the stairs, because the mother was enunciating clearly to the cockney *signora*. Alice Clara Forster and son. *Forster.* Yes, she said. *A room with a view.* The young man blushed as Evelyn passed. He was tall and gangly in ill-fitting tweeds. He had a sweet face, rather mole-ish.

Two days later, Evelyn was in the drawing room writing to her father.

My dearest H.W.,

The Italians do many things well except make tea. Tea is the only drink I take in the pensione. *It defines my nationality somewhat. For when I drink wine, or vermouth, or the vivid red bitters, the cloak of my*

Englishness is pulled away, revealing a young woman of startling Euro-
pean temperament. I gesture, I discuss, I argue freely, my appetite is sharp.
I scrutinize works of art with an eye polished by corporeal awakening,
rather than an eye blurred by the heavy words of male critique. I would
like to meet Mr. Paul Cézanne again, Father. I think I could discuss a lot
more with him since my travels to the Simi—

(A cough.)

Evelyn looked up and smiled at the young man.

Are you traveling alone, Miss Skinner?

I am, she said. Am I causing gossip?

A little, he said.

Jolly good, she said.

He laughed. May I?

Please do, she said, and he sat in the chair opposite her and clumsily
crossed his legs, kicking her in the process.

I do apologize, he muttered.

Di niente, said Evelyn. Have you escaped your mother? she asked.

Momentarily, he said. She had one of her heads. I wish I was the type
of man who could cheer her up. She thinks I'm utterly incapable.

And are you?

Yes. I've mislaid countless maps and missed trains. I'm always missing something.

Evelyn thought the only thing he was missing was a man to kiss.

I'm attempting to learn Italian, he said, and produced a pocket guide
to learning Italian.

Are you winning?

Not at all. Quite hopeless, he said, and picked at his sock.

An ordinary young middle-class Englishman, Evelyn thought.
Clever, without doubt. But with a head and a body that had yet to
meet.

Forster looked up, said, I think you're very brave.

Me?

Traveling without a chaperone.

I'm not brave, said Evelyn, I'm just ready for an adventure. It's you who are brave.

Me? he said. Oh no no—

Traveling with your *mother.*

He blushed and smiled. Yes, he said, somewhat distractedly.

How long has it been now? asked Evelyn.

Oh. Three weeks or so. Only another fifty to go.

Oh my.

We came down from Lake Como. We were only supposed to stay in Cadenabbia for one night, but we stayed ten. Mother thought I needed the mountain air. It was so attractive, Miss Skinner. Very few incidents. A purse that was lost and found, and a flea and a centipede that were found. But I was prepared for fleas. My friend Dent told me about ammonia. That sorts them. They're not keen on it. I mean, who would be? I'm not.

An electric tram rattled past.

Forster nodded toward the window. That keeps me awake at night, he said. Does it you?

No. That's not what keeps me awake at night, said Evelyn, suddenly catching sight of Livia in the doorway. You sound as if you're not having a good time, Mr. Forster, she said.

So far, Italy has been a rather timid outing for me, Miss Skinner. A little anticlimactic. I went up the cathedral at Monza and was spat upon from the people on the spire. Which is not so nice. Mother says I am "lamentably unfortunate." She thinks that if we went to Pisa it would be just my luck for the Leaning Tower to fall on me.

Evelyn laughed.

Mother and I have been entirely surrounded by English people, mostly of middle age. They have scrutinized us, most not sure whether my mother and I will do.

You'll do here, Mr. Forster, ten times over!

Thank you, Miss Skinner. I'm grateful. At one hotel, half the guests were playing poker patience and the rest were sleeping.

Evelyn looked about at their surroundings.

No change there, then, she said.

We could be in England, he said, looking at the patterned carpet and pictures of Queen Victoria and the new not-yet-anointed king, and the crude depressing watercolor of the river Thames.

I had *prunes* for breakfast, he added. *Prunes.*

Evelyn laughed.

Morgan! Morgan!

Mother, he mouthed.

You've been discovered, said Evelyn.

Indeed. I'd better go, he said, unfolding his limbs to stand.

I hope you find what you're looking for, she said.

Thank you, Miss Skinner. Knowledge is a great liberator. Good day to you.

The day after their encounter, Evelyn watched him in the drawing room over a cup of tea. He was an innocent in many ways, intensely naïve and hapless. He had the long slender hands of a pianist and many guests had commented on how well he played. And here he was, lost in Beethoven. At the end of his playing, Evelyn applauded (well, tapped her spoon against the porcelain), and he looked intensely uncomfortable in the aftermath of her praise.

If one day you live as you play . . . , she said.

He stood up from the piano and his body unraveled.

I've lost my Baedeker, he said.

Have mine, she said.

If only I could lose my mother, he said.

Andiamo, she said, and he followed her into the dining room, where the Baedeker lay next to a teapot and a plate of shortbread biscuits.

It was at that moment—how beautifully—that Livia entered from the kitchen and was stopped abruptly, by an arrow shot to the heart. (Evelyn put down her bow.)

Won't you need it? said Forster, flicking through the pages of the Baedeker.

No, I have all I need here, said Evelyn, staring adoringly at her lover.

Suddenly, Forster found the violet pressed between the pages.

What's this? he said, holding it up to the light.

A violet / *Una viola*, said Evelyn and Livia in unison.

His gaze went from one woman to the other. They were standing in the same pose, one hand on hip, the other held at the forehead.

There is at times a magic in identity of position, he said. He placed the violet back between the pages and missed the moment when the two young women squeezed hands as one passed in front of the other.

And you're sure you'll be all right today, Miss Skinner, without your book? he said.

Oh yes, said Evelyn. I'm about to retire to my Italian lesson that will take up most of the afternoon. And she wished him a good day, and he bowed and dropped the Baedeker onto the plate of shortbreads, scattering them across the floor.

Morgan! Morgan!

He left the room and walked into the hallway. He stopped momentarily by the stairs and looked up questioningly, the remains of Evelyn's scent hovering. He shook his head and dismissed whatever crazy idea might have been formulating there and loped defeatedly toward his mother's demanding voice. She was mentioning something about a mackintosh square.

In a room two floors above reception, Livia was naked and spread-eagled on Evelyn's bed. Evelyn was moving up between her legs, enjoying a lesson in Italian pronunciation.

Evelyn kissed her ankle.

Caviglia, said Livia.

Her calf.

Polpaccio.

Kissed her knee.

Ginocchio. (She giggled. Ticklish.)

Evelyn licked up her thigh.

Coscia.

Last one, thought Evelyn, and she moved toward the juncture of her legs. Livia groaned quietly.

La mia passera.

Mi piace la tua passera, were the last words Evelyn said before her mouth and tongue were employed in a far more enjoyable pursuit than talking.

A couple of evenings later as he followed Evelyn into the dining room, Forster said, I must say, your Italian's improving momentously, Miss Skinner.

I have a good ear, Mr. Forster. And I practice a lot.

By yourself? he asked.

Oh yes, occasionally. Livia the maid has been a great help on basic vocabulary. I find I'm much better when I practice with her, she said.

I think that's what I might need. Someone to practice with.

Oh, I do too, said Evelyn. It's much more fun. And you'll see Italy in a very different light. It will open up a whole new world.

I might even be able to throw away my Baedeker.

Now, wouldn't that be something? said Evelyn.

When they got to the table, a folded piece of paper was tucked under Evelyn's place setting.

Do you think it might be a billet-doux? said Forster.

I really couldn't say, said Evelyn, unfolding it.

What is it? said Forster eagerly.

It's a question mark, said Evelyn, holding up the note for him to see. What do you think it means?

I have no idea, said Evelyn.

Do you think it's sinister?

No, I don't. Rather I think it may portend the great question itself.

As in, Why are we here? he said.

Exactly.

Obviously not in the Pensione Simi—

No, indeed.

But fate.

Evelyn smiled. I think you're right.

Morgan! Morgan!

Oh dear. Mother, he mouthed, and left the dining room for the drawing room.

Evelyn looked down at the question mark. What are you asking me? Something about love?

The American commercial traveler coughed. Miss Skinner? You're in a world of your own. I said, Does Miss Skinner wish to partake in some *vino rosso?*

Yes, that would be lovely, said Evelyn in answer to his question. She looked over to the corner, but beauty had disappeared into the kitchen.

With three days left before Evelyn's departure, ponderous silences had advanced with the fear of absence and the future lurking. They held one another longer whenever they could, weary from sex and the recitation of verb declensions. The impossibility of a longer-lasting love intensi-fied the minutes and hours in a way freedom never would have. No promises were made. No return was spoken about by Evelyn. In truth, little was spoken about except the beautiful mundaneness of the present.

Evelyn was on her way out when she noticed Forster in the salon, writing in a notepad balanced upon his knee. She didn't say anything, simply watched—the poor man had so little time to himself, she would not disturb him. His cheeks were flushed, and she hoped he was writing something saucy. He looked up briefly and smiled.

Miss Skinner.

Mr. Forster.

My mother has an attack of lumbago, so I've been granted a stay of execution.

Would you like to join me? I was just—

Evelyn didn't even finish her sentence before he was out of his chair. He began to clap himself all over distractedly.

Have you lost something, Mr. Forster?

Probably, but I don't know what it is yet. Baedeker or no Baedeker? he added.

No Baedeker, she said grandly, and they walked toward the door.

Outside was a baptism of sunlight. Forster breathed deeply—looked intensely happy—and crossed the road without looking, and only the quick thinking of a cyclist prevented an afternoon at the *ospedale*.

Phew! he said. See what I mean? He looked at Evelyn.

Evelyn took his arm and pulled him into the small chapel of the Madonna delle Grazie.

We're going to light a candle, Mr. Forster.

Will that keep me safe?

Millions of others have attempted it. Why shouldn't we?

Faith is rather a numbers game, isn't it? he said, as he lit a taper.

What should I ask for? he said.

How about a long life?

Yes, indeed. And for my mother, too. Does she require a candle for herself, do you think?

I'm not an expert, Mr. Forster, but I think one will be fine.

The church echoed with the sound of coins dropping into the box.

My mother insists that the English have faults, and that we mustn't mention them abroad in case foreigners find them out.

Evelyn laughed. I think our secret's out. Foreigners know what we are. Quite horrid, I think. We must try and be different.

I could try and tip more. Porters always grumble at my tips. I'm sure that's why my luggage goes missing.

That would be a start, said Evelyn, and she magically disappeared into a bakery on her left.

When she came out, Forster said, I thought I'd lost you forever! A sleight of hand between street and *il fornaio*. But here you are again! And I'm very happy to see you.

Evelyn handed him a doughnut wrapped in paper and said, *Bombolone alla crema*, Mr. Forster. A lady poet friend of mine introduced me to them. She said they are the true elixir of life. A cure-all.

Forster put the doughnut to his mouth. He shut his eyes and a dribble of custard gathered at the corner of his lips. He said, Miss Skinner, your friend is right. I have no doubt that this creamy little bun could maintain life indefinitely.

He stopped, arms out wide. No pain at all, Miss Skinner. No pain. And I also think my Italian has improved.

By Palazzo Strozzi, Evelyn persuaded Forster to get a shave. (And that evening he would declare the natural genius of Italian barbers, and he would blush across his well-exfoliated cheeks.)

They doubled back and walked across the Ponte Vecchio to the Chiesa di Santa Felicità and stopped at a café for an aperitif. They moved under an umbrella before the rains came, and watched a tourist cab pass.

Two vermouth *chinato*s, said Evelyn to the waiter.

How do people not love Italy? she said.

Forster thought for a moment. Let's say Italy and I are slow to an amorous clinch, Miss Skinner, but we have, at least, moved to the chesterfield.

I think it's a country where things happen.

Things, Miss Skinner?

Love! she wanted to scream. *Where love happens.*

Yes, she said. *Things.*

You are mysterious.

Isn't life?

He thought about this. He said, Truth be told, I only feel at home in Cambridge. University life. I feel safe there.

The waiter came out and placed the drinks in front of them.

Cin cin, they both said, and clinked glasses.

Do you know R. H. Hobart Cust, the art scholar? said Forster. Author of *The Pavement Masters of Siena*? Published earlier this year?

Evelyn shook her head. No, I don't.

He has a flat on Via de' Bardi and fills his rooms with viewy young men to hear them talk on art. I visited him two days ago.

How was it?

The tea party was pleasant, the talk on art dull and the men awful.

Oh dear, said Evelyn.

But Cust has found an Italian teacher for me at last. A priest of all things. I saw him yesterday. *L'ho visto ieri.* We talked about wine and oil and the occasional view. Oh, and eggs.

That sounds . . . promising?

I suppose if I ran a restaurant in the Apennines, I would think so too. Mother said he looked like a man who'd have fleas. She checked me over on my return.

And?

None, I'm happy to report. And you yesterday?

Botticelli's *Primavera* at the Accademia.

Forster sipped his drink and said, The painter Roger Fry liked to lick the dirt off that painting whenever the custodian wasn't looking.

Really? said Evelyn. And she wanted to know why Roger Fry did that. But not wanting to appear unsophisticated, said instead, Ah, so that's why Flora looked so clean.

Forster laughed. Oh, very good.

They watched as a chain of paintings was carried from an art restorer toward the Palazzo Pitti.

I often wonder, Mr. Forster, when I see paintings carried to and fro like that, if in those arms is a Leonardo, or an Artemisia Gentileschi, or happenstance a Rubens.

Oh Lord, not a Rubens. I don't care much for Rubens.

Do you not?

Much too prudish for me. His nudes look absentminded, as if they've carelessly lost their clothes and need to go and search for them.

Evelyn smiled. But to have a masterpiece in my arms. I'd cradle it like a child.

I'd be worried I'd drop it.

You would, wouldn't you?

Yes, I would. Four hundred years of genius destroyed by butterfingers me.

He shuddered, as if he was reliving the humiliation, rather than imagining the worst.

He said, Mother has probably awoken from her siesta by now, and is bracing herself for dinner. Gobbling down the charcoal as we speak.

The food really is rather ghastly, isn't it? said Evelyn. Outside the Simi, food is life. It's a celebration. But inside, it's—

It's Dante's third circle of hell! Our punishment for the past sin of gluttony! said Forster. *Midway in the journey of our life, I found myself in the Pensione Simi, as the straight path was lost!*

You are funny, Mr. Forster.

Am I?

Yes. Wonderful company.

I have to say, I've never viewed myself that way.

They paid the bill, stood up and made their way toward the bridge.

But have you noticed, said Evelyn, how well even the poorest seem to eat? They're very knowledgeable about vegetables. You should see them at the markets.

We've tended to stay away from the markets, Miss Skinner, on account of the beggars. When I shoo them away they laugh at me. Mother thinks I'm very ineffectual. Outside Santissima Annunziata, a poor wretched soul threw herself prostrate onto my shoes. I had to empty my pockets into her tin before she released me.

So what do you *like* to eat, Mr. Forster?

Forster thought long and hard. Beetroot, he said. I *really* like beetroot. And he smiled, and his face lit up, his eyes shone, and the bells began to ring out across the impending dusk. Across terra-cotta roofs, past green and gray shutters and the ochre frontages and the jewelers on the bridge, far out to the dark, dark hills and spaces beyond.

Will I see you tomorrow, Miss Skinner?

'Fraid not, Mr. Forster. Last Italian lesson.

Ah. Well, *buona fortuna* with that.

They said nothing more on their walk back to the *pensione*. Forster glancing at men, Evelyn at women. Their respectability and middle-class Englishness a perfect foil for their hidden desires.

Come back to mine . . .

Livia had only needed to say it once for Evelyn's sail to change tack. They were taking a chance, but they were young and in love and about to part and if not now, then when? The door opened onto a steep flight of stairs dense with the smells of waste and cooking. The soft climb up to the second floor, skirts hoisted, the alibi of an Italian dictionary cradled in the crook of Evelyn's arm.

That momentary awkwardness as they entered Livia's room. It was sparse but clean, as Evelyn knew it would be, but there was a suffocating undercurrent to the space, a claustrophobic existence of little opportunity. Livia poured out a glass of water and handed it to her. They smiled at one another. No words had yet been said. Evelyn took the water to the window, and through the shutters she spied Santa Croce and the statue of Dante. The airlessness Evelyn had previously felt, she suddenly realized was hers. The disparity between their lives ever more obvious. She stood at the window to center her breathing. When she turned, Livia had undressed on the narrow bed. There was an equality in that. In the discarding of clothes. Evelyn put down her glass. She loved her even more.

Evelyn woke first. Shafts of afternoon light cut through the shutters and it took a moment before she realized this was not her room at the Simi. On the floor lay dresses, drawers and chemise. A bowl of dirty water that had collected a rime of dust, the rags with which they'd washed one another, the silken trail of discarded desire. Curls of orange peel, too. An Italian dictionary. A nub of bread, rock hard now. She saw everything as if it was framed. The fall of light on the bowl told the greatest story.

She looked at the long line of pale nakedness next to her, and was lost to that moment. Life was meaningless without her, without the life she represented. She would never be able to explain her gratitude without its sounding patronizing and slight. Livia stirred. Evelyn kissed her smile. I love you I love you I love you over and over, until it became a singular monophonic song.

That last afternoon they hauled themselves from the sheets and took a packed tram from San Marco to Fiesole. They stood at the back, on the windswept platform, holding on to bonnets and laughing with the children at the wheel-screeching journey. The tram shuddering, stopping, straining up the hill.

In Fiesole the weather was warm and fair, but shawls were wrapped tighter as autumn swept in off the Apennines in unexpected gusts. They walked arm in arm to a place where the views across Florence and the Arno plain were ravishing. The afternoon light had turned the valley gold and the roofs shone vivid red. And of course, that dome.

They walked down through olive groves and fig trees, through tall grasses where they held hands and picked up prickly casings under an unexpected stretch of nut trees. They bought *gelato* from a cart and walked a path down to the Roman amphitheater, where they sat and fed one another the sweet chocolate ice, and because it was quiet, and they were alone, they kissed one another's lips warm, their pockets full of chestnuts. On the air was the faint smell of rosemary and thyme. Evelyn stood up and walked to the middle of the stage area, and there recited one of Constance's poems. It was about discovery and astonishment and forgiveness. And all the while Livia watched, smiled, applauded. And then it rained—but there was still sun—and they both eagerly looked about for a rainbow, but that would have been too perfect, too unreal for a last day of love. They talked freely. About what? The taste of a pastry, this woman, that man; such unremarkable, trivial everyday things.

On the journey down, the tram was packed, and people were complaining and Evelyn and Livia pressed tightly together, front to front, breast to breast in uncomplaining bliss. The wheels screeched, the coaches shuddered, and men leaped on clinging to the outside, other hands on their hats as wind and speed lifted anything not tied down.

At San Marco, people descended, breathless and shaken as if they had weathered the wrath of God. Evelyn suggested a drink in a square, and they walked arm in arm, eyes glazed by sunshine and sorrow.

They became quiet as the counting down to dusk began. Evelyn watched Livia light a cigarette. How she screwed up her eyes when the wind changed direction and brought the smoke back to her. What? said Livia. I'm counting your freckles. Why? said Livia. Because no one else will, said Evelyn.

They agreed to say good-bye on a bridge. Dusk finally joined them. Lights reflected on the Arno joined them. The dome of San Frediano watching. In a sea of entwined naked limbs they'd said good-bye before.

But here they shook hands.

And smiled.

In thanks.

It was agreed that Livia would turn to leave first and she did.

She did not look back.

That night Evelyn took herself to the Teatro Verdi. It wasn't even a quarter full and her grief felt exposed. The audience found the first act of *Boccaccio* very funny and called three encores for the comic trio. But Evelyn didn't find it funny. She sat in the dark and wondered why she was there.

She got back to the Simi just before curfew and noticed Forster in the drawing room, writing a letter.

Mr. Forster. How are you?

Not so well. I didn't want to go to sleep straightaway in case I choked.

Evelyn sat down opposite him.

Your ears must have been burning, Miss Skinner. I was writing about you.to my dear friend Dent.*

All good things? said Evelyn.

No, not at all! How, rather, you led me astray the other day. My first Tuscan doughnut. My first Italian barber. What more could I learn from you, Miss Skinner, if time was ours?

What more? thought Evelyn.

---

* Edward Joseph Dent would never receive this letter about Forster's time with Miss Evelyn Skinner. Through the carelessness of Italy's postal system, this more avid account of life at Pensione Simi has been eradicated.

They became momentarily shy. Or quiet. Maybe both.

How was your lesson this afternoon? he said.

Oh, sighed Evelyn. We revised the narrative tenses. And touched on the future.

And how is the future?

Tricky. I expect we'll stick to the past.

You look sad.

Yes, she said. I walked back from Teatro Verdi tonight.

By yourself?

Yes.

Were you not frightened?

No. Entranced. Old women with candles were lighting the *porte co-chères* and shutting the grilles. It's as if they were closing down the city for the night. Putting it to bed like a child. I found it rather sweet. I think you would too. There is peace. And ghosts—

Forster shuddered.

—and something ancient and permanent. And I sense it will always be here. To come back to time and time again.

And will you come back?

Oh yes. Nothing will stop me. I've found myself here, Mr. Forster. That's a hard thing to let go of.

Mother and I are heading into the countryside tomorrow, said Forster.

And I head to my aunt Maria in Rome.

Tonight is our adieu, then. And Forster stood up. Evelyn did too. They shook hands.

Good luck, Mr. Forster. I see good things for you.

Do you really?

Wonderful things. And remember: cherish the body, and the soul will follow.

Who said that?

The Greeks, probably, she said.

Well, good night now, Miss Skinner. It's been such a pleasure. Have a wonderful time with your aunt. Think of me. With Mother. Oh, and do take care in the Pantheon. I heard it's rather slippy after a down-pour.*

The next day, under low rain clouds, a lone cab ride to the railway station and no cyclist weaving in and out. Evelyn wondered if Livia might come to see her off, but she didn't. She lost her book of poetry on the train journey to Rome and found it hard to look happy when Aunt Maria met her at the station.

You look different, said her aunt. And your Italian! So effortless. So grown-up.

Evelyn began to cry.

Two summers later, Evelyn returned to Florence, hoping to pick up where Livia and she had left off.

It would be a deepening of passion, she imagined. More as husband and wife—or wife and wife?—but it would involve a home, a job, a shared life of commitment. They could, others had. A secret life but no less fulfilled.

Letters of love they had sent to one another. Coded, of course. The letters had begun to fluctuate over the months till they stopped. But even then, Evelyn believed love could conquer all.

She arrived at the Simi only to discover Livia wasn't there. No letter had been left for her, although over the years she came to suspect there probably had been. Livia had disappeared months before and nobody could say exactly where to. The cockney *signora* was all discretion. Maybe she went back up north, maybe she went to work for a rich family, maybe she was married, had a child . . . Maybe maybe maybe. Evelyn stayed a week before moving on. She rarely left her room.

---

* During a stay in Rome in January 1902, Morgan Forster slipped and sprained his ankle and then later broke his arm on the steps of St. Peter's. Not the Pantheon.

———

She chose not to return to Florence for a few years. She thought the world would end, but it didn't. Thought her capacity to love would remain unfulfilled, but it didn't. She moved her allegiance to Rome and took to her bed, some days, like Keats. Didn't die (her appetite was far too robust) and she grew stronger and more handsome until heartache went into remission. Livia became a memory. Livia became a piece of art.

There were others for Evelyn, of course. There was the suffragette from East London who showed her that smashing windows was a marvelous amuse-bouche before sex. There was also a brief *en passant* with one of the Three Vi's that resulted in a bruise and a second-rate poem.

And there was, of course, Gabriela. Beautiful, darling Gaby Cortez.

And Forster? Evelyn wouldn't meet him again. They orbited in a similar solar system, milling around the sun that was Virginia Woolf. But the heavens conspired to keep them apart and to leave intact what they had been—a flawless chapter of youth.

Evelyn saw him, though, about ten years later in the Italian Lakes. He had grown a mustache by then, a small creature hibernating below his nose. He was in conversation with a handsome man with brown skin, who sported a similar mustache. She believed them to be lovers—wrongly, as it would turn out—so she didn't approach him, and they passed one another at a distance. She sat down on a bench that offered a superlative view of Lake Como. And from there she watched him disappear.

So, time heals. Mostly. Sometimes carelessly. And in unsuspecting moments, the pain catches and reminds one of all that's been missing. The fulcrum of what might have been. But then it passes. Winter moves into spring and swallows return. The proximity of new skin returns to the sheets. Beauty does what is required. Jobs fulfill and conversations inspire. Loneliness becomes a mere Sunday. Scattered clothes. Empty bowls. Rotting fruit. Passing time. But still life in all its beauty and complexity.

Evelyn and Ulysses stepped out into the dark square as the first light went on in Michele's. The big man standing behind the counter having his first espresso of the day.

Evelyn took hold of Ulysses's arm and they crossed the stones toward Betsy, leaving behind a *pensione* at peace and unstirring.

Massimo fast asleep with a letter from Jem resting on his chest.

Pete turning over and dreaming of his old life on the stage.

Alys and Romy entwined in a way they seldom could be in daylight.

Peg safe in body and soul.

Neither Ulysses nor Evelyn noticed the elderly contessa standing at her window or the spectral flash of blue darting around the statue of Cosimo R.

They drove east and met the sun. The flaming dawn caused Ulysses to pull over, caused the grape harvesters to pause whilst the sky flared pink and violet and gold in eyes of wonder.

Five hours later, they arrived at the Coriano Ridge War Cemetery, situated in a green valley between Rimini and San Martino. It came as no surprise to Evelyn, who'd long suspected where Ulysses disappeared to every year. They sat for a moment. The only sound was of an engine cooling, and through the railings they could see rows of white grave-stones. Ulysses squeezed Evelyn's hand and said, Shall we?

They walked across the grass. The cemetery was beautifully tended and the lavender bushes brought in the bees and that little nudge of toil lifted the murmuring of sorrow. Swifts, yet to depart, darted joyfully overhead.

Ulysses knew where to find Captain Darnley, of course, and it took him no time at all to say, Over here, Evelyn. Here he is.

They stood side by side. Small whisperings but not prayers.

Ulysses said that time ran backward for him whenever he came here.

That's how he described it, anyway. From the moment Darnley fell. Rushing him to a field hospital in Ancona, two others injured in the back, driving one-handed, the other hand pressed against the wound. Eddying time, Evelyn. Churches, frescoes. Sicily. That first handshake in the desert. All those moments, those years, were his now. To remember or to forget. That's what Ulysses said. So I choose to remember. The best man ever. And everything about him is vivid. And he is young. And he is laughing.

Acknowledgments

I would like to thank my editor Helen Garnons-Williams for her quiet wizardry and brilliance. It was an absolute joy to craft this book with you.

Huge thanks as well to the wonderful, dedicated team at 4th Estate for their ongoing hard work in presenting *Still Life* to the world: Kishani Widyaratna, Olivia Marsden, Naomi Mantin, Jordan Mulligan, Katy Archer.

Amber Burlinson, thank you for making me think twice. Sometimes three times. And thank you, Aja Pollock, for the additional luster.

Sally Kim, you know how much I love working with you and your team at G. P. Putnam's. Thank you for your keen eye and passionate response.

Robert Caskie. You are everything I could possibly want in an agent and a friend. The word "dreamy" comes to mind.

My immense gratitude to Arts Council England, who gave me the opportunity to spend time in Florence. The experience forged this story and changed me as a writer.

Thank you to the British Library as always.

Thank you, Peter Bellerby, globe maker extraordinaire, for teaching me how it's done.

Thank you, independent booksellers, for your wonderful support and all you do in making the world a better place.

Thank you, Jagir, Suresh and Lohri Ji. And thank you, Cristina Betto.

My sincere thanks to the Provost and Scholars of the King's College, Cambridge, and the Society of Authors, who granted me permission to use E. M. Forster's memorable words.

To my friends and colleagues residing in Italy who played such an important part in the realizing of this book: Thank you to everyone in the Palazzo Guadagni, my home away from home. Tara Riey, thank you for your friendship and the joyous welcome that awaited me whenever I got off a plane. Thank you, Jane Ireland, for the lunch that brought Eve Borsook to my attention. Thank you, Monica Capuani, for finding the answers that assuaged my fears. Thank you, Emiko Davies, for guiding me so rigorously through the many pitfalls of Italian food history. And for also teaching me how to cook. Stella Rudolph—thank you for giving me Evelyn. I'll be forever grateful for the time we spent together. *Alla prossima puntata*, Stella.

My love and gratitude to Sharon, David, Mel and Stix, Andrew, Madeleine, Joy, Rachel, Elvira, Ola, Charlotte, Urtema, Vanessa and Andrew, Dan and Clare, Lewis and Debbie, Sarit and Itamar, Fred, Leila, Sarah T and Mum. You were all part of this book and helped me get through a year none of us shall forget.

And, of course, Patsy, always.